Raymond Edwin

Who's the Foxglove?

I would like to dedicate this to my mum and dad.

Published by Mayanne books

Copyright © Raymond Edwin, 2008

This entire novel, which has been solely written by the author, is a work of fiction and any resemblance to actual people is entirely coincidental.

All rights reserved.

No part of this publication maybe reproduced, stored in a retrieval system, or transmitted, in any form or by any means, without the prior written permission of the publisher, nor be otherwise circulated in any form of binding or cover other than that in which it is published and without a similar condition being imposed on the subsequent purchaser.

ISBN   978 0 9559919 0 5

For any information contact : words@mayanne.com

Alan Young would sit around a roaring fire and listen to stories about the horrendous conditions aboard HMS Tanmouth, one of the strategic vessels his father had commanded in the Antarctic during his life in the Navy. The boy just sat mesmerized when hearing how every man, of the boat's crew, would battle for survival and how the drops of frozen rain would smash into the faces of the raw recruits manning their posts. He'd listen, open mouthed, to how the gusting winds would lance contorted bodies slithering across waterlogged decks and how the chill from violent storms caused mists of doom to envelop the living flesh. It came as quite a shock when one day after starting the school's Winter holiday that Captain Henry Young suggested to his only son that he would like him to endure the hardships of an outdoor life for the next week and hearing the request the young lad stood motionless. He thought long and hard while chewing over the idea and it was a moment later he smiled when realising that he'd never undergone any of the traumatic experiences so vividly described by his father during the tours of duty. As he thought about it a wondrous notion developed inside his head that caused a sudden impulsive shiver to race across his shoulders. Was this his father's way of preparing him for the life that was yet to come? He hoped not, because he'd become accustomed to the leisurely way of life he'd got and was very reluctant to partake in any such schemes. However, after prolonged badgering, mainly from his father, he finally succumbed to the inevitable and it was with some cruel twist of fate that the previous seven days had probably been the warmest December on record, and on waking the next morning and opening the bedroom curtains his dry mouth fell open when seeing the arctic conditions and the freshly fallen carpet of snow.

After breakfast and much complaining, which came to no avail, Alan walked a sorry path towards the largish shed which had been erected to house the garden implements, but which for the foreseeable future was to become his home. Having reached it and with his arms fully laden with the various items of bedding he'd find useful, as well as necessary, he hurriedly opened the wooden door and threw everything inside with the idea of arranging things at a later date. Through the driving blizzard and several trips later, and with everything he thought useful stacked in small piles within easy reach if necessary, he scanned his new home and smiled lopsidedly at what he saw. There were several thick blankets piled high on his make-shift bed because there was no way he was going to feel the perishing cold of night. There was a stove where he could prepare a warm menu of food. There was a gas lantern useful for lighting up the lonely and formidable darkness. A substantial supply of unopened tins of food. There were also several bottles of drink, both non- and alcoholic. And lastly, there was a small item of luxury perched high in a corner and was quite simply a radio along with a set of batteries because the fear of isolation was now lessened to some extent.

After a couple of days, with the constant flurry of snow his only companion, he'd somehow managed to eke out an existence with no guidance from outside. But, after finishing his daily tasks of tidying the piles of rubbish he sighed deeply while reflecting upon his self induced boredom. To reverse this rather pitiful attitude, and pass a few moments in time, he pulled his dry lips into his mouth and stood staring out of the ice coated window. He lazily shivered while looking upon the undisturbed expanse of virgin white and as he stared could not even muster a supercilious grin of appreciation when watching how expertly a single Black Tit clung to the half coconut while pecking for food. He felt nothing watching the ever hungry starlings fighting over any morsel dropped by mistake and the only effort he could muster was to sigh yet again. With the feeling of failure slowly surfacing he began to hope, and wish, that his father would relent and welcome him back to the warmth of the Family home and realising that this would never happen swallowed hard when feeling the resentment bubbling in the pit of his stomach. How many minutes he'd been gazing outside he never knew but out of the corner of his eye suddenly noticed two unidentifiable people trekking slowly, through the thick snow, but a short distance away. He watched as they cautiously approached, stopped and unhooked the black metal clasp before struggling down the untouched matting of white. As they moved Alan's mind went into overdrive as he tried to identify the two strangers battling to remain upright. With no clear picture forming, as well as an inborn curiosity, he gingerly opened the door and shouted, "Can I help?" Getting no response he scowled, rather menacingly, as they simply carried on. Shrugging his tired shoulders and feeling rather brave put on his coat, and having prepared himself plodded outside until standing in direct line of their progress. The leader of the two intruders was totally unaware of Alan until he, or she, collided with him. Instinct, a natural reaction, call it what you will, but the aggressor's two arms instantly raced out and dominantly caught hold of a body.

"Hey!" The soft feminine voice yelped. His grip immediately slackened on recognising who it was and the proof became obvious when Carol Forester lifted her covered head and spoke. "Oh! It's you," her voice whispered. And as he waited Alan's heart began to pound while remembering the stories he'd heard about her, and when she pulled back her shoulders to thrust her comely bosom forward he realised the truth. "Come here!" She teased dragging him and pressing herself into the proud chest of the young man.

The instant they touched Alan's heart exploded into the kind of youthful fantasising that teenage boys are prone to get. He took the moment to absorb the pure symmetry of her beauty and as his heartbeat continued his enthusiastic gaze roamed over her voluptuous body. Well, his stare lingered slightly longer on the only uncovered piece of anatomy, and that was her neck. He smiled, rather ineptly, when seeing the blood red scald of a love bite on the right hand side just above the collar.

Carol would be about eighteen the same age as his elder sister, Alice, but that's where the similarity ended. Where his sister is what is politely termed a late developer, Carol on the other hand had been sexually attractive since the age of fifteen. Stories abounded, from the many suitors she'd acquired and discarded, about the magnificence of her supple body and legend had even gone as far as to indicate the reality of a portrait exhibiting her nudity, but no evidence could be found to substantiate the claim to its actual existence. With his body trembling, like it always did whenever he came into her close proximity, he felt the watery drops of perspiration coating the skin of his forehead. Somehow he found the courage to whine his apology, "I'm sorry," and the tone conveyed he actually meant it, but all the time he was aware of the underlying desire to touch and fondle her.

It had all started one summer's evening that year when returning to his own bedroom, to do some homework that he'd caught a glimpse of her semi naked reflection in the large mirror that his sister had in her room. Having just passed Alice, on the stairs, he lecherously grinned as Carol dressed only in a matching pink ensemble of bra and knickers paraded about. As he stared at the rather pale sheen to her skin he became lost in time and only became aware of it again when feeling a hot breath against the moist nape of his neck. While cringing in embarrassment he swivelled to stare directly into the hazel brown eyes of his sister's frown. Not a word was uttered when realising that he'd just been caught ogling her best friend's body, and as time marched on she religiously teased him about what he'd seen and even went as far as telling Carol of her brother's infatuation. Knowing this Carol would play a little tease, and on one occasion had openly suggested that they meet in the old tumbled down cottage at the end of the village for what could be to his advantage. He never made it to the rendezvous because like all best laid plans something happened to force his father to rigorously ban him from going out that particular night, and try as he might he couldn't make Carol understand that it was purely unintentional. However, as time elapsed he'd managed to steer clear of both his sister and her friend until he felt the whole episode had passed into yesterday's dreams.

He'd been relatively successful until that particular moment, because while waiting she'd obviously remembered and pouted a kiss so sensual and explicit that the young man could feel his heart on the point of explosion. He panted, like a dog, when feeling the mysterious way her supple breasts were being pushed into his body and needing no encouragement thrust his broad chest, although accidentally on purpose, against the navy blue serge of her coat. She obviously knew exactly what he was doing because after lifting her eyebrows, in mock alarm, gazed down and focused on that part of a boy's, or any male's, anatomy that would ultimately give away exactly how he must have been feeling. A sudden thought swelled and smashed into his adolescent mind as the snow fell hard against his face. Would he? Could he? These two supercilious questions revolved inside his mind until realising that he now had the Golden opportunity he'd only ever dreamt about. His pulse rate quickened even faster as a small bead of sweat formed just below his nose that forced his snake like tongue to flick and taste the salinity. With hidden knuckles straining he calmly asked, "Would you like to come inside and have something warm to drink?" And as soon as the words had left his mouth his heart pounded wildly in the wisdom that he'd actually done it.

Carol, who rocked her head slightly to one side, carefully listened to the words. She must have approved of what she'd heard and so waited. As she waited Alan could feel the underlying excitement slowly building as soft and subtle changes flowed over the entirety of her face. There was a sparkle of something stimulating in her eyes. Her lips had the dilation of something luscious because they were full and eager. Her cheeks had the soft hint of rouge that attracted the innocence of the young man's wide-eyed stare. What broke the spell was when Carol's companion stepped forward and spoke. She was obviously her sister because the voice sounded exactly the same but slightly younger. "Are we going to deliver these," asked the question that prompted an instant answer.

"You go," was the simple response as a farewell hand re-enforced the instruction. Once this command had been given, as well as the usual complaints, both Carol and Alan stood watching the smaller girl treading diligently away. They remained rooted to the spot until the other girl had reached the Oak door of the house, and it was then that Carol turned from the waist. Her short crop of blond hair covered by a single red scarf and the flawless complexion of her face now pleaded to be cradled in a pair of strong hands. The icy blue green of her eyes danced with an energy that vibrated through the whole fibre of her body. "Come on then," she instructed while taking his hand. "I think I need that drink now." He closed his eyes, more in shock than anything else, as he listened to the tempting voice of this modern day Siren. Opening his eyes again saw the large smile racing to her beautiful mouth and watched as slowly, very slowly, she ran her wet tongue around the fullness of her lips and once they'd been coated in the shimmer of moisture blew the sweetest of kisses. Seeing how explicit this was he shuddered violently? Not from fear, but from the intoxication of her beauty and the inherent excitement that was bubbling like Champagne. His mouth had long since dried and it was painful to swallow, and while opening the shed door to indicate the way his pulse raced like the sprinting athlete, as he eagerly watched the pure poetry of her beauty when she easily passed his quaking body. She was directly level when he noticed again the inebriating allure of her perfume as it drifted and filtered through his senses to highlight the pure animal desire he now felt. It was as if he'd become petrified because he waited for Carol to move ahead, but was this just a ploy that would enable him to gaze upon the licentious curves of her rather plump but desirable arse. He didn't want the moment to end, but end it must as once inside she rotated where she stood and smiled. Whether it was the warmth, or some other reason, but with simplistic ease she took off the red scarf before her nimble fingers undid each button of her coat. While this was happening Alan stared with his eyes getting painful and his mouth falling open at what he saw. He gave a wry smile because it was winter and the need for thick clothes seemed lost on this young woman because her black bra was clearly visible through the paper-thin white blouse she had on and needing no permission stepped directly in front of the fire giving out its heat.

For a minute, or so, not a word was spoken as the lad's heart went into a spasm of uncontrollable panic. This bout became even greater when she calmly removed her coat and while allowing it to fall curiously enquired, "I hear from your sister that you've got this fascination with my body!" And as she spoke, well pouted, her mischievous gaze centred on his trembling body for the telltale signs of response. He was now embarrassed and to prove it he simply trembled on the spot, and when his embarrassment was about to become even greater he panted like a dog. His mouth drooled when catching the vision of perfection as her breasts rose with eager anticipation. He was unable to swallow the large lump that had now formed in his throat as her eyes sparkled in understanding exactly where his stare was centred and to emphasis just how hypnotic a woman's cleavage was she leant further forward. As he looked his heartbeat quickened. His pulse raced. His eager tongue snaked a crooked path to wipe away the pool of sweat forming just below his nose. Sensing something, Carol stretched out an arm and searched deep inside one of the coat pockets. Glancing down, Alan, instantly saw the artificial sprig of mistletoe temptingly silhouetted in her fingers. His mouth became very dry again. Indeed it was so dry he had trouble making any sound, and when she moved directly towards him the urgency became even greater. He began to panic when she halted in close eye contact and gave a smile so wicked that the feeling he had bubbled like the cheapest lemonade. "Give us a kiss," she encouraged with her tongue lapping at the imaginary lollipop that seemed to be on offer. Alan was hooked and needing no permission swung his two hands around her back to finally settle on the arse of her jeans. With urgency, he dragged her close and kissed her. It was a reasonable snog, but somehow it felt strange. It was not one of passion but more like a kiss from a long forgotten relative. Feeling that he might have been the cause hurriedly moved an eager hand before pushing it inside the front of her jeans. As he quickly ventured down, the naked flesh, she seemed unprepared when his spreading fingers bulldozed through her pubic hair. "No," stated the definite cry as she removed his trembling fingers. "That's not for little boys." Having spoken she bent away from his disappointed grimace, cocked a single eyebrow and clucked like a Vestal Virgin. "If you've got to grope anything," she offered taking his hand and placing it on the outside of her blouse. "Then try here!" As if by magic his hand moulded itself around the softness of her left tit, and closing his eyes realised that it would be in the next moment he would experience the maternal warmth of a woman.

"Hey!" Came a sudden proclamation, and the voice was spoken with the tone of certain knowledge.

Hearing this both Carol and Alan turned their blushing faces and glared directly at the young intruder who'd just disturbed their private escapade. Realising his selfish grope had been concluded he twisted his frame to look at whoever was standing there. The intruder stood motionless while allowing the snow to settle on the hood of her pale blue anorak, and there must have been a delay of about twelve seconds before Alan spoke rather reluctantly, "Oh! I suppose you'd better come in." This was all the invitation the other girl needed because she stepped, or rather hurtled, inside the shed before standing directly in front of the fire. Squatting down, she stretched out her two hands and quite simply rubbed them together as if trying to encourage the blood to circulate. Slowly, very slowly indeed, the whiteness of her cold fingers changed into the fiery reds of heat and while all this had been happening the light outside had partially disappeared resulting in the need to light the lantern. With Ernest endeavour Alan lit the wick sending out a yellow light of illumination that allowed his stare to concentrate on each of his two companions. First, his eyes flicked from the elder, until coming to roost on the younger one.

He had often seen this second girl in the playground chattering with her small group of friends and giggling as schoolgirls are prone to do whenever coming to terms with their own personal development. She would have been in the year below his which made her about fifteen although to look at her one would have sworn she'd reached the legal age of consent and it had become playground gossip that because she was particularly good at sport, especially athletics, then she was conducting an illegal rendezvous with the Sports Teacher. With these familiar pictures flickering inside his head, like an old silent movie, he went to pick up the kettle nestling alone in the corner and with it in his grasp filled it with water before setting it on top of the stove. For the next few minutes not a word was uttered, only the curious stares bouncing like a tennis match. A watched kettle never boils, is the common phrase but eventually the steam rising indicated that it had indeed boiled. Feeling domesticated he noiselessly poured the steaming water into the rusted can he'd been using as a standby teapot and placed it on the make-shift table. At last he left it to brew and sat directly opposite both sisters watching his every move. In the dreamy atmosphere of the firelight he noticed that his companions were becoming more, and more, agitated. The mood was eventually broken, and he was quite relieved, when he heard the younger sister utter. "I saw what you two were doing!"

And before she could add any further comment the other snapped, "You're only jealous."

"No I'm not."

"Oh, yes you are," teased the reply. "Because you just want to see whether he'll try to get inside your knickers."

"No I don't!" Snapped the definite proclamation as the younger one turned the colour of blood. "And anyway," she began. "At least my nickname's not open all hours."

Carol immediately understood the implication, and for that was getting angry. "Well at least mine's not healed up," spat her words. "And I do know how to use it."

Hearing this, the younger one grinned as if making fun. "And I presume you know all of their names," sniggered her taunt.

"Shut up!" Carol squirmed as her face twisted.

The atmosphere was getting tense by the second and as a result Alan tried to calm everything down. "Where's that piece of mistletoe," he wondered reaching for it. Having picked it up; he stood. "Who's first," posted the question.

"Go on," prompted Carol pushing her sister forward. "Because you know you want to!" After a little horseplay the younger one stood face to face with Alan with her pouting lips ready. He grinned as he placed his warm hands below her chin and drew her face towards his. Then, as her enthusiastic lips approached he adjusted her head, at the last moment, so as to manage a quick peck on her left cheek. Having fulfilled the festive obligation he stepped back and noticed some irksome hostility in the girl's eyes. Her eyebrows narrowed. She pushed out her bottom lip and tilted her head slightly to the right. Aware of this Alan waited for the inevitable rebuke about his virility, and with the atmosphere electric paused with bated breath. His gut twisted in agony. Every nerve within his body selected that moment to contract. The butterflies inside his stomach turned to vultures as he lingered in anticipation. As time marched slowly by, nothing, absolutely nothing was spoken and the silence was more damning to his male ego than any words that might have been spoken. Trying to defuse the situation, even further, as well as trying to focus reality asked, "Does anyone want a cup of tea?" The tone of his voice expressed that if neither wanted to accept then he would be glad.

Carol cast her eagle gaze around the assortment of varied coloured bottles, mostly containing undrinkable liquids, and focused on one in particular. Her questioning words were sharply spoken, "What's in that one?" And having asked the question pointed to a single bottle standing quite alone. The bottle in question was half full of a particular Brandy that his father would toast the World with, especially when he'd been banished from the house for some misdemeanour or other. Alan was still miles away when Carol again repeated her request, along with the statement, "Well it's nearly Christmas!" Her tone had a teasing alarm to it.

He knew from stories told in the classroom that Carol was often to be seen in the local pub with her latest boyfriend sipping a variety of drinks, mostly composed of alcohol, and afterwards stopping in various locations to sample the Earthy thrill of being humped. Feeling less than generous, he shrugged his broad shoulders and contritely lied, "That's not what you think it is." After a moment's hesitation added, "And anyway wouldn't you rather have a nice cup of tea." The tone of his voice, this time, hinged between the sublime and the ridiculous.

He was trying to disguise the truth, but unfortunately she saw straight through it and in that moment whipped herself around and literally snatched her coat before demanding, "Come on Erin." There was a pause until she reached the door and then added, "We're going!"

The other girl got to her feet and rather sluggishly moved. At the open door she stood her ground and roughly hollered after the disappearing figure marching into the blackness of night, "I'm staying here 'cos I'm cold," and to prove the point deliberately shivered. "And anyway I want a hot drink!" Her voice had that hint of defiance as well as annoyance at being told what to do.

The outcome was so predictable as without faltering in anyway Carol shouted back, rather sharply, over her shoulder, "Okay, you stay here with lover boy but don't let him touch anything you can't handle," and with that last dig vanished from sight.

This last remark, half heard by Alan, caused him to watch the way the young girl blushed. He naïvely watched as she shifted from one foot to the other, and for this grinned wickedly. The soft rouge in her cheeks spilt into the fiery reds of unease as she tried to camouflage the actual fact of the moment. The next comment to escape from her mouth was so quiet that he had trouble discerning the exact word being whispered, but he watched her lips making what appeared to be, "Shan't," and seeing the insolent mood of her body as well as seeing her short pink tongue being pushed out probably meant that he was correct. She snorted, like a ruminating heifer, the moment before twisting and grabbing Alan's hand along with the instruction, "Let's get that drink!"

Once prepared, he stood facing his only guest and handed the steaming mug of something closely approaching tea. She readily accepted it before quietly placing it on the table. The heat from the fire must have obviously caused the young girl some discomfort making her straighten her pose and solemnly unzip the anorak. Drops of melted snow fell to the floor as she removed it, but unlike her sister she carefully hung it on the only coat hook available, which happened to be a protruding four inch nail sticking out of the doorframe. With the feeling of freedom running through her veins, she casually fluffed her shoulder length auburn hair that flickered with life as it reflected the fiery red flames from the stove.

Having prepared herself, she sat next to Alan on his make shift bed. This wondrous piece of necessary furniture had been fashioned from the filling of numerous sacks with oddments of discarded clothes and various other items of bed linen. He, well it was his father actually, who'd obviously done a good job because at least he'd slept comfortably since the start of his internment. It was during this period of thought that he unconsciously noticed the way her hair perfectly framed the naïve beauty of her face. Looking with pure innocence his gaze took in every detail of her body. From the way she laughed at his inane attempts to be funny, to the puppy fat slowly dissolving to be replaced by the magnificence of a woman's curves. From the tenderness and fullness of her young breasts that were pushing through the lemon jumper she was wearing to the way her heavy jeans clung to the very flesh of her thighs.

"Sod it," she yelped as a wet patch began to spread over the blue denim of her jeans. With Alan thinking he'd probably knocked her arm watched as she stood in a flash. Not an utterance was heard as she quickly spun around and faced the other way, but with no hesitation rapidly undid her jeans and removed them before hanging them against the heat from the fire.

"Are you alright?" He quizzed as she turned to face him. His eyes stood out as if on stalks as his mouth instantly dried. His heart pumped wildly when he saw the frailty of her underwear. The pale apple of its colour was so tempting and succulent that he remembered the forbidden fruit offered by Eve in the Garden of Eden. She giggled with a certain knowledge that man has been trying to combat, this desire, for centuries and her laugh became louder when she realised that it still commanded that same promise. Trying to be discreet, if at all possible, he simply looked away but not before focusing on the illusive outline of her hidden cunt. "So you're Erin," he enquired rather stupidly knowing full well he was correct, and to make matters worse actually allowed his determined gaze to concentrate on her knickers.

She saw exactly where his gaze was centred and as a teenage torment asked, "What would have happened if the wet patch had got any bigger?" And to increase his undoubted embarrassment added, "Would I have had to take my pants off?"

Hearing this rather suggestive remark he closed his eyes and thought long and hard about such a possibility, and somehow under his breath muttered the answer, "If only." As the hypnotic mirage floated, like summer clouds, he was wondering how he'd managed to miss the subtle changes that had obviously occurred upon her body that took her from an under-developed schoolgirl to the sexually attractive temptress quietly sitting there. His answer to this conundrum was to quietly admit defeat and try to rectify his loss, and so with this dilemma bubbling inside his head set about discovering as much as he could in the time available. In fact he sat beside her and began the question and answer routine and it wasn't until the radio chimed ten o'clock that they realised the time. "Shouldn't you be going," declared Alan as he stood? Erin looked with a curious stare. Her carefree poise seemed exciting as she walked towards the crate and calmly felt whether her jeans had dried, or not. Obviously realising that they had put them on, but as she pulled them higher she smiled a smile so wicked; that it took all of his control not to reach and help her. Next, came the anorak which she put on before reluctantly manoeuvring herself towards the door and posing quite elegantly in the frame. Now there; she turned and faced the lad but not before a shiver ran across her shoulders.

"Aren't you going it see me home?" She prompted with a hand extended ready for him to take. He quietly grinned like a Cheshire cat and dutifully waltzed up to effortlessly accept the invitation. Together they struggled until they eventually came to a halt below a single lamplight and as they stood reflecting on various things he smiled at what he saw, and with his heart beating ten to the dozen escorted the young lady across the road and towards the closed door of her home which was reminiscent of a card scene that would be sent to an aunt or uncle with kind regards. Together, they reached their destination and stood staring into the other's gaze. He was quick to notice the slight tremble as he returned the given smile. He watched as she pulled back her shoulders and hastily moistened her luscious lips with the tip of her tongue. Not wanting to be unprepared, in anyway, sent his tongue across his lips in order to moisten them. Again they stood hopelessly terrified to initiate the first move, and as time marched relentlessly on the atmosphere became electric. With eager anticipation, it was the girl, who calmly reached inside her anorak pocket and took out a sealed white envelope. Alan's curious gaze focused as she hurriedly pushed it into his ready fingers, and with it in his grasp turned and started to walk away. With an underlying curiosity he tore apart the seal and pulled out the card with a rather silly expression rolling across his face. On opening the card his mouth dried, well it hadn't really been that moist, as he stared intently at the highly suggestive picture drawn inside. His eyes grew wide, when in the pale light he read the message so beautifully written directly below the representation of a kissing couple celebrating the dawn of Christmas Day. In fact he was dumbstruck when lifting his gaze to discover her young innocence peering at that same image and to add a little ridicule she started to giggle. He was not ready when in one smooth movement she reached, like a hungry octopus, and wrapped her soft arms around his shoulders. He was not prepared when she dragged him closer and pursed her lips the moment before their mouth sensually met. They kissed. This was by no means Alan's first but the others paled into insignificance compared to this one. It was soft, but held the unique underlying strength of passion that caused him to respond with vigour, so in one motion he readily pulled her all the more tightly. The body language oozed as he tentatively felt the way her soft femininity pressed into his steady torso. It was still snowing and settling on their motionless bodies as they continued their kiss. With their eager tongues exploring and their hearts beating as if one it was Alan's fingers that marched a relentless path until feeling the delicate firmness of her covered tits. He was contentiously inhaling the intoxicating scent of her innocence when the teenage obsession, of lust, compelled him to pull at the metal zip glistening in the pale yellow light. And once undone he sneaked an eager hand under the coarse material of her jumper until cupping the soft mass of a single bra covered tit.

His palm had been resting there for less than a second when Erin dragged the errant hand away because she was obviously not going to allow any tentative touches, and to add a fragile rebuff to the incident quickly added the word, "No!" But the tone in her voice was coloured with a slight feminine hesitation. Instantly recognising the intolerable error of his ways he reluctantly allowed his wayward hold to be guided around her waist, but as a compromise dragged her all the more tighter. They remained bound exchanging telling kisses and subtle touches that declared their hidden intentions. Time meant nothing as they snuggled contentedly together until the flickering of a hallway light halted the moment. Alan instantly recognised the importance of this beacon and simply panicked. His immediate reaction was to force his banned hand, once again, inside the anorak and beneath the woollen threads of her jumper. In a flash he'd moulded the palm around her tit again and with it there waited. The wait was fractional as a picture formed inside his head, because he'd become aware of just how nervous her body actually was. And it was getting more nervous the further inside the bra his eager fingers travelled. Was it fear? Was it anxiety? Was it an inbred trepidation? And worst of all was it something he'd done, and getting no complaint his eager hand forged a direct path towards its ultimate goal. His pulse raced when he felt the firm swelling that indicated the exact position of the nipple. His inborn masculinity compelled him to roll it between his fingers and listen to the soft natural purring rising from her throat.

The door started to open, which suggested the time had arrived to finish his little exploration of her body and so with that hint he quickly removed his hand but not before giving her nipple a quick pinch. She backed away in alarm as the pain she'd obviously felt forced her to stare daggers at his grinning face. He must have realised that he'd done something wrong because without a single word she turned and resolutely walked inside the house, closely followed by her father giving a rather authoritative scowl. But before the door finally closed he hopefully called, "Shall I see you again?" And getting no response simply concluded that the answer was probably no.

He hardly slept that night but in the morning over a tepid cup of tea, he meditated the incident from the previous night when something made him shiver. Was it the cold he felt or could it have been something entirely different? With his mind in a bewildered state he sat, or more precisely perched on the edge of the bed and took out the card he'd been given. He smiled, again, at the words written as the image of the sender formed inside his head. This smile quickly formed into a laugh when realising just how explicit the meaning was. Suddenly, something made him jump. For a moment he was petrified. His eyes blinked in shock and his heart stopped beating. His aggressive face twisted as if trying to pinpoint the cause and hearing another dull thud against the shed forced his heart to pump the adrenaline of fear. The realisation of this unknown terror mellowed as he realised that the sound was simply a snowball rebounding off the wooden shed wall. Now feeling rather silly, he opened the door and playfully shouted, "Okay! Who threw that?" His voice was tinged with a humorous tone and getting no response craned his neck to search the locality for possible hiding places. Knowing every conceivable location, because he used to do the very same thing to his sister, it didn't take long to appreciate that the culprit was lurking somewhere behind the barren looking skeleton of a Worcester Apple tree. Gamely returning inside the shed to await the arrival of another projectile, and hadn't long because as soon as the door closed the distinctive sound of a thud was heard. He was ready this time for as soon as he re-opened the door he caught sight of the culprit's shape rushing for cover behind the tree. A wicked smile raced to his mouth, and for this he laughed as he gently bit his bottom lip because he was going to capture whoever it was cowering in optimistic hope. He stood quietly listening and heard the rapid breaths that promptly indicated their exact position. Bending down, he swiftly rolled a sizeable ball of snow and needing no help charged around and was ready to hurl the white missile when he saw exactly who it was. His eyes grew wider as the increased heat from his hand melted the snow causing drops of water to fall softly to Earth. The culprit and reason for his hesitation smiled. The dimple forming on the right side of her mouth only seemed to hypnotise Alan as her name echoed inside his head. This short delay was to prove costly inasmuch as she turned and hurried away. "Right," hinted his friendly hostility as he tried to rush her while at the same time launching the small ball of snow. It missed, but the next one didn't. It duly struck the giggling youngster right between her shoulder blades and caused her to yelp in pain. This action only seemed to heighten the situation somewhat as her small tongue poked corruptly into view in a gesture of defiance. With her escaped hampered by the snow she was easily caught and when he snatched at the flapping edge of her coat she instantly came to an abrupt halt. With both panting, for the much needed oxygen, he twisted the breathless youngster until both were looking directly into the other's laughing eyes. His thoughts were elsewhere as she seductively ran the tip of her tongue around her lips, which had been coated in the magical rouge of lipstick, and gave a pout that exuded a message that needed no interpretation to understand. Seeing the intimacy of the moment his pulse raced and his brow began to sweat. He stared with wonder. He stared with a longing that had encouraged the male to dissolve with inborn desires. He was so engrossed with his feelings that he was totally unaware as her two hands whipped out and coarsely pushed him away. This sudden jolt unbalanced him to the point of making him totter, like a drunk, before falling into a rather deep drift of snow. He lay laughing at himself more for having been allowed to be distracted by the innocent smile of the girl, and what hurt more than that was the fact that she knew. No words were needed as each movement told a story of how she must have been feeling. The little tremble of her fingers on stretching out a hand. The little shiver as she tried to pull him upright and when she'd succeeded the prize was hers as they stood together. Their eyes met and danced with an unspoken desire.

"Can I go and get warm?" Erin asked as a shiver ran down her body, and not waiting for the answer started heading towards the shed.

Seeing this he simply shrugged his shoulders and for the first time realised that he was without the protection of a coat. Seeing the way she shuddered it was now his turn to feel the penetrating depth of a Winter's chill, and with this frosting his mind he dutifully followed close on her heels but couldn't resist the temptation of hurling another snowball as revenge. The scream was piercing when the white missile landed against the back of her head, and it must have been painful because when he'd caught her he noticed several teardrops running down her pretty face.

"You sod!" She whimpered while brushing away the drops with a finger.

"I'm sorry," he apologised somewhat playfully.

Hearing this declaration her bottom jaw fell forward causing her expression to change to that of a mother about to chastise a naughty child, and to prove the point placed her hands upon her hips before leaning from the waist. Her eyes grew wider and wider, and Alan watched as the dimple started to throb when the words were heard to order, "And for that, you can cook me some dinner!"

Once inside his temporary home he scanned the mess he'd created and laughed hoping she'd take the hint. With arms out-stretched in a sign of anxiety he sighed, "As you can see I've got no clean plates." His tone was reminiscent of those males not yet trained in the gentle art of housekeeping and was quite content not to be bothered.

However, he wasn't prepared when she calmly took off her coat, placed it on the hook and pulled up the sleeves of her lilac jumper. "Come on," she exclaimed busily moving various items of crockery and placing them in what he was using as a washing-up bowl. "Let's clean up and make it liveable," her expression teased. He was absolutely speechless at this request but for the next hour or so they managed to tidy the majority of the mess and it was when making the bed that they somehow managed to fall like autumn leaves to lay side by side.

It may not have been planned but neither moved whilst staring into the other's questioning gaze. "Do you remember last night?" His question fired.

She never moved. "When," asked the question.

"When we were outside your house," he hinted rolling onto elbow as if wanting to gaze at her. "And saying our goodnights."

"Oh! Yes," returned the giggle. "When you felt a right tit?"

He inanely smiled at her comment and then thought for a moment. "But I thought that's what you wanted," returned the justification of his actions.

"Is that right?" She smiled. "And I suppose you'd like to try again?"

Listening at the matter-of-fact tone he grinned, "Oh! Yes please." His grin was getting ever larger as he moved his insensitive hands beneath her jumper and forged a path higher until settling on the softness of a covered breast.

"That was a joke," she mused while realising exactly where his hand was and what it was doing. With her heart pounding; she intimately understood the intoxication of the moment as he began to knead the soft mass as if they were balls of sensitive dough.

With his sexual curiosity flowing he delved beneath the cotton material and captured the petite, but hard, structure of a nipple. "So would you like me to stop?" He lecherously grinned.

"Only if you want?"

He now realised that he had a choice. Did he stop and call a halt? The answer erupted instantaneously as he pushed her jumper that bit higher and exposed the seductive beauty of her lilac bra. His smile grew wider as he carelessly lifted the material and his heart stopped when both naked tits came perfectly into view. He drooled, like a panting dog, when seeing the bullet shaped nipples sitting within the two discs of salmon pink pleading to be kissed. Instinct now took control, or was it some primeval lust, when his mouth opened and into its moist interior a single nipple raced. Feeling the luxuriant texture he carelessly nipped the tender flesh, like a baby, and sucked as if drawing the reward. So with bold intentions and deliberate persistence his hand disappeared beneath her skirt and up her shivering thighs. He smiled when touching the damp material of her knickers. But he wasn't prepared when Erin quickly grabbed his wrist and pulled it away. He was, needless to say, a little put out but like a caring lover never said a word. Holding back the disappointment it was this little escapade that strengthened his lustful desire to discover if what he'd heard about the differences between a girl and a boy were actually true.

"Let's finish the jobs," she pouted while standing up.

They continued and managed to tidy the majority of the mess, and when at last they'd finished it was Alan who was again in for another shock because she simply turned and smiled, "You sit down and I'll cook us both something to eat." He needed no second invitation, and so lazily dropped onto the overturned packaging he'd been using for a chair and nonchalantly sat watching her undoubted expertise.

At last the meal was completed and with his stomach rumbling he was quite agreeable when she announced, "It's ready." Together, side-by-side, they sat eating the hot food with no words passing from their mouths. Having finished, they once again sat eyeing the other hoping someone might start something and it was Alan who'd remembered his sexuality.

"You know the card you gave me last night?" Started his careful challenge, and having spoken carefully watch for any private exhilaration that was now quickly colouring her face.

Her stare became soft. A smile rushed to her mouth to cause that little dimple to smile as well. "Yes," she knowingly answered while tossing her head back to highlight the autumn leafed colour of her hair.

His next question was rather supercilious but it had to be asked. "Do you understand its meaning?" He smirked rather wickedly as a very personal image sprang to mind, its clarity so precise that the picture was very much alive. He watched as her face turned a deeper shade of red and there was no need for any further confirmation as the fiery blush strengthening his belief that she knew exactly what it meant.

She looked him straight in the eye, sent the broadest of smiles to her mouth and calmly spoke. "I'd better be going now," and having uttered her words moved towards where she'd left her coat dangling and simply put it on. She walked away and on reaching the door turned. She stood apprehensively waiting for Alan to come and join her. He smiled because this is exactly what he'd been hoping and when it happened he sprang to his feet and raced to warmly escort her home. It was while on their journey that he offered his hand as a token of friendship and knew she'd accepted when feeling the warm strength of her grip.

Erin kept him company for the remaining days of his ordeal as they laughed and played like the two teenagers they were and their friendship grew with each passing day. Eventually the penultimate afternoon arrived and after bidding her an early farewell, something to do with her father wanting to discuss something or other, he sat shivering while at the same time stirring a saucepan of prepared food. With each rotation of the cooking spoon he reflected on what had happened during his supposed isolation with the outside world, and for that he smiled. The smile grew as with each thought the same pretty face danced into his imagination to play a delightful melody on the strings of his heart.

He suddenly smelt burning and peered down at the congealed mess that was supposed to be his latest meal, and seeing what was there felt less hungry. Depression chased into his mind when he opened the shed door. He sighed deeply and was about to hurl the sacrificial meal away when a familiar face stared straight back at him. "Hello," he responded rather cheerfully and waited with bated breath for her response.

"Can I come in," she enquired in a strange tone of voice that caused the hairs on the back of his neck to rise with some concern. He remained a trifle curious but did nothing as she pushed passed and manoeuvred towards the fire. There she stood, and it was a moment later that her shoulders started to droop. The pale yellow from the lantern only seemed to heighten whatever was wrong because she brought up her two hands to cover the entirety of her face and simply started to sob. He was quite taken aback. No, more than that, he felt a sense of pity for the young lady standing there inasmuch as it forced him to put down the burnt offering and go towards her. As a comfort he tenderly placed a strong arm around her trembling shoulders, and not quite knowing what to do pulled her unwilling body towards his. He couldn't understand why she hesitated because in their time together she would actively encourage his attentions, but this time she was reluctant. Feeling that maybe she needed some support increased his pull until her head rested gently against his chest. They remained like that until she turned her wet face and looked directly at him, and as he looked he could now see her red eyes pleading with an uncertainty clearly chiselled across her stare. She pulled away and slowly walked until dutifully sitting down. He didn't know what to do, and for the first time he wasn't sure how to react. In his gut the feeling of rejection tightened and only subsided when she extended her shaking hand for him to take. Accepting the offered friendship he sat beside her. He now feared the worst and to confirm the dread felt just how rapid his pulse had suddenly become. Her words were lost in the whine of her voice. "Father's just explained that due to his promotion at work," started the explanation, and with it came a trembling hand trying to prise itself into his protective grasp. "Then we've got to move!" And as soon as the words had left her trembling lips the ordeal was over because her head fell heavily against his broad chest and with it there started to weep yet again.

Alan's eyebrows rose in an elevated manner as he tried to defuse the sorrowful feeling galloping through her body by asking, "Where's it you're going?"

As the words left his mouth he noticed the frightened fidgeting she'd started. Whether it was the fears of isolation but her voice vibrated in a kind of melancholy apprehension as she begged, in the tone of a frightened child, "Please, hold me." He was ready as his protective fingers fanned and became entangled in the softness of her auburn hair. Her sad and tearful face was hidden as a single place-name sprang from her mouth, "Gibraltar!"

He knew all about the traumas of moving home and losing friends because of his father's occupation in the Navy. Thinking it was the best policy to try and defuse her anguish he quietly mentioned, "It'll be alright." Having spoken he was now conscious of using that same tone of voice his father would adopt when trying to pacify his own children when the same question was asked.

She lifted an eyebrow, stared him right in the face and flung that most annoying of challenges. "Why?"

"Because you'll find new friends," returned the condescending but standard answer. Hearing this Cavalier attitude she pulled away, looked up with those red eyes and gave a funny smile. Seeing how she appeared it was difficult for him not to laugh because it reminded him of the expression given by the old Bloodhound dog he'd once had as a pet. "When do you go?" He offered in an attempt to stay calm, and as a further incentive ran his fingers slowly through her hair causing a pulse of static electricity to crackle.

Before she answered he felt the cold shiver racing across her shoulders because was she aware of his anxiety as she softly complained, "Next Monday," and to make matters worse added, "At half past ten in the morning."

It was now his turn to panic. "But, that's two days before Christmas," his statement announced. He now partially understood why she was feeling the way she was and to assist in anyway forced her to look directly into his gaze. A brotherly grin spread across his dry lips which, with the flick of the tongue, changed into the softness of a boyfriend's pout. The remedy for the concern charging through his body was to act spontaneously, and this he did. Not wanting to dilute her strong emotions calmly stood and reached out a single hand for her to grasp. "I'd better see you home," he confidently offered, although his own heart was playing a different tune.

Hearing this dominant instruction she reluctantly got to her feet, twisted her moist face and smiled. From a pocket, somewhere, she removed a crumpled tissue and wiped away the congealed mess of the dried tears caked to her cheeks. Struggling to push out her pale tongue she hurriedly ran it around the colourless texture of her lips and limply pouted her thanks. Seeing this gesture he stood ready. He saw her home and as thanks for everything Erin gently kissed him on the cheek before moving inside the house. It wasn't the kind of kiss they'd been exchanging all week but was similar to the one given by her elder sister, all those days ago, and which held no emotion or comfort.

He awoke the next morning with one single mission paramount inside his head, and that was to acquire an offering that could be classed as both a Christmas present as well as a leaving gift. What could he get a fifteen-year-old girl? What could he indeed. He sat pondering every possibility until he simply decided to venture into town, which was about seven miles away, and look in the festive shop windows hoping for inspiration of some sort. He knew Alice would be getting her usual lift into town, from one of her works colleagues, and so sat waiting. Eventually, she appeared at the front door, turned and waved farewell to her parents before traipsing through the recently melted rivers of snow and towards the parked car, which had just pulled up, by the gate.

"Can I have a lift?" Alan hollered while dashing into view and towards his sister.

Without stopping for a moment she swung her face towards her brother and solemnly scanned his physique. He must have thought that Alice had received some good news because she rather graciously offered, "Yes I suppose it'll be alright with Colin." After some explanation, from his sister, it was decided to drop him at the bus station where it was a short walk to the shops, and it had also been decided that he'd make his own way home.

For all of the morning and for the majority of the afternoon he scoured the gift shops and likely places hoping to discover his ideal gift. Finding nothing suitable that would appeal to this young lady he ultimately felt morose and totally depressed. Having given up the idea of getting anything worth while and not caring where his tracks would lead he ventured towards a building where an exhibition was being given by a local artist. With nothing to lose he crept inside hoping to gaze at the standard portraits of a single vase festooned with an array of coloured flowers and other unimportant masterpieces that were obviously on show. Noting the prices and feeling generous he ultimately decided that if there was one picture that captured his attention then that would be his gift. Stepping into the small crowd, that was there, he began to mingle and admire the pictures. He was casting his rather hasty, and uneducated, appreciation at miscellaneous portraits when he saw variously dressed figures gazing intently at one particular canvas. Pushing through he literally stopped dead in his tracks when he saw it. That single picture sent a clear message that could be seen, like the Lighthouse of Alexandria, to warn of an innocent risk that might have to be taken in the hope of something greater. It pulled his wide-eyed stare and once directly in front of the picture it felt strange. The portrait itself was of a single woman standing at the stern of some sort of Naval Vessel allowing the wind to innocently fluff out her skirt. Even though the artist was clearly trying to disguise the hypnotic attraction of her unseen nudity it wasn't that which had attracted his attention. He stood transfixed, his stare absorbing the fine detail the artist had used to convey the woman knew that she was being watched. He grinned as a thought ricochet around his volatile mind. He laughed, and his laugh grew stronger as each moment passed because he was drawn, like a magnet, to believe that he'd seen this same picture somewhere before. Was it in a house he'd been in? Was it in one of the books that his father had acquired? Or was it just his imagination? He racked his brains trying to dislodge the flicker of knowledge he knew and when nothing came decided that the best option was to simply purchase it.

With it securely wrapped and feeling pleased in managing to barter a better price he carefully started on the journey home and was just about to hail an oncoming taxi when he noticed a familiar car pulling into where he was standing.

"Have you been buying something for someone special," Mrs Cathy Dunn warmly enquired seeing the present being carefully held as he struggled to open the passenger door.

He peered at the distinctly wrapped rectangle, gave a grin like a Cheshire cat and replied, "It's really a going away present."

"I hope they like it," smiled the sincerity of her answer and after his assumption that they would the conversation for the remainder of the journey concentrated on the fact that it was exactly three days until Christmas. "Shall I drop you here?" His chauffeur enquired on drawing next to the open gate of his father's home.

"Thanks for the lift," he mused while getting out, "And if I don't see you again," he warmly continued, "Then have a Happy Christmas." He stood smiling eagerly while watching the bright red lights of her car drive confidently away and towards its' own destination.

It was dark and the only illumination, to aid him towards the shed, was the glow from a single house light in the far distance. With the utmost care he endeavoured to make it without falling or dropping the gift he was going to give the next day. At last he made his ground, and once outside the shed noticed a slither of light running along the bottom of the door. Puzzlement. Curiosity. In fact amazement made his brow furrow like a newly ploughed field as he hurriedly pushed the door wide. Now open, he cast his gaze at whoever had decided to confiscate his isolation. His angry grimace changed when the culprit spun around and directly smiled at him, for in her hand was a solitary saucepan that could be seen to contain a fine array of vegetables. "You're back then," her cheeky expression announced, and when she saw the effect it caused continued in that self same patronising tone, "And here's me been slaving all day preparing your dinner!" He couldn't see the giggle racing along her lips when she turned away from his stare and calmly placed the saucepan back on the cooking stove. Alan, put down the painting before stepping towards her. Placing his strong arms around her waist he pulled her fresh and willing body into direct contact with his. "Not now," Erin teased as he easily flicked aside her auburn hair and began nuzzling the warm softness of her neck. This single comment, known the world over, had the desired effect and caused him to retract his drifting hand from reaching its intended target.

"Why ever not?"

The young woman pirouetted causing her skirt to fluff up like a rather pathetic attempt to get a kite into the air, and her smiling face had the expression of that she was in control. The language of her body oozed the authority needed to deny the animal lust Alan craved. "Because it's nearly time to eat," her words clarified and the delicious smile given spoke of an understanding that she knew exactly what she'd done.

In the shadowy light of the fire the meal was enjoyed as both youngsters watched the other with an understanding that their emotions were clearly on display. It may have been just a longer gaze, or the quick glance but the underlying message was there to be read. With the meal finished he stood and picked up the dirty pots, and then quietly announced, "I'll do the dishes in the morning."

This single statement concentrated the sensual atmosphere as they both smiled, and as they did she stood. The combined silence now caused her to move towards him and once ready lifted her moist lips. Alan was prepared to allow her advances and in doing so forced his lips onto hers. She was responsive, so responsive in fact; that she readily allowed him to intimately cup her covered buttocks. With his hands in place he moulded the inherent softness as he pulled her even closer, and as their impatient bodies touched he instinctively knew that she could feel exactly how he felt. His eyes closed as slightly sweaty palms began to gently knead the softness of her arse and she never objected when he urgently pushed both hands beneath the hemline of her skirt. Now feeling the soft cotton, of her knickers, his eager fingertips wormed inside the waistband before moving around her warm arse and pressing against her innocent cunt. Realising exactly what was happening he was eager to venture further, and by the positive thrust of her body, so was she. But as a solitary finger felt just how wet she'd become something deep inside caused him to suddenly withdraw his hand. Was it the fact that she was only fifteen? Was it the fact that he, himself, was unsure? Or was it for some other unknown reason? With a feeling of regret, both stood their ground with eyes searching for clues. Someone had to start and it was Erin who sensed his obvious reluctance to touch her and to counter the disappointment moved one step away. She stopped and in the passionate gloom Alan struggled to see the awkward expression on her face and it was this that forced his brow to furrow with doubt.

The feeling inside his stomach deepened as he watched just how eagerly she pulled the lime green jumper over her head, and allowed her hair to cascade as her head reappeared. With the jumper in her hands she casually threw it to the floor. He was instantly drawn to the simple way she started to undo the white silk of her blouse. First one button, and then the next, and then the next until all six had undergone the same treatment. Alan stood his eyes riveted on what was slowly coming into view. His lips dried as the bright firelight danced over the emerging canvas of her flesh. His own body trembled as his heart raced for there before his very eyes were the two covered objects of his adolescent desire coming perfectly into view. He bit his lip to concentrate his mind because he was literally dumb-struck as he watched how easily her hidden tits rose and fell with every breath. A large bead of perspiration formed just below his nose as Erin confidently started to unzip the short run of teeth that held together the waistband of her skirt, and in one complete movement pulled down the flowery material to delicately step from it. Seeing how she stood, hands on hips and seductively pouting, he swallowed twice hoping to dislodge the large blockage that had formed in his throat. He failed, of course, because of the pure eroticism coating her every move. For second after second he stood petrified admiring the intense provocation of her beauty. He was apprehensive, in a funny sort of way, at what he thought he could see obliquely hidden by the fine cotton of her pants. No words were spoken as she looked directly at him, but the smile gave away her innermost thoughts as she viewed the ever expanding bulge of his crotch and the twinkle in her eye made stronger the realisation that she knew exactly what was there. It was like two coiled springs being set free when at once their bodies crashed together, but of course they felt no pain. Only the complex pain of lust. Only the pain of need to explore the newness of the other's body, and it was Alan who first made the move when his shaking fingers struggled to loosen the Gordian clasp of her bra. Erin giggled mischievously as she expertly took over, so with swift dexterity she undid the hooks and eyes to allow the total exposure of her young breasts. The rhythm of the young man's breathing became erratic as he watched her semi naked body gliding effortlessly towards him. She halted. She thrust her tits at him and when he didn't react began to undo the line of his shirt buttons. Once she'd finished; she pulled the material from his sweaty body and stepped back. He looked at her and saw the welcoming pout. Being a man he wanted, so much, to hold the warm flesh and so pushed his hands higher until cupping her tits. Feeling the luscious weight he closed his eyes when finding both nipples. He instinctively rolled them between a fingers and thumbs while listening to the soft whimper she gave. Hearing this, it was a reflex action when a single hand reached between their bodies and fumbled for the material covered area at the apex of her thighs. Had he done wrong? Had he committed that most heinous of crimes against woman when he felt a protective hand stretch and cover his own. His heart stopped. Every movement ceased as he waited because in his mind it was a justifiable risk. He was quite prepared for her rejection, but it came as a bit of a shock when she backed away and stood in direct eye contact with him. The glow from the fire sent out wisps of colour to reflect against her near naked body. He could now see the magnificence of her cleavage as if she'd been painted on a living canvas of life. He watched as she closed her eyes the moment before pushing down the fine cottons of her knickers. Slowly, oh! So slowly he waited as his mouth felt as dry as any desert. His pulse quickened to new heights and his body trembled when the fine threads of her pubic hair drifted into view. She looked priceless standing naked, devoid of any of the clothes that ultimately added to the mystique of the female form. She was all woman and the only prize he could offer was to reach out his hands. She laughed as he grasped her wrists and pulled. Their bodies touched. Their blending nudity caused a laugh. It was not a laugh of resistance, but a laugh of timid insecurity, and as he held her close her uncertainty dissolved to such an extent that one of her little hands went on an adventure to discover exactly what it was looking for. The sound of Alan's trouser zip being pulled apart confirmed her intent, and it was when his stiff cock sprang to life that she smiled. Whether this was her first view of an excited male she never let on but her actions were slightly hurried when a warm hand encircled this strange erection and instinctively began to pleasure him. Her hand had been there but a moment when suddenly his body stiffened and a burst of spunk spurted high into the air. It landed with a hiss upon the heat of the fire and for that he smiled with a certain amount of arrogance, because he was not going to admit to any embarrassment that might be forthcoming. A small girlish chuckle began to rise from Erin's throat that probably meant that she was still a virgin and had never held an erect penis, or come to that matter seen the way it discharged itself upon achieving climax. Having gained his satisfaction he hugged the young woman so tightly that she could hardly breathe, but it was at that moment he clumsily pushed a finger inside her cunt to realise just how lush she'd become. Hoping to gain control Erin took and held his hand until she began to pant quite vocally. He was naïve to say the least, but continued until sensing that most, if not all, of her bodily muscles contracted. Suddenly, he became aware of tears splashing against his skin and the effect was dramatic. He stepped back in alarm, looked with some uneasiness at the young woman trying to hide her face.

"What's wrong?" He had to ask as a shiver ran down his spine. Whether it was a pang of worry that had forced him to quake he wasn't quite sure and so he repeated his concern, "Are you alright?"

She never recognised the consideration he was trying to convey. She never even looked at him. She never lifted her gaze to allow him to observe the intense mistake, she thought she'd committed as it rolled across her brow. In total silence she reached for the items of clothing that had been discarded and hurriedly started to put them on. He was flummoxed by the apparent agility she used in getting dressed. He was uneasy, as his keen stare never left her body as she covered each piece of her naked anatomy with the correct piece of apparel. Not a sound was heard and it was even quieter when she'd gone.

He never slept that night for the simple fact of the matter was he kept reliving every intimate moment over and over again. At long last the morning light drifted into the barren shed, and it came as quite a shock when the door opened. His surly attitude evaporated. His distorted point of view dissolved when the person that had been responsible walked straight towards him, and seeing the timid smile upon her lips a million questions rebounded inside his head. "Why did you leave?" Was the only one that escaped?

She grabbed his hand and sat beside him before giving half a grin while truthfully answering, "I was scared."

A set of deep lines chiselled along his brow as he considered whether he was responsible, and to add confirmation asked, "Of what?"

Hearing the question only seemed to make her blush as the soft pink in her cheeks became alive forcing her small tongue to poke momentarily into view before asking her question, "Can you remember what we did yesterday?"

"Oh!" He smugly laughed. "You mean when I played with your tits and fanny?"

"Yes," she blushed. "That's part of it."

"Didn't you like me doing it?" He teased as he saw the way her head tilted away from his strong gaze, and it was at that moment he understood the anxiety she must have felt.

"Yes," she stage whispered. "I did." And for the next couple of minutes nothing was spoken until her voice trembled as she pleaded, "I need you to hold me."

"Like this!" He suggested wrapping an arm around the soft flesh of her body.

"Tighter," sighed the plea as she snuggled into him. They were bound together and it was Erin who dramatically picked up his hand and guided it against her jumper. "Can you feel the way my body's trembling?" Her sincere voice begged.

"No," he lied.

Taking his hand she dramatically pushed it beneath her jumper and placed it just below her left tit before asking, "Now can you feel it?"

"Oh! Yes," he grinned when inadvertently touching the luscious material of her bra. With an inborn perpetual arrogance his hand suddenly clutched her tit. Glancing up; he saw a wide smile forming as she closed her eyes. He was also grinning when his fingers slipped under the single bra cup and discovered just how warm her flesh actually was.

"Kiss me," she pleaded as her arms raced around his shoulders. Their mouths met and the kiss was so powerful that the message sent was so clear that it caused both bodies to shudder. He was like an athlete hearing the starters' pistol when he gently pushed her until she lay on the bed. Then looking down he instinctively knew what needed to be done and in that moment carefully pushed her jumper higher. Leering with passion he wanted more and so lifting the cotton material, of her bra, his eyes stood proud when clearly seeing the intricate detail of her nipples which had been so shadowy lost in the firelight glow the previous day. With the certainty of knowledge he moulded his ready palm around their exciting shape only to feel just how rapidly her heart was pounding. "More," whispered her panting voice. Hearing this instruction it was Alan's adventurous hand which ventured beneath the hemline of her skirt and quickly rose against her thigh. Next, a sweating palm nestled comfortably at the apex of her legs and felt the fact that she'd forgotten, or more precisely not bothered, to wear any knickers. His breathing ceased as the gossamer threads of her pubic hair tickled, and the sensation was similar to touching the velvety down of the finest fleece. He licked the dryness of his lips as a finger slipped inside her cunt. He began to pant as he listened to the erotic instruction slipping from her mouth. "Please," her voice begged. "I want you to fuck me." Hearing this he stood and stripped. Holding his stiff cock he knelt between her open thighs and once ready glanced down to admire the welcoming slit of her wet and juicy cunt. It looked so perfect. It felt so private and for this his breathing panicked. Dare he? Would he? Had he the confidence to try? All these supercilious questions were answered when he watched Erin eagerly pushing her hips upwards to meet the downward jab of his. The pain felt was only equalled by the shriek of distress heard as she forced the nails of her fingers to scratch a line of terror along his spine. His eyes watered in confusion. His mind was a tangled web of wonder. "Not there," she yelped forcing her hand between their bodies to take hold of the cause of the pain. "Here," she instructed carefully shifting its intended path. Waiting but a moment he drove his hips hard against hers and felt the pure magic as he invaded her body. He never heard the slight whimper of pain she'd given, nor did he notice the glazed look in her eye and anyway if he had he wasn't particularly bothered because he was reaching that point in time over which he had no control. The cry of satisfaction erupted from his throat as in one final effort he pushed further and harder. He'd achieved his climax and for that he was satisfied, and so with no energy remaining rolled away to lie at her side. He lay, like a dog with two tails, while reflecting on the moment. He felt like Pandora who'd just opened that box and been given all the pleasures he'd only ever fantasised about. He hurriedly closed his eyes and was even quicker in opening them if only to strengthen the belief that this was not a dream. He smiled on seeing Erin motionless, her nudity so erotic.

For a time neither moved, and then it was only when the shed door suddenly burst open that both lovers turned as one to stare at the macabre figure silhouetted by the dull light of the sun. The intruder took one step forward, their arms crossed as a mark of disapproval. With Alan, and his mate, cowering a voice crisply announced, "I thought I might find you here." Its tone petered on the sarcastic as well as a sisterly tease. Hearing the proclamation both youngsters breathed, what could only be described as relief, and started to giggle when Alice simply grinned from ear to ear as if her lips had been glued in place. They watched as the newcomer's gaze very swiftly floated from one naked body to another, and it was while the eyes were staring that Alan tried his damnedest to cover the flagging extent of his cock. Seeing the embarrassment the invader caustically lifted the corner of an eyebrow and clucked like a mother hen. Her words were spoken with a modicum of thought as to the inevitable consequence, "I hope I've not interrupted anything!" Her tone was tinged with some slight unease probably realising that she may well have done.

Erin gave a wondrous grin of utter fulfilment and her response confirmed the declaration. "If you'd come a few moments earlier then you might have done," buzzed her reply as she turned and quite simply kissed her lover on the forehead. Alan coloured.

As if to bring a little étiquette to the situation, Alice smiled. She ran her tongue around her lips before speaking. "There's been a telephone call from your father."

Erin smiled. She calmly stood and dressed by first pulling on the discarded jumper. Then confidently moving to and fro pulled on the skirt while at the same time her question fired, "So!"

This act of flippancy seemed to ignite the friendly and sincere mockery that had been Alice's trademark. Her shoulders rocked as she patronisingly spoke, "Did he last more than three grunts?"

"If you must know," Erin began as she walked towards the door. "It was probably two," her giggling rebuff concluded. She halted in the doorway, spun around and calmly asked, "And, anyway, what did father want?"

"They're getting ready to go," Alice declared as she watched Erin start to disappear.

Suddenly, Alan propped himself onto his elbows as his mind turned a somersault when he remembered the painting he was going to give, and so rotating his still excited body pointed to the decorative parcel and announced, "Happy Christmas." Having spoken there was a pause. There was a silence. There was nothing until he continued, "And I hope you like it!" Without a word she picked it up and walked away. He was clearly upset when she'd gone. He sat reflecting what had happened when all at once he saw the large white package waiting by the fire. With eager anticipation he ripped apart the seal and pulled out a single watercolour that depicted a scene of debauchery set within the confines of a harem. He allowed a smile to travel to his lips when he read the small card attached.

It was over ten years later on the twenty first of March, to be exact, that Mother Nature had yet again got her weather conditions totally wrong. Today, officially being the first day of spring, was supposed to be where the temperature should rise but like the previous four days had in fact dropped. Alan stepped from the warmth of the house, in his usual winter drab, and set about the arduous task of scraping away the thick layer of ice glistening in the weak morning sun. So with a definite purpose he struggled for a few moments, against the apparent immovable, and knew it was a losing battle when his fingers began to lose all feelings with the resultant slowing of his efforts. Blowing out a deep breath, which instantly became frozen, suddenly heard the sharp yelp of a dog's bark. Remembering the amusing incident from the previous morning, something to do with the owner being comically dragged with limbs akimbo, decided to prepare himself in anticipation. He hadn't long to wait because that same russet coloured Pointer, with it's nose clearly glued to the ground as it constantly sniffed for scent, charged into view closely followed by it's owner. The young man was never one to miss the opportunity to break the ice when it came to stating the obvious. "Morning Marsha," he half laughed recognising the doctor's wife and seeing the way she struggled sincerely shook his happy face before continuing, "I see he's still in control."

"Don't just stand there," her demanding voice hollered. Hearing the plea, he decided to remain rooted to the spot as the dog and its intended path for freedom moved closer. Whether it was a deliberate ploy, or not, but the dog simply crashed into the prepared weight of the man standing his ground. Unfortunately, due to the Laws of physics concerning the application of inertia over a dead weight, he fell sending a shower of white crystals high into the air. The dog's owner just stood laughing as if she'd seen a Keystone Cop trying to apprehend a criminal inside a warehouse full of flour. "Here, let me pull you up," expressed the sincerity of her voice while at the same time extending a steady hand for him to take.

As he lay against the thorny bareness of the Hawthorn he could now see the funny side and gladly accepted the formality of her reach. He smiled and the harder he stared the faster the smile began to spread, like butter, across his mouth. Was the reason for this simply because the doctor's wife had lost control of her charge for the umpteenth time, or was it from the notoriety she had gained? With this little teaser drifting through his mind the inner warmth of knowledge forced him to reflect the little snippets of hearsay about her liaisons with a multitude of various men concerning her profession. And before you get any funny ideas about her being a lady of the night she was actually an illustrator of a well-known top shelf magazine, and the mealy mouthed gossips of the close-knit village had taken it a step further by implying of illicit relationships flourishing behind closed doors. Come to think of it there's not a lot of difference between the two.

"Who's taking who for a walk," he teased while dusting down his coat.

"I think it's the dog," her voice struggled as once again the panting animal took charge and hurriedly moved away on discovering yet another scent. Alan sighed forcing the corners of his mouth to bow forming a crescent while watching the lady gamely battling her away around the bend, and once she'd vanished listened to the constant shouts and curses being aimed at the dog. After this rather lengthy interlude he returned to the job in hand and having finished clearing the frosted windscreen trudged back inside the house to enjoy his recently prepared banquet of coffee and toast.

It was exactly eight o'clock when he started on his regular journey towards the office where he'd been employed since leaving college some eight years earlier. The main bulk of his work, within the small Haulage Company, was the payroll although he'd expanded his initial duties to be responsible for most, if not all, of the accounting functions. It had been a tricky drive, but with care and concentration he'd managed to complete the hazardous travelling and in doing so was happily surveying the snow-bound landscapes while on his trip along the deserted country lanes he knew. The only fly in the ointment was when coming to the main junction, and the only one across his route, that he misjudged the actual stopping distance and finished with his front wheels protruding a short distance in front of any on-coming traffic. As luck would have it, if he'd been but a few seconds earlier he would have been hit by the bulk of a transport lorry struggling along the snow-bound carriageway. He sat ashen faced. His muscles twitching with anguish. His hurried breathing was now being controlled by the adrenaline pumping violently through his veins. The fundamental fascination for survival, plus the good fortune, compelled his shaking body to sweat quite profusely in the cold atmosphere. At last he arrived in the car park where he cautiously drew up and sat quietly reflecting on what could have been an ugly incident. He'd been there for a few minutes when he literally jumped out of his skin. What had happened to cause this was when he heard the quick tap on the window. "I see you've made it," cackled Felicity Hooper his works colleague, and supervisor. He lazily stared at her and decided not to fight the forceful shudder which began at his shoulders and finished in his belly. Now ready he quite simply smiled at her. After allowing his stomach to settle calmly opened the car-door before getting out and standing in direct eye contact with the culprit.

She would be about forty-eight, and nothing spectacular to write home about. Since their original meeting, at his interview, Alan had never really taken a lot of notice of the woman. She may have been quite beautiful in her youth, but the ravages of time plus the auspicious application of make-up had over the years taken its revenge. She'd often talked about a husband somewhere but like most forgotten wives, of philandering men, had quite incorrectly assumed it to be their fault that they'd remained alone. Was this because her unfaithful companion had obviously roamed further a-field, to gather the greener grass and decided not to return to the marital bed? Or was it something more mundane? She had no children to speak of, but if the factory snoops were to be believed then she'd had more than one termination. Although she was no oil painting, it came, as a subtle reminder of the feminine charm she'd once possessed that occasionally, especially when he was feeling particularly dejected by his latest love, that he would glance up and wonder if some of the stories about her after-hours activities were true. His train of thought was suddenly side tracked when he saw her waiting for his response. "Only just," he replied while watching her standing motionless in the blizzard which still appeared to have travelled from the Russian Steppes. With hurried anticipation he cast an eagle eye at his watch and noticing the time, about eight minutes past nine, decided to venture inside the building and start doing some work. Puffing out his cheeks, in resolute abandonment, and hearing the muffled whine of another car walked away but as it neared twisted his gaze to watch Felicity carefully walking towards the newly arrived vehicle. Before entering the Main Door he gave a wry smile when the driver's door opened and out-stepped Simon Carlisle, one of the Directors. The elegantly dressed man had joined the Company about five years earlier and it was his job to search out new contracts to keep the flotilla of Lorries in work. He would be about fifty and had been de-commissioned; well that was his expression for his official retirement from the Army and according to his undoubted ability to talk had described that during his time, on active service, had nearly reached a similar commission as his father. Whenever asked to discus his role within the regiment in which he'd served, he became coy to the point of embarrassment and would never disclose his actual work. Unfortunately, after several drinks at the local pub, he would occasionally let slip little snippets of information which when analysed formed a picture. It was these little carrots of facts that ultimately led to the belief that Simon may have been in the army, but reaching the distinction of a senior rank seemed highly implausible. He may have been a corporal; he may have probably made it to sergeant, but to reach the dizzy heights of a Major definitely not. He wasn't married, but according to Simon himself, continuingly enjoyed the relationships of the fairer sex and had even gone to the point of disclosing that he had an illegitimate son somewhere in the Far East.

Alan glanced at both Felicity and Simon laughing, about something private, and for that he shivered slightly from the chill in the air. With the biting cold penetrating his very bones he pulled his collar that bit tighter around his neck and grinned while watching, both Felicity and Simon, bow their heads and marching towards the warm and sheltered domain of the rather cramped offices. Eventually both Alan and Felicity settled into the dreary pattern of their mundane duties, and come about eleven o'clock it was decided that Alan was to put away some files that had been deliberately left. With arrogant ease Felicity sat at her desk, in the corner, and contented herself with other tasks that were obviously unnecessary. Everything was going fine until realising the final file was to be placed in the box directly above her head. Taking the folder and rather noisily moving a chair to where it was needed quite athletically climbed up and pushed the bright red folder inside the box. Having completed his task and as if trying to keep his balance glanced down at his superior sitting directly below. What he saw when she leaned towards her rubbish basket, to sharpen a pencil, forced his mouth to drop open. Infact it compelled his eyes to grow wide, in appreciation, as he looked lecherously down the front of her reasonably thick turquoise blouse and the moisture in his mouth instantly evaporated when he saw that she was not wearing a bra. As he continued to look he undoubtedly found the whole experience totally intoxicating, especially when noticing that her somewhat large nipples were fully erect. Was she aware that he could see her uncovered bosom? Was she even bothered of him ogling her elfin like tits? Whether she was or not made very little difference because at that moment the telephone rang and after answering the call stood up. Carefully, she brushed down the crisp creases of her charcoal grey cotton skirt. Then without turning her head walked out of the office, but before disappearing shouted over her shoulder, "If Simon comes then the envelope he wants is in my top draw." And having finished her statement closed the door and wandered down the corridor. Having been given his instruction he climbed down and feeling confident went to her desk and pulled the draw with slightly more force than was necessary. He cursed under his breath when the whole thing slipped off its runners and spilled the entire contents onto the floor. He sighed in frustration, but with quick intentions started to replace the documents and legal paraphernalia, which had fallen out, and it was while moving things about something glistened in the corner of his eye. With hurried animation he lifted the objects and stared directly at them. Curiosity furrowed his brow because it was simply a set of photographs, but as he stared he quickly realised that they were more than that. With eager anticipation he scrutinised the five images depicting a different woman. It wasn't the perfection of model's nudity, though that might account for some of his admiration, but was the cost of each of the operations. "What d'yer think you're doing," challenged the Dickensian toned voice of the woman now standing in the open doorway.

    Hearing this rather obvious statement he blushed. "I'm sorry," he stuttered somewhat at a loss as Felicity entered the room. She held out her hand into which he hurriedly gave the set of photographs, and seeing the glance of devilment returned to the task of tidying up the mess he'd created. Having finished he went back to his own desk and commenced the task he'd been given that day, something to do with the auditor's statistics. After this little episode the atmosphere was electric and as they concentrated they never heard the office door swing open and Simon walk in. They were so absorbed, in what they were doing, that it was only when he stood in front of Felicity's desk that either knew of his presence.

"We're all going home," calmly announced Simon leaning against the tabletop and staring with eyes riveted at Felicity's expression. Hearing the declaration Alan turned towards the others and grinned. Without a single word, he stood and moved towards his coat. But, before he'd put it on the telephone suddenly rang. Realising that both Felicity and Simon were engrossed in their own little world he returned to his desk and answered it. Whether it was some slight noise that made him look at the couple disappearing through the door, or something else, but he instinctively became aware of Simon's hand urgently moulding itself snugly around the undoubted softness of Felicity's arse. Viewing at first hand the office gossip graphically concerning the shenanigans of his superior and a certain member of the management team he could now claim to its actuality. Seeing the evidence, so clearly demonstrated, he closed his eyes and gently shook his head from side to side. He was reminded of the present by the continual drone of the telephone.

"Hello," uttered his standard response to the grey technological marvel vibrating in his hand.

"Can I speak to Simon Carlisle," asked the feminine, but regimentally toned question.

"I'm sorry, but he's just left the office," he responded; and as an afterthought added. "Something to do with the weather!" This comical ad-lib, as well as the tone of his voice only seemed to ignite some sort of giggling fit from the caller on the other end of the phone.

It took a moment for any words to come back, but eventually they did. "I'll give him a ring at home," giggled the statement as a wonderful hint of the veldt bubbled and with that the caller quickly replaced the receiver. With the feeling of annoyance he posed telephone in hand and nobody on the other end.

The caller was totally forgotten as he walked through the office door, and once outside stepped into the semi blizzard. As the chill bit into his flesh he shrugged his shoulders, gallantly, while walking a direct path towards his car. Realising the journey home would be daunting, he sighed deeply while glancing around the deserted car park. With his cold eyes surveying the drifts of snow that were being dangerously supported by a garage wall he felt a shudder of worry coursing through his body and stood shaking his snow covered head in an act of defiance. He smiled somewhat lazily as he struggled while taking a couple of minutes to clear away the never ending deluge of white precipitation from his windscreen, and having succeeded commenced the journey home. If the journey that morning had been hazardous, then the return was downright suicidal. At one point when turning severely at a bend, just outside the village, he slid ominously into a stationary vehicle he instantly recognised. The crash was hardly noticeable but that wasn't what caused his pulse to race. His eyes narrowed as he looked about in the vain attempt to see whether the occupants had actually seen him do it. Seeing nothing untoward he stepped from his car and traipsed over to the other vehicle hopeful of being of assistance. Bending from the waist he peered inside but the car was empty, and for this his stomach knotted in compounded worry. Where had the driver gone? Where was his passenger? And why hadn't they continued their journey home, and more damning was why weren't they patiently waiting? With these curious challenges rushing through his mind it made him feel exactly like the weather, cold and indifferent, and for that he violently shivered. Suddenly, something made him look. Suddenly, something flickered in the peripheral vision. Suddenly, the outline of two people wandered into sight and as they neared Alan's heart pounded in wonder and curiosity. It took about twenty seconds before the two apparent Arctic Explorers saw him, and it took another second before they realised exactly who it was.

"Oh! It's you," Simon challenged while trying his utmost to appear debonair. The lady on this other man's arm gripped the lapels of her coat all the more intensely as if hiding something. As they neared, Alan pushed out his bottom lip and stared directly at Felicity. He was going to think nothing of it until she slipped slightly, and in doing so allowed the edges of her coat to fall open. His eyebrows climbed, in voyeuristic knowledge, when he focused on the fact that the usual standard of dress had been compromised resulting in her blouse buttons not quite aligning with the correct buttonhole. He smiled at the image and it didn't take a lot of intelligence to workout exactly what had occurred between the two would be Romeo's while in the infamous bungalow on the outskirts of the village. For his part Simon was completely unaware of what had just happened and so ushered his passenger into the car. Seeing this Alan simply smiled as he watched them start on their new journey and with them gone got into his car and drove home.

It was on the Saturday morning about a week later that Alan woke with a start and remembering the probable amount of alcohol he'd drunk, as well as the thumping headache he'd got, felt in desperate need to go and relief himself. Turning slightly he glanced at the alarm clock by the side of his bed and realising that it was rather late, which probably meant that his mother had gone shopping, decided to get up and go to the toilet. He wasn't particularly bothered that he was naked because he thought he was quite alone, and anyway if he wasn't then his mother would have seen it all before. So moving across the landing he rather brutally opened the bathroom door and walked inside. He'd taken exactly one and a half steps before stopping dead in his tracks because he saw someone lying in the bath looking straight back at him. "I'm sorry," he grunted with slight embarrassment, as well as the ignorance of a hangover. "But I desperately need a piss."

"Give me a minute," smiled the young woman obviously understanding his problem. "And I'll get out."

"I haven't got time!" He winced when realising the pressure in his bladder was reaching the point of explosion, and having spoken stepped forward holding himself ready because he wasn't particularly bothered whether she wanted to see or not. "That's better," he sighed when he'd finished, and like most men shook his cock hoping to remove that final drop. Now back to relative normality he opened his eyes and stared at the woman. He was staring because at that precise moment her identity flashed inside his head. "Carol," he stuttered. "Carol Forrester!"

"That's right," she smiled. "And I would stand up and give you a hug but as you can see I'm not dressed for the occasion."

"So," he stage whispered and while waiting for any kind of response he just stared and grinned, like any voyeur, when seeing her tits so clearly visible above the water-line. As he continued to wait he was becoming more infatuated by the fact that his gaze was being drawn towards the pair of nipples sitting quite divinely in the two discs of earthy brown.

"Can you please stop looking at my breasts?"

"Why?"

"Because there are other things to be looking at!"

"If you say so," he shrugged looking down.

Suddenly, whether it was pure instinct or not, but her hands disappeared beneath the water. "And you can also stop trying to see what's down there," Shot the warning. "Because that's not what I meant." Hearing the directive Alan grinned before looking up, and instantly noticed that her nipples had now become rock hard. "Cover that," exploded her words. "That thing."

Following her pointing finger Alan looked down. "Sorry," he lamely apologised when realising that his cock had now become fully erect. "I don't know what came over me?"

"I do," she challenged.

Realising that he'd been caught, with his metaphorical trousers down, they just stared at each other with neither giving any quarter. "So what if I've got a stiff cock?" He eventually mused and then rather churlishly added. "I bet you've got a wet fanny."

Hearing this, her eyebrows rose in a kind of irritation, "And I suppose you'd like to have a go at finding out."

"Why not?"

"Because, if I remember rightly," she smiled. "Then I once explained that what you're hoping to find is not for little boys."

"But I've grown."

"I can see that," she giggled. "But the answer's still no!"

"Spoilsport."

"That maybe so," she warmly admitted. "But I think it would be for the best." And having spoken quietly added, "And anyway I think you'd better be going because I want to get out." With that simple instruction Alan smiled, took one last look at the woman and marched steadily from the bathroom. Once outside, and obviously still in the intoxicating world of alcohol, gave a drunken smirk when probably realising that he'd imagined the whole incident. He got back into bed and instantly went back to sleep because when on re-opening his eyes and glancing at the clock saw that it was close to one thirty in the afternoon. Again, his bladder compelled him to venture across the landing, but this time he knocked just in case it was occupied. Finding it vacant, obviously confirming the fact that he'd probably imagined the whole sexual incident, walked inside.

"Look whose come to stay?" Alan's mother indicated as he walked into the kitchen.

"Yes, I know," he muttered refusing to glance at her. "We saw each other this morning."

"Hello again," Carol smiled while standing up and walking towards him. With her arms outstretched, like an octopus, she wrapped them around him and pulled him close. They hugged, and as their bodies met his mind went into overdrive especially when feeling her tits against his chest.

They remained bound for several moments until he pulled away with a question, "Why didn't you tell us that you were coming?"

Trying to regain her composure the younger of the two women smiled. "I had this sudden impulse to come and explain certain things," she started. "And so I wanted it to be a surprise."

Hearing this tender, if somewhat fragile, explanation Alan very quietly under his breath muttered, "Not as much as it was this morning."

"Okay, you two," his mother interrupted. "Let's go into the sitting room where we can discuss things." With that all three disappeared and it was over the next couple of hours that there were discussions concerning the various aspects of the other's lives.

There was the dramatic account of Captain Young, and the freak accident that had resulted in his untimely death. There were the untold years of mourning that had been finally laid to rest. The story of Alice, and her rather pitiful attempts at achieving a meaningful relationship with members of the opposite sex and the laughter that followed when it came to pass that she'd achieved her goal and had even produced a couple of offspring. There were tales of Carol's own sordid affairs that would grow towards romance, but which ultimately died the death. With him listening Alan became conscious of the fact that Erin's name hardly cropped up and for that felt his gut tighten. He never complained, as he felt the time wasn't right, but knew at some point that he had to. As time marched on and it was probably due to the excess alcohol being drunk that the talking was prematurely paused at around eleven thirty when it was deemed a reasonable time to go to bed. It was while standing outside their guest's bedroom that Carol admitted to the fact that what she'd neglected to reveal was of having walked out on her latest boyfriend after about a year of his continual beatings. "Why didn't you write and tell us," enquired Alan's mother as she again wrapped her protective arms around her guest. Wanting to express her concern, Mrs Young calmly took Carol's hand and excitedly escorted her inside the bedroom. Watching the door close Alan immediately understood that all would be explained, but not to him, and for this he smiled. Now feeling the power of the zeds drawing his strength he walked that short distance and disappeared inside his own room, and it was here that he simply fell into a wondrously deep and magical sleep.

He awoke the next morning with a start, as well as an erection, and feeling extremely randy started wanking. It was about thirty seconds later, although it could have been a lot less, that while cleaning away the mess he'd created the bedroom door suddenly swung open. Panic. Embarrassment. As well as the dreaded thought of being caught in the act rippled across his colouring face as Carol stepped into the room dressed in one of his recently ironed coffee coloured shirts which seemed hardly large enough to conceal whatever lay beneath. "Oh! I'm sorry," she apologised having stopped. "But I thought this was my room."

Seeing her standing there Alan, like most men, could only concentrate on the fact that she was in fact half naked and as he did an erotic image raced inside his head. "That's alright," he grinned when focusing on the fact that her nipples were definitely poking through the material and smiled when watching the way her tits wobbled as she cast her curious eyes around the room. Suddenly she stopped looking and grinned when seeing the painting hanging so prominently above his bed and her steady finger twitched, just the once, as she pointed directly at it. Not a word was uttered when she innocently shrugged her shoulders and turned to leave but not before blowing a kiss so full of innuendo that forced him to peer with lecherous thoughts, once again, bouncing inside his fertile imagination. With her gone, he waited a few minutes hoping she'd found the right room before getting himself out of bed. Putting on clothes, he quickly dressed and walked towards the stairs. As he neared the partially open door, of his sister's old room, he slowed his movements because a sudden flicker of something made him look directly through the cleft in the doorway. The feeling of déjà vu raced into his mind as the reflection of Carol's body was plainly seen in the large mirror attached to the wardrobe. Making not the slightest sound he stood perfectly still, as he did all those years ago and hardly breathed as his keen eyes absorbed the covered mystery of her body. Giving a mischievous grin of appreciation his heart pounded when she pulled the shirt over her head. It wasn't the way her long blond hair cascaded everywhere. It wasn't the way she stretched her arms while letting the shirt drop to the floor. It wasn't either of these but was the fact that she was not wearing any underwear and in that instant lecherously gulped when actually seeing just how seductive her beautifully shaved pussy was. As he kept on looking he grinned when remembering the invitation she'd given him all those years ago about going to the Observatory and discovering something to his advantage.

"Breakfast's ready," shouted his mother, rather crisply, from somewhere downstairs which was probably the kitchen. Hearing this statement and also hearing movement Alan waited until Carol joined him before escorting her.

"Morning," both youngsters proclaimed while sitting themselves on the vacant chairs regimentally arranged around the table.

The cook, the chef, the mother call her what you want turned herself around and gave the widest of smiles as she placed the ready plate of food in front of their guest, and the tone of her voice was tinged with a fundamental curiosity as she spoke. "Did you sleep okay," smiled the inquisitive question as she walked away and sat directly opposite.

Carol took a smallish bite of toast, which sounded similar to someone walking along a gravel path, and responded, "Like a log!"

Alan, who'd been busy eating his round, lifted his head and looked at both women doing what most women do best. Talking. Feeling slightly left out continued his breakfast until he'd finished and having been given the day off, something to do with a lack of work for both Felicity and himself, decided to venture around the village to see how much mischief he could get into.

Having left Carol in his mother's company he'd been walking but a moment when he saw a small crowd gathered around an incident of some sort and as he approached heard an order, "Go and fetch Dr Cooper," being given

"I'll go," he responded and having been given his instruction the young man hurried towards his destination at a rate of knots until finally halting outside the rather grand exterior of the doctor's house. At the door he halted and slammed his hand hard against the wood to make the occupants aware of his presence. A dog barked and it was about ten seconds later the door opened, just enough to allow a cold damp nose to be pushed through the ever increasing gap. His words were instantaneous, "There's been an accident." Having spoken he should have waited that fraction because it wasn't the doctor he was talking to but his wife.

"He's at Grandma Pond's," knowingly exclaimed Marsha as she hurried past the inert figure twitching on the spot. "So we'll call and collect him," continued the dominance of her voice.

Miss Pond had been a nurse in the War. She had not only served in the Second World War but had actually served in the First. However, for most of her life during Peace Time she'd lived within the confines of the village where she was well known for one small indiscretion that had grown out of all proportions with each telling. A sort of real life Chinese whispers and the version that Alan had been told was the one where she had fallen for the charms of a young doctor from the Unit in which she'd served and fell pregnant. Once the authorities discovered that Miss Pond was with child, and had infact lied about her age; as she would have been only thirteen at the time, had decided for all concerned that a termination be performed to save face. Having said that the only thing he knew with any certainty was that Miss Pond, he never did know her Christian name but rumour had it that it was something like Charity or Isobel, must have driven ambulances which possessed only one gear because whenever he heard a car screeching towards him he could guarantee that the driver could only be one person, and nine time out of ten he was proved to be right. Her rather prim and proper detached home was situated in about an acre of apple orchard just across the road at number Nine Thackeray Drive.

"Wait here!" Marsha shouted as she raced up the path before knocking on the door.

When it finally opened there was a short discussion. "Come on," the doctor shouted as all three returned to the small crowd of curious onlookers.

"Let him through," chanted several voices together. Watching what was happening Alan stood amazed because it was like watching the parting of the Dead Sea when a corridor appeared only to close immediately behind him. Feeling at a loss he lazily wandered back home only to find Carol still sitting at the breakfast table drinking a cup of what smelt like coffee. She must have heard his grand entrance because she raised her eyes and instinctively stared at him. Taking not the slightest bit of notice he went and sat directly opposite with a cup of coffee and it was over this that the standard inquisition started about what had taken place outside.

"What's just happened?"

Hearing the question Alan pushed his left index finger hard against his nose in the mode he'd often use to donate the fact that he hadn't the slightest idea and while shrugging his shoulders added, "I don't know."

Somehow Carol, like the majority of women, changed the subject without any hint or indication, and smoothly proclaimed, "I've just asked your mother whether it would be possible for me to stay until the end of April." Having spoken the atmosphere became electric because try as he might he simply couldn't put his finger on what it was but there was something. Something he'd often dreamt about. Something that even he considered impossible, but there as large as life and twice as beautiful was the symbol of one of his innermost fantasies. She must have noticed his sudden mood swing because she stood and quietly asked, "Let's go for a walk?"

Hearing this impromptu invitation he was timidly keen, but not wanting to give anything away licked his lips and acted with nonchalant ease before gallantly speaking. "Come on, then," he teased while watching just how readily she picked up her thick coat and hurriedly put it on.

As they stepped through the gate one of the neighbours walked passed shaking his head with the comment, "When will they learn?"

"Why," wondered Alan.

The man turned and raised both eyebrows in that condescending manner that people use before stating the obvious. "Youth and the Elderly do not mix," he mused as a supercilious grin spread across his mouth. After further investigation it appeared that the victim of the mishap was Barry Cowperthwaite, a War Veteran and Elder Statesman of the village who'd recently celebrated his ninetieth birthday, and had in fact been knocked against the Church wall by a rather rowdy teenager causing the old soldier to fall and cut his head open.

Thanking him for the information both youngsters continued on their walk, and because Alan wanted a different kind of answer from the one Carol initially had given grabbed her wrist and pulled her towards that final building at the very edge of the village. The desolate shell of that cottage, where during the summer months was constantly being used by courting couples to experiment with the various anomalies of the other's body, was today isolated. "Oh! I see The Observatory still here," she smiled, or giggled, rather amorously.

"So you do remember!"

"Of course I do," she frowned as a curious glint flashed in the whites of her eye. Her small pink tongue poked into view and rolled deliciously around her full lips. She grabbed his hand and pulled. "So come on," she exclaimed. "We've got some unfinished business."

"So we have," he smiled as she dragged him excitedly towards the dingy gloom of the building. Together they walked into a vacant room only to be hit by the smell of stale urine lingering like a damp mist on an October morning. Carol halted, and it was here that she turned in direct eye contact with the man at her side. Both stood motionless. Each gazing into the other's smile as the sensual heat from their bodies melted the frosty isolation that had obviously built. Carol sent her moist tongue around the rouge flesh of her lips and Alan watched as she pressed her fingers against the expressionless features of his face. He felt nothing as she seductively ran them down his cheeks. Again, he experienced absolutely nothing as she pushed her covered body against his stoic stance. His blood ran cold as she blew the kind of innuendo that had trapped the unwary since the dawn of time.

Suddenly, with dominance, he pushed her quite violently against the wall and looked at her with eyebrows furrowing in alarm. He was unrepentant as her head smashed against the solid brickwork, and he felt no guilt as a whimper of pain dribbled from her throat. "Why, exactly are you here," asked. No demanded his curious voice.

She allowed a cringing smile to develop along the rouge line of her lips, and with it the intimacy of the moment was his, but in that instant she reached out and caught his violent hands. With expert dexterity she moved and it was at that moment her tone sounded responsible if however coated with some slight regret. "Do you remember the night of Erin's Wedding," she whispered. This single statement caused Alan to shiver violently. He stared hard at her as those painful memories flooded back.

"Yes," he sighed. "All the time."

He remembered receiving a strange phone call one Tuesday afternoon and being told of Erin's forthcoming marriage to someone she'd recently met while at an Officer's Party. Things got even stranger when on the following Monday an invitation arrived, at his place of work, along with a return flight to Gibraltar. The letter inside, the brown envelope, simply told him not to explain his venture to anyone on the superficial grounds of the secrecy that was obviously needed. With a modicum of deceit and deception he'd managed to conceal his undoubted enthusiasm, and simply told his parents that he'd been called away on business. He remembered the feeling of subjective curiosity burning deep inside when he'd been ushered into the office, which over-looked the chapel, and was simply allowed to observe the entourage arrive. It was absolute torture as he remembered that moment once again because his gut churned with jealousy when watching Erin step, dutifully aided by her father, from the rear of that limousine. He shivered with dismay when watching her glide in the magnificence and sheer elegance of that beautiful Wedding dress. Heckles of panic raced through his body as the vows were being exchanged, and he cringed in envy when witnessing the solitary kiss she'd used to bind her to the groom forever. With the feeling of desolate isolation he returned to the hotel where he could not sleep as the mirage of his nightmare danced as if shuffling across the fiery coals of hell. The sweat was oozing from every pore when an unannounced knock was heard. Brushing his forehead, with his sodden forearm, he climbed from the bed and paced towards the door. On opening it there was Carol, and on her arm clung her sister. It was like a dream come true when his hand was taken and simply placed inside the young bride's trembling fingers. Not a word was spoken as Carol turned and disappeared into the night and with her gone the realisation of the moment flew spontaneously into his mind. Swallowing hard he knew what he had to do and so taking her hand they walked beneath the star studded sky until halting beneath the lightly flickering branches of a lonely palm. Time meant nothing as they looked into each other's eyes and it was when they kissed that they both realised that all the hopes and regrets of a forbidden love had gone forever. His heart was heavy when looking down and seeing that lop-sided smile running along her lips. He even noticed the glint of a solitary tear in her emerald eyes, and for this he pondered what might have been as he took her hands and stared at the golden band around her wedding finger.

It took a good ten minutes before he answered, and when it did come he still sounded as confused as he did before his recollections. "I remember when we held each other," he quietly mouthed. "That she asked me whether I'd still got the painting she'd given."

"And you have," confirmed the simple laugh. "I'm glad!"

"Why?"

There was a slight pause before Carol answered, "Because at least you've got something that will help you to remember her!"

Hearing this curious statement he frowned, "I'm sorry."

It was then that her mouth broke into a smile. "Obviously you've not taken a good look at it," erupted her next statement.

"What," he challenged roughly grabbing and shaking her shoulders.

"If you let go," she insisted. "Then I'll explain."

"Okay," he agreed while releasing her. "I'm waiting!"

"If you'd have looked more carefully at the young girl behind the sultan in his harem," she giggled. "You might have been surprised."

Hearing this he was totally confused so the journey back to Calder's was in absolute silence. She walking at least two steps ahead and him content to follow sheepishly behind. Along the path they trudged with Alan well aware of his stare being drawn towards the erotic pear shape of her buttocks, well he was a male when all said and done, so with his mind elsewhere he was totally unaware of the fact that Carol had suddenly stopped.

"Oh! I'm sorry," he apologised rather pathetically as his arms stretched out and caught her body. Whether it was some kind of misfortune, on his part, or not but after the classical display of trying to remain upright he ultimately lost the battle and was forced to drag Carol to the floor. What made it even worse was that he'd managed to pull Carol so that she was lying on top of him and staring directly into his eyes.

As she looked a very large smile spread along her pretty mouth. "I know you've always wanted to grope me," she grinned. "But couldn't you have waited until we'd got back to the house." It was probably embarrassment that forced him to quickly stand and offer his hand so that with one pull she stood. Suddenly, and with no restraint, she pursed her moist lips. "Thanks," offered the gift as well as a rather blasé snog. But again it still reminded him of being kissed by a long forgotten relation, probably an aunt. And it was a moment later something happened. He was not quite sure how it happened but his hand was taken and irresponsibly placed on her left tit. "There," she smirked. "Is that what you wanted?"

It had been there but a moment when someone interrupted his train of thought. "Because I saw you both fall," started the concerned voice Alan instantly recognised. "I was just wondering whether you were both alright."

With his hands still intimately entwined around Carol's tit he twisted his gaze and immediately focused on Marsha Cooper. "I think so!" He answered.

She laughed and then as quick as a flash continued, "I really shouldn't have been that worried because I can now see that you've got everything in hand."

"Oh!" He knowingly smirked while quickly stepping back and watched as Marsha walked away.

"Who's that?"

"That's the doctor's wife," he admitted while at the same time taking Carol's eager hand. "And according to local gossip," he lied, knowing full well he'd experienced the piece of knowledge he was about to confess, "She's known as ripcord!"

"She's known as what?"

"Ripcord," he replied as they moved away.

"Why's she known as that?" And before he could answer suggested her own explanation "Is it because she's always ready for a jump?" And having given her answer went into a kind of giggling fit.

Alan smirked on hearing her words. He gently snorted through his nostrils and in one simple move placed his arm around her waist. He pulled her close and whispered, "Nearly but not quite."

"Why then?"

"Because," he started, "With one pull her legs open?" After he'd revealed the reason they both laughed as they made crude gestures concerning the explicit usage of such appendages during any physical romp. They were still laughing when they headed up the garden path and entered the house where they found his mother dutifully preparing a fine assortment of home baked cakes for tea after the Church Service.

"Hello you two," spoke her somewhat cheery voice as she wiped her floury hands down the apron she was apt to wear on such occasions. "I'm glad you've come back because now I can go and visit Ethel." Having spoken she smiled while walking from view.

After the front door had closed, and after they'd removed their outdoor clobber they spontaneously returned to the kitchen where Alan walked over to the kettle and turned it on. "Tea," he asked.

"First," she started. "I want to show you something." Having spoken took his hand and led him upstairs until stopping directly in front of the painting. "Look," she smiled as a finger pointed.

"Where?"

"At the young girl holding a single yellow flower and wearing the rose pink veil."

He looked and stared. "It just looks like a naked young girl obviously waiting for the sultan to be of service."

"Look harder!"

"I am," he grunted. Suddenly something clicked. His mouth dropped open as he stuttered, "That's Erin!" And Carol's smile confirmed his assumption and so he simply stepped back and smiled. He quietly sniggered to himself when realising that she'd always been naked in his bedroom.

"Remember when we got posted to Gibraltar?"

"Yes!"

"Well," started the explanation. "She wanted to give you something special as a leaving present."

"She did that alright," he giggled when remembering exactly what had happened between them.

"And so after a lot of arguing with my father, as well as yours, it as decided that why doesn't she get her portrait done."

"It's that alright."

As he was staring at the painting, in a new light, Carol walked over to the window and simply stood looking at the infamous shed at the bottom of the garden. "She doesn't love him!" She rather quietly exclaimed.

Confusion was now sketched across the man's brow. Uncertainty was drilling through his body as a simple question raced towards his mouth. "Who are you talking about now?" He asked ninety percent certain of the answer.

"Erin!" She returned without twisting her gaze so as to stare at Alan smiling in the knowledge that he was in fact right. "It was you she wanted," continued her account. "But you never replied to any of the letters she'd send." Finished the damning exposé.

"What letters," demanded his disbelieving voice. Carol had now confirmed the ridiculous notion, which he'd harboured since that eventful day. It was simply that his parents knew of his relationship, with Erin, and had gone out of their way to distance the undoubted love that had grown.

"The ones she would send every week," admitted her voice, tinged with a modicum of jealousy, or so he thought.

He was pole-axed. He simply couldn't believe her words. His shoulders sank as a mark of disbelief and as if to expel his anger took three strides to reach Carol, still gazing out of the window, before sending hostile hands to grab her shoulders. He spun her around and with tears, of fury, welling in his eyes a single excuse exploded from his mouth. "But, I never got them!" He snivelled.

Her pink tongue slowly moved around her dry lips. She smiled. She cradled his face in the security of her hands. "For four years she waited," explained the solemn declaration. "And it was only when your father arrived to explain about your marriage that the truth finally sank in," her crisp, if somewhat contrived, words stated.

"He did what," cried his anger as he recalled his father going overseas to discuss the various strategic anomalies that would be faced by any Captain aboard the Tanmouth.

"You heard!" She declared, and then matter-of-factly added. "So when a young Lieutenant asked her to a dance one evening she readily accepted," admitted the warmth of her tone. "One thing led to another, and the rest is history."

Hatred. Anger. All the hostilities of vengeance surged through his body making the veins on his neck throb. In one pitiful act of defiance he turned and stormed towards the study where he knew that his father kept all of his important documents. Ever since his death, Alan had fought the compulsion to go and search the books and files hoping to discover exactly what his father did and up to that point he'd been successful but that was about to change. Down the stairs he raced. Inside that room he charged. Searching every nook and cranny hoping to find any answers that might lead to his father's reprieve, but there was nothing. Only the detailed drawing of Frigates and other naval paraphernalia. He wanted answers that might explain what was causing his head to spin. So turning page, after page, of detailed manuals he felt absolute loathing gnawing at the very heart of his soul. He'd been searching for about an hour when he suddenly delved inside an old suitcase, carefully hidden below a stack of military journals, and found a multitude of unopened envelopes tightly bound with a piece of cord. With the curiosity of a criminal he took one. His fingers trembled as he read the name and fought back the tears when reading the loving words. As he grieved, for the love he never knew, fury rekindled the spark for revenge. Like a caged animal being let free he sprang to his feet and saw his mother standing by the open door. With venom dripping from his open mouth he seized her shoulders and dragged her white face towards his own. "You knew!" He screamed at full volume waving the two pages of written words. He lost control. He lost all dignity when he pulled back his hand and made out to strike her across the face.

"No," groaned the instruction as well as his wrist being tightly clamped.

With swift dexterity he swivelled his fuming face and stared directly into the calm eyes of Carol. He was now panting like a savage beast. His teeth were clenched as an act of barbarism. His body trembled like a jelly because without warning he snatched his mother's shoulders, dragged her to his volatile gaze and demanded, "Why!"

Understanding his need she calmly announced, "It's what your father decided was for the best."

"And you let him?"

"It was a joint decision," spoke his mother.

"So who else was in on it?"

There was a lengthy pause before she quietly added, "Erin's father."

Hearing this Alan trembled as a forbidden truth fell from his dry mouth, "But I got an invitation to her wedding." And the tone of his voice petered on the sublime when he reflected the knotting torment churning inside.

"I know," confirmed his mother's voice.

Hearing this, his eyes grew larger in shock as he listened to the words. His heart had stopped in disbelief and only started again as his own request fired. "So, it was you who sent the tickets!" And as added confirmation his finger pointed straight at his mother holding out her arms. It was as if he was five again and just fallen from the garden wall, as his mother's protective arms cuddled the weeping figure of her son. For the remainder of that day, and well into the small hours, Alan was allowed to hunt for any leads that might explain why his father had done what he'd done.

"Morning," he smiled when entering the kitchen and was quick to notice both women sat talking as if they'd never stopped from the previous night.

They turned as one at his proclamation, but it was Carol who spoke first. "Can I have a lift into town," asked the pleasant question. "Because I'm hoping to meet an old friend."

"By all means I'll take you," he agreed feeling generous, and while reaching for his toast and coffee the sound of the post being pushed through the letterbox could be heard. Obviously hearing something land Mrs Young, dressed in her usual yellow dressing gown, rose from her chair and slipped from the room. With her gone the atmosphere became electric with neither of the two remaining people holding the courage to look directly in the other's gaze. With his mouth full of buttered toast Alan allowed the spontaneity of the moment to erupt, "I wonder who else knew about those letters."

"I don't know!" Whispered her words as the answer tumbled with no confidence. "And anyway," continued her solemn declaration.

"What!"

"That's all in the past," came her abrupt ending to the scene.

Was it that simple? Was it that easy? Or had a seed of wonder been planted inside his mouldy head making him tremble in self-doubt. The episode, as it stood, came to a premature conclusion when his mother returned waving what appeared to be an invitation. "I'm going to a party."

"That's nice," sniggered her son. "So who's the lucky man who'll be taking you?"

"The Colonel," she grinned. "And by the look of it then you've been invited as well," she smiled while handing over an exact copy of what she'd got. "And you haven't got a partner."

"But I have," he scowled. "Because according to my father I've got a wife somewhere."

The look of paternal annoyance spread across his mother's face. "As I tried to explain the other night," she grimaced. "He thought he was doing the right thing."

"Okay!" He conceded. "So who do I take?"

"Why don't you take Carol?" And the tone of her motherly voice had a definite tinge of something more than a platonic friendship.

"She may want to make other arrangements."

His mother turned toward Carol and smiled, "Have you?"

"I'll have to consult my diary," her flippant tease smiled. "When is it?"

"A week on Saturday."

"I'll let you know tonight," Carol shrugged. "And anyway I haven't got a dress to wear." Alan sighed as the two women began the usual discussion about the party details and realising that he wasn't needed decided to get up. "If anyone wants a lift then I'll be going in about ten minutes," he stated while leaving the room. He went to start the car, and having got it going sat impatiently waiting for his passenger to appear. Finally, after several furtive glances at his watch, the front door opened and out she stepped. He neither smiled nor cared when she got in beside him. The drive to town was quiet. The only sound to erupt from Alan's throat was a scowl, of annoyance, when Miss Pond pulled straight out of the junction over which he was about to cross. "Silly old bat," he sneered as his white knuckles clamped his fingers to the steering wheel. After he'd overtaken the constantly moving vehicle, in front doing about ten miles per hour, he felt the anguish of the hormonal adrenaline slowly subsiding.

Out of the village, passed the old derelict building that stood like a monument, and onwards along the country lanes until turning a sharp right and pulling into the Company car park. "I'll make my own way back," Alan's passenger admitted as she got out of the car and walked away.

"Morning," he announced as he stepped into the office but not before noticing that Felicity was actually talking to someone on the telephone. He shrugged his shoulders, as an act of apology, when no answer came back only the wave of a pale hand as ready acknowledgement. Realising the morning had got off to a poor start he puffed out his checks, and cast his eyes down at the pile of unopened letters that had accumulated. With no relish at all he began to open them before passing them on. He'd systematically opened the first three when suddenly his heart pounded. His brow began to sweat. His body began to twitch as he pulled out that single sheet of paper. His mouth became very dry as he read the first paragraph, and his mind was still debating the commencement of the facts when an unexpected hand snatched the paper clean away.

"It's not for you," shot the caustic words as Simon took the letter. He quickly read it before folding it in two and placing it inside his coat pocket. Nothing more was said as he walked over to where Felicity was sitting and produced another white envelope and like Houdini removed what was inside and placed it directly in front of Felicity still talking.

Finally, the telephone conversation finished and with it Felicity picked up the white sheet of card. "It's an invitation," she grinned while staring directly at Simon grinning back.

"It came this morning," he admitted replacing it back in the envelope, and like any shrewd person changed the subject. "Is everything arranged," he asked while allowing his bottom lip to roll over the top one.

Obviously understanding the text of his question she looked lop-sided at him and calmly answered. "The price is a little to high," began her answer. "But

I think we can afford it," she finished while lovingly placing her left index finger just below the newcomer's nose.

Alan hunched back, in some alarm, and focused on the diamond ring sparkling in the fluorescent glow of the office lights. "When's the wedding?" Teased his voice because he never dreamt, in a million years, that Simon was capable of such a spirited offer. For the next day, and the next there was little, if any, work done as the romantic couple waltzed around various offices in what could only be described as a romantic stupor. At last a certain Friday afternoon arrived and when it was time to leave Alan bid his happy associates a cheerful farewell and that he'd probably meet them the following evening. He slipped from the office with neither acknowledging his departure, and once he'd managed to start his car drove back home.

Through the boredom of that Saturday afternoon he sat watching sport on the television until eventually it became time to prepare himself for the undoubted good time he was expecting, especially after discovering that Dr Cooper would be on duty at the local hospital and unable to attend.

Down the stairs both Carol and his mother glided as Alan stood in the hallway, his stare captivated by the pure beauty of the women moving ever closer. First, he smiled at the artistic charm of his mother dressed as a Lady from the Court of King Arthur. The stunning beauty of her silver and pale peach costume highlighting every sensual curve she undoubtedly possessed. The tight bodice superbly lifting her stunning cleavage as the deep cleft emphasised the seductive fascination this period in time held. Carol, on the other hand, was wearing a pink and white gingham dress much seen on television worn by the intrepid Frontier womenfolk of Wild West America. Her unblemished face evoked the rugged lifestyle the women at that time endured. From the rising of the sun to its setting. From the intolerant drudgery of a Homestead and childbirth to the antics of its murderous men. Still no change there then.

Because, it was only a short distance and the need for a car seemed unnecessary it was decided that they walked. Together they strolled along the quiet road until arriving at the Colonel's house and as they neared the louder became the gaiety of the party as well as the music. Outside the front door they stood until his mother strongly knocked and calmly waited. It took about two minutes before their host dressed as General Custer cordially opened it. "Well! Howdy," began a rather good impression of an American accent. "Do come in." It was after the formalities, of the welcome, had been completed that they were shown into the large drawing room where it appeared the entertainment was to be held. "Drinks, and eats, are in the library," their host indicated.

As one they manoeuvred between the other guests until finally reaching the table where the stunning display of refreshment, as well as the drinks, could be found. When he'd reached across the table, to get himself a glass, someone whispered in his ear, "Have you seen where the Colonel's got his hand?" And the tone of this polite question was rather amorously hinted.

Without altering his intent of getting a drink he shrugged his shoulders as an expression of unconcern, and as if to confirm his attitude asked, "Where?"

"On your mother's bum," Carol exclaimed with great emphasis being placed upon that final word. Having got his drink he turned his grinning face and saw the frown of abject jealousy coursing across her brow.

Trying to defuse the apparent atmosphere Alan giggled, "He probably fancies his chances." And the comical tone of his voice appeared to have been lost on his companion as she shuddered at such a possibility. "Because if I was a dirty old man, like that, then that's where my hand would want to be." Carol looked daggers at him if no other reason than hearing the Freudian slip. When at last all three of them met up they walked through the double doors towards the other guests and as they moved all eyes seemed to be focusing on his mother gliding effortlessly across the wooden floor. Finding an empty table they sat down and it was about five minutes later that Tom Hasnik, the village store owner, walked up to his mother and warmly enquired of the Camelot Lady, "Would you care for this dance?" And before she had time to refuse the man had quite cleverly snatched her wrist and dragged her away.

Alan sat pondering for a moment until realising the opportunity that was now presenting itself, and so with a hopeful arrogance gallantly stood. He bowed his smirking face, towards Carol, and warmly asked, "Would you care for this dance?"

"If you want," she answered while fluttering her eyelashes at him as a sign of her undoubted playful naïveté. She held out her spindle like fingers for him to gladly accept. He ably assisted her to stand and they waltzed around the dance floor like perfect partners never colliding or touching others who were also dancing with precision. After the final chord had been played Alan escorted his partner back to her seat. "Thank you very much," Carol pouted as she fluffed out her dress before sitting down.

Was it the company? Was it the lively atmosphere? Or was it the alcoholic effect that after an hour, or so, various other people would come up and ask either for a dance. It was getting towards midnight when a complete stranger walked up to Carol and asked her. There was a bit of a discussion between the two of them but in the end Carol stood and disappeared from sight. Alan was now sitting quite alone because their host had, once again, asked his mother for a dance and it must have been a pang of childish jealousy when he saw the man quite arrogantly place his hands around the accommodating expanse of her motherly backside. As he looked Alan picked up his half empty glass, of whisky, and in one go downed it. The warm sensation tickling his throat caused him to choke slightly, and he was quite happy to allow some stranger to roughly slap him on the back and knock some sense into his body.

"Is that better," giggled the soft voice of Marsha as she finished the task in hand.

"Only just," he sputtered as he gulped for the necessary air he'd lost. It took several moments before he was able to thank her personally and with the alcohol inside he twisted his gaze and smiled. Also hearing the enticing melody of the music he quite simply had to ask, "Do you want to dance?" And the tone of his voice was one of charitable hope rather than expectancy.

"I've been wondered when you'd ask me," she pouted while squeezing his hand. Alan turned his head slightly and was instantly drawn towards the way the flickering reds and yellows of light reflected from the Hawaiian grass skirt, and bangles, she'd decided to wear.

From then until the closing ballad, both he and Marsha danced and talked away the evening as well as consuming more alcohol. It was about half past two in the morning when the leader of the band calmly announced, "It's now time to play some romantic ballads, so please find a partner and take to the floor." And all the while he was speaking the tempo of the music decreased in line with what he'd said. Needing no second instruction, Alan's heart thumped hard against his ribcage as he looked around the room. There was his mother, her arms wound around the Colonel's waist and him massaging the inherent softness of her rounded arse. There was Simon and Felicity romantically canoodling in a corner. There was Carol in the frantic clutches of that complete stranger, he'd earlier seen, and to make matters all the more odd was when Alan watched the way the man grabbed her wrist and pulled her towards the door.

"Well!" Marsha exclaimed as she helped him to his feet. He looked intently into her light tan eyes, because even in this light he could see the expert detail of her make-up, which highlighted the alcoholic beauty of her face. "Come on," danced her voice as she started to push through the congregation of bodies with her hand tightly gripping his. He was all to eager to follow close on her heels, but held back that fraction to observe the symmetrical sway of her hips and as he watched his heart started to pound with excitement. At last, they found a deserted spot amongst the happy revellers and it was here they joined together as a slow harmonic melody began to play. It must have been the surplus alcohol they'd drunk which caused the relaxation of all inhibitions. It was that, or something more basic, because as their hot bodies touched the young man's arms swung around the woman's waist and urgently dragged her willing body even closer. His sexuality ignited when feeling the intensity of her feminine physique pressing exquisitely into his chest especially the magnificence of her partially concealed bosom. The intoxicating smell of her body set fire to his cumbersome passion as he reached down and grabbed the lustful expanse of her arse. It felt hot as his eager fingers spread, like a Spanish fan, and began to massage it. With each moment she gasped with a salacious desire that forced her to reach and clamp him around the neck. It was the sexual perspiration oozing from their pores, or the heady scent of pheromones, that forced; no compelled him to kiss her? They were still kissing when he reached up and eagerly fondled her breasts. Their tongues probed each other as he cleverly lifted a single tit free from the bikini top and felt its magical weight. It was to dark to see anything erotic but his fingers soon located the excited nipple and it was instinct that now compelled him to happily roll it between his fingers. He was mesmerised by the rhythmic pulsation, of the music, and so with despicable courage pulled her until he knew that she could feel his stiffening cock against her naked belly. "I've always wanted to do this," she sighed taking the situation that bit further, and before he could suck in any air listened to the distant sound of buttons being prised apart. His pulse quickened as she roughly sneaked a hand inside his navy blue pantaloons before instinctively removing his stiff cock, and now feeling the erotic freedom he realised that this was the cue to send his own hand below the erotic hemline of her grass skirt. The sheer luxury of her smooth thighs lubricated the necessary path and needing no guidance desperately touched the sodden fabric of her paper thin bikini pants. She thrust her hips forward and allowed his impatient fingers to slip inside the cotton gusset and through the fine hair of her crotch. Panting hard he confidently found the sodden entrance to her cunt and promptly inserted a finger. "Let's find somewhere quiet," she encouraged as they rocked together just the once as the tone of her voice dripped a sexual intrigue.

"Come on then," he urged while struggling to re-house his impatient cock back inside his pantaloons and once ready walked away hoping to locate an unoccupied room.

The first closed door offered only company when opened, because both Marsha and Alan's eyes sprang wide apart as they stared at the couple basking in the nudity of the other. To the next they hastened, and it was in here they saw Felicity straddled across her lover and dictating the necessary motion she obviously craved. The lecherous agony swirling in Alan's loins urged him to simply snatch his partner's wrist and drag her towards that third door. It opened with ease and the quiet told its own story. Having found his paradise he flicked the light switch and the darkness instantly dissolved. His eyes popped like Champagne corks as he stared. His mouth immediately dried. His heart stopped and the lack of circulation caused him to feel faint, was the reason for this another couple making love?

"Look," he abruptly choked as his index finger twitched.

"Where?"

"There," shot the answer because his startled gaze had been immediately dragged towards the large oil painting hanging above the bed and as he looked he didn't know what to feel because the portrait was absolutely breathtaking. It showed a woman sitting beside a large clump of yellow St John's Wort reading from a book. Her hair may have been that bit longer and the face may have been that bit younger but the smile was unforgettable. It wasn't the fact that she was naked. Nor was it because of her left hand being cupped around her left tit and playing with the nipple. It wasn't even the fact that there was someone else's hand nestling and hiding the erotic image of her cunt. It was none of these but everything became clearer when he choked, "That's mother."

"Are you sure?" Marsha asked while standing behind him and taking a good look.

"Of course I am!"

"But she looks about twenty three," she concluded. "So how can you be so certain?"

"Because when I was searching through some old photographs that my father had kept I happened to come across one of my mother in her naval uniform," he smiled. "And it's exactly the same face."

"So, if the woman in the picture is your mother," she whispered into his ear. "Then I presume the man fingering her is your father."

"It had better be," he admitted. "But what's it doing here?"

"I don't know," she replied as she silently wound her supple arms around his trembling body. "Maybe your father sold it, or gave it away."

Alan quickly swivelled and looked at her. "Why would he have done that?"

"I don't know," she shrugged again. Realising that it needed some more investigation he stepped forward to look a little more closely at his mother, and although he felt as if he was invading her sexuality, he got as close as he dare. As he looked Marsha suddenly sighed, "Alan."

"What?"

"Give me your hand."

"Why?"

"Because looking at that picture, and seeing what your mother's doing, has made me feel horny," she moaned while guiding his hand under her skirt and pressing it against the gusset of her pants. "And I just wanted to let you know how wet I am."

"So you are," he grinned as he took her hand and pushed her onto the bed.

Looking down he became transfixed as she cleverly lifted the front of her skirt to reveal the pagan design of her lime green knickers and with her eyes tightly closed her words sounded even more explicit, "Remember the man beside your mother?"

"Yes!"

"Well, I want you to put your hand where he had his."

"What here?"

"No," she groaned taking his wrist and moving into the right place. "Here!"

"Really," he tormented as his palm again nestled against her covered cunt.

"Oh! Yes."

"Would this be better?" Asked the question as he climbed onto the bed, knelt between her thighs and moved his hand inside her knickers.

"Much."

"Then how about putting this in there," he smiled while quickly pulled down his own pantaloons and holding his stiff cock.

Her eyes opened the moment before a wicked smile ran along her lips. "That would be a much better idea," she whimpered as her eyes closed again. Understanding the moment he smiled when pulling down her knickers and slipping his cock up her cunt. "Harder!" She panted, as her own body arched in unison with each one of his thrusts. The combined smell of their bodies only urged him to be selfish and silence the throaty scream of pleasure as his climax caused every muscle in his body to contract with erotic severity.

Having finished, he looked down to give a wide smile of sexual gratification. He never looked at Marsha as she swiftly placed her own fingers where but a moment ago his cock had been. He walked away without ever turning back, and while moving listened as the intensity of the woman's own intimate satisfaction squealed like a suckling pig. Through the bedroom door he stepped and stood against the chiselled wood of the banister and gazed pompously down at the gathered crowd, of revellers, totally oblivious to what had happened in Marsha's private world but a moment ago. As he stood, his mind flickering over each moment, he smiled when Marsha came and joined him. She wrapped her arms, in the expression of friendship, around his strong frame along with the whispered words, "Who are you looking for?"

"Carol!" Burst the name as he kept swinging his gaze around the people below. As he kept looking various people drifted into focus. There was Brian Archer, dressed as Perseus, trying his hardest to get his hands inside the covering tunic of Diana the Goddess of Love. There was Florence Nightingale or Caroline Hills, attending to a wounded World War One soldier who wasn't her husband. He was sitting in the corner of the room with someone else's wife perched upon his knee. The recognised man was grinning lecherously as his hand was beneath the blue serge skirt of the look a like sixteen year old schoolgirl from St Trinian's. There were other couples in a variety of arrangements, but there was no sign of Carol.

"She's probably gone home," Marsha offered as a reasonable statement.

He shrugged his shoulders, in acceptance, and responded, "You're probably right." With this likely explanation sinking in he twisted his head and looked directly at Marsha. "I think that I'd better go and see if she's all right," he sweetly offered and with that left the party.

He rounded the corner. Walked up the loose pebbled driveway making quite a lot of noise and noticed the single light in his father's old study. Thinking that maybe she was in there or that they'd been burgled, hurried until he stationed himself in the doorway looking in. He was pole-axed. He was petrified with fear. He swallowed hard as if trying to force the large lump of suspicion to slip down his throat. He failed, and felt the rush of adrenaline cascading throughout his body. She was in that room all right looking quite relaxed and seemed totally unaware of the destruction that had happened. She appeared unconcerned at the mess as she sat at the desk scrutinising the contents of the book in front of her. Her gaze never faltered as he pushed his way through the broken furniture and glided towards her. She still continued to stare as he stood at her side. Eventually she turned her face and simply pointed at the red writing in that open book. Seeing what was being shown he suppressed his annoyance because he knew of his father's pre-occupation to detail and how little snippets of background information would find their way inside the covers of particular publications that would obviously assist in the man's work.

The untimely death of Captain Young had only served as a reminder to Alan of how precious the relationship, with his father, actually was. With the growing emotion of guilt shrouding each day he would go into the study trying to discover any gems of knowledge that might prove beneficial in his desire to understand his father. He would pick up several books from the in-house library and scan its undoubted reference. He would see the large amount of cryptic comments written in red and tried his damnedest to understand their intricate content. Of course he failed miserably because most, if not all, appeared to have been written by an unintelligent spider and there was no way that his modern mind could assimilate their concept. He had at times of ultimate boredom flicked through that same book, which now lay open in front of Carol, with complete indifference. No words were spoken as her forefinger, once again, ran along the red lettering underneath the boldness of the name. "Are you alright?" He asked as his strong arm raced around her trembling shoulders. He noticed the single tear rolling down her cheek and tenderly dabbed it dry.

Was it hostility that now forced her words to squeal? "Can't you see," sobbed the declaration as the acidic tone sounded like someone scrapping their fingernails down a blackboard.

A violent shiver crashed through his body. It seemed to start in his shoulders and ultimately raced down to his feet. He shuddered, again, as he looked down at the yellow flower. He harshly panted as if forcing the words from his mouth. "That's the second time that I've seen that flower tonight," he admitted.

She never twisted her face to look at him, but merely asked, "Where, did you see it the first time?"

The heady atmosphere was drawing him to answer. "On a painting," he responded while staring down at the picture. It was a moment later he added, "Of a woman reading a book."

"Where was that?" She repeated.

"In one of the Colonel's bedrooms."

"And what were you doing in there?"

Not wanting to admit anything shrugged, "Just looking."

"And I suppose the painting was of a naked woman?"

Under his breathe he answered, "And a bit more besides."

"Pardon!"

"Nothing," he grinned and then as if trying to change the subject added. "That flower seems to be getting everywhere."

"Why d'yer say that?"

"Because isn't it similar to one that Erin's holding in the painting she'd given me?"

"I don't think so," she shrugged.

"Come on then," he said while harshly dragging her up the stairs and powerfully pulling her inside his room. Together, they stared at the empty space where the painting should have been. His mouth fell open in disbelief. "Where is it?" Stormed his voice launched with the ferocity of an atomic bomb. There was no time for answers as the sound of racing feet could be heard scrunching across the drive outside. In an instant he'd pushed Carol away so that she staggered and fell upon his bed. He never looked back as the pent up anger, welling inside his mind, forced him to hurtle headlong down the stairs. Through the open door he chased and onwards. He heard no sound, only his own frantic breathes, and for this he stopped. He listened but there was nothing. The air was silent as he craned his neck as if to hear the slightest noise, and for the next few moments simply stood his ground with gaze adjusting to the shadowy glow from a single street light. Suddenly, he heard the quiet crackle of something in the black distance and as he moved closer it went deathly quiet. Like a hungry vulture after carrion he drifted towards the blackened shell of the bus shelter and stopped to listen. Slowly, he became aware of panting breathes but an arms length away, and so with the speed of an assassin reached inside and grabbed his victim. The scream was pitiful as their faces met. A second scream confirmed his mistake as Alan saw exactly who he'd caught, because even in the yellow light he instantly recognised his mother.

It took but a moment before either spoke and when they did it was her appeal that came first. "What's the matter?" She enquired as Alan watched the shadowy figure of his maternal parent adjusting her dishevelled costume. He was even more shocked when the Colonel moved into sight to expose the fact that his buckskin trousers were around his ankles. Seeing what he saw; Alan shook his head in apology as a knowing smile formed along his lips. For in his sober mind he honestly could not accept the fact that the Colonel had but a moment ago been shagging his mother. He quivered in disbelief as yet again he could not accept the fact that it was his mother needing, or enjoying the sexual satisfaction that two people could share. Embarrassment now controlled her son as he stepped away to allow both his mother, and her consort, the necessary time to make themselves presentable. In doing this Alan turned his back, as a mark of respect, and waited. The sound of zips and fasteners only highlighted the unnatural conception that it ought to be just the young who took pleasure in having the occasional fuck. Alan never turned as the Colonel's footsteps were heard to walk away and disappear into the isolation of the night, for it was only when he felt a soft feminine hand being placed upon his shoulder that he responded.

"We've been burgled," apologetically announced the excuse for his disturbance of their obvious pleasure.

Together they walked back through the gate and down the drive. As one they entered the house and made directly for the study where, on seeing the carnage, his mother simply collapsed. He struggled to carry her dead weight, but eventually he got her to the couch where he allowed her to remain. He was scanning the room when suddenly a realisation hit home. He remembered pushing Carol away before chasing after ghosts, so where was she? He recalled her falling safely upon his bed. But that was several minutes ago, so he couldn't quite understand the absolute quiet the house seemed shrouded in. Requiring some answers he left his mother and charged up the stairs yet again. To his room he raced and violently swung the door wide. He clenched his fist in aggravation at what he saw. His heart exploded with frustration because she simply wasn't there. Was it absolute panic that forced him to race downstairs and go outside to stand like the Colossus of Rhodes in the absolute pitch of night? Or was it something else that made him scream, "Carol! Where are you?"

It was the next day after dinner when Alan decided to go down to the river and contemplate the recent events. "I thought I might find you down here," his mother smiled as she walked up to him. "Because I think you deserve an explanation."

"If it's about what happened last night," he offered. "Then I really don't need to know."

"Oh! But you do," she half smiled and hearing this he hurriedly sighed because he obviously realised the possible content of the conversation. "I'd just turned eighteen when I first met your father and after a whirlwind romance we sent out invitations explaining that Miss Yvonne Parsons would like various people to attend her marriage on the Saturday with a full Naval service. After the ceremony my husband took me back to the Oyster Hotel, in Portsmouth, and insisted that I go upstairs to disrobe before getting into in the marital bed alone. Like the dutiful wife I obeyed and waited for him to join me. Eventually he walked through the bedroom door, gave a warm smile, and turned the light off. Hearing him remove his uniform I cowered when he eventually got in beside me. I was a virgin that night, and although I'd heard little snippets of information about what was supposed to happen between us, I was petrified."

"First night nerves I presume," he smirked.

"You could say that," she grinned. "But I needn't have worried because they quickly vanished as his expert hands started to caress my breasts and other naughty parts of my naked body."

"Please mother," he choked while shaking his head in Freudian horror. "I really don't want to know any of the graphic details."

"Sorry," she smiled. "I quite understand."

"Thanks!"

"But you have to remember," she warmly smiled. "That as a young girl I was starting out on my own personal journey of discovery concerning the pleasures, if any, that could be found in the sexual intimacy between two people."

As he listened to her words an erotic picture, of his copulating parents, formed inside his head which was forcing him to shiver and not quite knowing how to respond to what his mother had just explained answered, "So I suppose you learnt that there was more to just lying there and staring at the cobwebs on ceiling."

"Oh! Yes," she smiled. "Because from that first night I was on the beginning of an adventure that was to bring me fantastic satisfaction." Suddenly, she caught sight of his face. "And if you're thinking that while your father was away on board his little boat," she giggled like a schoolgirl. "Then I would take the opportunity to find solace in some other man's bed."

"Isn't that what you're saying," he stared. "Because it sounds like that while he was away serving his country you were being serviced."

"That's not what I said!"

"It sounds like that to me!"

"You've just got a dirty mind."

"No I haven't," he sulked. "But listening to you what other conclusion can I draw."

"Please," she warmly smiled. "I loved your father, and yes he would be away on a tour of duty but I was faithful throughout my marriage." There was a momentary pause before she continued her story, "In saying that, though, I would get many offers from the young cadets wanting to become my consort."

"You mean they simply wanted to get inside your knickers."

"Alan," she scowled. "There's no need for that kind of language."

"But I thought!"

"What, that you can talk to your mother like that!"

"I suppose so," he shrugged. "Because listening to the way you were talking then I thought that it'd be alright."

"Well it's not," she glared. "And anyway I promised to be faithful to your father as it was a wife's duty that came with the job."

"But, surely you realised that before you married him!"

"Of course I did," she admitted. "So after the initial apprehension, of that first night, I decided that when he came home I would go out of my way and make it a very special occasion."

"That's good to hear," he smirked. "And I presume he made up for lost time."

"If you're thinking about our sex life," she amorously smirked. "Then I had no complaints in that department."

"I'm glad about that."

"Henry even went as far as commissioning a painting that he hoped would keep me satisfied when he was away."

"And did it?"

"Oh! Yes," she warmly sighed as he instantly noticed that her right hand had now moved until nesting in the lap of her skirt. "Because I would often go into his study and stare at the erotic image of the picture while doing unspeakable things to myself."

Hearing this and taking a quick look noticed some slight changes in her appearance. Her face had more warmth to it probably due to the fact that her nipples had now become more pronounced and remembering the erotic painting lamely asked, "Do you still go into the study and do those sort of things?"

She looked at him with a modicum of horror. "No," she said. "Because after your father's death I just couldn't bring myself to keep remembering the happy times we had together and so I sold the painting."

"So, where is it now?"

"I'm not sure," she answered. "Because I left it at a London auction house and I remember getting some money from its sale and so as far as I'm concerned it's gone forever and I hope that whoever's bought it gets as much pleasure from it as I did."

"Do you know who actually did buy it?"

"No."

"So it could have been anyone?"

"I suppose so."

"So, if I'm hearing this correctly," he assumed. "Then you've allowed a complete stranger to keep looking at that picture?"

"Put like that," she mildly frowned. "Then I suppose I have."

"Aren't you bothered?"

"Why?"

"Because there's probably a pervert, out there, playing with himself while looking at you."

"I've told you before," exploded the reprimand. "About your language."

"Sorry!"

"Anyway," she started "Just because my sex life had fizzled out to nothing then why shouldn't I allow someone else to find erotic pleasure in seeing my naked body?"

"Okay," he huffed. "So, let's get back to what you were up to last night."

"What," she frowned. "That I allowed the Colonel to have sex with me?"

"Yes!"

"So what's wrong with that?"

He looked at her and realised that, although she was technically his mother, there was a good looking woman sat in front of him. Infact a very sexy woman. "Nothing I suppose," dribbled the answer. "But what made you change your mind about the sexual side of your life?"

"It may have had something to do with what Alice once said to me over the phone."

"So what's she said now?"

"To put it in her words," she smiled. "When was the last time I'd actually held a stiff cock in my hand and enjoyed having good shag?" He looked absolutely shocked to say the least, but then realised that he'd never been privy to the scandalous conversations that sometimes occur between a mother and daughter.

"Trust her."

"Why?"

"Bringing the conversation back to basics."

"I'm rather glad she did," smiled her reply. "Because, that night I went to bed and while laying there reminisced about the good sex I enjoyed with your father."

"Please stop there," he implored as yet again a vivid picture formed inside his head.

"Anyway," she smiled. "I decided that maybe your sister's right and to cut a long story short the Colonel has been my lover for the past four years."

What had happened to Carol Forrester? Well the CID hung around the house like leeches to its victim and come the second week had managed to finalise exactly what had happened.

The statement read. With Alan Young, arriving home early from a prior engagement, he'd unwittingly disturbed the attempted break-in of the house. Confusion, and fright, now ruled as the two intruders thought of a devious ploy. With no time to prepare for their escape it was decided that Miss Carol Forester was to play the confused woman sitting amongst the cowardly epitaph to a crime. She played it to full effect, and such realism, that Alan Young was totally fooled. This couldn't have been planned better because the second person now had more than sufficient time to remove the said item, or items, before making their escape. With the confusion of the situation slowly clarifying Alan Young sensed that something was amiss and with great urgency raced upstairs to discover that the painting was in fact missing. It was while searching the room, and attempting to gather information, that Mr Young thought he heard footsteps running over the gravel driveway outside and wanting to apprehend this second intruder raced from of the house. Now with Mr Young out of the way and recognising the opportunity, Miss Forester slipped from the scene of the crime and met up with her accomplice at an agreed rendezvous. Now together at the Observatory, the rather derelict building on the outskirts of the village, a quarrel took place between the two burglars that ultimately led to the more serious crime. Evidence to this hypothesis was everywhere. Detectives found pink and white threads of her costume clinging to splinters of wood. They found signs of an obvious struggle, which had occurred, and strands of black and blond hair matching both the victim and the suspect. They found a set of footprints matching those of a Mr Jason Hickling that pointed to the fact that something bulky had been dragged. A police cordon had been set up and the coroner's report confirmed that the time of death was between four, and five, o'clock in the morning. It was also confirmed that Miss Forrester had been involved in a struggle, and the lacerations to her face and body pointed to the perpetrator being a male, before suffering a severe blow to the cranium. Although this played a substantial reason of her death, the coroner pointed to the fact that she was still alive when she entered the water and the primary cause of death was in fact drowning. Indications also showed that she'd had sex before her death and analysis of the semen corresponded to the specific DNA of Mr Hickling. There must have been some sort of struggle because detectives found traces of the victim's skin under the accused fingernails. More corroboration of the facts emerged when skin was also discovered beneath the broken fingernails of the victim, and the line of scratches torn down the face of the accused only seemed to verify the facts. The police found footprints leading a direct path towards the riverbank and after dredging the water located a handle, of some sort, that was later identified as being the weapon used and discovered the accused fingerprints everywhere. There were several statements, especially the ones from both Mrs Yvonne Young and Colonel Michael Ledbetter indicating that there was someone at the gates to the garden of the Observatory and from the description given a photo-fit was produced of the suspect.

Mr Hickling's detailed account of events leading up to the time was so full of flaws that it would have taken a miracle not to have proved him guilty. Being from outside the village, he stood out like a sore thumb when seen on several occasions talking to Miss Forrester. He even went to the extent of admitting to having sexual relations with her but claimed that on the night in question he'd been drinking continuously all day after she'd expressed her desire to finish with him, which was collaborated in the hand written letter they'd found in one of his pockets. He stated that he fallen asleep and can only remember being woken by the sound of someone walking through the derelict shell of the room in which he'd taken refuge. He said that he was quite surprised to see Carol Forrester, as well as a man he'd never seen before, walking slowly into view. By the light of several torches they just sat talking, but he can remember watching Carol getting drunk until finally she collapsed and fell asleep. The two men continued chatting about various things until it was decided that they also went to sleep. He cannot remember the exact time but he suddenly felt a hand being taken and placed on a pair of woman's naked breasts. He obviously assumed that it was Carol Forrester having woken and for all intense and purposes wanted to have sexual intercourse. The DNA from the semen sample taken from inside the victim's vagina confirms that this indeed was true. Unfortunately, the forensic detail point to the tears in the membrane of the vaginal walls corresponding to the brutal repetition of the sexual act. In conclusion the probability was that she'd been raped.

Justin Hickling was accused of the rape and murder of Carol Forester, in a fit a jealousy, and also of the burglary of Calder's. Although, after an extensive search the painting was never found so it was assumed that he'd disposed of his ill gotten gains before his arrest. He was later sentenced to life imprisonment in one of Her Majesty's Secure Institutions where he'd spent exactly four months, always claiming his innocence, when the news was leaked that he'd been found hanged.

Carol Forester's funeral was a solemn occasion. There were only members of her family, and immediate friends, gathered around the graveside on that wet April morning. The rain came in torrents as the wet, but dutiful, vicar prattled on. "Ashes to ashes," droned his words as the fine particles of Earth were thrown. "And dust to dust," solemnly proclaimed the standard line as the vicar sermonised about the happy existence of the young woman being laid to rest in that corner of the graveyard. Alan's heart started to pound as he looked across at the mourners and saw a young woman lift her covered head and for a moment stare directly at him. Before he could even nod his recognition she'd bent away as a further mark of respect. It was in that second he felt the chill of the air while instantly recognising the sweetness of her smile. The drops of rain lashing against his face felt like lead shot, rattling against a length of board, as he stared at the long strands of her bleached hair cascading down her face. He never noticed the frosty atmosphere of the cortège as he watched the fullness of her figure that had blossomed from the teenage temptress he'd once known to the delicious beauty of the married woman standing gazing into the grave of her sister. When at last the service had been completed the ceremonial cortège moved away, only to re-assemble in the dining room of Calder's. There, in one corner, was Commander Marshal Forester dressed so reverently in the black of grief. Next to him was his wife, Kitty, also dressed in accordance with the day? Both were talking to Alan's mother, and both were holding cups of something a little stronger than the standard sherry. Feeling the isolation of grief Alan soberly walked up to the banquet placed upon the large dining table and began to gather what he needed to eat. He was doing this, not because he was hungry, but because he simply wanted something to do. He'd been there but a moment when Wayne, his nephew, ran headlong into him. "Are you okay?" He asked while taking a bite from the ham sandwich he'd recently picked.

The young lad seemed a trifled shocked, but took a step back and looked his uncle straight in the eye. "Yes," he innocently chirped, and with that he ran back to wherever he'd come from.

"Go and find your sister," barked a voice he instantly recognised, and looking at the guilty party saw Alice ushering her youngest son away. Alan smiled when seeing Wayne disappear from view and the child's smile was so reminiscent of the ones he would give whenever his parents ushered him away. With a feeling of déjà vu sweeping over him he began to walk towards his sister when the clatter of something fragile hit the floor somewhere. He closed his eyes in absolute dread, as all heads turned towards the commotion.

The corner of his mouth rose, like his father's used to, whenever he spoke after such a calamity. "It's alright," began Alan's docile prologue of recognition. "I'll go and see what's happened." His sister's hand waved in receipt of the offer, and with that he walked from the room. He shrugged his shoulders, more in relief than anything else, and on entering the study saw exactly what had happened. He laughed quietly to himself. He shook his head like most parents are apt to do when about to chastise whomever it was responsible for whatever had happened. On the floor, against the desk side was the painting, which his father treasured more than anything else in the room. Its frame seemed to be slightly cracked by the fall, but apart from that it appeared undamaged. He carefully picked it up and quite deliberately replaced it upon the hook that had been used since its arrival into the house.

He'd just put it in the right position before taking a step backwards to stare directly at the oil painting of HMS Tanmouth that had been given to his father as a retirement present. He was staring when suddenly feeling two warm hands encircling his stomach. Glancing down, he immediately noticed the single band of gold around the third finger of the left hand, and for this scrunched up his nose in an act of uncertainty. "Alan," sighed the sympathetic plea as he felt the softness of her hands so securely held within the strength of his own. He slowly turned and when they came face to face simply stared into the tear strained jewels of her emerald eyes. His pulse quickened as she wrapped her arms around his shoulders and simply pushed her head into his broad chest. It was as if the clock had been turned back when he felt the damp of her tears soaking his shirt, and for that he instinctively wrapped his strong hands around her sobbing head to coerce the sorrow to spill. It must have been a good five minutes before either spoke, or made any effort to part and it was only when a stern voice penetrated the atmosphere.

"Oh! There you are!" Harshly spoke the words of the military toned man. Alan looked and simply stared directly at the man responsible, and it was at that precise moment that he realised that this was probably her husband. As if to prove his assumption the lady in his arms shuddered, and he felt the way she trembled like a leaf. The man in question walked, or more exactly marched, into the room and stood in awe at the Warmongering paraphernalia hanging on the walls, or the collections of books restored to their undoubted splendour. The man walked across to the window and watched the rain driving relentlessly against the glass pane, and for this sighed at the thundering sound. As he posed with hands clasped behind his back, in the authoritative mode of an officer waiting for an incriminating report, the man's shoulders began to tremble. He thought for a moment, and with the clarity of his thinking so evidently on view, turned towards the two people still bound as one. "I think it's time we left!" He instructed and the tone of his voice dripped the insolence of a naval rating.

Hearing the command, well that's what it sounded like; Erin craned her neck and gently gazed into the comforting eyes of Alan. With no word forthcoming she glided towards the symbol of her marriage and stood like the irresponsible child waiting for the reproach of his anger. There were words spoken that Alan couldn't hear. There were gestures of an emotion he thought had died all those years ago. Finally, he watched the angry man walk from the room without ever casting his gaze back. His pulse slowed to a near stop as Erin followed. With her gone the room was quite desolate. The room was so cold and empty now that it caused a shiver to travel the length of his spine. He shuddered violently, but that lasted only a moment as Erin danced quickly into the room, once again, throwing her head from side to side as if trying to locate someone else. She hastened to his confused stance, pushed a single finger against his lips in the plea of silence, and just as swiftly opened her handbag to remove an envelope. Into his steady hand she pushed the offering, and when he'd clutched the gift she simply turned and fled. He was still clutching the envelope when he heard voices of farewell being exchanged. Deciding not to be intrusive went to the study window from where he'd be able to watch the grieving family drive away. Feeling as if his world had been turned upside-down he slumped laboriously against the wall and waited. He to watched the heavy rain falling into large pools of water that had formed on the driveway. He frowned. He smirked, like a naughty child, when he saw both Erin and her husband walk towards the blackened vehicle. Their raised umbrellas concealing their faces. They never turned to look back at the building as they drove away, but suddenly he gripped the envelope that bit tighter when she twisted her head. Was it a smile he saw, or was the look of a frightened child?

It was after that fleeting moment that things began to change. It was as if the words in Erin's letter, about their forlorn romance, compelled him to once again dig and delve through the books and leaflets that he'd discovered inside his father's study. He would spend many hours searching in the hope of finding whatever was there as clear as day. Night after night he would go to bed in the knowledge that he'd obviously missed that vital clue. He read books on military strategy, books on intrigue and espionage, pamphlets on HMS Tanmouth and its secret armoury; he even looked through the book that Carol had opened on that fateful day. There was nothing. Only the standard red ink indications of something, or other, but try as he might he could not fuse the obvious simplicity hoping to make a start.

His enthusiasm eventually waned and it was a couple of months later on a close and clammy evening, in early June, that Alan decided to venture down to the lichen covered schist where friends had told him an enigmatic stranger would recount his truly wondrous stories. Feeling bored and ultimately having nothing better to do, showered and dressed according to the weather, and after rummaging through his rather sparse wardrobe and discarding various items of clothing finally settled on a pair of white tennis shorts and flame red vest, with the words Hello Sexy printed across the chest. Now feeling like a million dollars sat beside the stereo to await the approach of the witching hour and when it finally arrived, at around eight thirty, decided to make steady progress towards the open-air auditorium. With his heart bubbling in anticipation he wandered down the lane, which followed the flowing waters of the river, and soon found himself on the tract of land where the village cricket team would play their games. As he sauntered, with hardly any cares, noticed several couples huddled together in their secluded hideaways obviously waiting for the commencement of the entertainment.

Having located the exact spot from where he could both see and hear he'd been sat, for some moments, totally bewitched by the fluorescent incandesce of the evening light when a familiar voice was heard to speak. "Is there going to be anyone sitting here?" She demanded and the tone of her voice was painted with pure acrimony as well as an underlying requirement for an immediate response.

Hearing the request, partially lost in the gathering volume of sound, Alan slowly aimed his curious stare at the culprit. His eyes were quick to focus on the shimmering beauty highlighted by the subtle changes of light and instantly recognised the woman standing, hands on hips, looking down at him. It was the one person he kept in his heart and for that a large smile raced to his lips. His pulse-rate increased to the point of explosion, because she was stunningly beautiful. Her auburn hair shimmered in the dusky evening light to resemble a lush carpet of carmine silk. Its' shoulder length superbly framing the beauty of her face. Its elegance subtlety enhanced by the wide brimmed sun hat she was wearing. Eagerly moving down her body he absorbed the fact that she was simply wearing a blouse of the thinnest pale lilac material tied in a knot which highlighted the fact that her two erect nipples could be claimed as being obscene. Licking his lips while realising her figure absolutely mirrored the perfection of Diana the Greek Goddess of hunting, and with this thought provoking his imagination he continued down her tanned belly and was shocked to see the single gold ring piercing the luscious texture of her navel. He gulped. He carried on further down until settling on the flimsy material of the cerise wrap around skirt that hid the pure seductive length of her legs.

    Suddenly, a small cough as well as a sharp kick against his shin caused his clouded mind to be dragged mind back to reality and it was this moment that alerted him to the fact that she was impatiently awaiting an answer. Now feeling decidedly annoyed, he looked directly into the challenge of her emerald green gaze and for that confrontation bit his bottom lip. The pent-up frustration, the lovelorn unease soon evaporated as she ran her pink tongue over her cherry red lips which seemed to pout an offered apology. He had now decided to return his answer in the same way as he'd received the question, full of flippancy. "Not yet!" He delivered and as he spoke felt a strange sensation starting to build inside his gut that began to slowly climb and force his heart to beat harder against his ribs. Since she'd left, on that fateful day, he'd rarely felt this kind of sensation and was utterly bewildered as to why he felt the way he did. Was it the warmth of the evening combined with the pure freshness of her femme fatale? Was it the way she kept hitching about while waiting for his answer? Was it the thought that he'd probably never get another opportunity to actually come into contact with her, whether accidentally or not? Or was it something more unmistakably simple. With this conundrum spinning wildly inside his head he sat and pondered, and as each moment flashed he realised exactly why he felt the way he did.

She collapsed by his side and having removed her hat pushed her nimble fingers through the fluffy strands of her hair causing the light to reflect the coloured texture. "Hello," she smiled as her voice sounded sugary and tasted like the sweetest caramel.

"Erin!" Half coughed, half spluttered his response. Having identified the usurper of his space he was a trifle unsettled. Was her husband somewhere watching for his reaction? Was her husband even aware that she was there? The anxiety bubbling through his stomach set off the alarm bells inside his head that proved just as chaotic when scanning the area around.

"Aren't you going to welcome me," she pouted. Again, he twisted and seeing nothing untoward paused before giving a quick kiss upon her cheek. "Is that it," carved the damning rebuff.

"I can't," he implored pulling back and feeling the anguish. "Your husband might be looking!"

"But, he's not here," she announced as the look of formal relief swept across her face, and having spoken clutched his hands. "He's in Gibraltar doing some work."

"So, why are you here?"

Alan was speechless, if not a little bemused because whether intentionally or not, her next words only seemed to ignite some dormant infatuation that lay hidden. "I just wanted to get away," she smiled while leaning forward. "And have the chance to think."

"What about?"

"My life," she frowned as they kissed again, but this second had more passion to it. He responded in the only way he knew, and that was to wrap his arms around her shoulders and pull her close. His eyes closed with the memory he held. His heart pounded as he kissed her for all the years they'd spent apart. Suddenly, he stopped. Hesitantly he pushed her away and looked into her eyes. They stared, with no one daring to make the first move until finally Erin reached out her small hands as if trying to snare him. Having caught hold she pressed her luxurious, but trembling, frame into his torso and teasingly held herself there. It was at that instant; with both looking intensely into the others eyes something wonderful and definite happened. Had a seed been planted that was now beginning to flower in their fertile imaginations? Had she deliberately rubbed herself against his broad chest? Was it the fruits of his own fantasy, or was it something more risqué that forced him to arrogantly push against the softness of her breasts? Together for the next few moments they touched and played like inexperienced lovers, but again it was Erin who first reacted by pushing her small tongue wickedly between the fullness of her lips. Then as if to encourage his response readily thrust her excited body at him. "Don't you remember the day before I left for Gibraltar and how you felt my heart pound?" She smiled.

"How can I forget?"

"So would like you to feel it again?" She pouted demonstratively while taking his hand and placing it securely against the straining fabric of her blouse. Now with it in position he could feel exactly the softness and warmth. As the evening progressed the not so subtle interchanges between them grew with each moment, and as they became lost within their friendship a large crowd gathered to listen to the storyteller's words. But tonight, which was to be his last not a word was heard as they sat fidgeting with their thoughts swirling inside their heads. For moment upon moment and with his world turning somersaults Alan sat inwardly reflecting on what he was doing because the years of pent up passion finally exploded when he quietly placed a trembling palm against the covering fabric of her skirt. Like a forgotten lover he gently fiddled until feeling the sensual softness of her naked thigh and then, like an army on manœuvre, his fingers moved until feeling the guarding cover of her taut lingerie. His pulse raced exponentially as he wormed across the smooth, but moist, fabric of her pants. He held his breath while creeping beneath the right elasticated edge and sighed, with pleasure, as his fingers foraged through the prickly strands of pubic hair and found the sodden entrance to her pussy.

Suddenly his wrist was strongly captured. "Not here!" Dramatically whispered the words as her face came close to his and having spoken she stood. Watching for any reaction she held out her hand for him to accept. "Let's go for a walk," she pouted while increasing her leggy stride and scurrying away. Alan simply watched as she moved and was instantly drawn towards the rhythmic sway of her hips and his parched mouth became painful as he tried to lick the sandpaper texture of his lips. His heart began to beat in rapid time as her body pulled his lecherous gaze like a magnet. Needing no second invitation he nonchalantly hurried to catch her quite dramatically by the shoulders, and then with underlying passion twisted her so that he could stare directly into the softness of her smile. Seeing him frown, her smile quickly became a giggle when noticing the exact direction of his stare and to reinforce the sensual temptation that was obviously on offer pulled back her shoulders.

They walked, like good friends, down the well known bridal path that ultimately led to the sounds of water rumbling its way towards the sea. Occasionally, they would make meaningful glimpses as they giggled and laughed on the journey to wherever they were heading. On one such event with a five barred gate blocking their progress and him being the gentleman of opportunity watched as she easily climbed to the top before jumping to the ground. Thanks to the law of physics and the resultant air resistance causing her skirt to resemble an open parachute, he watched as her feet hit the floor first. He felt wicked. He felt privileged as a grin, as wide as any valley, sped across his mouth when the display of her peach coloured lingerie came intimately into view. It was only a momentarily glimpse but that didn't matter because the seed of optimism had been planted inside his mind that forced him to take a calculated risk. Biting the corner of his lip he climbed to the top rung and posed like a great Trojan Warrior. Feeling the time was right he plunged to Earth knowing full well that his fall would be broken by the woman standing laughing at him. Of course everything went according to plan and as luck would have it they collapsed together onto the soft grass below.

"Right for that," she giggled while scrambling to her feet and instantly straddling his body. "I'm going to squash you."

"Oh! No you don't," he administered while unashamedly sending two hands to nestle softly against the hidden flesh of her arse.

"Try and stop me," giggled the daring citation as she moved her weight quite dramatically. Feeling the pressure she'd applied a single realisation swept into his head. It was either now or never, and so with a modicum of playfulness bulldozed his errant hands beneath her skirt. It felt heavenly as his fingers ran over the smoothness of her skin. It felt wondrous when touching the silky threads barring any further progress. "Right," she smiled on standing. "You men are all the same." Hearing this statement his brow furrowed while watching her. "Because all you ever want to do is to get inside a young girl's knickers," focused the damning truth.

Alan grinned knowing full well that he'd been sussed, "Is that so wrong?"

"I'm not sure," she teased. "So, you'll have to catch me to find out." And having spoken she raced away. He was up like a shot and started giving chase. It didn't take long before he reached and grabbed her hand before pulling her into the intensity of his desire. They stopped. They turned to each other. Their eyes dancing. Their eager bodies trembling while waiting for any clues that might be there. Erin accepted and softly squeezed his hand before smiling her words, "Let's stop here!" Having spoken she collapsed onto the soft bed of grass while at the same time patting the area next to her. Alan was watching carefully as she casually lay and closed her eyes forcing her breathing to become more exaggerated. He stood motionless, but all the time the pounding of his heart gave away the basic thoughts welling inside his head. He smiled at what he saw and could feel the excitement beginning to build while noticing the exquisite beauty that was laying there. He already knew from his previous examinations that she wasn't wearing a bra and so licked his lips when seeing just how excited her nipples were. As he stared, Erin opened her eyes and the glint spoke volumes of how she must have felt because as if to prove the point her breathing became more intense. He watched as her excited breasts strained against the taut material and in that moment he knew. The feeling inside his stomach was churning. The primeval instinct forced his next action when, like a stone, he fell to lay at her side. She knew what was to come and so lay perfectly still as his agile fingers searched to locate the bound knot of her blouse. He smiled in triumph when with precision he pulled the two folds apart. His mouth formed a crescent as he could now see her naked tits. He smiled, with lust, when seeing the two nipples standing like triumphant climbers inside the discs of salmon pink. His breathes became a pant when watching the tip of her tongue poking deliciously from between her lips before racing around the fullness of her mouth. Seeing this unspoken invitation he approached a single breast and comfortably ensnared the warm flesh in the guarding palm of a hand. A spontaneous reflex forced him to start and roll the rigid nipple between excited fingers and hearing no complaint, only the purrs of sexual pleasure, continued while allowing his open mouth to suck upon the other before gently nipping it between hungry teeth. Slowly, his kisses moved down her trembling body until halting at the waist-band of her skirt. For that moment he paused and waited. The wait lasted but a fraction before confidently lifting her arse and pushing up her skirt. Now seeing the frailty of her knickers he bent his head to kiss the wet gusset and as he did he closed his eyes, if for no other reason than fearing the erotic shock of what might be there when realising he'd just won first prize in the lottery of lust. Then like a butterfly rising from its chrysalis he tugged and removed her knickers before holding them aloft like a trophy and with not a care in the World simply tossed them away. With his heart beating ten to the dozen he shoved his hands beneath her arse and quickly lifted her cunt towards his waiting mouth. As his tongue rushed inside it felt hot with the blistering heat of passion, and as he lapped it felt luscious as if her body had been smeared in an earthy lubricant that gurgled like thick syrup. After each caress her throaty sighs became a deeper melody forcing him to search the exact position of her clitoris. Having discovered its location, he lapped like a kitten as her vocal sound bore witness to the nearing climax that would ultimately race throughout her body. Suddenly, she pushed him away and sat up. He felt cheated. He felt aggrieved, but above all else he felt uncertain. As he glanced at the saliva sparkling on the gossamer hair like the dew on a spring morning he became aware of her sudden panic. As he waited he needn't have worried because it appeared that the reason for this abrupt finish was quite simple inasmuch as she'd obviously heard someone approaching with a heavy cough and seeing exactly who it was had closed her legs in a modicum of embarrassment.

"Shouldn't be allowed," the anonymous man huffed, but like all critics of visible flesh was only to impatient to keep on staring in the hope of seeing more and not wanting to be caught enjoying what he'd seen the man playfully tugged at the dog's lead before disappearing from sight, with a vocal display of chuntering about how it was all so different in his day.

The moment of their unified excitement passed into yesterday's memory, and to reinforce the point Erin liberally purred her definite words with the underlying sense of regret. "No more," she apologised somewhat reluctantly while standing to start brushing down the pleats of her skirt. Her head moved from side to side as if trying to locate the forgotten pair of knickers he'd previously thrown somewhere and having discovered their location walked to where they were and gave a wicked smile the moment before turning her back. Seeing this innocent action Alan watched as he now knew what he had to do, because in one stride he'd positioned himself directly behind her. His heart was on fire as he reached and cradled both tits before feeling their wondrous weight. "Stop that," she sighed.

"Why," smiled the grin as he instinctively reached between her legs and started playing with her sopping cunt again.

"Because I need you."

"To do what?" He teased as she pushed him away and turned. They stood apart as if time meant nothing with each dreaming and thinking of what to do. Then as if to break the moment Erin reached and started fumbling with her cotton blouse. He was hypnotised when she'd removed it and exposed both tits for him. Next, with a quick flick of desire she stripped away her skirt and posed with hands on hips.

Not a word was spoken as she groped for his shorts and the sound of his zip being pulled confirmed her intent, and when her eager fingers reached inside his underwear he understood. Feeling the urgency he grinned, like a dog with two tails, when she seized his stiff cock and expertly guided it into the chill of the evening air. Suddenly with no hint, or clue, she shoved him violently away. He tottered backwards with astonishment spinning wildly inside his head. He was dazed and confused as he stumbled and eventually fell to Earth. He lay with his expression becoming serious when all at once she grabbed his shorts and pulled them down. She smiled when he was naked and it was then that she straddled his belly, because in that moment she bent from the waist and offered her pouting lips as the eternal offering of friendship. Their mouths met and they kissed in a frenzied display of courtship. Her hungry tongue probing every inch of his mouth. Sensing the underlying passion Alan manipulated a free hand and searched for the hidden secrets that had been released. He smiled with a lover's greed when fondling the fullness of her tits. He panted with desire when she grabbed his cock and held it ready. "Please," she begged. "I need you to fuck me!"

"You only had to ask," teased his words as she urgently started to increase the pace.

"Oh! Yes," she panted as the combined rhythm culminated in the throes of ecstasy surging through their bodies. Exhaustion, now forced both to simply lie side by side with not a word being spoken. Erin was the first to recover as she slouched on her elbows and smiled. She leaned forward and pushed her perspiring face intimately close to his so that he could feel the warmth of her breathing. He was astonished when her words were stage whispered, "It's been over two years since Patrick has seen me naked, and I can't remember the last time he fucked me!" And the basic language used and it's unprovoked admission caused him to rear back in some consternation but when she warmly added, "And I would like to thank you for making me feel like a woman again," prompted him to playfully nip the engorged texture of a single nipple before moulding his hand easily around the remaining bulk of that tit. She grinned with eyes growing wider in mock alarm and for that she giggled like a schoolgirl.

It was about twenty passed midnight when they finally arrived back at Calder's and it was only the noise, coming from the sitting room that indicated that there was anyone still up. Opening the door they walked in and were quietly surprised to see Alan's mother sitting on the settee chatting on the phone. "Look who's come to stay," smiled his opening gambit.

His mother turned and saw them. Then without hesitation immediately finished the conversation, and with a warm smile running the whole length of her mouth, quickly stood to extend her arms in obvious welcome. "Come and sit next to me," smiled the offer as the two women hugged. "And tell me all about what's happened to you." It was over the next hour, or so, that both women became totally engrossed in their own conversation and in doing so Alan was totally ignored. In fact he felt so left out that he decided to take a quick glimpse at the television screen, which was probably what most men would have done when being caught up in the middle of this kind of exchange, and saw the standard drivel being shown.

As if to make himself feel slightly better asked, "Does anyone want a drink?"

As one both women turned. "Yes please," smiled the standard reply and having answered returned to the chit-chat.

Shaking his head in mock annoyance he calmly walked to the drink's cabinet and once there poured his own before enquiring of his mother, "What would you like?"

"A Vodka and lime," she returned without looking. He gave a deep sigh and picking up the correct mixture strolled back and simply handed it over. "Thanks," she grinned as she put it on the table.

"And yours?" He enquired when tilting his face and looking at Erin.

"I'd like a sweet Martini," she answered with a mischievous smile. Puffing out his cheeks, like an over fed hamster, he did as he was asked and with a couple of overfull glasses in his hand wandered back. Again, he sat and tried his hardest to become part of the frivolous dialogue that was being exchanged, but like most men failed miserably because he either lacked the basic ability to talk at that level, or more likely lacked the necessary intensity. Now feeling even more rejected he sighed while turning towards the idiot box in the corner of the room and looked at the blond haired presenter talking to an elderly woman about the tattoos she'd had done on her body. The whole thing may not have been that interesting except for the fact that the over-sized lady, being questioned, was naked from the waist up and for that he grinned like a dirty ole man at a nudist's convention.

Suddenly the unmistakable tone of his mother's voice ripped apart his concentration. "Alan," she belittled. "What are you watching?"

He replied in the standard mode of male survival, "I'm not sure!"

And as usual the quick response was just as destructive. "Whatever it is," she lambasted. "It's disgusting."

"What is?" He casually shrugged.

"Seeing that old woman without any clothes on."

"Hadn't really noticed," he lied. "And anyway what's wrong with that?"

"She old," awkwardly shivered his mother. "And you can see her bosom."

"But it has gone passed the watershed!"

"He has got a point," Erin giggled in his defence as she noticed what they were talking about.

"I realise that," Alan's mother confirmed. "But it's not a pleasant sight seeing that woman's saggy breasts completely covered in tattoos." There was a pregnant pause before she continued. "And I hope mine don't look like that when I'm getting toward senility!"

"They might do," he muttered rather jokingly and having stated the obvious felt rather stupid. "But from where I'm sitting then I don't suppose you'll have any worries."

As soon as the words had left his mouth his mother immediately cupped her breasts. "You can stop looking," she scowled. "Because it's not something a son does to his mother!"

He was about to respond when Erin looked daggers at him and so changing tact. "I suppose the old biddy," he indicated. "May have just had a fetish about being covered in coloured ink."

"And you think that natural?"

"But isn't it traditional that some sailors look like that," he smirked.

"I know," she smiled as her eyes closed.

"So it's alright for men to have tattoos?" He asked when remembering the faded anchor on his father's lower arm.

"Not at all," she offered. "Because I do remember, from my time in the navy, that there were a few women who'd had them done."

"Really!"

"Yes really," she grinned. "But at least they had them discreetly placed."

"So you couldn't actually see them?"

"No," she admitted. "Because they would always be hidden under their uniforms."

"So I presume," he hypothesised. "That we're not discussing the kind that the lady on the television's got?"

"What d'yer mean?"

"Well," he pointed at the elderly woman's breasts. "Just look at the size of that dragon across her tits."

"Alan," his mother chastised.

"Sorry," he sulked. "So I don't suppose any of the wrens were ever allowed to have anything as flamboyant as that?"

"No," spoke the definite statement. "Most definitely not."

"So what were they allowed?"

"You have to remember," she grinned rather coyly. "That I was a young Wren at the time."

"So you're admitting that you had one done," he asked with a modicum of amazement.

"Maybe," she dramatically answered. And as soon as the word had fallen the atmosphere became thick, and for that she dropped her gaze to look at the floor. Both Alan and Erin watched just how easily his mother twitched like a broken toy.

"Now look what you've done," Erin scowled. "Because can't you see she's embarrassed?"

"I'm sorry," he offered. "I didn't realise." No one spoke as Erin strolled up and wrapped her arms around the other woman shoulders as if to comfort her. The look she gave forced Alan to make his excuses and leave both women talking like church mice. Understanding the indignity he'd caused quickly climbed to his room and lay listening to the radio hoping to pass the time and as the music played inside his head small fragments of something whirled around his mind. He was still reflecting when, about ten minutes later, a soft knock was heard on the door. It opened and in walked Erin who smiled as she neared his bed and once there sat on the edge.

"Is mum alright?" He asked looking at her.

"Yes," she smiled. "But!"

"What?" He snapped.

There was suddenly an awkward moment until she whispered, "I don't know whether I should be telling you this but can you remember what you were discussing downstairs."

"What," he wondered. "Whether mum's got a tattoo somewhere?"

"That's right."

"And."

"Well," she admitted. "She has got one and it's quite a nice design."

"So, you've seen it?"

"Oh! Yes."

"What's it of then?"

"A polar bear."

"That's a bit of a strange choice," he suggested.

"She wouldn't tell me the reason why but she did say that your father insisted that she had it done."

"What, like a secret emblem of some sort," he giggled as he thought about it.

"I don't think so."

"Why then?"

"If you knew where it was," she giggled. "Then you might have a better understanding."

"So where is it?"

"Somewhere rather personal."

"What, on her arse?"

"Nearly," she cooed. "But do you remember where you kissed me this evening?"

"What, down by the river?"

"Right idea," she smiled with a wicked grin. "Wrong place."

"Oh!"

"Oh! Yes," she smirked with a wicked glint. "So now can you picture it?" Hearing this he shivered as a strange sensation, the kind Oedipus must have felt, rippled through his mind. "And there were also some words above it."

"And what did they say?" He joked. "Touch me if you dare."

"No," she corrected. "Bears are in the Arctic."

Because she was a married woman it had been decided by Alan's mother that Erin should sleep in Alice's old room to prevent any shenanigans, or the like, when it came to a single man with hormones as well as matrimonial étiquette. This arrangement worked fine until the second night when he was suddenly woken; well he wasn't really asleep, by Erin climbing eagerly into his bed. "Fuck me," she urgently whispered while grabbing his stiff cock and guiding it into her wet cunt.

"Sleep well," Mrs Young asked as they both walked into the kitchen the next morning. "Because I thought I heard something banging about!"

"Like a log," her son announced as he optimistically placed his hand on Erin's arse and as he gently rubbed she wickedly gave a frantic jiffle.

Completely oblivious to what had happened his mother smiled, "When you're ready then can you drive me into town to get some new things for the party a week on Saturday?"

"Do I have to?" He complained.

"Yes," returned the answer. "And anyway Erin might like to come along."

Hearing this, the young girl's ear pricked up. "I was thinking of buying a new outfit," she smiled. "And seeing as he's got the day off work then he can be our taxi."

"I'd rather be at home!"

"I know you would," started the guilt trip. "But I thought you'd be willing to fetch and carry for us." The rest of the morning was taken up with various conversations, mainly between his mother and Erin, concerning what pieces of clothing they undoubtedly needed.

Eventually the seven mile car journey to town was in complete silence; well it was for him as you would expect, which also continued while he parked the car. "Okay, we're here," he shrugged as he got himself comfortable.

"Right," his mother started. "Don't you want to come with us?" Realising that he couldn't refuse followed them like an obedient dog and watched as they kept disappearing in and out of various shops until walking towards Knickerbockers the infamous lingerie emporium.

"Wait out here while we go and get some new underwear," Erin instructed and having given her order went inside, with his mother, to leave him looking at the erotically dressed manikins in the shop window. It was a good twenty minutes later, it may well have only been five but the wait increased the idea exponentially, when they eventually reappeared carrying various bag of something or other.

"Got everything," he hopefully enquired.

"Not quite."

"Now what," he asked looking a bit dejected.

"We need new dresses," they both explained when entering Perfect Style the best dress shop in town.

"So you don't need me," he hoped when spotting the shop's self service café.

"I may do," smiled the words from Erin he didn't really want to hear and with a sense of dread followed them towards the huge range of clothes in the women's section. He stood, like a leper, as they flittered from one rail of fantastic looking evening gowns to another until eventually moving towards the changing rooms clutching just a small sample. "Wait out here," they insisted and for the next half an hour kept trying on different designs. Eventually getting bored with the whole idea, especially when they kept appearing and asking his opinion, decided that the next outfit would be the one he'd unwaveringly declare to be the best. Watching the cubicle curtain open he watched as his mother marched towards him in what could best be described as a set of curtains.

"I don't think that suits," he choked with half a snigger.

"Okay," she sneered. "Then go and fetch me one you do like." Taking exactly two steps, to his left, grabbed an outfit and handed it over. Then like a judge, at a beauty contest, she held it at arms length. "There is no way that I'm wearing anything like that," she fired handing it back for him to replace. The outcome of this was that she brought the initial one which Alan had said made her look decidedly frumpy. Erin on the other hand had chosen well. Especially when she emerged from the cubicle for his honest opinion. His eyes sprang wide apart when seeing just how revealing the apple green and cherry red bodice was. Having finished, at long last, they went home and once inside it was his mother who spoke first. "Alan," her voice commanded. "Can you please carry the boxes upstairs and put them in my bedroom?" Lifting his eyes heavenwards he struggled up the stairs, with his mother, before moving inside the one room he'd very rarely been in. In fact he couldn't remember the last time and so when the door opened he stepped inside, like the obedient son, and dropped the parcels onto the bed in the untidy mess of youth. "Careful," snapped the word.

"Okay," slouched his response, and as he spoke instantly noticed the large painting above the bed. "Your father gave me that before he went on his last tour of duty," she admitted when noticing where he was staring. The painting itself was a scene of his father standing on the ice pointing at something in the distance. There was his boat, the Tanmouth, anchored behind but it was the two rather large white blobs of paint, in the foreground, that drew his attention. "What d'yer think those are," he challenged.

"I imagine they're probably penguins."

"Bit big for penguins," he smiled.

"Then, what d'yer think they are?"

"Some sort of bear."

"Maybe," she agreed. "But that's how I received it and do you want to know something else?"

"What!"

"I'm not bothered," she grinned. "Because I can't take it down."

"Why ever not?"

"It was the last thing your father gave me before his death," she confessed.

It was three days later when Alan woke with a start. Not because of who was beside him fast asleep, because she'd kept him company since that second night, but because he suddenly realised something. "Wake up," he demanded while violently shaking Erin.

"What's wrong?"

"I need to see that painting again!"

"What painting?"

"The one in mother's room above her bed."

"Why?"

"Because I want to examine it," he insisted.

"But, there's nothing wrong with it."

"Oh! Yes there is," he claimed when remembering the words he'd been told were above his mother's tattoo. "You don't get polar bears in the Antarctic."

"So!"

"Well maybe it's been done deliberately," fired the suggestion.

"Why?"

"I don't know," he hypothesised. "That's why I need to have a look at it again."

"Just look at the time," Erin sighed forcing her tits to flop against the white T-shirt she had on.

"I know it's late," he whispered. "But something's not right."

"So what are you asking?"

"I need you to go and wake mum so that I can go into her room and take a good look at the picture."

"What," she moaned. "Go and wake your mother."

"Yes!"

"And tell her what?"

"Anything," was his suggestion. "Something about the dress you brought for the party being wrong."

She looked at him and sighed, "But, surely that can wait till morning."

"If I don't do it now," he pleaded. "Then I'll probably never get another chance."

Hearing this Erin forced her eyebrows skywards. "Okay," she half heartedly agreed and with that very quietly left the room. By this time Alan had positioned himself by his own bedroom door and watched Erin disappearing. It took exactly two seconds before she reappeared looking quite shocked. Then as if passing a relay baton she grabbed Alan's wrist and dragged him back inside his own bedroom. "Just go and take a look," she vigorously suggested. "Because I think you'll be in for a bit of a shock."

With this piece of information he casually crept up to his mother's bedroom door and very quietly pushed it ajar. Then like a peeping tom looked inside and saw his mother asleep on her back. It wasn't the image of her pale pink nightie that was so erotic. Nor was it the fact that her nipples were poking through the material. But what made it obscene was when seeing the naked figure of the Colonel, complete with an erection, lying at her side also asleep. "I wonder what they've been up to," Alan asked as he and Erin got back into bed.

"This," she giggled while romantically removing the T-shirt.

"You could be right," he agreed as his hands massaged the pert firmness of her tits. They kissed, they fondled and he was particularly excited as he began to fuck her.

"Careful," Erin instructed watching him take the painting off the wall. "Your mother's only popped out for a moment!"

"I know," he said while urgently studying the picture.

Suddenly, they heard the front door open and quickly shut. "Hurry up," Erin urged. "She's back!"

Whether he wasn't quick enough, or more probably he thought he'd seen something, but the bedroom door burst open and Mrs Young strode in. "What do you think you're doing," asked the question.

"Just looking!"

"I can see that," returned the answer. "But why?"

"Because there's something wrong with this painting."

"Really?"

"Yes really," her son insisted. "Because I've decided that those white blobs are too big to be penguins."

"So what if they are," she scoffed. "It's my painting and there's nothing wrong with it!"

"Okay," he offered while climbing off the bed. "But I still say that there's something not quite right."

"Like what," she inferred. "That Henry was a spy and had hidden important details in the painting."

"I suppose so," he smiled when realising what a fool he'd been.

"Now can you please get out because I want to get changed?"

"Okay," he agreed while moving towards the door and then he suddenly turned because something had metaphorically hit him. "What went there?" He demanded as his finger pointed at the blank space on the wall where his father was also pointing.

"Nothing," she shrugged.

"Are you sure?"

His mother looked away and Alan saw the concentration whirling inside her mind. "Oh! Yes," she finally admitted. "I remember now."

"What was it?"

"A model of the Tanmouth in a glass case."

"So where is it?"

"I never did like it, and so after his death I had it removed and put in the garden shed." In the pitch of night, plus a rather dodgy torch, both he and Erin searched until it was decided that it would be far better if they tried the following day. The next morning he was up bright and early. So early in fact that he had time to go and search the shed, with that same dull torch, on his own. Whether it was because of his renewed enthusiasm, or more likely because they'd moved something, but it didn't take him long before discovering the glass case with a ship inside hidden in a corner.

"Is this; what was on the wall?" Alan asked when at last the kitchen door opened and his mother appeared.

"That's it," smiled her confirmation.

"So where's the key?"

"What key?"

"The key that opens the case."

"I didn't know there was one," shrugged the reply. As he stood thinking it was as if someone had switched on the light, in his head, because at that moment he was up and away. On the landing he bumped into Erin, who'd obviously just woken up, and having given her a quick peck on the cheek rushed passed into his mother's bedroom. Now inside he stopped and stared at the two unidentifiable blobs until a possible solution rippled through his mind. He gave a wicked smile as he gently touched the oils before applying a greater pressure. What did he feel when obviously pressing a little too hard and forcing his index finger through the canvas? Was it horror that triggered his trembling fit? Was it panic that forced the blood to drain from his face? It was neither of these but it was better than a poke in the eye.

"What have you done," scolded his mother when she saw what had happened.

"He's ruined it," Erin added standing at her side and looking at the picture.

"But I had to do it," flew his defence. "To see whether I was right."

"About what?"

"When you said that there wasn't a key," he twitched. "Something inside my head clicked."

"So you came up here and destroyed the picture!"

"Put like that," he admitted while gingerly fumbling inside the hole he'd created. "I suppose I did." And it was a moment later when touching the distinctive outline of a key that he felt vindicated in his action. He felt even better when the key turned, just the once, and allowed him to remove the beautifully detailed model of the Tanmouth.

"Now what are you going to do," asked his mother getting closer.

"I'm not sure," he shrugged holding the model at arms length. In an instant his gaze rushed from the model and then towards the picture and then back again. "Look," he demanded.

"Where?"

"At the funnels in the painting," he insisted. "And then look at the funnels on the model."

"There's an extra one!"

"Correct," he laughed while snapping it. "And look what's inside!"

"A couple of pieces of paper."

"Oh! Yes," he grinned unravelling one and trying to read the words.

"Have you seen this?"

"No," he answered. "Why, what is it?"

"It's a small photograph of a naked woman."

Hearing this Alan immediately snatched the photo and scrutinised it. "Has anyone got a magnifying glass," he hoped.

"Why?"

"So that I can have a better look."

"What at her naughty bits," flew back the statement?

"Not at all," he refuted while picking up the other piece of paper. "So that I can read the words on this one."

"Here," his mother said while handing her son a magnifying glass.

With care and precision he clumsily stage whispered the words, "Find St John's Wort."

"What's that," demanded Erin looking a bit confused.

"It's a lovely yellow flowering herb!"

"Never heard of it."

"I don't suppose you have," his mother laughed. "Because it's not your everyday cooking one." Having spoken she closed her eyes. "But it was your father's favourite," she said. "Because he could make an oil to use from it."

"So why's he wanting us to find it?"

"Follow me," she stated leading the way into the garden and towards some flowers. Picking a sprig, of leaves, she held it to the light and asked, "What can you see?"

"Little red dots."

"Correct," she agreed. "Because they are supposed to represent the holes that Christ had upon the cross."

"Where did you learn that?"

"In one of the books Henry had."

"Can I see it?"

"If you like," she shrugged as they wandered back towards the study and once inside found the right book. In fact it was the very same book that Carol had been looking at.

Alan took it and found the correct page before studying it. "Get a pen and paper," shot the instruction. "And write these letters down as I call them out." It took a good few minutes but eventually after handing it over he could make out several words and so read them, "In the place where the caddie will find more than his tea and toast there'll be an ensign amongst the violets."

They went to bed and slept. If slept is the right word because whether it was Alan who started proceedings, or Erin for allowing it to continue, but there was an awful lot of grunting and groaning going on as well as bed springs making funny noises. It was even worse the following morning because they just seemed to continue from where they'd left off the previous night but eventually they did manage to make it downstairs. "Morning you two," smiled Mrs Young reading the paper. "Sleep okay?"

"Morning," they replied together. "Perfectly."

"Alan!"

"Yes."

"As you're taking Erin to town?"

"I know," he grumbled. "Something to do with her changing her mind and wanting to pick yet another dress."

"That's right," Erin butted in. "Because, when I got the other one home and had a good look at it I didn't feel that it was quite apt for the occasion."

"Weren't you showing enough cleavage?"

"Alan," snapped his horrified mother. "There's no need for that."

"Sorry."

"It's alright," Erin grinned. "He's just being a man."

"Yes he might be but there's a time and a place for that kind of thought," his mother inferred. "And it's not at the breakfast table."

"Okay," he lamented. "Okay."

"Anyway," continued his mother brilliantly changing tact while casting her perceptive gaze at her son, "Seeing as you'll be in town can you please go to Libby's and pick up the book I ordered?"

"What's it called?" He sighed.

"How to make delicious fruit cakes."

"When I get my new dress," Erin suddenly smiled.

"Yes."

"Would you like to take some photographs of me?"

"Of course," he smirked with a wicked glint in his eye. "So does it matter where I take them?"

"Not really," she grinned.

"Maybe she'd like you to take some of her in the country," smiled his mother. "Like down by the river."

"Sounds like a plan," Alan agreed.

"It most certainly does," Erin smiled. "But I'll decide where."

"Okay," he shrugged. It was about two hours later. It would have been one but for the fact that he'd forgotten to switch off the headlights so the battery was flat and the car wouldn't start.

"I'm not going to push," Erin whined while getting into the driver's side. Eventually they managed to get it started and drove into town knowing full well that the journey would charge the battery. "Go and have a cup of coffee," smiled the instruction as he watched her disappearing towards the flotilla of dresses. After his third cup; she reappeared carrying a rather large bag with the store's name embossed across it for free advertising.

"Where you been?" Fired his flippant question. "Timbuktu?"

She looked at him with eyes resembling daggers. "I had to make sure that it was right," pouted her words.

After yet another cup of coffee they were heading back to the car when Alan walked through the doors of Libby's, and collected his mother's cookery book. "So what now," he asked while starting the engine.

She knew exactly what he was thinking because it's something women can instantly do. "When we were coming to town," she smiled. "I saw a nice spot that would make the ideal background for the photographs."

"And where's that?"

"You just drive and I'll tell you when to stop."

"Okay," he answered knowing full well that she wasn't going to tell him.

They'd been driving for about eleven minutes when she suddenly said, "Just pull over into that layby!" Hearing the instruction he stopped, switched the engine off and turned toward her. "Let's go for a little walk," she chuckled while picking up the bag.

"But that's the golf course."

"Is it," she smiled. "And there's me thinking that you've always wanted to play around." With this double entendre his heart started to beat that bit quicker. Picking up his camera they strolled through the wooded edge and as they neared the fairway a sudden chattering forced them to conceal themselves behind a rather thorny hawthorn bush. Watching a group of players walking over the small rise, their overfull golf bags clunking with the various clubs they were never going to use, both youngsters listened to the discussion about the forthcoming championship at St Andrews in Scotland. Alan was totally engrossed when watching one of the players chip a bunker shot onto the green when he suddenly felt a hand resting upon his shoulder. "I'm going to get ready," she grinned as the ball rolled menacingly towards the hole but stopped about four inches short.

"Where?"

"Over there," she indicated.

"Okay," he stated as they both walked towards a small copse of trees and as she disappeared added. "And I'll stand here so that I can keep a look out." It was about five minutes later that Erin reappeared wearing the sexy ensemble of a French Can-can dancer, from the Moulin Rouge, complete with black stockings and frilly knickers. "Wow," was the only expression he could muster for the erotic image before his eyes.

"So, are you going to take my photo?"

"Certainly," he snapped.

"How's this," asked the question as she wafted her skirt at him.

"That's perfect," he admitted with a click, and to say that he was erotically thrilled would be putting it mildly. His jaw dropped, his growing cock pushed against his jeans as his finger worked overtime on the camera shutter button. Suddenly, as if dancing to an imaginary tune, she spun around and lifted the dress to show off the hidden delight of her saucy underwear covered arse before giving a little wiggle. "Hold it." he leered as the camera shutter clicked.

"Did you like that?" She asked moving closer

"Of course," he admitted looking at her. "Especially when you started rubbing your arse."

"I thought you might," she laughed as she spun still holding the hem, and watched him smiling like the Parisian man must have done all those years ago, when she instantly fanned the skirt. Click. Letting go; the hem dropped compelling her to bend, from the waist, to display the full beauty of her partially hidden cleavage. Click.

"You see that fallen tree trunk over there?" He indicated with his finger pointing.

"Yes!"

"Can you go and sit on it." Click. "Hands on knees and lean forward." Click. "Lean back and thrust your chest out." Click.

"Would this be better?" She asked putting her hands under her tits and lifting them."

"Of course it would," he smirked with a click.

"What if I take them out?"

"Great," he clicked. "And I hope you realise that these photographs won't be seen by the general public."

"I'm rather glad about that," she smiled. "Because I wouldn't be doing this for anyone."

"Okay," he leered while looking around and seeing no-one continued with a modicum of hope. "Right, follow me."

"Where are we going?" Asked the question as Alan strolled towards that same copse of trees.

"Just here," he finally admitted when finding a good spot. "Right," he smiled looking straight at her. "What I'd like you to do is take everything off!"

"What," she giggled. "Strip!"

"Yes," he leered. "So that I can take you looking oh so natural."

"Really," she sexily agreed.

When at last she was totally naked Alan simply couldn't focus on anything except for her tits and cunt. "What I'd like you to do," fired the instruction. "Is to go over to that log and place your hands on the trunk."

"Like this."

"Yes," he drooled while focusing on her arse. "Now spread your legs." Again he clicked as the sight of her wet cunt came deliciously into view. "Now turn round and face me!" Click. "Put your hands under your tits and lift them." Click. Time was irrelevant as each pose seemed to be getting more, and more, explicit when suddenly he thought he heard rustling of undergrowth a short distance away. "Quiet," whispered his instruction when realising that maybe they'd be caught and so quickly added while picking up the dress, "Here, put this on!" Once ready they both moved until spotting a single girl, of maybe thirteen or fourteen, getting closer before walking away. "I wonder who she's going to meet." He pondered.

"What d'yer mean?"

"Just look at the way she's dressed!"

"Just because she's wearing a short skirt."

"That's not a skirt," he implied. "That's a belt."

Hearing this Erin quickly looked at him. "Just because she wants to look attractive," uttered the female's standard defence. "Doesn't mean that she's on the pull."

"Doesn't it?"

"No," she snapped.

"Well," he leered. "We'll just follow her to see who's right."

"Okay," she answered and with that they kept track of where the girl was heading until finally coming to a complete stop close to a well known location much used by local reprobates for immoral practices of one sort or another. Then as if waiting for someone the young girl became more agitated as she kept looking back from where she'd come.

Suddenly; when Alan saw who the man was he reached and grabbed Erin's hand. "That's Ratty," choked his startled words.

"Who?"

"Simon Carlisle," he corrected. "One of the managers at work."

"Why's he called that?"

Alan swung his head and stared at her. "Just look at what he's got under his nose," started the explanation. "It just looks like he's sniffing a rat's arse."

"Some women find that sort of thing attractive and a big turn on!"

"Well," he pouted. "I hope you're not one." There was no time for an answer because the couple in front now resembled a scene from a love story as they kissed and cuddled with the man's hands going everywhere. Then as if by magic the girl stepped back and gave an innocent smile as she slowly unbuttoned her blouse and dropped it to the floor. Her smile became wicked when stepping out of that infamous short grey skirt and standing, hands on hips, in her virginal white underwear. Next, she unclipped her obvious training bra and took it off. Both men were now staring at the girl's immature tits as they appeared. Alan because he was in effect a dirty old sod, and Simon because he actual was a dirty old sod. Finally her tease finished as she yanked her knickers off and stood quite naked so with one step Simon moved to cup her left tit with his left hand. His other hand had moved, with lightening speed, to cover her rather childish fanny.

"Just look what he's doing?" Erin stated as she'd wriggled herself in front of Alan.

"I can see," he leered while feeling the way she pressed her arse into the bulge in his jeans. What did they feel as the two voyeurs witnessed the sordid, and illegal, act of Simon fucking the girl?

Both Erin and Mrs Young had been invited, by Mary Haslem, to a lady's only dinner with the instruction that they dress according to the female characters in

Greek Mythology. Erin, who having changed the dress for the umpteenth time, decided that Persephone would be perfect and when she'd walked into the sitting room along with the necessary pomegranate and saw Alan's reaction realised that she was correct in her choice. His mother, on the other hand, had always intended of going as Antiope the queen of the Amazons. The meal was fantastic as they sat, with the other guests, until finally they began chatting over drinks and cigarettes. It was at one point that the host calmly announced a little snippet of tittle-tattle that she'd heard somewhere, or other, "I wonder if she knows?"

"Who," asked Judy Fretsum who happened to be dressed as Aphrodite?

"Felicity Hooper."

"About what?"

"That her fiancé's being a bit of a naughty boy behind her back."

"In what respect?"

"From what I can gather," she carefully whispered. "Then he's been seen with one of the teachers from the girl's school."

"Has he?" Returned the knowing, but smutty, innuendo from Cathy Thorpe dressed as one of the Muses. "And I wonder which one that is?"

"I cannot be certain," spread the malicious gossip. "But I'd hazard a guess at it being the Geography teacher."

"You don't mean," sniggered Mandy Appleton, dressed as one of the harpies, sitting on the far side. "The one who's got no chin, got a voice that grates as it goes through you and looks like she's just sucked a lemon?"

"Yes, that the one," confirmed Massie Birkenhead as Hera. "Because hasn't she got a rather descriptive nickname."

"Oh! Yes," chimed several of the ladies in unison. "Because she's better known as Hoover as she's quite capable of sucking any man dry!" And having given this rather disgusting description the sound of school girlish giggling erupted which bore an uncanny resemblance to a pack of wild hyenas.

"Ladies," the hostess grumbled. "A bit of decorum!"

"You started it," sang the chorus before there was silence, if you could call it silence, because there were still pockets of soft voices everywhere. "I wonder if she's ever done it behind the bike shed," hinted Sarah Kirkland as Artemis the goddess of chastity.

"Never mind about that," stage whispered Bunty Cheswick dressed as Demeter looking directly at Natalie Eastern made up to resemble a gorgon, or more precisely one of three sisters, Medusa. "I understand that you've had another complaint from one of your workers about the unfair treatment they've allegedly received?"

"Yes," wafted Natalie with a contemptuous wave of the hand.

"What's it about this time?"

"Something about me bullying them."

"That's a bit serious," agreed the four women dressed as Sirens. "But I suppose your husband's managed to iron things out in your favour."

"To right."

"But, isn't that a bit immoral?"

"Why?"

"Well surely being the managing director he should be on the side of fair play and getting an honest result."

"And if he ever does," Natalie smiled. "Then, the chances of him getting inside my knickers again are nil."

"So you're using the sex angle to keep in trouble?"

"To right," she giggled. "And it works!"

In another small group Abigail Stanley-Smythe, as another of the Muses, smiled while staring at Sarah Kirkland, "I've been wondering all evening whether that's an all over tan you've got?"

"Most definitely," returned the captivating grin.

"So where did you go to get it?" She asked. "Clarkson's the chemist."

"What d'yer mean."

"Well from here it looks like a bottled one."

"Silly girl," flew the giggle. "Remember me telling you about Frank wanting to celebrate our thirtieth wedding anniversary by going to the places we visited during our honeymoon?"

"Oh! Yes," Abigail answered. "You said that you'd gone camping along the River Tay and visited the villages before going shopping in the local city."

"That's right," she confirmed. "So when the actual day arrived and we set off I was a little surprised to discover that Frank had actually booked a holiday in the south of France.

"So you weren't going to Scotland?"

"It appeared not."

"Weren't you disappointed?"

"Not really," she smiled. "As I'm getting to old for be pitching tents and pissing in buckets; and besides I need my creature comforts."

"So Frank played a trick on you?"

"You could say that because it got even better when arriving at Heathrow and meeting Sandra Cunningham one of my old school friend."

"That was nice."

"Yes, it was," she answered. "Since it appeared that her husband had got in touch with Frank to organise a dual celebration for their silver wedding anniversary."

"So were they were going with you?"

"Yes," she grinned. "Though it did feel a little strange when Sandra, who I sat next to on the flight, asked me whether this was my first time."

"First time for what," enquired Abigail. "The mile high club!"

"I wasn't sure what she meant," Sarah smiled. "But it all became clearer when she simply explained that the holiday was going to be at a nudist beach."

"How erotic," giggled Amy Bright? "Seeing all those naked men and their little willies."

"After the initial shock," Sarah smiled. "I realised that maybe this was Frank's idea of restarting my libido."

"Didn't know you'd lost it!"

"It's not something I like talking about," she admitted. "But, when Frank kept going on about the lack of physical intimacy in our marriage he felt that he had to do something."

"And taking you on a holiday to a nudist colony surely beats taking pills and getting counselling."

"It most certainly does!"

"Come on then," expressed the willing audience. "Let's hear all about it."

"Well," she began. "When we arrived, at the site, it was late and after booking in we were shown to our chalets. Sandra and Mike in one and us next door."

"Hurry up and get to the juicy bits!"

"If you let me continue," Sarah grinned. "We woke the next day to the sound of children playing outside and when Frank got up to open the curtains I just sat up in bed. As I watched he suddenly indicated for me to come and join him so I got out and wandered across the room."

"What did you see?"

"Looking out of the window I saw several children playing with their parents."

"Obviously they were all naked?"

"Yes they were."

"And what was Frank doing?"

"He'd obviously seen something that had excited him because when I looked down I spotted that he'd got a stiff cock."

"So when you saw what he was doing did you start to feel sexy?"

"No," Sarah looked away, "I felt absolutely nothing."

"But your husband must have done?"

"He's always like that."

"Typical male," interrupted Abigail who suddenly continued. "Now here's a catch twenty two question for you."

"What's that?"

"Was his erection caused by him looking at the mother, the father or the children?"

"Now what are you chuntering about?"

"It's quite simple," fired the legal conundrum. "Would he have been classed as a paedophile if it was children that had caused him to get that erection?"

"I don't know," smirked Celia Crosby as Hera. "But it sounds like the kind of subject that'll be worth grabbing and massaging to a positive conclusion?"

"It doesn't matter how he got his stiff cock," added Rhea. "Because I know exactly what I would have done with it."

"I know you would," suggested Sarah. "Because rumour has it that you would have been up and down on him like a pair of whore's knickers."

"That's a bit unkind," she retaliated. "Just because my fanny's not healed over and I like having a good fuck."

"Never mind about your sordid lifestyle," Betty Harper smiled. "I just want to know whether Sarah got excited when seeing all those naked willies cos' I know I would have been." There was a giggling pause until she continued when seeing the way Sarah blushed. "So you were getting turned on," erupted the collective laugh.

"You have to remember," returned the stage whisper. "That in all the years of my marriage to Frank I'd never actually seen another man naked in real life."

"So, when you saw all those strangers," enquired Bunty. "With their lambing tackle hanging down you obviously understood the meaning of the old adage about familiarity breeding contempt."

"Yes," Sarah smiled. "I most certainly did."

"So what was your precious husband doing," Demanded the question. "As if we couldn't guess?"

"You're right," Sarah confirmed. "He'd started wanking."

"I'd a loved to have seen that," a hidden voice stage whispered.

"Anyway, his explanation for doing it was to reduce the chances of getting an erection later on."

"What poppycock, because according to the biology lessons we had at school we all know that men can get stiff cocks' at any time," fired the argument. "And anyway more to the point what were you doing?"

"Nothing because at that moment there came a knock on the door."

"That was a bit inconvenient."

"To right," she sighed. "Because I was actually starting to feel a little excited watching Frank playing with himself and seeing those other naked men outside."

"So who answered the door," begged the question. "Because I don't suppose it was your horny husband."

"No," admitted Sarah. "As he'd suddenly became very embarrassed and was trying to hide his cock by jumping into bed."

"Serves him right," laughed some of the ladies. "Because when we women get excited all that normally happens is that our nipples become hard and pretty obvious."

"That's right," Sarah giggled. "And even those were hidden under the nightie I was wearing."

"So who was at the door?"

"Mike and Sandra."

"Were they in the nude?"

"Yes they were," Sarah confirmed. "And as revenge for what Frank had schemed I warmly invited them in."

"That's what I would have done," announced Ruth Cottrell dressed as Pandora. "And anyway was Mike floppy?"

"Of course he was."

"Shame," Ruth giggled and then asked. "And Sandra?"

"When I saw her standing without any of her clothes, and showing the world her naked body, I instantly became conscious of the fact that why should I be embarrassed by my figure."

"Why what happened," asked the curious question.

"She'd obviously undergone a mastectomy to remove her left breast and to be conscious of the fact that everyone could see that took a lot more courage than I would ever have."

"Didn't it look a bit odd," wondered Bunty. "Only having the one tit."

"It's like Sandra said," smiled Sarah. "You can hide away for only so long before appreciating that you are still a woman. Okay you're a woman with only one breast but at the end of the day you are still a woman with other naughty bits and it's not your fault that you've had to endure the prejudice that people are eager to give because they live in the kind of society where everything has to be perfect."

"So what did you do?"

"I smiled as I listened to her words and understanding exactly what she'd obviously been through realised that just because I'm a grandmother, with wobbly bits, doesn't mean that I should be embarrassed with my own figure."

"So you stripped?"

"Of course I did."

"What was Frank doing while you were taking your nightie off?"

"Oh him," smirked Sarah. "He was still in bed and anyway it didn't matter because once I was naked both Sandra and myself walked up and pulled the bedcovers away."

"Was he still hard?"

"No, but it was pretty obvious that he had been."

"Were the others shocked?"

"Not really," she began. "As Mike explained that because of the biological nature, of the male, then an erection will occasionally be seen by the other naturists."

"So what happens when it does?"

"Nothing, but what they do frown upon is the continual exposure of an erection."

"So my Brian wouldn't be welcome there," asked Sylvia Winters.

"Why's that?"

"He's constantly thinking of sex," she smiled. "And always got a stiff willy."

"So I've heard," sprouted a mysterious voice somewhere along the table. "And anyway I thought we were going to hear about Sarah losing your hang ups about the sexual side of her life?"

"It was on the fourth day, if my memory serves me right, that when I was strolling along a secluded section of the dunes with Sandra we thought we heard some strange grunting in the distance."

"Bet I know what sort of noises they were!"

"Okay clever clogs," Sarah issued. "What kind were they?" Having asked the question the culprit, who happened to be Natalie, went very red.

"Was there a couple having sex out there in the dunes?"

"Yes there was and so very quietly we crept up the sand dune to look down at a rather elderly couple below us having a game of parking the porker," Sarah smartly announced. "And seeing the passion they were using I immediately went back to the cabin and allowed Frank to basically fuck the arse off me."

Back at work it must have been the straw that broke the camel's back, because Felicity Hooper immediately stood and walked directly at Alan looking blankly into space. In four strides she'd reach her target. Slamming her smallish hands hard against his desk she screamed her words, "I've told you before that I'll go and see Simon the next time something like this happens!" He wasn't bothered when she hastily spun around and stormed from the office. She'd been gone for exactly ten minutes before returning. "Simon wants to see you," commanded her statement some three octaves higher in pitch.

He sniggered on hearing the order and deliberately pushed the un-opened file that was on his desk forward. He stood and brushed down the imaginary lapels of a jacket before strolling from the room. Down the never ending corridor of power he paced until coming face to face with the white named plaque on the closed door. His stomach never felt better as he violently pushed it open and stepped inside to stare at the man sitting behind the desk. Once inside the two men simply eyed each other ever hopeful of detecting any motive for their encounter and it was Alan who was the first to speak. "You can stick your job," he forced as his hands smashed on the table. Before the papers had time to settle he'd turned, walked and slammed the door with the pure hatred he obviously felt. He never looked back as he drove from the yard. He never saw both Felicity and Simon staring, from the office window, at his departure. The only thing that he seemed able to do was drive erratically along the country roads as the adrenaline pumped violently around his body. He was halfway home when he'd calmed enough to reflect upon the spontaneity of his actions and for that he turned the radio on and listened to whatever was being discussed.

"Jack Blossom has just driven his second shot into the front bunker of the eighteenth hole here at St Andrews," solemnised the commentator as he prattled on about the prestige of the modern game. "And the pin has been positioned towards the back of the green," the faceless man continued.

Feeling decidedly bored at hearing this, Alan switched channels until finding yet another station. "Let's listen to Scrappy Pads latest single," the false jollity of the young voiced celebrity whined as the music started to play. Even though the song was basically rubbish it still had that annoying beat that compelled either your feet to tap along, or your fingers and voice to sing.

"Hello," welcomed the rather surprised chorus from both his mother and Erin.

"I've quit," he huffed walking passed.

He never saw the two women's expression as they turned towards each other and nor did he feel the atmosphere at that moment in time. All he was concerned about was disappearing inside his room and lying on his bed to replay each moment, of his actions, over and over again. Left to wallow in his own self satisfaction he was a trifle startled when the door opened and in strode Erin looking as radiant as ever. Her long hair tumbling down her shoulders as the bright sun enhanced her beautifully tanned skin. The small dimple was so gorgeous that his eyes were immediately drawn towards her smile. "You okay?" She wondered sitting beside him on the bed.

He never answered, but at least he did smile. It wasn't the smile of victory, but was more like a smile of irrational behaviour and probably realising the magnitude of the situation sat against the wall to give a clammy grin. Obviously feeling generous Erin leaned forward her lips ready. They kissed. They were still kissing as he reached inside her bra and groped a single tit. It was as he was fumbling a different hand moved with spontaneity below his waist and inside his trousers. Suddenly there was a regretful cough at the door and so with reluctance they separated. With both youngsters going the colour of beetroot they simply stared at the culprit and waited for the apology. "I'm sorry," announced Alan's mother standing in the doorway scrutinising their dishevelled appearance and looking straight at her son continued. "It's the phone and it's for you!"

"Who is it," stuttered Alan's rather stupid question. There was no reply as he hurriedly tried to tidy himself because his mother was simply standing watching his every move. Whether she'd seen anything, a bit naughty, didn't really matter because without a word she turned and walked away. "Hello," he responded having picked up the receiver, and for the next ten minutes spoke to whomever it was without giving any clues as to their identity. At last the conversation finished and he was rather relieved when walking into the kitchen to see a ready prepared mug of coffee waiting.

"Who was that," asked the two women together.

"Work," laboured his nonchalant answer, and before any other questions could be asked added. "And they want to see me tomorrow at ten o'clock."

"Will you be going?" Asked his mother knowing full well the inborn arrogance, and stupidity, he'd inherited from his father.

"I'll have to sleep on it."

"Right, if you're staying," began the formal statement of his mother. "Then we're going shopping." Having spoken he watched both women pick up their handbags and walk from the house. He sniggered lamely as he now felt alone, and so decided to settle inside the study to try and figure out the clue he'd discovered.

It was about half passed six when Erin and his mother returned from their shopping spree and it was about an hour later, after having put away the priceless trinkets they'd bought, that it was decided that they all go to a restaurant and sample the much publicised cuisine that was on offer. They drove to town, but not before going to pick up the Colonel. The meal was perfect. The conversation during, and between, the courses was taken up by the Colonel recounting his adventures in the jungles of Borneo, Africa and other equally exciting settings. They left around midnight, and with Alan driving Erin sat next to him so that his mother and the Colonel were in the rear. The moans and groans, erupting from the back seat, caused Alan to keep a watchful eye in the rear view mirror because was it pangs of disgust, or was it pangs of jealousy, that he felt when watching the other man's hands disappearing inside his mother's unbuttoned blouse before sleazily removing a single naked breast. Alan tried to concentrate on the driving but would occasionally allow his gaze to be drawn towards the erotic scenes being staged and as he watched the acts of immorality he knew that there must be something a little more than friendship between the two passengers in the back. This was confirmed when he stopped to drop off the Colonel; and his mother got out as well with the announcement, "I'll be staying so don't wait up for me."

Hearing this rather sordid declaration Alan drove the car directly home, and once there escorted Erin inside. The door closed with a thud as an inner voice compelled him to stretch out his two hands and drag her towards him. Not a sound was heard as she readily accepted his embrace and not a word was spoken as he formally placed his trembling hands either side of her dress. With the strength of a lover he tore it from her body and watched as it fell so slowly to the floor. Now with his gaze urgently fixed on the erotic symmetry of her partially covered body his eyebrows rose as his carnal needs dictated how he'd react. Then like most males he was only to eager to gaze upon the pure beauty of her nakedness and understanding his desires, as well as her own, Erin carefully removed her bra before taking down her jade coloured knickers. She looked beautiful standing there. He licked his lips, with desire, as he quickly removed his own clothes. Now naked they both stepped forward and hugged each other. His hands went everywhere. He played with her tits. He kneaded the softness of her arse. He slipped an eager finger inside the wetness of her cunt. "Oh! Alan," she moaned as he pressed his stiff cock against her belly. Then without warning she fell to her knees and in one quick movement took his cock in her mouth. Her eyes were tightly shut as he allowed her to dictate and govern the positive movement of her head and it came as no surprise when her explicit action resulted in him shuddering to a climax. It was at that moment, as she glanced up, that he shoved her away. No words were exchanged as if like a rag-doll she purposely collapsed to the carpeted floor and lay to await his action. She never moved when he fell between her knees and violently reached beneath her arse and lifted her to lap like a slavering dog. As he licked he was prepared when her thighs clamped his head tightly in position. She shivered, but it wasn't from any cold. She screamed, but that wasn't from any pain and once released Alan stood looking down at the luscious sheen, of sexual seepage, that now coated the fine pubic hair around her cunt. He smiled at what he saw, and for that reached out his hands. Together they climbed the stairs and instantly understood what needed to be done as they collapsed upon the bed.

They awoke next day to the haunting sound of silence and as they lay naked upon that dishevelled bed their minds remembered each passionate moment from the previous night. Their desire was strong as Erin, once again, straddled his sexually active frame and guided his stiffened cock into the freshness of her cunt. "Look at the time!" She moaned with each of his thrusts.

Hearing this he enthusiastically moved his hands and massaged her tits and quite simply contemplated his future. He panted somewhat dryly, "It takes about eighteen minutes to get there and it's twenty to ten now."

"You're late," corroborated the twin voices of Felicity and Simon as they prepared themselves. "We said ten o'clock," Simon managed twisting his wrist and glancing at his watch. "And it's now three," his acidic voice confirmed.

"I'm sorry," the condemned man shrugged as he stared straight at Simon who could be seen twitching. "But, something came up," he added with a smirk as his eyes closed while remembering exactly what had been the cause. The atmosphere was electric as it attached itself to everyone. It prickled. It clawed at their flesh until the moment was broken by a sharp knock on the door.

"Yes," snapped Simon's voice.

The door opened and in walked his secretary carrying a silver-plated tray upon which had been arranged three cups of coffee and a dish of fruitcake slices. They were like vultures grabbing the morsels and clutching them as if their lives depended on it. After they'd eaten and the disciplinary had started again Alan was totally unaware of his accuser's voices as he concentrated on his own thoughts. Suddenly, and with no prompting he stood and began to laugh. He shook his head as a mark of indifference and bent forward so that his two hands pressed on the desk. He leaned forward and swivelled his glare, first at Felicity and then at Simon. Neither saw the apathy twinkling in his eyes, but they felt the caustic chill of his presence as he delivered his clear incitement. "You can stuff your job," he stated and the atmosphere hadn't the chance to become barbed before smiling. "Because I'm going to Dundee," he confirmed, and having given his intent left. But before finally shutting the door he caustically delivering his stinging barb. "You'd better ask lover boy here," he smiled while staring directly at Felicity. "As to whether he used a contraceptive when having sex with that underage girl last Thursday." Having spoken he paused but a moment and watched as the blood in Simon's face vanished and Felicity twitched like a vestal virgin on her wedding night.

The train pulled effortlessly and silently into the gloomy atmosphere of the station and as Alan peered through the grime-stained window saw the large clock displaying its constant time with hands indicating ten past one in the morning. The changing motion was slowly subsiding as he resolutely nudged his hibernating companion who had somehow managed to get comfortable by sprawling on one of the dust covered seats. The corners of his mouth rose in pleasure as he leaned back and simply waited for the expected response. He quietly laughed when she began to twitch in recognition because this simple action resulted in a continuous shockwave cascading over the entirety of her body. It had started in her right shoulder forcing her tits to wobble like jellies and finished when she sat up with white knuckles rubbing the sleep from her eyes. "Have we arrived?" Asked the sleepy question as she carefully brushed the array of creases from the creamy white floral skirt she was wearing.

"Yes!" He responded in that most patronising toned drawl that the male is apt to use when replying to a woman's rather stupid discussion of the obvious, and not waiting for the undoubted comeback stood to take the single suitcase they'd packed.

"What's the time?" Continued the rather supercilious question as the carriage suddenly swayed making their hot and sticky bodies fall against each other, so that with the resultant forces of inertia and gravity both youngsters collapsed in a jumbled heap.

"It's obviously past your bedtime," he sarcastically responded as his gaze floated down. Seeing exactly where his eyes were focused she gave a lop sided smirk when instantly understanding exactly what thoughts were drifting through his mind, which really didn't take a lot, and forced her small tongue to rush around the dry texture of her lips. He grinned lecherously as he instinctively cupped her smooth chin and pulled her towards his waiting mouth. They kissed, and as they kissed his hands began to wander over her body.

"You can pack that in," she rather abrasively snapped while trying to stand. "Because shouldn't we be going?"

"I suppose we'd better," he smiled and on the scale of one to ten, in the chances of doing something immoral, the answer was probably zero. Understanding this he stood and wandered towards the carriage door. He then found that the handle was a trifle stiff, mirroring exactly how he felt, but eventually after a little brutal persuasion it swung violently open and onto the desolate platform they both stepped. Shivering, the cold grey of night was illuminated by the fluorescent glow from the dozens of yellow neon lights as they watched a lonely mother scouring the empty carriages with concern. Suddenly, a welcoming smile was seen radiating to her face as towards those waiting arms, and carrying his laundry, a young uniformed soldier ran. Both Alan and Erin watched as the boy dropped his laden bags as the show of maternal love, which had been his since birth, glowed with an aura of warmth that ultimately calmed the young man's anxiety.

"Tickets," demanded the solitary word spoken by the man huddled in his little box, like a ferret down a drainpipe, and having given his requirement a single hand stretched to claim the offering. Hearing the ransom for the ride Alan twisted his gaze to stare directly at Erin who'd had the good fortune to locate the two lilac pieces of paper, which she'd safely kept inside the unexplored territory of a woman's handbag, and watched as she graciously handed them over. The little man gave a desperate sigh, and a somewhat cheerless expression, as he took them in exchange for the freedom they'd paid for. Through the guarding gates of the station they both walked, and once outside realised that the weather hadn't improved since the start of their journey north. In fact it had probably got slightly worse.

"I'm getting wet," she sulked as the near monsoon started to penetrate the light anorak she'd had the misfortune to use even though the weather forecast had quite clearly stated that it would be raining heavily the further north you went.

Feeling gallant, or stupid depending on your point of view, he unbuttoned his thick coat. "Here's mine," he volunteered whilst chivalrously handing it over.

"Thanks," she murmured while anxiously trying to dance the quickstep and put on the heavy coat all at the same time.

"That's alright," he sombrely smiled but was actually thinking why on Earth did I give it away. As the rain soaked through his shirt he felt cold, but when twisting his gaze and seeing Erin totally hidden from view except for the very top of her head he couldn't help but laugh. They reluctantly trudged into the desolation of the empty car park and it was here that they kept finding the vast array of overflowing puddles to eventually reach the classic situation of passed caring whether their feet were wet or dry. Feeling like the proverbial drowned rat he shivered violently when Erin grabbed his sodden arm, and was about to give the customary words of annoyance when spotting exactly what she was looking at.

"There," erupted her defiant voice as water cascaded down her face. Her pointing finger indicating the probable dark outline of a taxi, and it was truly unbelievable for there waiting like an oasis in a desert was an unoccupied vehicle obviously expecting a fare.

"Where to," questioned the unrecognisable accent of the man who simply refused to turn his head. Realising that it was drier inside the car than it was out Alan who hurriedly pushed Erin towards the interior, and once there jumped in and sat beside her. Having made himself as comfortable as possible he shivered when once again feeling the cold water against his flesh. "Where to," repeated the Scot's emphasise that could now be just understood.

"The Emerson Hotel," drilled the words as Erin instinctively wrapped an arm around the shoulders of Alan and pulled him close, as a mother would a child. The drive to their destination was uneventful except for spotting several pubs with their lights still on with the invariable drunks leaving and wobbling their way down the street. Eventually; as they pulled up outside a partially illuminated hotel the driver informed them of their exact fare and it was then that Alan remembered exactly where the money he'd brought was. With this realisation the corners of his mouth rose as he shot Erin a crafty glance and giving no quarter quickly thrust his hand inside the tightly bound lapels of the coat he'd given her to wear. Once in position he inadvertently, or was it deliberately, made contact with the soft weight of a breast and started groping it. He wasted no time in rubbing, rather harshly, the fullness of her tits. As he continued he suddenly seemed a little concerned when she jumped slightly when realising exactly what he was doing. As a silly grin spread along his mouth she shot him a stare, but in doing so must have understood his dilemma because not a word slipped from her mouth only the scowl of a diplomat.

"I'm only after the money," he chuckled.

"But, you won't find it there will you," she instructed as her own hand moved to cover his.

"Maybe not but it'll be fun finding out," he smirked as he allowed his hand to be removed. Eventually the fare was paid in full plus a little extra to which the taxi driver was heard to tut his disbelief at such a meagre gesture.

As they watched the disgruntled man drive away rainbows of diffused light were seen glimmering in the equally spaced streetlights. "Come on," she instructed with unaccustomed cynicism while at the same time trying to run. With the rain still pouring they ultimately reached the small porch-way and huddled together before entering the bright interior. Like two drowned rats they made soggy progress towards the front desk, and once there it was Erin who pushed the rather ornate bell and waited. No answer, and so she tried again. No answer. She was about to try once more when a door opened and towards them strode a rather formal looking lady dressed in a cream and pink uniform. There was no expression on her colourless face. There was no look of knowledge as she surveyed the two strangers at the desk, but there was only the single word. "Yes!"

Erin's expression showed signs of an underlying calm but by the perspiration along her brow, or was it the rain dripping from her hair, her heart must have been pounding with excitement. This was ultimately confirmed when her voice had the tone of a frightened child, "A double room has been booked in the name of Mr and Mrs Young!"

Alan flicked his head and stared. He narrowed his eyebrows in wonder at what he thought he'd heard, and when he looked at the receptionist, as well as Erin, realised as to the reason why. The receptionist also understood because was it a smile of smutty knowledge running along those colourless lips when studying both shivering youngsters, or was it the fact that she'd been disturbed. Whatever the reason her Scot's voice had the tone of complete indifference as she announced, "We weren't expecting you until tomorrow."

Hearing this Alan regained his jocular insight. The corners of his mouth rose as he strutted like a fighting cock. "It is tomorrow, and it's pouring with rain," he began as drops of water splashed on the ink written names in the register. "And now you're telling us is that there is no room at the inn," came his rather silly expression.

The receptionist, who was pushing Alan's shoulder away, never changed her expression. "It's alright," she announced running her finger over the smudged names. "There's number twenty seven." And having authorised their stay turned and took one of the many sets of keys hanging on the board behind. "Here's the key," she announced handing it over.

It was a long walk up the stair and along the corridor, but at last they stood outside their room. "Where's the light switch," questioned Alan as his unsteady fingers searched the wall. He'd been trying to locate it for some moments without success when Erin gave him a gentle shove that proved to be a little more dramatic than she'd anticipated. The sound of him tottering and then collapsing to the floor only seemed to cause a bout of hysteria instead of the concern he deserved. Suddenly, the room was illuminated when a short click was heard and once she could see Erin stepped inside and closed the door. Once there she manoeuvred herself until towering over his motionless body, and after she'd looked down quite simply burst into laughter. The laughter became infectious as he began to join in, but this was just a ruse to get her to reach out a hand to help him get up. With pathetic movement he did exactly that and after standing; and feeling generous extended his hand to once again congratulate her on her achievement.

As they posed at arms length she stood to her full height, all five foot six and three quarters, and smiled. She ran her lush tongue around her lips before stepping forward and swinging her wet arm around his shoulders. "Thanks for letting me come with you," quietly whispered her words as she reached onto tiptoe and kissed him full on the lips.

"That's alright," he admitted as he allowed her hot lips to crush his, and for that he responded. "You could have picked a better time," he half heartedly whined as his husky voice sounded like treacle dropping from a hot spoon. Whether it was the cold, or whether it was the consequence of her actions but with her heavy breasts looking wholesome and good enough to eat he stared at their unmistakable beauty. Now with their hands clasped together and with one strong pull he dragged her against his body.

"Come on, let's get out of these wet clothes," she sighed.

Hearing this invitation, and with no apparent cares in the world the man began to strip away his water-logged clothes. First, his shirt, which he allowed to drop to the carpet and land like a sponge being thrown into a bucket. Next, he undid the buttons on his trousers and easily dragged down the drenched fabric. Once finished he stood, half naked and half ready, with his wet hair shimmering in the bedroom light. Now feeling like a million dollars, or was it more like thirty cents, he could not condone Erin's actions when she started to undo the line of buttons of her transparent wet blouse before carefully removing it. He was beginning to tire and was therefore immune to the splendour of her emerging nudity. He was on autopilot when his heartbeat quickened on seeing her large and succulent breasts straining inside the housing material of her flamingo pink and black bra. He felt like someone in the audience of a strip show when she expertly unfastened the buckle of the belt around her waist and allowed her skirt to fall. His eyes exploded in pure hunger and he wept with an inner lust when seeing the flimsy threads of her knickers hiding that one piece of feminine anatomy that had caused many wars to be fought.

It was at that moment and with an inner strength he, again, tried to seduce her. With controlled aggression he took her in his arms and pulled. As their wet bodies touched he felt the exhilarating pressure of her tits pressing against his naked torso. He waited but inkling before pushing a single hand hard against the fine silk material that covered his undoubted destination. They kissed, and the undeniable enthusiasm with which she responded compelled his breaths to become a pant when pushing a hand deep inside her knickers and having a spontaneous grope of her cunt. With cumbersome reality swiftly sapping her obvious resilience Alan rather abruptly and enthusiastically asked his question. "Shall we go to bed?" Stammered his immoral suggestion and the words needed no explanation of his intent.

"You go and lie down," she smiled. "And I'll be with you in a minute!" Hearing this request he swivelled on the spot and gazed upon the luxury of the double bed that politely requested their presence. Needing no second invitation he ran, at half gallop, and fell onto the generosity of the covers. He gave a broad smile, as he thought about his immediate future, and with it dancing deliciously inside his mind his head touched and sank into the fluffy down of the pillows.

"Good-morning," announced the cheerful voice as the pale earthy brown curtains parted and the morning light crept through the dusty window as Alan, who was still half in the land of nod, stirred momentarily until finally waking. Still feeling somewhat tired he ultimately managed to get himself onto his elbows, and saw Erin standing at the bottom of the bed looking straight at him. Now seeing that he was back in the land of the living she walked with a flourish and sat at his side. "Did you sleep well?" Asked the question peppered with a certain amount of curiosity, as well as a little je ne sais quoi and having spoken she leaned over his body and kissed him.

Remembering absolutely nothing he gave a rather good impression of a knowing smile so with an air of uncertainty he looked directly into her eyes and as he scrutinised her deceptive charm his dry mouth instantaneously became even drier. "Why, what happened?" Having uttered those immortal words he waited, with bated breath, for the response as ripples of apprehension crawled across his naked shoulders.

She looked, at him, and started to give half a smile. She pointedly rested a slender finger against his twitching nose and slowly, very slowly, emphasised her words to great effect. "When I'd finished undressing and got in beside you," and it was here she paused. The delay. The anticipation was agonising as he waited for her to continue and to make the statement even more damning she pushed his nose with slight playful force ahead of standing and walking away. Having reached the bedroom door she twisted her head, looked over her shoulder and condescendingly laughed, "You'd fallen asleep."

Hearing this he fell back and simply thought of what might have been. After a moments reflection he gazed at the alarm clock, at the side of the bed, and noticing the time leapt out to get dressed with as much enthusiasms as a rabbit with myxoamatosis. He gave a wry smile when realising that he was completely naked and that all of his clothes including the underwear, he'd worn to bed, had been placed on a chair beside the dressing table. With a cautious laugh he dressed and once ready wandered to the top of the stairs and listened to the sounds of chatter emanating from somewhere downstairs. His eyes were instinctively drawn towards the shape of Erin as she moved across the foyer and inside one of the rooms below. Feeling guilty, as well as rejected, he walked towards the delicious smell of cooking until finding himself inside the dining room and once there had the chance to survey the other occupants chatting and conversing to each other. There were several couples sitting together, some with children some without. There were three or four single men sitting on their own reading papers or doing the crossword. There was a single lady who Alan noticed to be fidgeting with insecurity, but her attitude finally changed when her partner from the night before finally joined her. Feeling decidedly happier he diligently shuffled his way across the room and towards Erin, who happened to be sat in the furthest corner, and it was over breakfast that their itinerary for the day was discussed. "What do you want to do," asked his rather stupid question.

Erin drew back her shoulders and lifted her pretty face. Then while staring her sarcastic statement challenged, "Why, on earth, are we up here?"

Alan's blood ran cold and caused a shiver to race across each and every bone of his skeleton, and then like the condemned man answered with the weight of guilt dripping from every word, "To try and find the answer to my father's riddle!"

A smile as large as any canyon spread, like butter, across her lips before responding. "And how are we going to do that?" Asked her voice so full of wonder, and having given the question slouched back to await the answer.

There was hardly any delay because he duly admitted, "I don't know!" And to reinforce the point added with slight flippancy. "And anyway it must have something to do with the Navy!"

"So what're you saying?"

He shrugged his shoulders as he answered, "Why don't we just walk up to the docks and simply ask them!" And the tone of his voice petered on the sarcastic as well as the stupid.

Erin thought long and hard about her answer. "You know exactly what'll happen if we do that," giggled her words.

"We'll either be told to go away," he admitted. "Or get locked up." Having spoken he tried to hide the smirk, but when his lips trembled he knew that he'd been unsuccessful. He thought for a moment and allowed his gaze to float around the room. Blowing out his cheeks because he'd seen nothing as inspiration returned his stare while leaning on his elbows before offering with a shrug, "Why don't we just go down there to find out whether it works?"

"What and get accused of treason!"

"Now there's a thought," he cackled. "So what do you suggest we do?" They were about to discuss various possibilities when a trolley, obviously with a single wonky wheel, rolled up to their table and breakfast was served. While eating they tried to fathom out the necessary course of action they would have to use in gaining entrance into the base and they were still contemplating, their method, when they caught the bus and travelled to the docks.

"Halt!" Declared the uniformed Rating with his rifle discreetly levelled at his thigh. Both stopped. Both looked the aggressor straight in the eye but were well aware of another coming to join the discussion.

The new man, who had three stripes down his arm, barked out his intention in a voice that had obviously been trained, "This is a Government Installation and is not open to the general public."

"But, I want to see the Commanding Officer," interjected Alan as he started to move forward. There were no words spoken when with a quick gesture, from the sergeant, the Rating's rifle came pointedly into view. Alan halted on the spot because he knew, from his father, that the sentry's training was quite simple. Shoot when told!

As they walked away both he, and Erin, looked directly at the three women walking towards them. Neither party acknowledged the other on passing but Alan stopped and turned. He gave a snide snigger when they walked through the Main Gates, without being stopped but showing the necessary passes, and continued to wherever they were going. He smiled when realising the compulsory route needed to gain entry, and so hurriedly grasped Erin's arm and pulled her close. "What's that for?" She squealed.

"I know how to get inside," he chirped as his footsteps got quicker. They were silent as they walked back into town and seeing a café decided to have a drink to relieve the parched feeling in their mouths.

Having got their drinks, and a couple of slices of the Town's infamous cake, they sat by the window and watched the World and his wife saunter passed. It was during this time that they discussed Alan's plan to gain entry to the docks.

"You want me to do what!" Her slightly aggravated voice drilled as he smiled at her.

"All I'm asking is for one of us to get a job there, and since you're married to a sailor then you're probably better qualified," his response explained. Her eyebrows rose in consternation as for the next half an hour or so; there came argument and counter-arguments as to the possibilities of any such an idea. Having reached a compromise, in Alan's favour, they stood and walked into the murky weather conditions.

It had been raining on and off since their arrival in Dundee, about five days earlier, and the prospects of it getting any better looked decidedly grim. "Bloody weather," announced Erin as she hurriedly pulled her coat collar that bit tighter around her neck. "And anyway what are we going to do now," asked her rather disillusioned voice while blowing out her cheeks.

They were soaked to the skin when they entered their hotel room and the heady smell of their wet bodies prompted Erin to disappear, plus some dry clothes, down the corridor and towards the communal bathroom. From their initial day they'd discovered that the door wouldn't shut properly and so if there were any pervs about then all they had to do was look through the inch wide gap and ogle whoever was in there. It was on the second morning, in fact, that Erin came hurriedly back to inform Alan that she thought there was someone spying on her, and it didn't help matters when he rather insensitively smiled, "Well, what do you expect shuffling around with no clothes on."

Realising that he probably wouldn't be seeing her for the next fifteen minutes stripped and simply lay on the bed to wait her return. In fact it was about thirty minutes later that he was getting a little concerned about her non-appearance when he suddenly heard a piercing scream. As quick as a flash he raced from the bedroom and ran in the direction of the bathroom at the far end of the landing. Having got there he posed by the door looking in and saw Erin sitting on the edge of the bath with a turquoise blue towel wrapped around her hair that resembled a hippy beehive.

"What's wrong?" He stuttered as he moved forward and placed his strong arms around her trembling shoulders.

"When I got down here and found it empty I simply walked in and tried to shut the door," her tearful explanation began. "And as you know it doesn't close properly."

"I know."

She continued, "And hopefully thinking that everybody was out I started to remove my clothes."

"There's nothing wrong with that," he tried to comfort.

"I suppose not," she admitted. "If you don't mind the possibility of some pervert staring at you." Alan thought carefully about how he'd answer and like most men quite simply refused to be drawn. "Anyway, after I'd stripped and part way through washing my hair something happened," she dramatised with a cold shudder.

"And that was?"

"Someone tried to molest me."

Trying to make a joke out of the situation he smiled, "They probably got further than I ever would have done?"

"Stop it!" she cringed as her tone was getting rather melodramatic. "The person, I thought was you, never said a word as they placed their hands around my waist."

"This sounds interesting."

"Be serious," she countered.

"So, what happened next?"

"It all happened so fast," her tearful account continued.

"Take your time," he condescendingly offered and it was at that moment other residents started to appear, as if from nowhere, and simply gathered. It was at one point when seeing two elderly ladies staring; well actually they were watching how things were developing, that he suddenly remembered that he wasn't wearing a lot. Anyway Erin was completely oblivious of this and so continued, "As I stood; this pair of hands reached up and cupped my breasts."

"What like this," he offered as he quickly placed his own in what he thought was the correct position.

"A bit higher," she sighed. "And not so rough."

"Is that any better?"

"Oh! Yes."

"And did you," he wondered. "At any time try to reach out and grab anything that might have grown out of all proportions?"

"You mean," she grinned. "Like this."

"That's close enough."

"I was quite enjoying what was happening when I looked down and saw the signet ring," her words described. "And it was then that I realised that they weren't your fingers inside my fanny."

"So what did you do?" Asked that most stupid of questions.

"I just screamed."

"Now here's a silly question," he asked. "Did you see his face?"

If looks could kill then he would be dead. "No," she fired. "Because the man just turned and ran."

While all this was going on there seemed to be a lively debate between the two old biddy's in the background. "I never saw any man running," announced the first. "But, if I had then maybe my dreams might have been answered."

"Why Betty," the second one laughed. "Would it have something to do with one of those?"

"It could have," the other replied with a giggle staring at Alan's predicament.

"What would you like to have done with it?" The second woman's declaration continued. "That's of course you can remember that far back."

"I don't know what you mean," the other woman answered as she turned and began to snigger like a teenage virgin.

The obvious younger of the two, who Alan thought to be in her middle sixties, spoke again. "It's a pity my old man couldn't have got like that when I needed him," her mocking tone announced. "And anyway it wasn't that big when he did get excited."

"But, size isn't everything," her friend declared closing her eyes.

"No," came back the retort. "But it helps!"

"You're only jealous," laughed the predictable comment.

"And why's that?"

"Because Ted," returned the answer. "If I remember rightly was never big enough to fill your twat."

"I'm not that big," declared the woman as she sniggered aloud. "Because at least he didn't need a plank strapped across his arse."

"What," laughed the other grandmother? "To stop him from falling in." Having spoken they turned and disappeared down the corridor.

After a rather boisterous discussion the general consensus was that a sexual fantasy had gotten a trifle out of hand. "She probably just wanted a good fucking," stated another women looking expectantly towards the man at her side. "And the way I'm feeling so do I."

"I'm open to any offers!" Another voice was heard to volunteer. "And I can promise the lucky lady a jolly good time."

This style of vulgar banter continued for maybe five minutes before everybody started to disappear and it was when they were alone that Alan offered Erin his hand and pulled. They now stood quite isolated in their private thoughts and as if to lighten the moment Alan touched his forelock in the mode of an obedient servant. "What is my Lady's pleasure?" He enquired as his skilful hands cupped the erotic structure of her panty covered buttocks.

She joined in with the theatre they'd started. "To find a wealthy man, with a cough, who could keep me in the lifestyle I deserve," she smiled. "So do you have a cough?"

"No my Lady," he implored. "But, I do have this." Having indicated exactly what it was quickly forced her to twist around and once ready pushed her shoulders to make her instinctively grab the edge of the bath. Looking down and seeing what was there his desire was complete when he fucked her doggy style.

It was three days later when Erin had begrudgingly gone to work. She'd actually started the previous day because her application to join the civilian workforce at the Naval Base had been successful. She was to be employed in the canteen serving the ranks, and didn't she look a picture in her nice neat uniform, and it was while dishing up the meals that she'd have the opportunity to keep her eyes and ears open for any hearsay that might be useful. It was on the Friday evening that she arrived back in a state of agitated panic obviously bursting to reveal exactly what she'd seen, or heard.

"If we go down to the swimming pool," her hurried words flew before the door had time to close.

Alan lifted his curious face, from the paper he'd been reading, and furrowed his brow. "Slow down," prompted his remark as he watched just how flustered she was. He stood and strode towards her. He took her coat and flung it to the floor before quickly placing is hands upon her shoulders and forcing her to sit. "Right," he encouraged. "Tell me all about it."

She went into a lengthy prologue about her day which included the following sentence, "There were four young Ratings sitting, at a table, eating their dinner when I overheard one of them talking about a certain Lieutenant."

"So!" He uttered with a modicum of boredom because if this was the best she could offer then he really wasn't interested.

"But, it wasn't a bloke they were discussing," she squealed as if trying to keep his attention. "It was one of the women Officers," she insisted. "And they were saying that she's got a sort of white flag tattooed, in a rather private place, as well as some funny looking mauve and yellow flowers." And then to add a little mystery added, "And the way they were describing the artwork reminded me of the tattoo your mother's got."

His ears picked up. "This could be worth investigating," he flippantly answered. "Especially if it's in the same place."

"Don't be so crude."

"Why not," he lecherously grinned. "Because, how do we know whether it's the right person that my father wanted us to find?"

"What d'yer mean?"

"Well according to his riddle," he scoffed. "We're looking for someone up here with a tattoo that's of an ensign amongst the violets."

"I know that!"

"But do you know what a violet looks like?"

"Sort of," she shrugged. "A funny kind of bluish flower."

"That's one variety," he mocked. "But think back to when we were in father's study looking through that book of herbs and seeing a sweet violet as well as the heartsease."

Her eyes closed as she tried to remember. "Okay clever clogs," she bit. "Why don't we try to see whether she's the person we're looking for?"

"What," announced his patronising tone? "Just go up to her and ask whether she'd be willing to drop her pants so that we can take a quick gander at the tattoo she's got."

"Of course not," she sighed.

"What then?"

"From what I've heard then she'll be at the public swimming pool tonight."

"And?"

"Because my sweet numpty," she smiled. "If I'm there in time then I might be able to see whether she's the right one when getting changed!"

"So what are we waiting for?" He smiled because at that moment he grabbed her hand and pulled. It was a quarter passed seven when they entered the reception area and it was ten minutes later, having purchased their costumes that they strolled into the chlorine stench of the pool. "Is she here?" He demanded.

There was a moment's pause. "You see that women!" Erin dramatically emphasised with finger pointing to one specific person dressed in a one piece black swimsuit.

Alan who was now sitting at one of the poolside tables, where they'd placed their towels, looked along the line of her finger and answered, "Yes!" And then remembering why they were there asked, "And was you in the changing rooms at the same time she was?"

"Yes!" She confirmed with some slight hesitation. "But, only after she'd got into her costume."

"So you didn't see the tattoo?"

"No!"

"That's a bit unfortunate," he admitted while looking at just how sexually confrontational Erin was standing, and posing, in the pale gold bikini she'd just brought. He grinned when realising that she was blatantly aware of the way it emphasised every sensual curve of her body; but like most young women she was naïvely unmindful to the fact that the lecherous glances given, by the majority of the men and he being one of them, were only being used to applaud what was visible and not to create any sexual impetus or overtone. He was still away with the fairies when the woman in question got out of the water and walked around the edge of the pool and took about fifteen seconds before she squelched close enough for Alan to regard her with furtive curiosity. "I need to see that tattoo," he quietly mentioned as she walked away. "Just to make sure she's the right one."

"And how exactly are you going to do that?"

Suddenly he heard half a conversation to his left. "I told you it was the wrong changing room," the giggling female voice explained to her friend. "But it was worth it when seeing all those naked men."

The idea was fantastic. Infact it was brilliant. Everything about it was perfect, but the only fly in the ointment was how he could get inside the women's changing room unnoticed and remain there unobserved. With this voyeuristic challenge they sat discussing the possibilities when they saw the woman standing by a chair drying her hair. "She's about to go and get changed!" He exclaimed as his pulse quickened, and it was then that they settled on the fact that it was either now or never. Deciding it had better be now they stood and walked from the pool and down the corridor. As they neared the changing rooms, one on either side, they came face to face with that single problem. There sitting at his desk was the duty receptionist obviously making sure nothing untoward happened.

"Wait here," instructed Erin as she disappeared inside the women's changing room. "It's empty," she whispered on her return. "And there's a small storage room at the far end where you can go and hide."

"What about matey," he emphasised with a flick of the thumb.

"Leave him to me," she smiled. "But, be ready to disappear when he's not looking." He stood by the door and watched as she approached the desk. Suddenly, she gave a yelp of distress as she appeared to slip on the wet floor. The result was spectacular as she threw out both hands hoping for better balance and this action proved vital in alerting the attendant. The plan worked a treat because the young lad, on the desk, raced around ever hopeful of being of use and with him being otherwise engaged Alan slipped inside the room to stand looking at what was there. But, what she hadn't explained was that there were rows of clothes hanging, in full view, on the pegs. His eyes widened, in bestial depravity, as he strolled between pair upon pair of differently coloured knickers hanging quite openly, and he was about halfway along when he stopped momentarily in front of a delicate ensemble of mint green lingerie and as he looked at the luxurious material he simply imagined the young woman who'd actually worn such an erotic outfit. With this fanciful illusion spinning wildly inside his mind he walked up to the other end of the room and opened the door before stepping inside that little hidey-hole. Once there he closed it. It was quiet and the smell reminded him of a male changing room after a sporting event but it was a sort of softer smell. Less, the harsh male testosterone and more the soft female oestrogen. With hurried investigation he soon located what appeared to be a man-made breach, which was just wide enough to enable him, to observe some of the women getting changed. He was thinking about shifting position when he heard the sounds of happy voices entering, and then as quietly as he could Alan pressed an eye against the slit and looked into the room. Was it bad luck, or something else, because all he could see was absolutely nothing?

"I wonder where they are," he speculated as he moved about the fissure ever hopeful of seeing something a bit risqué. Suddenly, he saw them. It was a group of four schoolgirls prancing about displaying their young femininity and seeing the immaturity of their bodies the peeping tom estimated that the average age was no more than twelve. He didn't want to continue looking, but their obvious innocence attracted him like the lecher he portrayed. For what seemed an eternity he quietly listened to the constant barrage of blasphemous dialogue, concerning the inevitable loss of their virginity, and he was rather grateful when at last they'd gone.

For the next five, or six, minutes he watched various women substituting one set of clothes for another, and he smiled when seeing one particular elderly woman standing next to that mint green ensemble that had previously attracted his attention. He stared, at her slender body, as she stripped off her wet costume and allowed it to fall in a soggy heap. With vigorous strokes of her bath towel she quickly dried herself. Then with meticulous ease she quickly pulled on the pair of knickers that seemed just adequate to cover the smoothness of her sexual skin. Next, a pair of fishnet stockings that were simply clipped to a mauve and pink suspender belt. Then, with penultimate skill she securely housed both petite breasts in the equally flimsy strands of her bra. Now ready she finally wriggled into the frumpy design of her dress and glided from view. He watched her disappearing through the doors and into a world where only she knew the sensual thrill of her underwear.

He was beginning to succumb to the vivid illusion of every man's fantasy when the door opened, yet again, and in strode the specific woman he wanted to gaze upon. His heart pounded as she walked instantaneously to where he was hiding and stood in direct eyesight of his gaze. There she posed, her shoulder length grey hair perfectly contrasting the black material of her costume, and as she endured his stare he had the opportunity to study her facial features. It was like being in a strip joint as the woman slowly started to remove her costume. As he watched he was becoming more excited especially as her tits came perfectly into view. He stared at them. He admired them. He wanted her to continue but gulped, in frustration, when before she'd completed the necessary removal there was a shout from somewhere in the distance that prompted her to turn and face the other way. Now, with her back to him she finished taking off the costume before allowing it to drop to the floor with a squelch. She was naked, except for the two dancing tigers, one on each cheek of her arse. "Turn around," he very quietly mouthed. She never, of course, heard but at least she did turn. His eyes grew wide. His tongue, that was as dry as a barber's strap, fell from his mouth. It was like that because just above the line of her pubic hair was a tattoo showing a white ensign and on either side of the flag fluttered a couple of sweet violet flowers.

"You're the one!" Squealed Alan's words as he stepped from his hiding place and pointed at the tattoo. The scream was piercing. There was hardly any delay before the door swung open and the young attendant rushed in, but that was all the time Alan needed. Blind panic required him to think on his feet. Fear forced adrenaline through his body compelling him to race towards the door and knock the woman to the floor.

"Bloody pervert," hollered a chorus as they watched him disappearing from the building and up the High Street.

Erin didn't return that night or the next but finally appeared around ten o'clock on the third. "I've been staying with Olivia," she announced as she sat on a chair. There was no kiss of welcome. No apology. There was nothing, but that statement. And even then she struggled to even look him in the eye.

"Who," choked his words as he realised something was not quite what it seemed.

"You remember," her hostile chronicle challenged. "The one you were going to molest."

He smiled while shrugging. "Oh! Her," declared his rather nervous expression. For five minutes nothing was said as he looked at her, sitting bolt upright, and staring towards the open door as if expecting someone. Finally, the tension became too great and so he marched up to her and violently grabbed her shoulders. With the strength of ten he twisted her face and lifted her unresponsive body before drilling her with raging eyes. "What's wrong?" He bawled with his mouth two inches from her face. He knew he'd frightened her by the trickle of tears rolling down her cheeks, but he didn't care. And to prove the point screamed his next words, "And who's this Olivia?"

The door opened and in marched that same woman. "Hello Alan," she greeted as she neared the shaking lad. Was she a lost relation he'd never met because she cuddled him with pure affection?

"Who are you?" Escaped the only words he could muster.

"From what Erin's told me I'm the woman you're looking for," she explained. Holding out her hands, in the mode of friendship, she warmly took his. Now ready; she led him to a chair and promptly sat him down.

He sat and felt his heart pound. He sat as a million questions raced around his head. He sat and thought is this the woman his father was on about? He sat and thought about what, if anything is her involvement? Finally, as his reflections vanished like a mist a single question exploded from his dry mouth, "Who are you?"

The woman came and stood directly in front of him. She looked down with an air of knowledge. "Erin," she began. "Has explained that you're looking for someone, who has got a very distinctive tattoo about their person, and who personally knew a certain Captain Henry Young."

"You could be right," he intervened trying not to give anything away.

"She also went on to explain who you are," slipped her confirmation. "And so knowing that I'm here to tell you what I know."

"I'd just joined the Wrens when I got posted to Singapore for a tour of duty, and it was while out there that I became very friendly with a certain group of sailors."

Erin suddenly burst in with her words. "She was more than bloody friendly," she accused. "It was more like trying to sleep with them." And the acid tone of her voice stripped any goodwill that she might have had for the woman. "And by her own admission she succeeded."

"Why?" Alan directed as he now turned toward Erin as she sat fuming. "Who were these lucky men?" She never answered, but the anger welling in her body forced her to tremble like a leaf.

The woman turned to Alan. "First, there was your father," she clinically announced.

"And then it was mine!" Interposed Erin snarling with a face as red as a beetroot.

"Is this true," the apparently unconcerned voice of Alan queried, although its tone was some two octaves lower in pitch.

"Yes!" The woman sulked but after admitting the truth there was no signs of regret as she turned her head so that she couldn't face her audience. "But you have to remember that none of us were married at the time."

"And that makes it alright," Erin challenged. Hearing this; the other woman never replied but the expression she gave was more damning than any words could have been, and when Erin violently blushed both women understood. "Anyway," she continued. "I'd been out there for about six months when your father," here she looked at Alan, "Asked if he could have a portrait done of me."

"What as a memento of getting inside your knickers and rutting for the empire?" Erin snarled.

"I'm not sure."

"And why's that?"

"Because after he'd taken the photographs, which I presume were for the artist, I was posted to Dundee and I've been here ever since."

"So you made your life here?"

"I suppose I did."

"And did you ever marry?"

"Yes," she flippantly answered. "I went from being Miss Olivia Whitehouse to Mrs Olivia Thomas." During this narrative her attitude seemed rather churlish, and the reason for this became blatantly obvious when she added. "But the bastard found himself a girl half my age and set up home somewhere, or other." There was a pause before adding with a hint of spite, "And I hope the weasel's willy drops off!"

"That's not a very nice thing to say."

"He never used it much while we were married," she cursed. "So I don't suppose he'd notice if it does."

"Let's get back to the painting."

"If we must."

"Have you ever seen the actual painting he commissioned?"

"No," she quickly answered but then after a moment's pause added. "But I remember being sent a photograph of it."

"Have you still got it?"

"Yes," she answered. "But it's at home and I'm not quite sure where it is."

Changing tact quite skilfully Alan smiled, "And what about this tattoo everyone knows about."

"Oh! That!"

"Yes," the two answered together.

"You've got to remember that it was an awful long time ago," she began. "And from what I can remember I went with some friends to a downtown bar."

"What, in Singapore?"

"Yes," she confirmed. "And I'd obviously had a bit too much to drink because when I woke up the next morning apart from having a really bad head I felt extremely sore around my vagina."

Hearing this Erin suddenly looked concerned. "So did you think that you'd been raped?"

"That was my first thought," she shivered. "But when I saw the tattoo I realised that I'd probably had it done in one of the many notorious backstreet clinics that they have down there."

With this type of conversation going on all three sat until the early hours, with a variety of drinks, reminiscing over the good times and bad. It was probably due to the flow of alcohol that at one point Olivia suddenly giggled, "Would you like to see the tattoo?"

Erin instantly glared at Alan probably because he was smiling like a Cheshire cat. "I don't think so," she humbly offered. "Because we wouldn't want to give him a heart attack!"

"Spoilsport," dribbled his word as he stared intently at Olivia's crotch.

"Maybe later," returned the stage whispered smile. This kind of unsubtle innuendo continued until around four o'clock when it was finally decided to call a halt to proceedings but before leaving Olivia invited both youngsters to come and stay at her house. "I need some company," she told them while slipping from sight and into the never-ending bustle of the City's nightlife, or more precisely the early morning life. They awoke next day from the drunken stupor, at around four o'clock in the afternoon, and discussed what they thought had happened.

"I think we've been invited to go and stay somewhere," queried Alan as he tried to speak even though his mouth resembled the bottom of a bird cage.

"I think you're right," Erin responded as her eyeballs strained painfully in their sockets. As her head spun, like a windmill, she dropped a couple of fizzy tablets into the beaker of water and drank it in one gulp. Her eyes half closed as the realisation of instant relief passed into tomorrow's dreams, for now she quite literally understood the phrase piss-holes in the snow. Alan was no better as he slouched around the room like death warmed up and by early evening their collective consciousness had managed to untangle itself to hold a moderate conversation, but this was only undertaken as long as no-one raised their voices and it was around six thirty that the telephone rang. "Hello," softly welcomed Erin's voice as she struggled to answer it.

The voice on the other end sounded perfect, "Are you alright?" It asked and it took a moment before Erin's brain fathomed out exactly who it was.

"I think so," she whispered in case the hostility of her own words caused her head to start spinning again. There was a pause and then she spoke again. "Am I right in thinking that you've invited us to come over and stay with you," spilled her sentence as her eyes closed from the alcoholic pressure throbbing inside her head.

"That's right," came back the chuckled declaration. "Everything's been prepared for you!"

Well it was around eight thirty that evening, when they stood in front of the reception desk and paid their outstanding bill. They climbed aboard the taxi and were driven to number 31 Chestnut Road. They paid their fare and staggered along the driveway to ultimately stand outside the closed door. Alan carefully pressed the bell and stepped back to await the answer. "Welcome," smiled the elegantly dressed woman who opened it. They were led inside and up the stairs. Along the landing, Alan carried the single suitcase, and was taken to the third door. "You're in here," the woman declared with a wave of the hand. "And I'll leave you to get ready." She'd taken probably a couple of steps when she turned and smiled, "I'm about to have my dinner so if you want you can come and join me."

Seeing as neither had the stomach for any food and just the thought of it started a nauseating sensation to begin upsetting their stomachs they replied, "I think we'll give it a miss." Having given the proclamation the colour in their faces vanished like the setting sun and so it was decided that a good nights' sleep would probably be a better prospect.

It was sometime next morning that the growing urgency in Alan's bladder forced him to leave Erin asleep and venture along the landing hopeful of discovering the whereabouts of the bathroom. Like a mouse he passed an open window and seeing the bright sun realised that it was well passed getting up time. He neared a door and thinking it was the right one gently pushed it ajar to carefully look inside. His heart pounded with a fundamental desire when seeing, as large as life, their host bent double in the sink washing her hair. He stood studying her covered arse before watching her stand up straight, reach for a towel and cover her wet hair like a turban. With no obvious cares in the world she twisted around and stood like Aphrodite rising from that clam shell. The inborn fascination of seeing her half naked in just her knickers prompted him to forget exactly where he was and come to think about it; exactly why he was there, so with hormonal urgency his hand reached down to cover the developing bulk in his underpants and feeling his excitement growing closed his eyes. Suddenly, she turned as if to leave and as she did his eyes sprang lecherously apart. "Oh!" She smiled knowing full well that he was staring at her, or more precisely at her tits. "Do you need the toilet?"

"Please," he sighed while rushing passed. When he'd finished he wandered back along the landing. But when passing the second door, which by careful deduction was Olivia's room, a sudden craving hit him and so going back to his room quickly put on his clothes. Now ready he returned and carefully knocked, on the bedroom door, just the once.

"Yes?"

"Can I ask you something?"

"Okay," the soft voice said. "Come on in."

Feeling extremely curious, in voyeuristic sort of way, he opened the door and stepped inside. His heart started to quicken when seeing Olivia sitting on her bed drying her hair. "Hello again," she smiled without turning. "And what can I do for you?"

"I was just wondering," he lied rather unsuccessfully. "Whether you've had a chance to look for the photograph we were talking about the other night." And as he waited for her response he simply couldn't focus on anything except her reflection in the large mirror directly in front of him.

"Let me just see whether I can find it in here," she confirmed while leaning towards the bedside table. Now with the drawer open she began to rummage around. "Oh!" She giggled while quickly placing, on the bed in full view, a sleek and smooth silver vibrator. "You weren't supposed to see that." He wasn't bothered in the least because as she was speaking she'd turned to face him. He smiled, with pure voyeurism, as he now had a wonderful naked panorama of her upper body. To you and me he saw her lovely tits. Suddenly she stood and glided passed him. "I know where I put it," she announced walking towards the wardrobe and opening the door. With it open she bent and reached inside. "There," she smiled when finally handing over a rather creased photograph.

He took it and studied it. He smiled, in a lecherous kind of way, as it showed Olivia sitting at a desk in her uniform. But what made the whole thing erotic was that below the table top was the fact that she was not wearing any underwear and there as clear as day was the specific tattoo so perfectly visible.

"Very nice," he smiled.

"Why thank you," she blushed.

Suddenly, he felt a chin digging into his shoulder. Twisting slightly he saw Erin looking down at exactly the same image. "Is that all you ever think about," she cursed while grabbing his wrist.

"Yes," he laughed as she pulled him away.

Today was Sunday the 20th May and it was around eight thirty, in the evening, when everyone simply sat around listening to the hypnotic melody's that reminded Alan of his misspent youth while at college. The conversations flowed like the alcohol, both stimulating and totally pointless, and as the intoxicating beverages were drunk the rational process of thinking disappeared to the point of stupidity. It was about half passed ten when he suddenly noticed that both Erin and Olivia were talking as if they'd been the best of friends for a lifetime. They were laughing and joking, telling stories of their most intimate secrets, and as he sat feeling left out of their frivolous conquests glanced around the room. There were pictures of various designs but the one that captured his attention was the naked view of a woman walking towards the shipwrecked hull of a galleon. She left footprints as the haunting moonlight cast long shadows in the sand. Once he'd become bored by the image his eyes dropped and focused on the collection of tatty looking books that had been stacked by the antique writing desk. He grinned in appreciation because with the women's attention still otherwise occupied he wandered over and picked a thick volume at random. He picked another and read it. He didn't actually read it; more like just looked at the pictures. Then another until finally discovering that the collection, of various journals and reports, concerned one specific mariner who'd claimed the salvage rights to the seafaring vessels that had floundered, upon the rocks, around the World and its Seven Seas. It was after an hour, or so, that he selected what appeared to be the final journey of Captain Brendan Masco. He took the papers and sat. Reading the spidery words he remembered the stories his father would recount about a particular stretch of water that had claimed the many lives of the unwary. His attention was immediately drawn when he read the name of that final vessel that had come to grief around the Cape of Good Hope and felt the chill of terror rolling along his shoulders as he quietly read. "The Tanmouth," he stage whispered. "Was lost on Wednesday 24th December 1766 near to The Devil's Brooder with its treasure of Spanish gold and Italian jewels." The picture instantly focused as he sobered. His thoughts rushed forward for he simply couldn't believe what he'd just read and so instinctively raced to his feet. "Got it," he squealed waving the watery brown parchment as if on fire.

Both women turned as one and stared at him as if he were a freak. "Now, what have you found?" The two voices asked in unison.

He couldn't contain himself. "What the whole thing's about," he sang waving that single article.

The women looked at him. They looked at each other. Then like two peas, in a pod, strutted to where he was standing and peered like hungry vultures at the stained words being held. Erin, suddenly, snatched the document and coldly looked at it, and then like a mistress lifted her eyebrows in the mode of indifference. While wrapping her arms around her lover's waist calmly announced, "Can't it wait until tomorrow?" And having spoken walked across the room.

Thinking that he might be onto a good thing swung around and stared directly at the seductive sway of her hips and thought, "Why not!"

And having reached her his hand quickly covered her arse. "If you're thinking what I think your thinking then you'll be out of luck tonight," her giggling voice proclaimed, although tinged with some slight regret. He sighed with frustration as he didn't need the biology lesson to understand what she meant and so gripped her hand that bit looser.

"Goodnight!" They both smiled as they left Olivia on her own pondering over what he'd found.

Erin was asleep, but he couldn't rest as his mind roamed the Oceans and he was still awake when hearing footsteps along the landing. He listened to a door as it opened and then just as quickly close again.

After dinner, and dressing the part, it had been decided to go and watch a rather saucy play being given at the Dominican Theatre. They'd paid good money to sit in the balcony seats and watch the show, about a hospital, that contained both bad language and full-frontal nudity. It was in one of the scene that the leading man, already down to his underwear, was taken to the wrong ward. This hilarious cock up had occurred when the night shift sister misread the patient's notes and instructed one of the junior nurses to find him a bed for the night. In the morning and waking in the hysterectomy ward, all the sexual innuendo flew like chaff in the wind. The audience had a good laugh as the other patient's tried their hardest to keep this nubile hero from the constant surveillance of the nurses. They kept hiding him in their beds beneath the covers. They stripped him naked and in keeping with the location dressed him in women's clothes and it was especially this scene, plus the rest of the play, which concentrated on both the voyeuristic as well as the comical situation and come the final curtain the applause, was both loud and enthusiastic.

After meeting some of the performers, of the show, Alan and Erin walked the streets of Dundee as they headed back holding hands. It had just starting to rain, yet again, as they turned the final corner to see the darkened outline of their abode for the night. Feeling over-zealous, as well as getting wet, they half scurried along the path until standing in the deception of the Georgian Porch. "Have you got the key," solemnly announced Erin as she cuddled closer to him.

"What's this?" He systematically chortled pushing it into the lock; and once free the door swung open. The hallway was dark, but was soon illuminated with a flick of a switch and once inside they shivered as the house felt uncomfortably cold.

"Let's go to bed," sermonised Erin as her voice now sounded rather frisky, and having given her instruction waltzed towards the stairs wiggling her sumptuous arse. He followed with the knowledge that if he played his card right he might be onto a good thing and probably knowing what was to come disappeared up the stairs as well. Once inside the bedroom they kissed as hands went everywhere and it didn't take long before his clothes were removed and thrown to the floor. Very quickly he started on her attire. He was relatively successful until wanting to remove that final piece of clothing that was hiding his ultimate desire.

"No!" She soulfully explained as his hands were removed.

"Why," he hinted. "Is it still like the Somme?"

"What!"

"Bloody."

The alarm went off at around six thirty only to be picked up and thrown against a chair because although the blasted thing had done its job Alan was still tired. He lay motionless and through the dreaded eyes of sleep listened for any sound that might give away the fact that he'd not yet died. He panicked when he heard absolutely nothing. He felt slightly better when hearing Erin snoring as she usually did, but as he listened something felt wrong. Sitting up in bed he concentrated on the life outside. There were the sounds of milk bottles rattling against each other. Arrogant drivers sounding horns to imply of their existence. People chatting and walking dogs. "Wake up!" He demanded while rocking Erin by the shoulder.

It took about two minutes, this may have been a slight exaggeration, before a single eye began to acknowledge the request and the grunt of disapproval confirmed her annoyance. When at last both eyes stared at the man responsible; her lackadaisical enthusiasm was clearly on display. "What is it?" Muttered the standard three words as she pulled the cover that bit tighter around her throat, because there was no way that she was going to feel the icy chill.

"Can't you hear?" He uttered while getting out and standing in exactly what he'd gone to bed in which was a slightly grubby pale green T-shirt and nothing else.

"What are you on about," asked another of the standard questions. Alan wasn't listening, or he may not have heard because he speedily vanished through the bedroom door. By the time he'd reappeared Erin was sat up rubbing her eyes. Her hair, which last night looked immaculate, now showed signs of needing some repair and her brow furrowed in wonder as she spoke her words, "What's wrong?" The smudged traces of make-up made her look a trifle comical as she tried to look somewhat serious.

"I'm not sure," his direct statement shot as he quickly pulled on his clothes, and once dressed disappeared once again. The sound of hurried footsteps racing down the stairs, two at a time, indicating the apparent urgency. Listening to the commotion Erin ultimately decided that curiosity was probably the best plan and so got out of bed. She found him at the writing desk pushing sheets of paper as if it were rubbish. "She's fucking took 'em," snarled the vicious blaspheme as he kept on searching.

"Who's taken what," asked the early morning question inasmuch as her thinking hadn't quite caught up with her brain.

"Olivia," returned the name in a tone that wouldn't have been out of place on the Quarter Deck of a Tea Clipper. "She's also taken the scroll of paper about the Tanmouth," his ill-tempered manner declared. "And she's nowhere to be found," he whined as once again he stormed off. They turned the house upside down looking for clues that might tell them where she'd gone, and finding her car-keys missing decided that she'd obviously planned it once she'd discovered the truth. He gave a wide sarcastic smirk while reflecting over every detail both he and Olivia had discussed since his apparent discovery. He'd used her knowledge, as well as the nautical charts she'd borrowed from the Admiralty, to try and locate the last resting place of the Tanmouth. He sat and tried to recall the intricate detail they'd discovered, but the memories in his head spun like the gossamer threads of a spider's web. He closed his eyes as if concentrating. The anger welling in his gut forced him to admit defeat as only miniature fragments cruised and came to rest in the harbour of his mind. Feeling like a leper he skulked around the disorganised sitting room until lethargy compelled him to sit. It was frustration that now forced him to hyperventilate and he felt faint as a single idea bounced inside the windmills of his mind. Somehow getting a second wind he calmly reached across the small table and picked up the telephone. He dialled the set of numbers, etched on the stones in his brain, and waited.

"Hello!"

There was no introduction as he simply went for the jugular. "I need you to look for something," he craved.

"Who's that?"

"It's Alan," his shocked reply uttered. "Your son!"

"Oh! It's you," she returned. "I'm so glad," whinged her next frightened statement.

"Why, what's wrong?" His next question prompted as he imagined all sorts of disasters.

There was a long pause. There were sounds of her trying not to be frightened, but when she spoke again the tone was clearly plain. "I've been getting threatening calls," she stage whispered.

Hearing the words the hairs on his back stood and prickled. His fist clenched tightly around the phone as all of a sudden his own thoughts of the charts and maps dispersed into the vacuum of concern. "We're coming home," he offered as he quickly replaced the receiver.

"Who were you talking to," demanded the sweet voice at his elbow.

He twisted and looked into the Emerald green fragments of her eyes and smiled. It wasn't the smile of serenity, but was more like the smile of necessity. He cleverly cupped her chin, pulled her eager face towards his own and kissed her forehead. "Something's happened at Calder's," he sighed. "And so we're going home."

They rang the station to find the time of the next train. "It's the Highland Express that leaves at a quarter to eleven," repeated the female Scot's voice on the other end. Alan looked at the clock and noticed the time. Even with his basic mathematical brain, and realising they had hardly anything to pack, knew that they had about two hours to waste and so decided to watch the television. They perched together on the settee and started watching a programme about the Amazonian Rain Forest and its abundance of wildlife. It concentrated on the unique balance that the dwellers within the forest had with the animal kingdom.

"Just look at that," quoted Erin as the documentary now focused on a couple of naked Amazonian girls walking into shot and continuing into the village. Having spoken she turned her head and looked at Alan smirking with a rather stupid, and vulgar, grin. "I know that all you ever think about?" Her statement exploded in the tone much used by women when having just caught their husbands ogling a younger model of themselves. "But try being a little less obvious."

He shrugged his shoulders in acceptance, and to add salt into the wound looked across at the portrait hanging above that writing desk. "What about that?" He suggested with finger pointing at a print of a classic nude.

"That's different," her impartial voice offered. "It's art."

"So what's the difference?" He teased. "She's showing everything!"

There was a pause as she thought. Then a smile a mile wide appeared upon her lips. "But, she's not real," concluded her answer, and having given her response nodded her head just the once as a mark of finality. The argument was far from finished as he stood and walked over to the painting of footprints in the sand. He positioned himself directly in front and simply stared at the image of the woman and his eyes narrowed as he stared. He pushed his tongue out while concentrating. "Well!" She bated while standing next to him.

"I'm still looking," he struggled, and to help concentrate his argument looked earnestly at the picture. Whether what he saw was what he wanted but he suddenly grabbed her elbow and forcibly made her look. "What can you see?" His eager voice charged.

She made the face of an irritated child, scrunched up nose and all. Then following the line of his finger furrowed her eyes. She tilted her head as her gaze focused on the stern of the shipwreck and four letters escaped from her mouth, "O.U.T.H."

"That's the Falmouth," he insisted and for pure devilment ran his finger down the canvas, where the funnel was, and sure enough an invisible patch came away. With renewed urgency he squinted at the tiny letters written and like the last time read them, "Look for a tailed cat in the place that will skin your life and its here that you'll find the stony burdock."

It was a glorious hot Saturday afternoon, at the beginning of June when Erin decided to wear the most inadequate set of clothes she'd recently brought. Alan was waiting in the kitchen when she made her entrance, and the way his eyes popped simply confirmed he liked what he saw. He gulped his appreciation as the transparency of the sky blue blouse resembled a waterfall cascading over the bawdy exposure of her mustard yellow bra. He had trouble forcing his open mouthed gaze to drop, but when it did his heart exploded because the length of her light sapphire skirt seemed to halt some six inches above her knees and to make the whole spectacle even more moving, in an erotic sort of way, was that she wore no stockings to hide the cinnamon colour of her legs. It became even more explicit when she turned around and bent to put on her white sandals because the hypnotic intensity of her apple coloured knickers came perfectly into view.

He could have stayed, all day, admiring the luscious texture of her body but like the sulky vixen she appeared unconcerned as his tongue hung from his parched mouth. The in-explicable attraction of her femme fatale caused a coating of perspiration to cover his forehead and made his pulse race. It appeared to be even worse as she moved towards him because her movements, which had been expertly choreographed since time immemorial to lure the stupid male, worked perfectly as he gazed like a rabbit caught in the headlights of a car on the sexual attractiveness of her body. "Let's go for a walk?" he implored when realising the fundamental desire throbbing through his body.

"Okay!" She answered with a knowing smile. Through the village, they walked, which looked exactly the same as when they'd left for Dundee, except the summer flowers were now starting to display their undoubted beauty.

"Hello!" Cordially announced Marsha as she walked passed obviously on her way to an illicit rendezvous somewhere; and in her hands were the obvious tools of her trade. I know what you're thinking but this time is was a box of coloured pencils because she was an artist when all said and done.

"There she goes," grinned Alan as he watched her disappearing down the garden path of number 24 Mill Lane.

The girl, on his arm, gently nudged him. "She's probably wants to do a quick sketch for her next painting."

"I suppose she does," he replied. "And I wonder what sort?"

"What d'yer mean?"

"Well it could be a landscape. An abstract," he mocked. "Or more likely a naked study?"

They'd walked precisely eleven paces, further on, when she ran forward and promptly stopped. "I've decided," she grinned while turning to face him. "I want a painting done."

"What as a replacement for the one that was stolen?"

"Yes."

"But this time," he suggested. "I just want a full portrait of you in that beautiful dress you had on when I took your photo the other day."

"Okay," she giggled remembering what had happened afterwards. They kissed, and having agreed continued their walk.

Cars kept passing on a regular basis, and when one stopped they cheerfully gave direction to the aptly named Oval where the village cricket team were about to play their latest match. "It's just down there on the left," Alan smiled having given the instruction to the man leaning from the open window.

"Thanks," returned the appreciation as he drove away. Having done their bit for good relations both he and Erin continued along the road before stopping in front of the gate that led towards the infamous cottage at the end of the village.

"Let's go in here!" He smirked as he strongly grasped her hand.

Probably understanding his intent she pulled back and smirked like an innocent virgin waiting to be shown the facts of life. "Righte-o," she responded as her smirk suddenly became the smile of desire. As they moved his heart was pounding. His pulse was racing as they hurried towards the broken door and once inside a room, which was once probably the sitting room, they stopped. Standing fractionally apart he watched as she gave a little shiver from the ever present chill and smiled, like a perverted rascal, as her tits quivered like upturned jellies. His eager tongue circumnavigated his lips as he watched just how steadily her nipples had expanded to stand out like a couple of chapel hat pegs. He waited but a moment before placing his arms around her shoulders. He pulled her close and as she responded pushed his eager hands beneath the skimpy design of that skirt and began to fondle the covered bulk of her arse. With each caress he was getting more, and more, excited. Suddenly, he stopped. Something was wrong! Something, or someone, was out there moving closer. As he twisted his head to listen; it was as if his body had become petrified. The sound of scrunching leaves verified his concern and when that same man, he'd previously given directions to, walked clearly into view it was confirmed. When seeing the courting couple the stranger stopped. He grinned, somewhat apologetically, as he began to walk closer. From the jacket he was wearing produced a letter and quite simply handed it to Erin. Nothing was said while she read its contents. "I'm not going back," she cursed while passing it to her escort.

"What is it?" Alan demanded as he quickly took the piece of paper and read it. For approximately ten seconds no-one moved or said anything, then rather abruptly the other man stretched out his hand and clamped Erin's wrist like a vice.

"Just doing my job," he explained as he started to pull her away. Erin muffled a scream which forced Alan to panic. The battle against the adrenaline, pumping through his veins, took a moment but he finally gained some composure. As his body trembled he scurried a direct path towards the stranger and stood in direct eye contact. He lashed out with a fist and missed. The retribution was swift and the pain felt forced him to fall against the wall and crack his head. He wasn't going to be a loser so licked the blood, from his hand, and charged.

It was dark when he woke. He was alone, but there beside him was that damning announcement with three words added in bright red lipstick that had obviously been hurriedly written. With care he eventually stood and rested against the wall. His eyes closed in agony, both from the pain and the realisation that she'd gone. It took all of his effort before staring at the piece of paper, but when he did saw I'm so sorry scrawled across the page.

"So, she's gone back to her husband?" His mother calmly stated when he explained as to why Erin was no longer with him. This sort of conversation continued but the underlying reaction Alan felt from his mother's tone was simply, I told you so! Then taking her conversation in completely the opposite direction she cordially announced, "I'm just popping out."

"Why," asked his rather apathetic question. "Where you going?"

"To see the Colonel," she returned while walking from the house. Hearing who it was Alan really didn't care and the house was silent as he lay on his bed thinking about what had become of his life. It didn't matter what he tried to remember because it always seemed to come back to Erin. How she kept asking questions. How she wanted to know things that seemed a little trifle at the time. There was one particular occasion when they were laying in bed and his mother walked in to explain that she was wanted on the telephone. He thought nothing of it when she never answered his question about who it was and to read what she'd written on that letter only made him feel that maybe he'd been used. Was he on the verge of destruction as the thought of total rejection cruised through his body forcing him to tremble momentarily as he recalled that everything had started with the theft of a certain picture? Realising that he needed some fresh air, to help clear his mind, simply went for a walk. He didn't know where he was going but suddenly found himself outside the Colonel's house. He wasn't sure why he did it but he knocked on the door and waited. No response. He tried again and still no response. He tried a third time and getting no reply acted like a curious thief because someone should have been there and so with stealth, and urgency, tried the door and was a trifle bemused when it opened. Through the hallway he carefully moved while listening to the damning silence and having no luck downstairs decided to try along the landing. Flitting from room to room he eventually opened the master bedroom door before stepping inside to see what, or who was there. What he saw wasn't what he expected. It wasn't the Colonel and his mother but was infact someone else. It was actually Simon Carlisle and someone else. The naked woman, at his side, who should have been his fiancée Felicity Hooper, was in reality the notorious Janet Palmer-Jeffery. As he hovered, with one eye looking at that picture above the bed and the other on the woman, a sudden movement rippled along the two sleeping bodies that prompted the would be intruder to quietly steal away.

It was several days later an anonymous letter, plus a press cutting, arrived addressed to Alan that sent a cold shiver of panic across his shoulders and down his spine. The letter simply instructed him to read the torn page, and as he read it a lump formed in his throat.

Found today. The partially decomposed body of a woman, later identified as Olivia Thomas, was found floating in the Irish Sea off the Calf of Man by fishermen. Investigations have found that she'd arrived on the Main Island a couple of days earlier, and in her hotel room were maps and charts. Sources at the hotel went on to tell of her eagerness to search along the coastline hoping to find treasure lost from a Galleon at sea, but the irony of this was that after the police had informed the Admiralty they were later told that the charts were of an isolated atoll in the Pacific Ocean. When asked of its whereabouts they were informed that a volcanic explosion in 1834 had destroyed it.

He read the cutting again, and again, allowing a smirk of delight to flow along his mouth because what she'd stolen had been her undoing in more ways than one.

It was about a week later on a warm evening that Alan wandered towards the pub for a cooling drink, and he'd been walking for about two minutes completely engrossed in what he was thinking about when suddenly, a car horn sounded which made him jump somewhat. Spinning round, with aggravation, he looked at the culprit in an unfamiliar car drawing closer. As it neared he scrunched up his nose in modest innocence and shrugged his shoulders as an act of reverent nonchalance. Having nothing better to do began ambling towards the car and as he got closer his pulse quickened. A grin a mile wide formed around his mouth as the driver pushed her head out of the open window and cordially announced her word of welcome. "Hello," she smiled with her hair cascading down her face to give the impression of a fresh morning in spring. Alan, having already recognised whoever it was, bent from the waist and glanced directly at her. He grinned, from ear to ear, when their eyes met and as they clashed he dropped his subordinate challenge to immediately focus on the rather large amount of visible flesh slowly rising and falling with every one of her breaths.

"So you've had it done," he stage whispered when realising that she'd gone and had a boob job.

Always observant, Felicity instantly recognised the voyeur in his gaze and for that returned her own greeting by licking her glossy lips to seductively coat them with a moist shimmer of saliva. Having finished, she gave an impish grin that spoke volumes of the way she must have been feeling because her pink tongue protruded from between her ruby red lips. "Simon wanted me to have bigger breasts," she acknowledged. "And so I agreed."

"They are nice," he admitted while still looking at them.

"They'd better be," she smiled and then metaphorically added. "Because they cost me an arm and a leg."

"So, has he seen them yet?"

"Yes," she giggled. "He was playing with them last night."

"Lucky man," he teased with a certain amount of jealousy.

"So would you like to see them," begged the question. "Because the way you're staring at me I'm sure you would."

"If only," quietly dribbled his words when realising that the chances of seeing anything a bit risqué ranged from zero to absolute zero.

"I'm sorry," she grinned. "I didn't quite catch that."

"Nothing," he muttered.

"Anyway," started her next sentence when seeing the beads of perspiration coating his brow. "Aren't you a little hot?"

"If I wasn't before," he admitted when looking down. "Then I am now." What had caused this statement was when seeing the fact that Felicity was naked from the waist down except for the pair of paper thin charcoal grey knickers that were being used to hide her modesty.

Seeing precisely where his gaze had finished she laughed. "It was hot in the car and so I decided to do something about it," she smiled in trying to justify her appearance and then after a moment's thought added, "And anyway you shouldn't be looking."

Realising that attack would probably make the best line of defence he laughed, "A cat can look at a King!"

Hearing this, the corners of her mouth rose into a crescent. Her words flowed easily as she parried his jocular lunge, "Well, all I know is that there's a young knave standing there hoping to see my pussy," and having spoken blushed at having given such a crude response and promptly pulled her colourless thighs together as if closing the curtain. She shifted around rather awkwardly until asking with a smile, "Would you like to get in?"

"If only," he thought and shuddered with an unknown embarrassment as he backed away to stand pondering his destiny. Suddenly, with a Cavalier attitude glanced at his watch and noticing the time moved around the car. He waited patiently for the woman to lean across and unlock the door. When at last he'd settled she turned and quietly asked, "Well! How far do you want to go?" And the tone of her sweet voice dripped pure innocence.

Probably realising the Freudian slip he responded in kind, "As far as I can!" And after saying the words waited.

He hadn't long because her smile was infectious as she cottoned onto his train of thought. "You naughty boy," came the laughed reprimand, as she clearly understood his rather blatant insinuation. "And anyway what would Simon say?" She suggested.

A wicked smile erupted along his mouth as he remembered what he'd witnessed the other week and trying to be discreet answered. "I'm not sure," he rather tentatively lied. "And anyway you can drop me here."

Alan's mother had arranged to stay with a friend she'd known, and kept in contact with, from her husband's days in the Navy. He'd driven her to the station, that morning, where she would start to enjoy a well earned holiday on the Isle of Man. "I'll see you in a fortnights time," she cordially announced while picking up her suitcase and waddling across the platform towards the waiting train.

As it vanished Alan puffed out his cheeks, more in relief than anything else, because since the fourth day of his return from Dundee his mother had badgered him about getting a job. "Fresh air won't pay the bills," was the constant moan he received whenever another brown envelope slipped through the letterbox. In the relative freedom of his isolation the day itself passed fairly quickly and come the evening it was decided that a good drink was required to help pass the time. Once ready he walked towards the pub and as he passed a certain house lingered slightly longer than was necessary. He was doing this inasmuch as Marsha Cooper, because that's whose house it was, could according to village gossip be seen in various states of undress standing next to the easel in her workshop. He was fourteen when on a warm and clammy evening he'd actually witnessed this for the first time when seeing her in a mauve bra and a pair of scanty knickers. He smiled, and his smile became even greater when searching the old hiding place where he knew an old mangled pair of binoculars should be. Looking through the battered eyepiece, which had to be cleaned, he could focus perfectly. Well it was slightly better than with a naked eye but he didn't really care and feeling in desperate need of some diversion, or other, crouched beneath the hanging branches of the over-grown Elder that he'd once used to conceal his immoral activity and once there simply waited. He'd just checked his watch, for the umpteenth time, when eventually his ordeal was about to come to an end. He now concentrated his stare as the studio light was switched on and his heartbeat started to increase as into the room waltzed Marsha dressed in a figure hugging camel coloured cat-suit. He drooled with anticipation because it had apparently been sprayed onto her body like a second skin as every one of her sexual contours stood proud. With the one good eye-piece he could study her as she went towards her easel and gathered her brushes. He was watching when she walked towards a wardrobe, in the corner, where various other pieces of equipment were obviously stored and once there opened the door. He had an appreciative ogle, of her highly provocative arse, as she bent and ferreted around looking for something she might be after. Having gathered whatever she required stood and walked back to the easel. He could have followed her erotic movements, but didn't. He didn't because he was staring open-mouthed at what was hanging on the inside of the wardrobe door. He simply couldn't believe what he saw, and as his recollections started to build he made himself a promise that he would investigate and gather the proof of its existence.

In the pub he sat alone in his favourite corner, drink on the table, going over the plan that might allow him to discover if what he'd actually seen was the painting that Erin had originally given him. The plan itself was quite simple, because like all good ruses it was so easy that it hinged on being absurd. He decided that since he'd taken several breathtaking photographs of Erin he was going to ask Marsha to paint the portrait he so desperately wanted. He bided his time carefully until he thought it right, and so on the Wednesday evening knocked on the door and simply waited. He shivered, though not from the cold, as he stood waiting for an answer. It was after a couple of minutes and getting no response he decided to give it another try. He knocked and waited, but this time he was lucky because a bedroom window opened and Marsha's head appeared. "I'll be down in a moment," she giggled before disappearing again. He waited for the door to open. "Hello!" She smiled now dressed in a paint stained artist's smock. "Come in," came the offer as she indicated the way forward.

Once inside he stopped and turned. He regarded her with interest as he produced an envelope from his jeans pocket and coughed just the once, to clear his throat, before asking. "I've been thinking," his jovial announcement started. "Whether you'd be willing to do me a painting."

She rolled her right shoulder clockwise just the once. Gave his body a thorough stare and answered, "Of course!"

"Thanks!"

She shrugged her shoulders. "Do you know the type of style you'd like?" Asked the obvious question.

"Not really."

"How would you like to see my latest creations to help you decide on the impression you want me to give?"

This was it. This was the chance he was looking for because he knew that the portraits would be waiting for an audience. "Oh! Yes please," he smiled.

"Okay," she beamed as her smile became infectious. "Just follow me." She led the way as she guided him along a rather dark passageway and up some stairs until finally stopping outside a closed door. "I hope you're not easily shocked," her hinted warning declared.

"Not really," he replied as she opened the door. The bright light illuminated the room adequately for there on every wall were paintings depicting every corrupt facet of human nature. He wasn't bothered about the immorality of her subjects because all he wanted to do was look behind that wardrobe door.

"Bugger," exploded the blasphemous phrase used to denote that he'd obviously forgotten something, and the hurried search of his pockets confirmed the fact? "I've left the photographs I wanted to show downstairs on the table." He lied knowing full well he'd done it deliberately.

"Wait here," smiled the offer as he watched her disappear from the room. With her gone he hadn't long to discover the truth, so very quickly opened the wardrobe door and stared wide-eyed at that portrait. He did nothing but stare. He would have stared all night but quickly closed the door when hearing footsteps returning, and was just in time before she entered the room holding the elusive envelope. Over the next hour, or so, they discussed the terms and approximate costs.

"Let me sleep on it," he offered as he left the house.

Back in Calder's he climbed the stairs and stood looking at the space where that painting should have been hanging. He closed his eyes as a vivid memory developed inside his head. The painting itself was of five, or was it six, women in various states of undress. There was Erin in the background behind the sultan who appeared to be watching the women at play. But what drew Alan's gaze was did he recognise the first women's face, and if so was it Olivia Thomas?

He went to bed with that question and was awoken the next day by the continuous knocking on the front door. Now fully awake he sat bolt upright and as his head cleared quickly jumped out of bed to pull on his jeans. As if in a race he bounded down the stairs and looked through the frosted glass hoping to identify whoever it was and was rather startled to recognise the blue uniform of the police as they stood waiting.

"Can I help," erupted the standard opening to his conversation.

The stoically built man dutifully removed his helmet, placed his hands by his side and legally asked, "Mr Alan Young?"

"Yes," confirmed the reply with his eyes narrowing in wonder.

"Can we come in?" The policeman asked without the flicker of anything on his face. Hearing this Alan twisted, with a feeling of trepidation, and looked directly at the young policewoman at the other man's side before giving his welcome. They were led into the kitchen where Alan was offered to sit. The policeman paused, as if trying to find the right words, and then depressingly continued. "I'm sorry to have to inform you," he began.

He never had the chance to complete his sentence before Alan raced to his feet and slammed his flat hands upon the table. "What is it?" Demanded the frightened voice as it could be seen that a thousand and one questions raced through his mind.

The policewoman calmly placed her arm upon his shoulder and pushed him until he was sitting again. "It's your mother," she began.

As soon as those words dropped Alan choked as wretched visions swirled inside his head. "She's not," stuttered that most grisly of questions.

"No," calmly announced the male voice. "But she has been involved in a hit and run accident."

Alan was grateful as he sank back in the chair. He closed his eyes and kept breathing as deeply as he could. "How is she," dribbled his rather stupid question.

"She's out of danger," offered the policewoman as she just sat and stared. "But, she's still on a life support machine," calmly, although somewhat dramatically, continued her report.

"Where is she," escaped the next question after a lengthy pause.

"In Douglas on the Isle of Man," again replied the policewoman, and it was over the next couple of hours that he was told of what might have happened, but it was only circumstantial for there were no witnesses and that they were still waiting for her to regain consciousness. Eventually they agreed to make preparation because he expressed his intention to leave, straight away, and go across to be at her side.

After the police had left he disappeared to the garage and climbed aboard the high powered motorcycle that he'd kept in working order, and his father would have been proud to see again the sleek movements as it took corner after corner. Up towards Derby he headed and then onto the breathtaking panorama of the Peak District with its rolling mists lying in concealed valleys and tumbling downs. Through the full face helmet the smell of newly mown grass wafted until the intoxicating stench of ozone replaced the fragrance. Having reached the outskirts of Liverpool, in fairly good time, and weaving through the bustle of everyday life he eventually located the docks. It took another twenty minutes before his machine was duly handled and loaded, and after biding it a discreet farewell made his way forward until finding solace in the spacious cafeteria. He knew all about boats, from the gigantic battleships of yesteryear to the passenger ferries of today, but he still felt the nauseating undulation as it rolled over the calmness of the Irish Sea. He knew that the only way he could control the feeling was to actually watch the bow slicing its way through the water. With great effort he struggled on deck, but eventually stood where he could see the grey nose forming the backwash that rippled away to sea. It took a moment before he felt able to look around and when he did grinned when noticing that he was not the only one to appreciate the view. It didn't matter their reasons for being out there, but he smiled in return for the one they gave. He'd been there for about half an hour when he was presented with the kind of dilemma that had caused many a war to be fought. It had started to drizzle and he auspiciously watched as the two girls, he'd been seriously surveying, simply disappeared inside. Realising the consequence of remaining outside, like getting thoroughly soaked, he finally succumbed to the inevitable and paraded back inside. Now in the cafétéria he roamed and was pleasantly surprised to see both young women standing at the counter hoping to be served. With a rush of blood he stepped forward and stood directly behind the two as they picked up the plastic beakers containing the weird concoction of something drinkable. They swung around and very nearly collided with him, spilling what he guessed to be coffee.

"I'm sorry," he apologised as he bowed like a doting servant. This rather childish act seemed to unlock their giggles as they smiled and continued on their journey. He returned the smile and watched the seductive sway of their hips that were beautifully encased in figure hugging leathers. His enthusiasm soon waned as they went and sat with a couple of Real Bikers. You know the ones with long flowing locks of untidy hair, tattoos up each arm and probably over other pieces of their covered anatomy. He gave a quiet grunt of jealousy because he knew that although the biking fraternity had gained an unfounded reputation for being a trifle wild they would often help in times of strife.

It was about twenty to three, in the afternoon, when he finally clambered onto his bike and started it. It had stopped raining as along the promenade he raced although slowing and veering to miss the trams that constantly plied their trade. On his right was the beach quickly filling with holidaymakers as they claimed their pitch with the sea slowly ebbing away? The squawking gulls a constant menace as they dived for any thrown away scraps of food and it was about halfway along the front that he indicated left, cranked his bike and followed the signs for the hospital. Into the relatively small car park he rode and stopped. Into the hospital foyer he marched like any tearaway son. "I'm here to see Mrs Yvonne Young," he smiled as pleasantly as he could.

"Visiting times are at ten in the morning and seven thirty in the evening," replied the Dickensian attendant behind the desk.

"But I've just landed," he snorted like the proverbial bull crashing his helmet on the desktop causing what few papers there were to fly.

This apparent ingratitude did little to soften the rigid poise of the middle aged woman still bound inside her own little world. "As I've already stated," she began. "The visiting."

She never finished her sentence because his volatile words superimposed them. "She's been involved in a serious accident and I'm her son," he grunted while staring red-eyed at the impression of a certain teacher, from his old school, who clearly indicated that the resistance of the immovable against the forces of time was completely futile. This statement was further reinforced as a bony finger stretched up to indicated the hand written poster behind his back. He left, the building, with the feeling of pure malice surging through his veins because back into Douglas he stormed, twisting and winding his machine as if there was no tomorrow. Eventually he turned and raced to the very end of a cul-de-sac. He stopped directly in front of the Ashton Hotel and dismounted. With his black helmet in his hand he walked directly into the foyer and strode over to where the receptionist sat at the far end.

"Can I help," asked the slip of the girl manning the desk.

"I hope so," he returned forcing her to look up and stare. "I believe that the police have arranged for me to stay here."

The young girl must have known all about it because she got up, reached across and picked a set of keys from the rack. "Mr Young?" She asked with confidence as she kept hold of them. "Mr Alan Young!"

"That's right," growled his unassuming response as he partially unzipped his leather jacket and searched for something. "And here's my driving licence as proof," he smiled as she took and scrutinised it.

Having convinced her of his identity he took the keys and trudged up the stairs until halting outside the correct door. Once inside he showered and waited. He paced around the isolation of that room, like the prisoner waiting for the day of their release, but eventually seven o'clock arrived and with it he went downstairs and returned to that institute of graceless humour.

"I'm here to visit Mrs Yvonne Young," he again stated to that same woman who appeared not to have moved since he'd left.

It was as if a sprinkling of magic dust had rejuvenated the uniformed crone into action. "She's up in The Trafalgar Ward on the second floor," grunted the articulate response while being unable to look up from the register of patients.

"Thanks!" He cheerfully replied while turning and walking towards the Georgian replica of a staircase. He took the right curve, although he could have taken the left but there were several people going either up or down. The antiseptic smell hung, like a constant cloud of doom, as he marched passed the uniformed nurses and several doctors with stethoscopes dangling around their necks.

"Yes," demanded the rather agitated voice of a nurse walking from one of the wards.

Alan stepped back in apprehension. He noticed the rather large badge, on her uniform, that identified her name and her rank. "Excuse me sister," he politely opened. "But, I'm here to see Mrs Young."

She stood to her full height, about four foot two; both up and wide, and indicated him to follow. They walked along the cheerless corridor passing various doors that he presumed led to the wards until finally stopping outside the one at the very end. "She's in here!" Her rather official voice announced. "But, you can't go in," she concluded as she looked through the viewing porthole on the door. Alan followed suit and viewed his mother lying on the bed apparently fixed to wires and the suchlike that were obviously being used to keep her alive. His gut churned when seeing the electrodes and pipes dangling, especially the rather thick tube hanging from her closed mouth, and rolled his head in a desperate gesture of forlorn hope. He stood petrified. He just didn't know what to do and it was the sister who came to his rescue. "She'll be given the best treatment," her standard line echoed with the stock medical formula. "And we hope to see some improvement."

He stood alone, for about an hour, simply looking through that porthole as the hospital staff continued their priceless work. It was at one point that he thought that he saw movement and rushed away to inform anyone willing to listen. "It's just a nervous reflex," smiled a nurse walking passed carrying a tray with something hidden beneath the starched whiteness of a towel. He felt alone, and unaware of the time, when a hand touched his shoulder.

"You go and get some rest," subtly offered the white coated doctor at his side. Alan twisted and was quite staggered when remembering exactly where he'd already seen that face before. Appearances can be quite deceptive was the truthful phrase that rolled around his head as he left the hospital.

Back at the hotel, where he stayed downstairs in the bar and drank himself senseless before retiring to bed. He awoke the next morning with the kind of head that resembled a large and ugly looking baked potato, and it would have been around midday before feeling capable of doing any menial task let alone ride to the hospital. Looking at his watch he realised that he'd missed the first visiting time and so decided to tour the island particularly the infamous Race Course where the spectators are such a welcome diversion. Out of Douglas. Over Braddan Bridge. Through Union Mills and onto Crosby. Head straight towards Peel, but bear right at Ballacraine. Onto Kirk Michael and over the suicidal Ballaugh Bridge. Ramsey's next before the Gooseneck. Then up the mountain passed The Guthrie Memorial. Along the Verandah and down to Brandywell. Speed passed Kate's cottage until Signpost Corner gave directions towards the finish.

Friday came and there appeared to be little or no change in his mother's condition although there was some concern shown at one point when it was noticed that the wrong strength medication had been administered. The day itself was typical for late June inasmuch as it had been chilly the day before but today the sun shone, in fact the temperature soared into the high seventies with the result of the beach becoming overcrowded. Having nothing better to do Alan strolled along the promenade hopeful of locating the perfect spot in which he could roll out his towel to do a spot of sunbathing. His eagle-eyed surveillance soon located the ideal position from where he could watch the other bathers and so onto the hot sand he jumped. Treading carefully amongst the sprawled populace his gaze was often drawn towards the many female bathers having very little costume concealing their bodies; I know that's a bit of a chauvinist idea but were the women studying the young athletic men with their oddly shaped bulges as well. Anyway, whatever your point of view and thoughts, he trudged very close to a group of teenage lads playing football. He smiled when a gangly blond haired youth rose to head the ball and superbly sent it crashing into the back of a young skinny teenage girl sprawled on a towel. She screamed and turned. A wild yell of appreciation erupted from all the lads as the girl, who'd obviously forgotten to do up her bikini top, exposed her rather immature bust. Alan smirked; as well he might because he could now practise his dirty ole man routine while discreetly ogling the flustered girl. Suddenly with a laugh of embarrassment, or was it a smirk of feminine knowledge, she blushed when realising exactly what the boys were looking at and so with lightening speed her hands whipped up to cover the small, but truly sexy, exposure of her tits. He was still smirking when he found that ideal spot on which to spread his towel and so stripping down to his trunks he lazed and listened to the frantic, but joyful, noises that an afternoon on the beach brings.

  He'd returned to his hotel room where he could apply some cooling lotion to the red areas of his body where the sun had done its worst. Normally, he tanned fairly easily but occasionally he would burn and today was one of those occasions. However, he knew that with a shower and a good night's sleep he would awake with a beautiful tan. Going to the shower he turned it on. Stripped and after taking a deep breath ventured beneath the spray. Stepping from it he quickly dried and slipped between the sheets and dropped into a deep sleep. He was woken, rather brutally at around three in the morning, by the constant wailing of the fire alarm. Down the stairs he was ushered along with the other scantily dressed guests. However, walking with precise urgency he became fully conscious that the majority had managed to salvage either dressing gowns or coats but there were a few, mostly men and Alan was included, that had reacted with self preservation. Out along the pavement they were massed and counted. Blankets were dutifully wrapped around the naked evacuees and Alan smiled when being given his. It took approximately an hour before anyone was allowed to re-enter the hotel and that was only after being given the all clear by the fire service. Now feeling the chill of the air Alan followed that same group as they made their way up the stairs. Whether it was done on purpose, or accidentally, didn't really matter because about halfway up someone must have stepped on the edge of the towel that a plump woman had around her body. As she moved forward the towel stayed exactly where it was; with the result being her rather large build came into view and with it came the classic chuckle of voyeurism dribbling from various male throats as she abruptly, and unsuccessfully, tried to hoist the grey towelling tighter. "Who's the bloody pervert," she exclaimed while twisting around and giving the blanket an almighty tug.

"See," snapped a male voice which was probably her husband's. "I told you to put some underwear on."

"But, it was a fire alarm."

"So," he bullied. "You had time to hide your bits!"

"But you told me to get out."

"Don't answer me back," he snapped. "I was just telling you."

"What," she answered. "That I'm an embarrassment?" He never answered but the look said more than a thousand words. Nothing more was spoken as she and the rest of the party returned to their rooms. Alan lay on top of his bed trying to go to sleep, but of course failed as the pressure in his bladder became too great. Wanting to know the time he turned and reached for his watch that he'd left on the bedside table. It wasn't where he'd left it and not being able to find it started to panic. He sat bolt upright and turned the light on. With careful investigation he soon spied it on the floor, and thinking he must have knocked it when leaving earlier thought nothing of it. Glancing at the time and seeing the slight brightening of the darkness realised that dawn was fast approaching got up. To the window he went and opened the curtains. Looking down he thought he saw someone lurking near the parked vehicles, but then when looking again simply saw a couple walking together holding hands.

At the breakfast table the conversation, on every table but one, was taken up by what happened the previous night to a certain Mrs Prentice and especially the unfortunate exposure of her body. As he sat contemplating the events Alan looked across at the disgruntled victim and regarded her with a little more interest. She would be about forty, or thereabouts, with a figure that could be described as being a little overweight, and that's being rather generous. Her husband, well that was the assumption, looked as if butter wouldn't melt in his mouth. He looked both arrogant and suave. He looked like someone who could change with the winds to better his life. But remembering his comments from the night before, or more precisely this morning, could he when all said and done be classed as a bully. But in saying that an immoral thought flashed because behind the facade of the bedroom door, where there was just him and his wife, was he just a willing slave to a matriarchal and domineering leather clad mistress with a whip. Having finished his meal decided that now was as good a time as any to go and check the condition of the bike. Having tidied his dishes he stood and walked towards the gleaming paintwork of his machine.

"Is that your bike?" Asked someone he'd never met, but assumed was a guest as well.

"Certainly is," returned Alan's joyous response. Hearing this, the other man knelt beside the frame and scrutinised, with tattooed fingers, the intricate detail of the twin cylinder overhead camshaft.

There was no further conversation until the man stood. "You wouldn't mind doing me a big favour?" He asked a trifle anxiously. "Because when we were out here last night," he added. "And Amy saw this bike she pestered me to see whether its owner would take her for a ride."

Alan grinned in self-satisfaction. "Of course I will," he answered as his heart started to flutter with pride, "When?"

"Why don't we ask her," returned his pleasant tone and it was at that moment the lady in question walked from the hotel and headed towards the two men talking.

"So you want to feel the throbbing power of this beast between your legs," Alan smiled as she neared.

"Oh! Yes please," she answered with a smile. "Give me ten minutes to see whether there's an outfit I can hire." Having spoken she waved as she turned and disappeared. The two men waited and talked about nothing in particular until she returned, and when she did their mouths fell open because she'd obviously been successful. The gold and black leather one-piece snuggled elegantly around her body and the fawn coloured helmet complimented the effect. Once ready Alan sat and started the engine, and as it purred with life his passenger clambered behind. Her husband, who obviously held no qualms, waved their departure as they sped away. Up through the gears he raced until hitting the correct speed. Cranked it left at the corner, and then immediately right. Straight on with the power of the wind against their progress until finally hitting Laxey and its infamous Wheel. They stopped and dismounted and walked towards that obelisk where the three legs appeared like the propeller of an aircraft. To the top they climbed and stood alone.

"Please take my photo," asked the woman while delving inside the bag she'd brought. Having found the camera she handed it over and posed. Alan looked through the eyepiece and smiled. He pressed the shutter and smirked. "How about this," she sniggered while unashamedly unzipping the front of the suit. It fell open showing the uneven texture of her pale ribcage, and although he knew her breasts were somewhere they didn't show enough to make it an illegal photo, and so he clicked the shutter again. "Thanks," she charmed retaking the camera.

"That's okay!" He grinned because as she bent to replace it back inside the bag he looked straight down the front of her outfit and realised that it really wouldn't have mattered if he'd have taken a picture that included her tits because talk about being flat chested as he'd seen a couple of fried eggs on a plate that were bigger. Having finished she stood and watched him.

"I saw you looking," she teased as she quickly zipped up the leather front.

Listening to the truth he blushed, and as if trying to steer the conversation on a different tack asked, "Where would you like to go now?"

Whether she wasn't particularly bothered, or not, she shrugged her shoulders. "I don't know," her sweet voice said. "You decide."

"How about along the mountain," returned the offer as they walked back to where he'd parked.

"Why not," her reply agreed, and having chosen their destination they rode until sweeping along the path that led them higher. It was while twisting and turning that Alan became aware of his passenger pressing her upper body into his back, and it was near The Black Hut that he pulled over and both dismounted.

"This is for letting me come with you," she thanked while at the same time stretching onto tiptoe and kissing him on the cheek.

"That's alright," he acknowledged with a crocked smile. "And anyway I needed some company," he truthfully declared as he returned to the waiting machine. They continued around the island stopping here and there to take in the breathtaking landscapes. It was getting towards four o'clock when they finally arrived back at the hotel, and departed company.

Alan had been lying on his bed for about a quarter of an hour when there came a gentle knock on the door. He rose, with a sigh, and wandered towards it. "Can I come in," Amy, because he remembered her name, announced while quickly scanning the corridor before pushing passed.

"Do," he proclaimed watching her move. She still wore that outfit of racing leathers that clung to her like a second skin and once inside turned on the spot and stared at him like she'd done that afternoon on the mountain.

"We're leaving tomorrow," she confessed. "And I just want to thank you properly for what you did."

Alan was embarrassed. "It's alright," he mumbled. "I didn't expect any payment."

"Who said anything about money," her sexual tease hinted. "And anyway I saw you looking down the front of my leathers." With this torment he watched totally amazed as she promptly unzipped the top half of her leathers and slipped it passed her shoulders. He shuddered as his gaze was instantly drawn towards just how grotesque, in a sexual way, her thick nipples were. They were standing inside large disks of dusty cherry that seemed to cover the entirety of her non existent tits. "Oh! I see," she sniggered. "You want to see more!" Her tease announced taking off the rest of the leathers. She was now naked and the pheromone lure forced him to allow her to undo his jeans and drag them to the floor. He now looked comical in just his socks but he didn't care as he took her offered hand and lay beside her on the bed. They never once kissed as she expertly rolled a contraceptive over his stiff cock before straddling his eager body. He knew there was no excitement as he struggled to slip between the somewhat dry folds of her cunt. The grunts and groans of the act lasted less than twenty second, but he wasn't bothered and if she did then he wasn't particularly bothered either, because after his somewhat selfish performance she jumped to her feet and dressed. She disappeared only to be remembered as a metaphorical ship that passed in the night.

He slept well as the memory of her body raced inside his head and it was eight o'clock, next morning, when he woke. Feeling so full of life he danced towards the window and looked out to see that the sun had risen and a glorious day beckoned. With energy he dressed and charged down the stairs two at a time. He rushed through the doors and onwards towards his parked machine. It started first time and for that he sped away. Up through the gears, and then down at each turn. To the left he leant as his knee scraped the road. To his right; before accelerating away. The fresh wind blowing against his visor recharged his riding skill as he cruised onwards along the empty road. Was he worried that his brakes felt spongy speeding onto Union Mills. Passed The Highlander and down through the gears was his first response and it was then that his brakes failed.

His stomach churned as the adrenaline surged through his veins as he tried to keep the bike in control. Visions of his past flashed as a solid wall approached, and it was a split second later that he dropped his shoulder forcing the purring machine as low as he dare. Was it his skill, or was it simply good luck that prevailed as he finally slowed to a stop. He trembled like a leaf when he dismounted and sat along side the stricken machine still purring like a kitten. It took a good ten minutes before he even thought about looking at what the problem was, and when he did the brake fluid reservoir was bone dry. He collapsed in frustration as over, and over, in his mind spun the doubt as to whether he'd checked its level. Eventually, he decided that because of everything that had happened he'd probably forgotten and like all good bikers shrugged his shoulders and started to push it. It was heavy and with no vehicles on the roads it simply got heavier and heavier. Had his prayers been answered when in the distance he saw a single headlight approaching and the throaty roar of an engine confirmed the fact?

"What's wrong," queried the highly educated voice that belonged to a scruffy looking man still sitting astride his machine. Appearances can be misleading because the man himself had been with those girls on the ferry and was also one of the doctors that had been at the hospital.

"It appears that I've got no brake fluid," Alan replied feeling a bit silly at having to admit to such a fundamental mistake.

The other man simply couldn't hold back the laughter as well as the snigger, and after he'd settled offered his suggestion, "I got some back at the house, and if you like I'll give you a lift and let you have some."

Accepting the gracious offer Alan hesitated for a moment. "What about my bike," he suggested with a wave of a hand.

"It's all right I'll look after it," came the unselfish motion of the passenger slowly dismounting. She took off her helmet and allowed the flowing beauty of her coal black hair to cascade along her shoulders. The unblemished texture of her skin looked delicate with the flighty application of her make-up. She stood like a goddess with the well fitting light green and ochre racing leathers increasing the hypnotic value of her body. It had been several years since Alan had dared to ride pillion, and the experience was truly exhilarating. He knew how to sit. He knew which way to lean, and eventually they cruised through Peel until stopping outside a detached house at the end of a long avenue of Maisonettes.

"Shan't be long," spoke the man as he quickly got off and walked towards the open garage. With him gone Alan sat looking at the picturesque scenery that was there. Wanting to stretch his legs he dismounted and began to wander about. Amongst the brickwork of the wall he'd occasionally notice carved motives, with names, of various flowers and other plants. "Are you ready," hollered a voice moving closer with a bottle of something in his grasp.

"Ready when you are," returned the cheerful expression as he put on his helmet. Back to the stricken, and useless, machine they rode where several more bikers had gathered obviously trying to help an apparently helpless woman.

"Strange," muttered the concerned voice of one of the group of mechanics as he held both parts of the bleeder tube.

"What's wrong?" Alan asked as he knelt beside another scruffy biker inspecting the slippery evidence of a leak.

"Have you recently been hit," asked the dirty looking stranger holding a length of tube in his hand.

Alan thought. Shook his head in rejection and replied, "Not that I can remember."

"Well," started the answer. "I don't know how you did it but there's a hole in the tube."

Alan stood; his body limp with horror as he relived that awful moment yet again and as he looked skyward muttered, "Thank you."

It was the following day the bike was repaired, and once ready he visited his mother again. There was not much improvement from what he could see but the medical fraternity seemed to think that she was well on the road to recovery. "Is she going to be transferred?" Alan asked when they explained that maybe at the end of the week she could be moved.

"If there's any further improvement," started the diagnosis from a doctor. "Then I see no reason why she can't be sent back to her local hospital." This was possibly the best news Alan could have heard and so decided to return to the hotel where he was going to celebrate in style. He arrived only to be hailed by the receptionist on the desk.

"Mr Young," called the slip of a girl manning the desk.

"Yes."

"There's been someone looking for you," her lovely Caribbean voice announced. Hearing the statement he looked around the foyer and seeing no-one half shrugged his shoulders in wonder. He twisted his puzzled face towards the girl who quickly advised, "And said that they'll be back later."

"Did they give a name?" He asked as a multitude of unwanted faces developed in his mind.

"Alice Hodges," came the declaration, which forced him to remember that he'd forgotten to tell his sister about their mother's condition.

"Thanks!" He grinned with eyes closed in despondent shock. He was upstairs and while having a wash there was a knock on his door and opening it came face to face with both Alice and the Colonel. Alan shivered because he could justify Alice knowing his whereabouts but why oh! Why was he here? "Come in," he cordially, although arrogantly, offered indicating the way. They accepted, marched and sat on two vacant chairs.

Over the next hour a heated discussion took place mainly from his sister who was getting angrier as she listened to the countless feeble excuses given. The hostility smouldering suddenly exploded when she finally raced to her feet and vented her spleen. "Why did I have to find out from Felicity Hooper," she surreally spat. "And then that was by phone!" There was no hiding place from the verbal attacks and the physical prods from his sister's angry finger as well as the eyebrow beating he got from the Colonel. Alan was much relieved when they finally decided to leave, but he knew in his heart that the whole episode was to be continued at a later date. With the room empty he did absolutely nothing for ten minutes while staring at the blank lilac green wall. There was no comprehension as he tried his hardest to understand his error, but like a black hole in space there was definitely nothing and with this abhorrent pressure of guilt he walked out and wandered towards that magical water garden he'd found by accident one day. Through the rusted gates and into the cool arbour of bamboo he soulfully stepped. To the slow running stream he silently crept and sat on the bench but a stones throw from the edge of a fairly large pool of water. He sat alone and pondered his existence. He was in a different world when a Manx cat scurried from its hiding place, stopped and simply looked him in the eye. Alan smiled as it spats with contempt, at having lost its tail, before disappearing from sight under the trusty green of the many ferns. He buried his head in his hands as if trying to hide his shame and was completely oblivious to anything, or anyone. Broken fragment, of his life, ricochet around his head and so never heard the footsteps softly approaching. He could hear affectionate breathes, but his stagnant mind was unsure of the person standing at his back. Her voice was soft, but necessary. "Mr Young," asked the warm tone of Heather Cole the young hotel receptionist.

He slowly turned, looked into her hazel eyes and responded, "Yes!"

"I saw you walking in here," her sweet Caribbean charm began. "And I thought that I might come and join you."

"Please do!" He offered indicating the seat next to him. She accepted and sat. They hardly spoke as the cool evening closed around, and as the light decreased the full moon cast sultry shadows amongst the fluttering foliage.

Suddenly, like a jack-in-a-box, the young girl raced to her feet and hovered. Her long trestles of black hair fluttered in the gentle breeze. The softness of her angelic face beckoned. She smiled as she quietly stated her ambition, "When I'm feeling depressed I sometimes come here for a swim." And having spoken started to undo her blouse. Alan's depression was total because he remained seated while listening to the ruffled sounds of various garments being removed, and he was in no mood to appreciate the close proximity of her naked body. He even brushed away her hands when feeling the girl reach and pull his solid frame. He sat for twenty minutes listening to the happy frolics of her play and occasionally when moving into a bright moonbeam, rippling across the water, saw just how succulent her dark but opaque nudity was. It was well passed midnight when they returned to the hotel and went their separate ways, but not before Heather confidently took his two hands and pulled so that she could kiss him on the forehead. Alan smiled as he watched her disappearing along the passage.

He awoke next morning, from his troubled sleep, with a dense cloud of depression just above his head. His stomach embarrassingly gurgled to indicate that he'd not eaten for some considerable time and like the man sent to Coventry strolled into the dining room. Sitting alone he ordered what he thought adequate and when the spotty waiter brought a plate of toast with a freshly made pot of tea he just poured himself a large drink and set about the banquet with abandoned relish. "Can I join you?" Asked the warm voice he recognised.

He looked up, on hearing the request, and saw Heather hesitating by a vacant chair. "Of course," came the response, and as she sat his hand went up to attract the waiter's attention yet again. It was about half past nine when Alan, as well as his new acquaintance, walked down to the promenade and along the shops lining the front. In and out of the many souvenir arcades they laughed and joked. They'd just left The Little Owl Restaurant, after having eaten lunch, when Heather snatched his hand and pulled. Obviously knowing her destination it was down a narrow passage and between some rather cheerless shops they danced until halting in an isolated doorway with the statement "Closed for lunch" stencilled on a scrap piece of paper. They stopped quite alone. They turned and stared at one another. They hesitated hoping for the other to react and then almost immediately she pursed her lips and kissed him.

"You can touch my tits," she explained. "Because I know you want to."

"That's nice," he replied when he expertly lifted a single breast in the palm of his hand.

"Why don't you get it out," she cooed as her eyes closed.

Having been given permission he undid the short line of buttons, on her apricot blouse, before glancing down and seeing the erotic splendour that was housed inside the white thin cotton bra she was wearing. Licking his lips with a debauched sense of urgency he quickly rummaged until finding a single nipple that reminded him of a nugget of toffee he'd once had at school, and like the last time he simply wanted to suck it. He wasn't going to discus whether there were any religious implications about what he intended to do and as for her virginity he really didn't give a damn because all he wanted was to get inside her knickers and feel a cunt. She panted with erotic passion as his fingers probed deeper forcing her hips to instinctively push excitedly against his every thrust. With nowhere to go he impulsively pressed his equally excited body against hers and smiled with a fundamental desire. They continued to kiss but it was only after a couple of moments that she apologetically pushed him away, in the universal standard prick tease manner that has frustrated the male for centuries, and with the classic smirk stencilled across her face gave the excuse. "I've got to get back to work," she teased while pulling her clothing together and then calmly walking away.

Probably realising that he was just going to be another notch of her many conquests smiled. In fact he laughed at the ease in which he'd succumbed to her skill. "Shall I see you again?" He shouted watching her disappear.

"Maybe," she returned, and having given her answer walked that same passageway they'd used and when she'd finally gone he felt isolated. He started to walk a sorry path to wherever and it was exactly one minute later that the thundering sound of a car was heard to approach. The noise of squealing tyres made him look behind and freeze as a pair of bright headlights; well it was the middle of the day, made a direct route towards him. His athleticism came into it's own as he jumped from its intended path. He landed and rolled away, but the vehicle screeched to a halt and with the swiftness of mercury reversed. Panic compelled him to stare and watch as the car once again motored directly at him. Again he was lucky as he dived, away, the moment before they touched. It was now a matter of life or death that forced him to sprint to his feet and race to where ever, but with each step the hostile sound of his pursuer kept getting closer. Was it salvation that came to his rescue because directly in front, of his fleeing body, was a doorway and seeing it a dramatic question stuttered inside his head? Could he make it? The answer was simple. He simply had to run as if his life depended on it, which of course it did. His heart exploded as he dived that final fraction and felt the torrid draught as the vehicle sped by and disappeared. Now alone and needing the quiet of preservation he rested against the brickwork of the shop where he'd finished and noisily gasped for air. Now settled; his bloodshot eyes focused on a face staring directly at him. It took a moment, but smiled his stupidity when realising that it wasn't infact the face that was causing him to tremble but was the beautiful shape of the boat in the background. The face could have been anyone but the boat was certainly the Tanmouth. Realising that he may have discovered the answer to his father's next riddle stepped back to read the name above the shop. "The Orange Shop of Pictures," he smiled as he staged whispered the words. He began to laugh because whether it was coincidence, or not, but around that shop window were displays of things both Naval and Military. There were examples of Galleons in full rig. There were water stained documents lying there to be read. There were maps and charts showing coastlines of somewhere, or other. His eyes were everywhere, but they always seemed to come back to that portrait.

"You alright," questioned the man who'd just opened the door and marched out. His character would not have looked out of place on any quarterdeck, from the full growth of beard to the distinctive tattoos upon his forearm.

Picking himself up Alan brushed down his clothes. Shook himself rather vigorously and answered, "I'll be fine." And then like quicksilver his finger pointed to the woman standing at the quay alongside the Tanmouth, "Who's that?"

"That was my wife," the man replied with a modicum of pride as well as sadness.

"Can I see her," asked the question.

"I'm sorry," slouched the big man. "But she died when we were out in Gibraltar!"

Seeing the sorrow welling Alan quickly offered his condolences, "I'm sorry to hear that." And then full of remorse asked, "When was that?"

The man standing his ground looked Alan straight in the eye, and quietly answered, "Eight years ago."

Hearing this statement something clicked inside the listening man's mind and his next question only seemed to confirm the assumption, "Was it an accident?"

"Yes!" The man replied as his brow furrowed. "Why?"

Alan's next question erupted without delay, "Was she the only one involved?" And as he waited a paper's epitaph floated into his mind because he instantly knew the answer.

The response took a little longer, probably because the man was getting suspicious of something, but finally it arrived, "No!" Then there was a pause as the man scrutinised Alan before continuing, "There was someone else." And for a moment, while considering the effects, lines of wonder ran across his brow, "Let me think." Having spoken the man rubbed his bearded chin in the forlorn hope of stroking the answer. "Oh! Yes," he remembered. "His name was."

"Captain Henry Young," Alan imposed.

"That's right," the apprehensive looking man admitted, and obviously sensing that something not quite right asked. "Who are you," fired his first salvo. "Some sort of investigator." Having asked the questions, and obviously not wanting to hear the answers, the man turned and disappeared inside the shop. He closed the door as if closing a curtain on a rather painful chapter.

Alan's heart pounded. He stood astonished as frightful recollections filtered through his mind. He saw the Military Police stripping every fragment of his home. The intimate questions they'd asked had caused his mother many sleepless nights. The detrimental insinuations usurped the validity of his father's commission. The investigation took six months in all but when finding no evidence to substantiate the apparent crime they left leaving the case files open.

Why were they looking? What were they searching for? What had his father done? What had that picture got to do with anything? Realising that maybe another piece of the jigsaw lay on the other side of door he opened it and stepped inside. The man he wanted to speak to was standing with his back to him and so Alan walked up and placed a steady hand upon his shoulder. "I'm Alan Young," his rather quiet voice announced and to add a bit of authority quickly added, "Captain Young's son."

The man hesitated momentarily, and then spun around. He deliberately scowled as his gaze focused on Alan. The tobacco stained corner of his beard quivered with doubt as his tongue rolled along his bottom lip. Whether he saw Henry's genetic make-up in Alan's body, or not, but after a lengthy pause there came several nods of recognition as a warm smile developed along his lips. "So! How's your mother?" He asked as his eyebrows narrowed.

Was this a test question? If it was then he answered straight away. "She's in hospital!"

The other man simply scratched the back of his head. "I hope she's alright," the question master added with a little concern.

Trying to inject a little jollity to the situation Alan grinned, "Well, she should be."

"Why's that?"

"Because, she's being looked after here on the Island," he teased in his normal mode of stating the obvious.

"I know," the man admitted.

Alan could do nothing but stare open-mouthed at the man. Amazement. Shock. Disbelief. Were some of the words used to describe exactly how he felt? Lines, a mile deep, furrowed along his brow as he stuttered, "How, do you know?"

It appeared that Frank Sutherland, because that was his name, had been a serving Sub Lieutenant on board the Tanmouth at the same time as his father. It was even more of a coincidence that Alan discovered, due to Maritime

Traditions; that his father had officiated at Frank's marriage to Irene Tunnicliffe and as a wedding present that painting had been presented to the loving couple at their reception. As he studied the picture he remembered exactly where the other patches were and so very carefully felt near to the ship's funnels. "There's nothing here," he whispered to himself as absolutely nothing came away. "Maybe," he stage whispered. "It's somewhere else!" Looking about to make sure he wasn't spotted gingerly felt every inch of the canvas until finally admitting to the fact that this was obviously a red herring.

"Shall we go and discuss things over a drink," Frank enquired as he walked towards the door.

"Why not," Alan returned as they left and went to the café that was just around the corner, and it was in here that they sat discussing various things over cups of coffee. "Did you ever get another painting of your wife," he enquired at one point. "That shows that your wife may have had a tattoo done somewhere on her body?"

Frank looked at him with utter amazement. "How did you know about that," returned the question.

"Because there seems to be some sort of correlation between a certain group of women with a tattoo somewhere on their body, the paintings they may have received and the riddles that my father obviously left."

"Really?"

"Oh! Yes," Alan smiled. "And I was just wondering whether I could take a quick look at it?" Having asked he waited, and watched, for any indications that might be important.

Was it something he'd said, or was it something he'd implied that made the atmosphere suddenly become extremely heavy. "What," clearly stated the man in a tone of anger? "And have you staring at the picture of my Irene naked."

"Not at all," Alan tried to pacify. "But I just need to check something out."

"Won't a photograph work just as well?"

"Not really," he replied as several pictures were offered. It was when one showing his wife, along with their son, that a cloudy picture started to clear. Alan had studied the other pictures for maybe three seconds, but on looking at this particular one spent well over five. It wasn't the woman's beauty that was dragging at his memory but it was the happy smiling face of a University graduate holding the scroll of parchment. "Your son's a doctor!" His definite conclusion spoke with clarity.

"Yes!"

"And he works here at the local hospital."

"That's right," smiled the proud father. "And he's told me all about your misfortune the other day." Listening to this little dig Alan gave a rather smug laugh when realising exactly who'd helped when his machine had broken down.

Feeling he needed to thank him personally for all he'd done, Alan looked at the man somewhat cock-eyed and offered. "If I ever see him again," he grinned. "Then I'd like to buy him a drink!"

"You can do better than that," the other man declared while putting some change in the collection box by the till.

"How?"

"Well, Jeremy's celebrating his engagement to Polly Sanders this weekend and I'm sure another guest won't be turned away." Having given the invitation they both walked from the café.

Having organised the following night's entertainment Alan disappeared, and it was the middle of the afternoon when wandering along the seafront looking at the various ferries docking below the crumbling remnants of that castled bastion that he saw a mother and child. "Now, go and pick that up," chastised the young girl to her toddler son who'd just thrown some orange peel to the floor. Alan sniggered uncontrollably as he walked towards the curly haired culprit who was now simply standing his ground. The youngster's bottom lip protruded in the mode of defiance, but he was never going to win the battle of wills so turned and scampered to pick it up. He raced to the litterbin and grumpily hurled it inside. "There's a good boy," praised his mother as she took the child's hand, and with that they disappeared down the flight of steps that led to the beach. With the heat of the day forcing him to consider standing in the long line of people waiting for an ice-cream he checked his pockets for the right money. It took about five minutes before getting served and then with the single cone held securely he swivelled on his heels.

The scream was deafening. The push was violent. The comment loaded with medieval venom, "What the fuck do you think you're doing?" Alan was pole-axed as he watched the cone's topping sliding down the front of the victim's body. He smiled inanely as gravity forced the white trail to negotiate the hilly contours of her bust. "Give us a hand," she encouraged when in a flash she'd snatched his wrist and quite dominantly began to scoop the remaining ice-cream before it dropped to the concrete floor and was lost forever except as food for the gulls. Now, with his fare partially in order he offered his apology and headed towards an unoccupied bench where he'd intended to sit while eating what remained of the ice-cream cone. He sat for a moment with his gaze fluttering around the holiday makers and his stare took a while before becoming accustomed to the brightness, and when it did the first thing he saw was a group of teenagers doing exactly what teenagers are supposed to do! The four girls had run up to one of the lads, grabbed his trunks and gave an almighty tug obviously hoping to pull them down. The victim, on the other hand, was desperately trying to prevent this and not reveal the anatomical difference between a boy and a girl. He was saved when a couple of his obvious friends, dressed in the hideous design of Bermuda shorts, silently crept up behind one of the aggressors and yanked her bikini bottoms to the sand. This in turn forced the bandy legged girl to shriek with embarrassment. Alan shook his head and smiled before turning his gaze towards a childless couple sprawled on their towels. He was on his elbows surveying that same teenage girl, while the woman was face down with her bikini strap unclipped for that all over tan. Further round he probed and saw a motley collection of individuals made up of various age groups. There were maiden aunts dressed in accordance with the Victorian rules of the day, and that was no naked flesh visible above the knees and below the neck. Their thick woollen cardigans and long skirts made sure of that, but when they collapsed to the sand their billowing skirts gave a quick flash of something immoral. There was grandma and granddad sitting in deck chairs surveying the others and quietly reminiscing about their own misspent youth and sordid experiences. How they'd chase each other on a moonlight night and once caught engage in that timeless practice that keeps the population going. Laughing quietly to himself he turned away slightly and saw a couple of naked children, of no more than four, playing blissfully unaware of the Peeping Toms who might be ogling their innocent bodies. The silent observer raised his awkward eyebrows when spying another young girl, of about eight, removing her wet costume and standing in full view of anyone who was prepared to look. She obviously didn't care that her immature figure sent the wrong signals to those unwelcome agents of depravity gazing at her innocence. Suddenly, an older guardian rushed and threw a towel around the younger one's body as if trying to hide the nudity. This obvious chaperone, who Alan guessed would be between the ages of thirty and thirty five, caused him to laugh to himself when seeing exactly how she was dressed. All that was hiding her own modesty was the bottom half of a white bikini. The lad's eyebrows rose in wonder because there in full view were her extremely large breasts. Was it an inborn infatuation that pulled his gaze towards the two circles of reddish brown, or was it the fact that double standards were being used?

  Having finished the ice cream he stood and started to walk away. He'd taken exactly two steps when a familiar figure walked directly at him.

  "Fancy seeing you here," Felicity Hooper greeted as she wrapped her enthusiastic arms around his body, and the hug she gave reminded him of the ones his mother was apt to give when welcoming friends.

  His mouth opened but no words escaped until, "What are you doing here?" And his tone resembled a criminal who'd just been surprisingly apprehended.

  "We've come for a holiday," she smiled, and as soon as the words had left her mouth Alan's stomach tightened. It became even tighter when over her shoulder he saw Simon struggling with several suitcases.

"Hello," stated the hasty welcome when at last they met. The cases must have been heavy because the man simply allowed them to fall to earth with a typical thud.

Alan sighed for there in the distance was Marsha Cooper, with her husband, marching with the small party of tourists. He was quick to spot several more people he knew and the depression became total when Major General Otis Chaney appeared. Loathing. Revulsion. Absolute resentment chiselled at his gut because it had always been assumed that it was this man alone that had been responsible for the malicious accusations that had created the investigation concerning his father's loyalty. With damning finger pointing Alan's hatred boiled. "Why's he here," screamed the question.

The accused man had reached the accuser and for that replied. "It's a free country my boy," came the condescending retort as they passed.

With the weight of the world upon his shoulders Alan walked back, and into the quiet of his hotel room he crawled. Total disillusionment was rampant inside his head as he laid contemplating his life and thinking about what was yet to come.

Saturday morning arrived fresh and impulsive. Having slept he felt restored, and like the new man walked enthusiastically into the dining room of the hotel and abruptly sat down. Taking the local paper he opened it and simply read each headline. Having digested each piece of news, as well as his breakfast, and with nothing better to do walked to his bike, checked it over, and went to visit his mother. A great improvement, in her condition, must have occurred because he spent the entire morning discussing various topics, and it was only when the police arrived to ask their questions did he finally disappear. He toured the island, especially Peel, because he wanted to know his exact destination that night.

He went back to the hotel and sat waiting. Eventually the time arrived for him to depart for the celebration, and having dressed accordingly stepped into the pouring rain. He nonchalantly sighed as he pulled on the pair of yellow waterproofs he carried for any such emergency and the raindrops felt like buckshot as he cruised towards his destination. Having arrived he parked his machine beside several of the others that were there and strolled with determined arrogance where he knocked on the door. It opened, and there together were his host and his lovely fiancée. "Congratulations," announced Alan's affectionate word spoken with a definite shake of the hand as well as a quick peck upon young woman's cheek.

"Go and help yourself to a drink," Jeremy offered as he met another couple dashing to get in from the rain. "My father said that you'd be coming."

Alan followed the noise and walked into the sitting room. In there, after getting the drink, he scanned the room and saw about thirty people congregated together exchanging various topics of conversation. He looked hopefully around and scrunched up his nose simply because he knew absolutely no-one, that wasn't quite true because sat in the corner at the far end, was Heather Cole. Hoping that she might want to start a conversation walked over to where she was. "Hello," smiled the introduction as he looked down at her.

"I don't believe it," she smiled, in a mode of shock, as her brow furrowed while stretching out her hands. Alan confidently took them and pulled her up. Into his clutches she fell and with his eagerness somewhat improving kissed her on the cheek in that mode of continental welcome. They stood apart and discussed minor points of detail about the majority of guests. How some were dressed in the black leathers much renowned by the biking fraternity, but the majority superbly clothed in the flowing gowns of sparkling colours.

The celebration was in full swing. The lights had long since dimmed. The company divine as the alcohol flowed like a river and thus allowing the usual inhibitions to dissolve. With his glass half full, or was it half empty, in one hand he staggered close to a couple of people and when nearing them heard this rather contradictory statement. "It's not what you wear that counts," quoted the elegantly dressed woman who was speaking to a rather scruffy looking man with a beer glass grasped like a drunken yob. "Because it's what we have underneath." Having given the elegy she turned and walked away but not before a wicked smile raced along her mouth while at the same time her pencil thin eyebrows rose in a mode of explicit excitement. "Not here! You naughty boy," her smooth voice exclaimed, as though she'd got a rather large plum in her mouth, while quickly removing the spread fingers of the man who'd obviously just groped her arse.

 With everybody otherwise preoccupied with the party Alan decided to do some crafty investigations of his own. He left the multitude of revellers and started with the first room. Opening it slightly, and finding it in partial darkness, was about to walk away when he became aware of some sexual grunting and groaning going on in the shadowy corner on the far side of the room. Realising that he didn't want to be intrusive turned and left. Now leaning against the door, in a righteous kind of way, he was a little shocked when the door opened and that scruffy looking man walked out closely followed by that posh looking lady adjusting various pieces of her attire. Opposites really do attract he giggled as they simply went their separate ways and joined their obvious friends in other various corners. Now ready he went along the passage and opened another door. The light shone brightly as there was a group of people hugging, kissing and doing unspeakable things to each other. There were women dressed in long flowing skirts, but there were others dressed in costumes leaving little to the imagination. There were bottles of drink lined along the sideboard and up against the wall as there were several people all but naked playing cards at a table. Alan stood amazed when one of the card players, a man, simply stood and quickly removed his last piece of clothing. His excitement was prominent as he was simply led away by a group of semi-naked women. Leaving them to their own devices Alan climbed the stairs and went inside the first of a long line of rooms. Once inside and like a crook he rummaged around personal drawers hoping to locate anything that might show him the way when suddenly the door handle twitched. As quick as a flash the would be thief dived towards the wardrobe and hid inside with his heart beating ten to the dozen. While waiting he panicked at the thought of being caught, but when nothing happened he felt safe. Carefully, he opened the door just enough to spy on what was out there and what he saw simply took his breathe away because directly in front of his eyes were two, unknown, women undressing for his unobserved entertainment. Finally, after stripping down to their seductive underwear they hugged each other before exchanging long passionate kisses as well as fragile explorations of the other's body. Alan's heart pounded when watching how they moved towards the double bed that must have beckoned like a powerful magnet, and as he watched their passionate embraces getting more erotic his eyes grew wide in pure lust. Here was a voyeur, pervert, dirty old man call him what you will but how could anyone not be excited by the fascinating struggle that these two women were obviously enjoying. It took an awful lot of self control when watching these naked women caressing each other, well it didn't really because after the initial shock he simply got his lambing tackle out and started playing with himself, and it was some time later when they'd left that he emerged from his hidey-hole trying to rationalise exactly what he'd seen, and of course he failed. Anyway with them gone and having no interest in that specific room anymore he walked out. To the next he moved, and it was inside here that if the other room was quite an eye opener then the contents of this left him totally amazed. He'd entered what appeared to be an artist's gallery, and once inside saw numerous abstract landscapes hanging on walls. They only made up part of the collection because there were several portraits of women, both naked and fully clothed. There were pictures displaying scenes of horrendous mischief. There were artistic scenes depicting seafaring adventures, but it was one specific oil painting, that instantly caught his eye. Why had it done that? Well, to be honest it showed a young woman dressed in all but nought with a small tattoo about four inches below her belly button. The design cleverly showed two burdock flowers in full bloom with their stems rising from the prickly area of her pubic hair and looked absolutely perfect. His mind exploded when realising that here before his eye was maybe, more evidence towards his ultimate goal, whatever that maybe! He was careful as he bit his bottom lip in anxious irritation as he ran his finger down the textured canvas. He cursed when there was nothing. He was even angrier as he tried the other corners one at a time. Nothing. Knowing what to do he took a good minute, or so, going around each painting in turn trying exactly the same technique but ultimately discovering absolutely nothing. The answer's here he kept telling himself, but where!

His mind was elsewhere when the door suddenly burst open and someone touched his shoulder forcing him to spin wildly around. "What the hell do you think you're doing," demanded the stern voice of the man who'd invited him to the party.

"I was looking for the toilet," started his alibi. "And I must have opened the wrong door." He looked at the scowling man hoping he believed his attempt, and trying to add some more credibility added, "And I saw these."

"I think you've seen enough," the man declared as he escorted Alan out. "And there's the toilet," he indicated with a pointing finger. The apprehension had caused Alan's bladder to fill to bursting point and so went inside to relief himself. Realising he'd found absolutely nothing the cloud of doom was heavier than ever when Heather approached and rather drunkenly asked in a tone that was sweetly coated in curiosity, "What's wrong?"

"Nothing," he lied.

She never heard his word but smiled anyway, "Do you want to know something."

"What."

"I'd like to go outside and dance in the rain!"

"Well," he teased. "Why don't you."

"What by myself?"

He pondered for a moment and then asked, "Why not?"

"Because I'll need someone to dance with."

"Surely you don't mean me," he realised as she took hold of his hand. Outside they went and the rain wasn't cold as it seeped through their clothing.

"Come on, let's dance!" She proposed. There was no music but it made no difference as he felt perfectly entitled to wrap his shaking arms around her waist. The water quickly penetrated their clothes when he became conscious of his hands being grabbed and placed over luscious extent of her sodden arse. Was he dreaming when she forced her hot, but wet, body hard against his and started to gyrate her hips to the methodical, but silent, West Indian rhythm of desire? In doing that she pushed her voluptuous breasts against his strutting chest and the water percolating through the thin material seemed to ignite his passion. Realising the sexual power she oozed he felt the urgent desire to stretch up and catch a single tit. His pulse momentarily stopped while confidently lifting its weight, and as he shaped his palm around the mass he closed his eyes expecting the lecture. When nothing came he pulled her even more tightly against his own trembling body. The fullness of her nubile physic beckoned, and like a slavering eunuch he waited. She simply looked him in the eye and smiled as drops of water fell to earth. This was all the permission he needed, so with rough intent his hand hustled inside her drenched blouse and cupped a single, but absolutely soaked, tit. It felt hot inside his palm and it felt right when finding the erect magnificence of her nipple.

"Please," she moaned. "I want you!" Not a word was spoken as he rested against the garden wall and pulled her close. Suddenly, he twitched as a funny shaped outgrowth bore into the small of his back and his face grimaced, in abject pain, while turning and tracing his curious fingers over the smooth lumps of stone.

"What is it?" Heather coyly asked as she watched him spelling out a word inside his head. He said nothing but ran towards another block of stone that looked promising. Then to another and stopped. His heart was pounding as, in the pouring rain, he spelt out the exact word he wanted and hoping he was correct clawed at the sandstone block with ever increasing vigour. His fingernails hurt when loosening the sandstone paste which allowed the stone slab to totter forward, and then like the illusive thief stretched behind and touched that single box.

"Got it," he passionately exploded and as the wet material, of his clothes, clung to his flesh he grabbed her hand and dragged her back inside the house.

Once there Heather grabbed his arm and quietly spoke. "Let's go back to the hotel!"

Alan was all for that, and so they went to find their host to wish them well on their future life together. They found them canoodling in the drawing room and when they explained their intent were told that they couldn't possibly leave without having dry clothes. Polly escorted her guest away and Jeremy took Alan to a private room. It was in here that his host gave some dry clothes, that didn't quite fit, and left him to dress. It was while waiting Alan opened the box and took out the crumpled piece of paper and quietly read the words, "Look for the thyme in the rhyming slang for stairs because that's where you'll find the model you need." Shaking his head and hearing the door open hastily replaced the scrap of paper and stood.

Eventually, after being told that Heather was making her own way home Alan said his farewell and moved towards his bike. Starting the engine he confidently raced away occasionally glancing in the mirror to see whether anyone was following because he'd somehow become paranoid about the possibility. Up through the gears his foot moved in swift succession. To a bend; and rapidly down through the gearbox he flicked. Applying the brakes they seized. The solid wall approached and he had but a moment to respond. He dropped the full weight, of the bike, and slid along the road as sparks flashed lighting his way.

How long he was out he never knew but the aches and pain made it painful to stand. With adrenaline rushing around his body the severest of agonies were ultimately banished as he limped, like a lame dog, towards the bike that lay crumpled under a streetlight and against the wall. Finding the superhuman strength he lifted the twisted wreckage and prayed to the blackened sky above. The reason for this was quite simple inasmuch as with it still raining he'd had to curtail his speed somewhat so the chances of survival had greatly improved. How long he was sitting there he wasn't to know but eventually a car dramatically pulled up and out stepped a rather concerned member of the public. "You, all right," quoted the rather stupid question.

Not wanting to explain what had happened, especially to the local constabulary, he shrugged his aching shoulders and asked, "Can you please take me to the Ashton Hotel?" The man, who genuinely looked concerned, tried to persuade him to go and visit the hospital to check the possibilities of lacerations. It took a good deal of persuasion before the man finally agreed to Alan's demand and dropped the unwilling casualty outside the front door of the hotel. How he climbed the stairs Alan never knew. How he managed to get into bed again he never knew, but what he did know was that on waking he found that someone had ransacked his room.

He'd returned from the Isle of Man with a memory that needed the swift application of pen to paper. He knew the answer to the cockney rhyming slang but as to its relationship to anything that might prove a little more difficult. However, on the third day and having driven into town noticed a small postcard highlighting the fact that Bowler's the Sports Equipment Shop needed an assistant. Deciding rather forlornly that the need for employment was paramount strolled inside and asked Stuart, who happened to be the owner as well as the captain of the village cricket team whether he could apply for the vacancy?

Stuart cagily scrutinised him. Probably realising that he may not get any other offers, something to do with the crap wages and his poor man management skills, gladly welcomed him into the fold. With both feeling a little happier they walked to the rear of the shop where there were posters displaying several of the County Cricket Clubs motives. There was Warwickshire with its dancing bear. Derbyshire with its rose and crown. Worcestershire with its three pears. The single fox of Leicestershire. Glamorgan's yellow daffodil. And there were several others. There were signed photographs of the legendary heroes of yesteryear, and the present.

"It's an important match on Saturday," smiled Stuart while tossing Alan a rather battered looking ball. "And the selection committee have asked me to ask you whether you'd be willing to play." Hearing this Alan tossed the ball back and gave a wry smile because he and Roger Ovens still hold the club's highest opening wicket partnership, and that was a breathtaking two hundred and nineteen as both players rattled up their highest ever score. When Roger had had a little too much beer, which was most nights, he would go into dramatic detail about every shot he'd played. His cover drives got more spectacular. The fine leg sweeps more impressive and as for each of the square cuts they had to be heard to be believed. But in the end the partnership came to a hilarious conclusion as Alan was unfortunately stumped when missing a donkey drop that might have brought up his maiden century.

After agreeing to play Alan was told to start work the following day at eight thirty prompt and so with the whole afternoon free decided to visit his sick mother, who'd been transferred to the local town's hospital. "How, the devil are you?" His whimsical tone asked as his mother sat, in a light green dressing gown, on the sunny veranda. She smiled through her broken and chipped teeth. The lacerations had started to dissolve from the deep mauve. The line of stitches hardly showed below her hairline. The inflammation around her eyes, although visible, looked a lot better than it did when he'd first seen her. The bald patches were starting to be covered by fine hair, but apart from that she looked absolutely fine! He spent all afternoon discussing the tragic repercussions of her accident, and try as she might she couldn't remember anything except for the final five seconds. She still had nightmare as the car ploughed into her. She still cried herself to sleep, as she lay in agony unable to move. She would wake up screaming as she relived those last few seconds over and over again. Feeling depressed he made for Calder's where he decided to have a refreshing bath before going down to the local for a drink.

He walked into the snug, if that's what you'd call it, and after getting his drink sat in his favourite spot next to the rather grubby window. The place was empty but Ginger, the landlord, rather arrogantly smiled, "You should have been here about half an hour ago." Having spoken lifted the glass and gazed through its shape. "You couldn't move." Having finished his slightly inaccurate statement he quaintly replaced it under the bar along with all the others. Alan smiled at the comment. He'd been there a good length of time when the door swung open and in waltzed the doctor and his wife.

"Good evening," Marsha smiled when seeing Alan by himself. She turned and quietly talked to her husband, and must have given some kind of instruction because she moved across the room and sat in the chair opposite. From then until closing time all three huddled around the table exchanging little snippets of information, or telling jokes, which happened to get cruder in relation with the alcohol they'd supped. Eventually when Ginger shouted last orders, at about a quarter to twelve, the trio of merrymakers left and commenced their stagger home. It had always amazed Alan that no matter how much beer the doctor had drank he could always remain upright and walk a straight line. "Years of practice while at Nottingham University studying for my medical qualifications," the doctor recalled. "And walking to my digs, after closing time, from The Trip." Whether it was the surplus intoxication that was making Alan feel a little more fruity than usual but as they walked, the fifty yards or so, he hopefully placed his hand against Marsha's arse and began to sexually rub it. Getting no rejection he, rather clumsily, moved his hand higher until supporting her right tit in his left hand. Suddenly, whether it was because he'd over stepped the mark but Marsha swung around and stood in direct eye contact with him. Watching, she grinned as he fought back the belch of alcohol, and of course lost the battle as a loud burp erupted. "We'll be no good for each other," she grinned.

"Why's that?"

"Because you'll be suffering from brewer's droop," she explained. "And I'm at that time of the month." Understanding that age-old quotation as well as the biology lesson he smiled and watched as she disappeared. Now feeling decidedly unclean he was about to move away when a bedroom light suddenly flashed on. Its intensity bore into his eyes as he watched Marsha prancing around before starting to unbutton her blouse and quickly removing it. He licked his lips because he was actually interested in watching her undoing her white bra that ultimately allowed her rather pointy tits the freedom he himself had craved. Seeing them he sighed with infatuation as she innocently cupped the naked flesh and began to gently massage the nipples. She walked to the window and looked out. She smiled when catching sight of him leering at her and because of this gave a lovely wave before closing the curtains.

    He awoke, the next day, at around twelve thirty which obviously made him late for work and so with his mouth feeling like a parrot's cage with the bird still in it decided to ring in sick. Down the stairs he struggled, and was rather glad of the wooden banister that was there, but he did fall the final three to land in a crumpled mass on the beige carpet in the hallway. His eyes looked like piss-holes in the snow and the yellow coloration of his clammy skin pointed to the onset of a Liver complaint. Realising what needed to be done picked up the telephone and dialled the number. "Hello," Stuart answered.

    "I can't make it in today," oozed Alan's voice coated with deceit. "I've spent most of the night on the loo with diarrhoea."

    "When will you be in?"

    "I'm not sure," he whispered and it was at that moment he put the icing on the cake with a single quote. "Oh! Shit." No more was said as he put the receiver down and went into the kitchen before looking around at the variety of dirty plates and decided that food was probably the last thing on his mind.

It was the next day when a sudden knocking on the door announced that somebody was there. Feeling somewhat apathetic he opened it and stood staring at a well dressed lady hovering with a man at her side who looked as if they were a couple of Jehovah witness's plying their trade. "Hello," Alan grinned as his halitosis breath could have flattened the entire human race. Well he had been living on mushy peas and swilling copious amounts of beer.

    "We've just heard about your mother's condition," the woman warmly answered in a pleasant West Country voice that he didn't instantly recognise. "And so we thought that we'd better come and visit."

    Alan felt his gut churn with inborn curiosity while listening to her words and still being none the wiser shrugged his curiosity. "I'm sorry!" he apologised. "But, who exactly are you?"

"Oh! I'm sorry," came the tender mocking of her voice. "But I'm Catherine Hill."

Taking the hint the man, at the woman's side, stretched out his hand. "And I'm her husband," he offered with a cordial shake. "Gordon."

Had his mother ever mentioned the names and if so were these the same people? Deciding to give them the benefit of the doubt he bid them welcome into his untidy realm. Walking through the hallway the woman kept glancing at the mess until laughing her remark, "It seems that we've arrived just in the nick of time."

"I think you're right," her husband agreed as he nearly fell over what appeared to be a basket full of dirty washing.

The woman suddenly stopped, pulled back her shoulders and simply removed her thin pale cream coat. As she posed pushing up her sleeves Alan wondered at her age, and being a fairly good judge decided that she was between fifty and fifty-five. "Right that's it!" She concluded and started to tidy.

The other man grabbed Alan's shoulder, pulled him to one side and quietly said, "It's easier to leave her when she's in this mood." Having offered his advice they both strolled into the sitting room and sat discussing the forthcoming cricket match between Alan's village and another from down in the West Country somewhere.

They never left that room until the door swung open and a flustered face appeared. "Dinner's on the table," spoke the woman as she entered. The meal was the best he'd tasted in a long time, and the conversation very stimulating. After it had been eaten all three vanished to the sitting room where glasses of spirit were consumed on a regular basis. Deciding that an early night was best it was around ten thirty when Alan eventually showed his guests their bedroom, and it was about a minute later that he fell into a deep sleep. He awoke next day to the sound of hectic cleaning occurring somewhere. Feeling like a million dollars opened the curtains and looked out. The branches of the apple trees were swaying in what breeze there was. Swallows were diving to catch insects on the wing. The frantic buzzing of bees flitting from the mauve sage flowers to those of the red and white clovers. On the washing line hung various garments that billowed like air socks on a runway. He dressed in a set of new clothes, which just happened to have appeared on the chair next to his bed as if by magic, and wandered downstairs.

"Morning," welcomed Catherine's sweet voice looking over the top of her glasses as well as the front edge of the paper. "Would you like a cup of tea?" Alan sat opposite and stared directly at her. He could now look and assess her in the cold light of reality. She'd applied just enough make-up to highlight the possible attraction of her face. Her hair had lost its youthful buoyancy, but the impregnation of subtle colours enhanced the dark mystery she held. She was bordering on being heavy boned in stature, but the fullness was held superbly in place. Having given her the once over turned his stare and looked around the kitchen. He smiled when noticing the mucky pots and pans had all but disappeared. He ate his breakfast, and once finished stood and walked out leaving both his guests talking together. He marched towards the garage, got into the car and drove to work. Over the course of the day it reminded him of being back at school, or even worse as it felt as if his mother was there because Stuart kept treating him like a child. Where have you been? What are you doing? Don't forget to be pleasant with the customers. Don't forget to tell me where you're going. These were just some of the rather annoying questions asked and Alan could now understand why people didn't want to work with him. Finally he got home and found, on the table, a letter that had been addressed to him. If he wasn't feeling decidedly pissed off before reading it then when seeing the signature at the bottom he certainly was afterwards. His heart pounded as Patrick Carlton wrote about the wonderful holiday he'd just enjoyed with his wife and daughter. His eyes expanded painfully as he stared, open-mouthed, at the photograph showing Erin lazing on a beach somewhere with a girl of about seven years of age at her side. He gave half a laugh when undressing for a refreshing bath and so crept towards his door before carefully opening it to quickly scan the vicinity just to make sure that no one could spy on him. Seeing that the coast was clear he strolled across the landing and entered the bathroom before turning on the hot water tap. He got in and simply lay there contemplating the fluff in his belly button, as well as doing other unmentionable things that men are expected to do, when the bathroom door suddenly burst open. "Don't look!" A woman's voice cried in desperation as she rushed towards the toilet. Hearing the plea he simply couldn't obey the command as he gazed at the reflection of Catherine in mirror on the door. Unfortunately the mirror, itself, had become covered with steam so the chance of seeing anything immoral was somewhat limited. However if he concentrated on a small area, and used his imagination, he could watch just how easily she lifted her light autumn leaved coloured skirt and pulled down her knickers. He thought, and hoped, that while she squatted to allow the golden stream of piss to squirt into the ceramic bowl he wouldn't react. How wrong he was because his subconscious instantly reacted. He smiled in an awkward sort of way as they both looked at each other. He; concentrating on the opaque reflection of the woman in the mirror and Catherine staring directly at his stiff cock sticking out of the water like a submarine's periscope. He closed his eyes and thought that she may become excited by seeing what was on offer and then realising that he'd never know smiled? Anyway it didn't matter what they were actually thinking because that moment passed into history as not a word was uttered as she wiped herself dry and pulled up her knickers.

All evening they'd been successful in avoiding each other but he was upstairs when at about half past seven Catherine walked into his bedroom and bluntly asked, "Can you take me into town tomorrow?"

"Can't your husband?"

"Unfortunately not," she rather awkwardly answered. "Because he got to go to Nottingham to meet somebody and anyway what happened, in the toilet, was purely accidental as I desperately needed to go." Realising that this might be taken as an apology and deciding that as he was going to work anyway agreed. The drive to town was mainly taken up by her reminiscing over the good time both she and his mother obviously had whilst being free and easy. One such story went on to explain that they had been prizes in games of cards. Another went on to discuss how they'd managed to get stashed aboard a certain frigate. How the well respected Sub Lieutenant had been caught, by the retiring captain, with two partially clothed woman inside his cabin, but at the Court Marshall the excuse given was that their uniforms had become soiled while inspecting the engine room, and so not wanting to get them into trouble decided that the best coarse of action was to get their livery laundered. The unfortunate outcome to this was that the Lieutenant was demoted, and the two Wrens were overlooked for promotion. At last they pulled into the car park, and started towards the shops. They were about a quarter the way along the path when passing a certain kind of shop Catherine frantically gestured. "I've got to go in here," she giggled. "Because I need some new underwear."

"Okay," he smiled as he carried on walking.

"Aren't you coming in?"

Looking at his watch he smiled, "I'll be late for work!"

"So another ten minutes isn't going to hurt," she grinned. "And anyway I may want your advice?" Hearing this he felt awkward, not because of the fact that he was going to be late as he could live with that but because he suddenly had a quick flash of that moment in the bathroom. He was lecherously smirking as he followed and once inside Lucky Pearl's Lingerie Emporium his heart started pounding. All around were manikins, and other dummies, modelling what could only be described as a voyeur's delight. There were suspender belts of every colour with sheer stockings clinging to the clips. There was the highly erotic magic of black and red knickers. Varying sizes of bra that went from the exotically skimpy to the totally enclosing vacuum of every teenage boy's nightmare. There were transparent negligees that hid absolutely nothing. French knickers. Petticoats. Girdles and every lover's fantasy; the black lace and red satin Basque. "Alan, I need your advice," Catherine sang as she walked from the changing cubicles. Even from the distance he was Alan could see exactly what, if anything, she was wearing and it took a further six steps before she stood in direct eyesight of the drooling man. "Well!" She exclaimed pirouetting on the spot. "Do you like?"

"Of course I do," he shuddered as he simply couldn't take his eyes off what was partially hidden beneath the negligee she'd decided to try. His heart pounded as he grinned at the tattoo sprouting from the waistband of the cobalt blue knickers she had on. Lifting his gaze, slightly, he stared at the faded bunch of small mauve flowers that he thought he'd seen the previous evening. He tried to look away as he couldn't find the words he needed to confirm his thoughts, but when she looked at him she may have understood. Like a model she returned to the changing room and gave a quick glance of welcome. His heart ruptured when storming into the small cubicle with head twisting and turning. His jaw dropped as he saw the woman standing ever hopeful. His lips dried when he saw Catherine provocatively sniggering at his basic eagerness. That eagerness vanished as he marched up to her and threatened, "Don't make a sound!" While grabbing her shoulders.

"Why?" The frightened tone of her voice asked as sexual fear scorched across her brow. She trembled as he brutally ripped the transparent negligee. Looking at her, with pure hostility, he instantly reached and dragged her knickers to the floor. He stepped back and simply stared with his gaze travelling both up and down her plump, but naked, body. He leered at her large tits with her somewhat tiny nipples inside the discs of claret pink. It took a moment but his eyes moved down her body until with some slight difficulty focused on that small sprig of thyme rising from the pubic hair. As he stared was she ashamed? She must have been because the pale colour of her cheeks exploded in the fiery reds of embarrassment as both her hands stretched out to cover both areas of her sexual femininity.

"Get dressed!" He coarsely ordered throwing her clothes directly at her, and once finished he walked out.

It was ten to eleven, on Sunday morning, when Alan pushed his mother to church. Through the great archway of the door the wheelchair only just fitted, and having negotiated the single granite step manoeuvred her until finding the ideal place. Once comfortable he sat dutifully on the wooden pew and discussed various items of news, both local and national, with her. It was about five minutes later that Mrs Catherine Hill nee Hargreaves, dressed in the splendid formality of a summer's day, and joined them. Standing at her side was her husband, Gordon, dressed in a dark navy blue jacket and around his neck was a Paisley cravat. As Alan looked he saw Catherine hovering closer as if wanting him to move. "Do you want to sit here?" He politely enquired while starting to shift further along and in doing so felt the sharp stab of a splinter digging into his arse.

"If you don't mind," she returned while advancing into position. With both women occupied he sat gazing at the walls of that hallowed sanctuary. There was the stone epitaph to the fallen of any war. Around the alter were words of Latin. There were a couple of flags draping their loyalty. A large brass eagle where the bible so full of hope and belief rested in the pulpit. There was the organ. The bell ropes dangling, which when pulled called the congregation. There was the vicar, so full of pomp and circumstance. The collection box where the poor could give their last farthing. For about an hour, well that's what it seemed like, they sat listening to the vicar prattling on about something or other but it was about a minute into the sermon that Alan lost interest. His concentration usurped by the heady display of hats that only made their dutiful appearances at a Sunday morning church service. There was Anne Barclay supporting a large floppy ensemble of green and yellow that if anyone had the misfortune to be sitting directly behind would find great difficulty in seeing what was going on in front. There was Denise Appleton with a silk and velvet creation that had him wondering about the old joke of having a red hat. Violet Turner, with her husband and clan of five, trying not to look flustered. Feeling bored he focused on the Colonel sitting quite alone at the front where his family had been members of the congregation through generations as their name could be found on the scroll of parchment that hung inside the door to highlight the fact.

Eventually, the service finished and as they left shook hands with the waiting vicar who seemed to have a word for everyone. Into the hot sunshine Alan stepped, allowing Catherine to push the wheelchair, when a voice called. "I'll be with you in a minute." Hearing the statement the party halted and Alan became curious when watching the Colonel walk up to a stranger, who'd been sat at the back during the service, and began talking with him.

The incident was easily forgotten as they sat in the regimental splendour of the Colonel's dining room. The meal was perfectly cooked and the wine flowed as they talked. The conversation was principally idle chitchat, but somehow Alan was drawn towards one specific painting that dominated the far wall. Feeling slightly left out, of the discussions, he stood glass in hand and walked towards it. He shivered in wonder as the haunting picture clearly showed a single soldier, with his back to the artist, standing ankle deep in the death and filth of a war somewhere. The isolation was superbly captured as the moonlight cast shadows across the battle scarred and blooded uniform that seemed like a distressing epitaph to each of the friends he'd lost.

"We're just going for a walk," smiled the group of four sitting, like the horsemen of the Acropolis, watching the way Alan suddenly shivered. "Are you coming?" Someone asked.

He turned, looked at the Colonel beginning to push his mother and then gestured with an airy-fairy wave. "You go," he decided. "And I'll meet you back at Calder's." Once at home he crept into the sitting room, and it was here he simply crashed out on the settee and it was probably the heat of the afternoon, as well as the wine he'd drank, that he felt absolutely shattered because putting his head to one side he went to sleep. He awoke to the sound of an empty house and glancing at the ornate clock on the mantelpiece saw that it was a quarter passed seven in the evening. Feeling decidedly hungry went to the kitchen and helped himself to some food. With enough to feed an army he wandered back to eat his meal and was about halfway through when the sitting room door opened. Thinking that everyone had returned thought nothing of it. "Did you have a good time," declared his sincere words as he continued to eat.

"Yes, thanks," returned a single voice. There was a pause until she spoke again. "And anyway I need your help!" Hearing this plea he swivelled and looked at Catherine standing about two feet away. "Your mother tells me that you've got some photographs of your father," she continued.

After finishing the mouthful of food, he thought for a moment and asked somewhat uncooperatively, "Does she want them now?"

"If you don't mind," returned her words. "She wants to show them to someone," her sweet voice confessed as she smiled rather impishly at him. He gazed at her, and then blowing out his cheeks in mystification stood. Without any hints he walked from the room and headed up the stairs towards his bedroom. Now deliberately frustrated he busied himself hopeful of locating the shoebox where he knew they were. Under the bed he looked. Nothing. In the drawers of his dressing table he looked. Again nothing. He'd searched practically everywhere and was about to admit defeat when he suddenly thought of its possible hiding place. He gave a worried grin because he now remembered exactly where they might be, and for that his smile became even greater. It had grown simply because he didn't want to be discovered having a collection of rather naughty, and sleazy, magazines. Hoping Catherine was still downstairs he climbed onto a chair and stretched beyond the pile of naughty books.

"Are you alright?"

Hearing this unexpected question he wobbled slightly forcing him to over-stretch. The result of which was that some of the magazines fell to the thick carpet. Hearing them land he looked down hoping they'd fallen closed, and as luck would have it they did. He sighed his thanks, but it was then that another slipped and landed open. Alan looked at the imported glossy photograph displaying a naked model reclining on a cherry coloured chair. As he stared he hoped the lady, standing in the doorway, hadn't noticed the magazine fall let alone land open. How wrong he was as she began to move, and having reached the male intended book simply bent to pick it up.

He cringed as she awkwardly started to thumb the pages. "That's disgusting," was one of her favourite expressions used when studying certain modelling techniques. Another was, "It shouldn't be allowed!" And this was usually muttered after seeing a photograph displaying the carnal act in all its glory. Nothing but, absolutely nothing was going to stop her from studying every picture, every act, and every naked body inside that magazine. It finally came to a conclusion when she thrust a specific snapshot directly at the young man shivering on the edge of his bed. "They're not real," she announced with words struggling towards jealousy.

Alan smiled, rather stupidly, as he ogled the forty-five inch bust of that German fraulein. They were huge as they sagged dangerously close to her navel, but to some men they were a special gift of succulent pleasure. He thought for a moment and still staring gave his predictable response, "They could be!"

Her answer was swift and direct, "So you like big tits!" Hearing this slanderous remark he blushed, and as he watched the way she regarded him didn't know which way to turn and so looked at the floor. "Are mine big enough?" She demanded while thrusting her ample cleavage at him. Again, he didn't know how to react and so said nothing. Catherine was now on the attack and seeing the way he was went for the jugular. Like a matron at boarding school she placed both hands either side of his head and pulled his trembling face against the apparent softness of her covered bosom. Suddenly she pushed him away and in doing so he closed his eyes, more in shock than anything else, when she quickly removed a single tit for him to look at. "This one's real," she explained as he just sat there looking at her. Then the feeling that had built inside his gut exploded. His muscles tensed as he stood up and grabbed her shoulders before pushing her towards the bed. She fell and simply lay looking up at him. His fingers twitched with nervous anxiety as he reached and gripped the front of her cotton blouse. His eyes were emotionless as he forced the seven pearl buttons to fly apart. He panted uncontrollably as he stared at the white bra and it was after the fourth pant he wrongly assumed that she would allow his assault. With his pulse exploding his fingers tore at the material and he smiled, with sinister intent, watching the way her tits fell perfectly into view. He had no control as the sexual hormones racing through his body forced his large hands to grip the hemline of her skirt and lift it away. He stepped back again and drooled like a dog as he looked at the pair of flame red knickers she was wearing. His heart was pounding as he tore the fragile threads until finally exposing her cunt. His brain was on the point of explosion as he saw, yet again, that sprig of thyme and it was then that something twigged. It was that or when seeing the panic etched on the woman's face that forced him to shiver in abject horror. He cowered back. His face pained at the violent thought thrashing through his disturbed mind. He closed his eyes as he fought the primeval urge to defile her body, and with that he breathed as deep as he dare. For exactly nine seconds nothing was said as they stared at each other. She on the bed looking up and him looking down. At no time during those moments did anyone make the slightest gesture? There was nothing, and when the time had elapsed he calmly walked to the forgotten photographs of his father and picked them up. He said not a word as he passed Catherine, still sprawled on the bed, and dropped them at her side. He walked from the room and was downstairs, drinking from the actual Brandy bottle, when she walked into the room. He didn't turn to watch her, but he knew she was there. The silence was more damning than any words spoken because both understood exactly what had just happened.

Over the next couple of days the atmosphere, between both Catherine and Alan, was cold and hung like icicles on a frosted gate. Very few if any words were exchanged, between them, until the Wednesday morning and it was as they were both sitting at the breakfast table trying not to look at each other that it was her husband who unknowingly chipped at the walls of silence. "I'll be late back tonight," he frustratingly promised as he gazed at his wife sitting but one place away.

    Catherine was quick as she turned her head. "How am I going to get to the Antique Fair?" Her statement clearly asked.

    Her husband shrugged his mobster like shoulders, rolled his bottom lips in the mode of uncertainty and simply suggested. "Can't Alan take you?"

    "He maybe busy," her rapid rejection countered.

Gordon replaced his cup on the saucer, and then gave a genuine reply of wonder. "Hadn't you better ask him?" And having spoken shrugged his shoulders with curiosity. Understanding her reluctance Alan grinned rather stupidly and feeling somewhat silly cast his gaze across at Catherine who was blushing slightly.

No one commented on her obvious embarrassment, but when Alan noticed he pompously grinned while lifting his right eyebrow. He felt in control and so feeling that the time had come to start building that metaphorical bridge calmly asked, "Where is that you want to go?"

She leaned back in the chair, gave a formal smile and answered, "I really wanted to go to the Antique Fair at Rutland Hall this afternoon." She paused momentarily before saying, "But anyway you'll be at work." Having given her reply waited for any response that might be forthcoming.

Alan, who'd become bored at work after about the second day, decided that today was as good as any to simply jack it in. With this racing around his head he stood and walked from the room. He returned, some five minutes later, and cordially gave his cynical revelation. "I've just phoned to tell Stuart that I've quit," he half laughed while sitting at the table. "So I'll be taking you."

"Then that's settled," came the polite remark as Gordon left the room.

"What about mother?" Alan asked as he looked at his maternal parent sitting quietly struggling to eat her food.

A faint voice suddenly rose above the clattering crockery. "It's all right I've arranged with Marsha to come and start doing a painting of your father," spoke his mother, and it was then that her son instantly knew why they wanted the photographs.

It was about half passed nine when things started to happen. First, Marsha arrived with various designs she already started and secondly Alan carefully drove his passenger to her destination. It took about three hours, along various motorways and side roads, before pulling up in the car park and leaving the silver grey vehicle outside the auspicious design of that Grade One Listed Building. Into the rather plush interior they stepped, paid the entrance fee and started to meander around the various stalls that were on show. "I'll meet you in the cafétéria at about half past four," Catherine smiled as her attention was suddenly overwhelmed by something in one of the many rooms. Glancing at his watch and seeing that it was only one o'clock realised that he had plenty of time to waste. With this in mind he wandered around eagerly viewing anything that might attract his attention. At the third table he spotted a motley collection of sepia photographs going back to the Realm of Queen Victoria. With no intention of any purchase he casually flicked through them and smiled as the young ladies seemed so open about displaying their nudity although some air brushing had taken place to prevent exposure of certain parts of the naked body. To the next room and it was in here that he saw old manuscripts about the history of something, or someone. There were relics adding to the atmosphere. There were suits of armour showing off their splendid crests of royalty. There were paintings of whatever, or whoever. Silver bracelets going back to before the Romans. There was everything necessary to make the whole thing profitable, and it was getting near time to rendezvous with Catherine when he neared a table that was showing armies of tin soldiers with coloured cards indicating their appropriate regiment. As he looked it was one particular set of eight magnificently attired pieces of the 29th Foot that caught his eye. The official military badges printed on the information card, as well as the three pears, told of the gallant efforts of The Royal Worchester's during the Sutlej campaign. Was it instinct that forced him to pay good money, or was it some foolhardy idea?

"What have you brought?" Was the question Catherine asked as they sat down to their well earned drink?

"I don't know," he shrugged as he carefully examined the pieces one by one.

"Aren't you going to ask me what I've got?" She egged while tipping the entire contents of all her bags, except one, onto the table. The corners of Alan's mouth rose as he saw those same photographs he'd seen. There were intricate pieces of jewellery in all sorts of colours from deep aquamarine to pale sapphire. Letters sent from soldiers on duty at the Western Front. Medals, and their ribbons, regrettably offered for good money. Stamps from the differing countries of the British Empire.

He'd fought the feeling for about fifteen minutes but finally his curiosity became intolerable when he pointed and spoke, "What's in the other bag?"

"It's a secret!" She grinned rather wickedly. Whatever it was seemed to force her to shiver, because the gentle trembling started at her shoulders and ran the entire length of her body.

His curiosity was so potent that he simply couldn't let it lie. "Who's it for," asked his question while playfully trying to see inside the bag.

She thought for a moment, gave a smile that ran the full length of her mouth and then answered. "Someone, who's special," she admitted in a voice that dripped authentic tease. Realising the unwillingness, in her tone, no more was spoken about the gift.

It was getting late when they finally left to make their way home, and it had gone midnight when they pulled up outside Calder's. Catherine, who'd been asleep for most of the journey, had instinctively, woken as they drove along the gravel driveway. Together they stepped from the car and headed for the house. Into the hallway they stepped, and it was at the bottom of the stairs that she grabbed his hands and pulled him close. "This is for taking me today," she quickly thanked as she kissed him on the left cheek.

"That's okay!" He responded while hugging her.

It must have been around three thirty, in the morning, that Alan suddenly heard the front door open, and as he lay listening someone was moving downstairs. Now, being fully awake and feeling decidedly brave clambered out of bed. Going to the top of the landing to see whoever it was smiled when realising that Gordon had returned. Suddenly, a violent voice was heard to bellow and scream. "Did you get it?"

"No," returned the woman who was beginning to tremble. "But I know where it is."

"That's not what I sent you there for," Gordon's harsh tone threatened.

"But," she stammered.

"No buts, I needed that painting," he spat and having silenced her excuse whipped the back of his hand hard against her face. She tottered; blood running from her mouth, and Alan felt the pain as the woman staggered back and fell against the stairs. The aggressor took two steps before posing directly above his victim.

"Please," she sobbed while wiping away the blood and looked up at the aggressor.

"What!" Drilled his word as his fist clenched.

"Why do you need that stupid painting," her tear stained voice asked. "It's just." She never finished the sentence. The man's fist pummelled into her face, and as she crumpled to the floor there were no apologies as he looked down. There was no acknowledgement of his crime as he walked away and left her.

Alan was trembling as the man climbed the stairs and not wanting to be discovered hurriedly went back inside his room. His pulse raced with fear as he listened to the footsteps approaching, but sighed when they kept going. He went back to bed as pictures of what had just happened flashed across his mind, but eventually he must have dropped off because the next time he opened his eyes the bright sun was stealing the dreary gloom of night.

At the breakfast table the silence was damning. It was finally broken when Catherine stood up, clutched her husband's hand, and dramatically addressed her audience. "Both Gordon and myself feel that we've outstayed our welcome," her opening sentence delivered. "And so we have decided that it would be better for all concerned if we left and went back to Worchester." Having spoken it was around midday when they drove home.

There were gale force winds battering the coastline as the white-topped breakers breached sea walls. There were severe weather warnings for high-sided vehicles stupid enough to be on the move. There were uprooted trees pining broken telegraph poles to cause the necessary electric to be lost in the isolated regions of Britain. Slates from roofs injured those pedestrians foolish enough to be outside struggling home to be with loved ones. The news was full of the destruction when showing pictures of battered houses. The unforeseen deaths of foolhardy people eager to sample the killing strength of the winds and it was two days later, with the winds still battering, that Alan received a press cutting.

"…. The crumpled wreckage of a car was recovered from the river Avon yesterday, and inside were the bodies of the two people believed to have been missing since Thursday. Their identity was later confirmed as Sub Lieutenant Catherine Hill and her husband Gordon and it is believed that they were caught when the Lansden Bridge, near to the village of Caldecott in Worcestershire, collapsed sending tons of limestone into the swirling torrent of the river…."

Again, dressed in the black of grief both Alan and his mother were crowded inside the crematorium where the many people had gathered to pay their final and dutiful respects. After the service of condolence everyone gathered at number 47 Champion Crescent for the traditional wake.

"She was such a pillar of society," addressed a pristinely attired woman, whose black ensemble put the others to shame. Her face had been lacquered with enough foundation to support that very bridge. The bright red of her lipstick blazed a fiery beacon that could have been used on a foggy and dank afternoon. Alan studied this woman with some slight curiosity. Had he seen her before, and if he had when was it? Was she one of the women in the paintings that Erin had given him? Had he, perhaps, seen her in a photograph somewhere? Or even worse, was she the victim come back to haunt him? With various ideas whirling inside his mind he sipped from the glass, in his hand, and probably thought it was a case of déjà vu and shrugged his shoulders in wonder.

"Hello," greeted a strange, but familiar voice. The startled young man's concentration was pulled back to reality when Marshall Forester marched dominantly forward. They shook hands, and stood chatting for some moments. Their conversation was as friendly as could be expected, but held the underlying tone of distrust. Fortune favours the brave as Alan held his ground until the man asked, "Where's your mother?" And all the while his gaze was straining around the room.

"She's somewhere," Alan answered with a modicum of certainty. A grin of relief raced around his dry mouth when suddenly pointing at that same group he'd first seen. "There!" He responded. Marshall looked, smiled and left. In four strides he'd reached the women and introduced himself.

Understanding that his presence was not required the young man ambled to the table and helped himself to the cold buffet that had been prepared by expert caterers. The spread was mouth watering, and he was helping himself to another sausage roll when a hand rested upon his shoulder. Instinctively, he turned and looked directly into the bloodshot eyes of a member of the grieving family. She was dressed in accordance of the day. The black hat perched precisely on the flowing length of brunette hair. The fine layer of mascara discreetly smudged with tears. The pale lipstick highlighted the acute paleness of her mouth. "Hello!" She struggled to smile.

Hearing the introduction he narrowed his eyebrows in the mode of curiosity, and being unable to put a name to the woman returned his smile of youthful tact as he probably realised that it was the customary walk of a family member at this period of their mourning. "I'm sorry to hear of your loss," his polite words offered.

The respectfully dressed woman shook her head several times before giving half a smile. "I'm sorry," she apologised while masquerading in the grief of the moment. "I've not introduced myself," she started. "I'm Brenda Holst the daughter of the deceased." Having made the introduction gave half a smile, but it was such an emotional effort that her shoulders drooped with the exertion. It took a moment, but finally her words slipped from her quivering lips, "Can we talk?"

Hearing this Alan was taken aback, and for that he stared open-mouthed as she held out her black gloved hand to wait his grip and like a frightened child felt the protective handhold of the woman. They left the congregation of mournful folk and disappeared inside what appeared to be a study. The man's heart stopped as he stared at the painting showing the exact likeness of the Tanmouth. While staring he noticed two blurred figures standing beside the heady outline of the hull. "Who's the man?" He wondered with finger pointing. "Because, that's your mother," confirmed the certainty of the woman's identity.

Having spoken he turned and watched the way she gulped back the obvious grief. "I was never told," she half smiled. "But it could be my father." The mourning daughter gave a knowing smile as the corners of her mouth became raised a fraction to allow half a laugh to escape. She tried her hardest not to look at him, but failed as his curious expression demanded more answers. Not a word was uttered as she carefully stepped towards the desk and unlocked it, and from the inside pulled a sealed envelope. Her hand was shaking as she handed it to the surprised man. "My mother gave me instructions that if anything happened to her then I was to give you this letter," her pitying words explained. Reaching out he felt the eruption of curiosity flowing through his body as he took the offering, and as he did his fingers tightened.

Had he the confidence to ask that single question that was racing inside his head, and as he watched the woman he realised he hadn't. He sighed in torment as he tore the envelope apart. "How did you know who to give it to," he asked when realising that they hadn't been formally introduced.

The woman spun on the spot, causing her dress to pirouette like a parachute, and once again reached inside the desk. And after moving various papers she found a single photograph which she thrust at him. Alan allowed his eyes to focus on the picture and remembered Catherine taking it the day after she and her husband had arrived at Calder's. The victim's daughter, having done her duty, went and sat on a chair to begin explaining whatever was on her mind, "It was about a week before the accident that I remember receiving a telephone call from mum asking me to come and visit her," she dramatically started. "And it was just before the storms that she told me about the letter, and the photograph, and what to do if anything happened," she stumbled as her grief was heard to penetrate the tone. "I could sense that she was scared, but when I asked why she just laughed it off as an old woman's fancy. And now she's dead." Alan was reluctant, but walked to where she was sitting and wrapped his strong arms around her body as comfort. He said nothing as she wept into her hands. The tears felt warm, but the mood was cold.

Suddenly the door opened and a head appeared inside the room. "Oh! There you are," the man quietly stated as he came perfectly into view. The lady in question shuddered, stood up and after brushing down her dress walked away into the hustle and bustle of grief. The young man was now alone, and so with an incline of mystery read the letter. He shuddered because its contents were stark to the point of certainty.

Alan,

If you're reading this then my daughter's done as I requested, and you're probably standing in the study wondering why! Well, it's quite simple inasmuch as certain people have found and killed me.

Who are they? I hear you asking and my answer is again quite unnerving, as I simply do not know. But what I do know is that they were the people who were also responsible for your father's death.

How do I know? Because as a serving Wren I once worked with your father on a project of National Security, and it was during a quiet moment that he told me that the people he was after were trying to destroy all the evidence he'd gathered. We'd been investigating something irregular about certain documents that the War Ministry had, and before you ask no I don't know who it concerned only that it involved some high ranking official. Everything seemed to be going okay as we worked well together looking through files and documents and it was on the 25th August 1950 that your father took me for a celebration meal. Thinking that we'd completed our work I was very disappointed when he simply told me that for my own safety it would be better that I got posted for another tour of duty. I was really upset because working so close I found myself falling in love, and had freely agreed to his fanciful suggestion of having the tattoo done. Some three days later, which was pretty quick for the Navy, we stood on the quay saying our goodbyes. Now at Portsmouth and over the next couple of months I would cry myself to sleep thinking of what might have been.

I'd just turned 20, and beginning to sort out my feelings, when a surprise package arrived with the words happy birthday anonymously written inside a card. My heart pounded as I looked upon the painting that's hanging on the study wall, and I assumed it was your father that had sent it. Realising that I may never meet him again, except for the press cuttings I'd collected, it came as a complete shock when one day I read about his premature death. What can I tell you about your father? Only that he was very secretive, and very precise to the point of being fanatical. He never mellowed once, but it was completely out of character and a bit of a surprise when on that final evening, before I was transferred, that he asked me to join him for a stroll. It was nearly midnight when we walked, hand in hand, along an isolated beach in the moonlight. Our laughing footprints leaving a double trail and it was at one point we halted with the sea washing our feet. We turned to one another as the pale moon light flickered across our bronzed bodies and it was as we gazed into each other's warm eyes that he asked whether he could see the tattoo I'd had done. I readily agreed as he slowly removed the painted silks of my dress with his strong hands until I stood naked before his eager eyes. As I looked at him I so much wanted him to kiss me with just the moon our only witness. But as we stood apart he smiled before softly whispering the words I would never forget.

"…. Look but do not touch

Break but do not shatter…."

Sorry for that bit of reflection, but you can't imagine the hypnotic authority he held. Anyway getting back to the present all I can offer is that you have the painting as a momentum of our memories.

He sighed as he read the letter again and again. On the fourth reading he even managed to look at the painting. His eyes narrowed as he noticed absolutely nothing, but it was at one point he thought he'd seen a clue and staring even harder at the image realised that it was a flicker of nothing. How long had he been there he was not to know but it came to an abrupt end when a voice drifted across the room. "Oh! You're still here," exclaimed the concerned voice walking closer. Alan, turned to look directly at his host for the day and as he smiled she politely explained herself, "You're mother has asked me to tell you that she's ready to leave."

Hearing this he calmly looked at his watch and noticed the time. His pulse raced, because understanding his mother's condition to still be a trifle frail he didn't want her to become exhausted. He smiled while starting to move away, and he'd taken exactly one step when he stopped. He apologetically glanced at the woman standing her ground. He felt a shiver of doubt rolling down his spine as he tried to find the courage to speak his request. "I think you should read this," insisted the instruction as the letter was given.

Not a sound was heard as she read it. "So she wants you to have that painting," dribbled the tear stained voice.

It may not have been diplomatic but softly, as if stage whispering, he found the words he needed. "Is it alright if I take it now?" And as soon as he'd spoken he felt the cold of a winter's day rippling through his frame.

He stood waiting for her response, and when it came he wasn't prepared. He wasn't even ready when she flashed her hand across his face, and he wasn't expecting the flow of blasphemous expletives to flow from her mouth, "It's your fucking family's fault that my parents are both dead." And the tone of her voice dripped acid that instantly bleached his skin. The anger that had been trapped inside through out the service oozed as she ripped the painting from the wall. "Take it," her bitter words cast as she hurled the picture through the air. "I never want to see it again."

On the journey back Alan had this suspicious feeling that they were being followed. Whether he was being paranoid or not but the same set of headlights always seemed to be following. They would turn left where he turned, then again right at the next junction. Then thinking that he'd lost them by taking a short cut through a village he knew his heartbeat increased as there they were, in his mirror, yet again. It was midnight as he pulled into Calder's and was he relieved as those headlights kept on driving passed and into tomorrow.

It was a hot Saturday afternoon as the two cricket captains walked to the middle and performed the ritual act of tossing the coin. It landed tails and with Stuart winning decided to bat. Alan prepared himself in the familiar stance he'd often use when opening for the village team. Once ready, he glanced up and watched the solidly built bowler start his run ready to deliver that first ball. In his usual confidence he watched the deceptive flight of the red projectile as it left the opponent's hand. It swerved slightly towards the on side, and so with gallant abandon flashed his bat in the perfection of a cover drive. "Howzat," screamed the tight cordon of fielders waiting for such a chance. Alan, understanding the complexities of the game, stood to attention to await the umpire's decision. His heartbeat quickened when seeing the index finger pointing skywards, and the feeling of total rejection surged through his body as he walked the lonely path back to the pavilion, and to bring the point home nobody offered their commiserations. With the isolation gathering momentum he calmly decided to go for a walk if only to relieve the apparent boredom he was going to face. He deeply sighed as he moved away and towards the flowing waters of the river.

"Can I come with you?" Called a warm voice he didn't instantly recognise and hearing the request turned and spotted Brenda Holst waving her arms like a semaphore. Alan was somewhat taken aback, but feeling isolated waited for her to catch him up and once together she reached out her arms for him. "Your mother said you'd be up here," she greeted while embracing his frame and pulling him close so that their intimate bodies touched. "And I just want to say how sorry I was for my behaviour at my parent's funeral."

"I quite understand how you must have felt," he responded. "You had every right to be angry." And as they continued to cuddle it was at that moment his mind was on a different planet as he became very conscious of just how soft and yielding her comely bosom was. The thinness of her summer blouse perfectly enhanced the euphoric ecstasy of her nipples straining their escape. Realising the hormonal activity inside his body was causing a slight, well it wasn't slight if truth be known, growth of his cock he pulled away not wanting his sexual predicament to be discovered and as they separated he shuddered with slight embarrassment.

She smiled when obviously understanding. "Oh! You are sweet," came the warm words as they started to walk around the boundary and it was at one point that Brenda skipped ahead to collect the ball that had just been hit, by Stuart, for four runs. Once ready she bent, from the waist, and picked it up. Alan laughed as he watched the way she threw it back, all arse about face with no rhythm and having returned the ball they continued their meander until reaching the wooden bridge. "Let's go across," she grinned taking his hand.

With hopeful curiosity surging through his body he stepped onto the crossing and with dramatic elegance strode across, but on the other side he breathed a deep sigh that caused his skin to bubble like goose-flesh. He turned and watched just how easily his companion tiptoed across to join him and she would have been about halfway when a sudden up draught caught her skirt to make it to resemble a flowery wigwam. As he looked Alan's heartbeat quickened because for a brief second the delicate threads of her sweetly coloured underwear came perfectly into view. "If I'd only had a camera," he teased while pressing the imaginary shutter of the invisible contraption he was holding.

She blushed and turned her head away. For a moment she said nothing. "Can you please stop imagining that you're taking my photograph?" She instinctively snapped while quickly brushing down the errant skirt. "Because I know exactly what you're thinking."

"Do you?"

"Yes!"

"And what's that?"

"What's the colour of my underwear," her condescending toned voice preached as she stepped off the bridge.

He gave a silly smirk of adolescent knowledge. "They're pink," he replied knowing full well he was right. "And aren't they pretty."

Hearing this she instantly looked daggers at him. "Is that all you can think about," asked the question.

"Yep!"

"So it's true?"

"What is?"

"That the majority of men," she lectured. "Have only got one thing on their mind!"

"I can't answer that!"

"Why ever not?"

"Because," he nonchalantly said. "It might actually prove that you're right." Having admitted the belief there was a pause until he added, "But occasionally we do think of other things."

"Like what?"

As quick as a flash he replied, "Why are you here?"

She was rather startled, but not surprised, at the swiftness of his question and so gave a little smirk. "I'm here because when I was going through an old suitcase, that I'd discovered under my mum's bed, I found this letter that she'd obviously kept explaining exactly what happened with your father on the beach that night," Brenda admitted as she awkwardly looked skywards. "And it's very graphic!"

There was no time for him to ask his question because her final footstep seemed to get caught on something which made her stumble. Watching the way she tottered he was so eager to help that he was on autopilot. He made a grab and as their bodies touched his heart instantly pounded. He was completely unaware when his hands reached around her frame and cradled the soft bulk of her arse.

"What d'yer think you're doing?" She suddenly snapped.

"Trying to prevent you from falling over."

"Well," she preached. "There was no need to have put your hands where you've got them!"

"Why ever not?"

"Because it's not very pleasant," she stated rather condescendingly. "Having some strange man fondling my bottom."

Realising that he'd been chastised, for his actions, gave a comical smirk as he offered his apology, "I'm sorry." And then stage whispered. "And, anyway, it's a very nice bottom!"

"What did you just say?"

Not wanting to admit to anything continued, "You know the letter you were just talking about?"

"Yes!"

"What's it actually say?"

"Read it yourself!" She scowled while handing it over and sitting on the grass.

He sat next to her and read it. "All it appears to explain, in rather graphic detail, is what she wanted my father to do to her," he shrugged when he'd read it and as a joke added. "So all I can conclude is that she was just as sexually corrupt as the next man."

"Don't be so vulgar," her contrite words accused. Then after rummaging inside her handbag she suddenly exclaimed, "Got it!" And then to prove the point waved a small black book in the air.

He gulped his question. "What's that," erupted his curious challenge.

"It's my mother's most up to date diary," she grinned. "And you're in it!"

The sound of pages being turned were heard and she must have found the correct place because she stopped and gazed at him like a lawyer at a trial. "Do you remember what happened that second day when she saw you in the bath?" Her precise words demanded.

Deciding to be economical with the truth as protection he answered, "I'm not sure now!" But while he was speaking the tone gave away the fact that he did indeed remember.

She turned some more pages. "What about when you took her to get some new underwear?" A few more pages. "The day when she wanted you to find some photographs of your father?" As he listened it was Alan's turn to blush, but at the same time a strange sensation bubbled inside his gut. He gave half a laugh and knowingly sniggered when realising that what he'd done had been entered into that most personal of journals and kept as a memory. He looked at Brenda and gave an impish smirk. Suddenly she got onto her knees and immediately gave him a push. He fell backwards and was quaintly surprised when she quickly knelt across his chest. She picked up the diary. Flicked a few more pages. "Do you remember the night you came home drunk?"

"That could have been any night," he shrugged.

"So you don't?"

"I suppose you're going to tell me all about it," he encouraged completely oblivious of any such incident that might have made it into the diary.

She started, "I was woken by something, or someone, moving about in the bedroom at about two thirty and knowing that Gordon would sleep through the end of the World turned the side light on."

"And what did she see?"

"If you listen," she sniggered, "Then you might find out."

"Okay!"

She carried on. "It was a bit of a shock when seeing Alan trying to get into the wardrobe and I was just in time to prevent him from using it as the toilet. Realising he obviously needed some help, in that department, I led him across the landing and towards the bathroom. Once inside I did something a little bit naughty as we both stood in front of the toilet."

"And pray, what did she do?"

"Listen," she said. "He had his eyes wide open but I knew he was sleepwalking so I held his cock while he had a piss."

"I don't remember that."

"I don't suppose you do," she smiled while giffling about. Feeling the erotic movement of her arse over his chest he suddenly became aware of the fact that he was beginning to get excited. Needing no prompting he unceremoniously, and very quickly, placed his hands beneath the hem of her skirt and grabbed both cheeks of her arse and started fondling them. If looks could kill then Alan would have died at that moment but as a compromise he instantly withdrew both hands. "There's a good boy," she grinned. "Right back to the diary." Having spoken she continued, "After he'd finished and I shook him dry I helped him back to his bedroom and placed him on his bed so that he could continue in the land of nod. I know I shouldn't have done it, and I know it was wrong of me, but I just couldn't help myself as I just stood there looking at him."

"Bet that was nice!"

She never heard the comment and so continued, "Whether he realised that I was watching but he suddenly started getting an erection."

"But," he shrugged. "According to what she'd put in her diary she'd already seen it stiff?"

"Had she?" She asked looking somewhat shocked. "Because there's no mention of what state your penis was in, only the fact that she'd seen it." Realising that he'd just shot himself in the foot smiled. Brenda continued reading, "As I stood looking at him I was trying to remember the last time Gordon showed any signs of interest in the more unconventional side of sex in our marriage and realising that I couldn't a wicked thought flashed across my mind."

"And what was that?"

"I simply wanted Alan to wake up, strip me naked and make wild passionate love to me."

"I never realised!" He admitted. "That she wanted me to do that!"

"Why should you," she hypothesised. "Because people will only see what they want to see and not what's there."

"How true," he grinned when noticing just how firm her nipples had become.

Suddenly her mood changed. "This next bit," she shivered. "Is absolutely disgusting."

"Why, what's it say?"

She looked awkward. "I can't possibly read it aloud," she shuddered making her tits wobble.

"Okay," he shrugged. "But can I read it?"

She hesitated before handing over the little black book and then watched as he quietly read the words. "Oh! I see what you mean," he lecherously grinned.

"Don't you think it's disgusting," her coy words announced. "Putting your thingy in her mouth."

"But, if you remember I was in a drunken stupor so I don't think I had a lot of say in the matter." Changing tact he asked, "Anyway have you never tried it?"

"No!" She objected with a shudder. "It's just the thought of having a thingy in your mouth."

"If you've never done it then how can you be so judgemental?"

"What do you mean?"

"Well," he smiled. "Can I ask you a question?"

She thought for a moment. "If you must," she frowned before adding. "As long as it's not going to be rude."

"I'm not promising," he smiled. "You know when you have sex with your husband?"

"That's a bit personal," she answered.

"That's as maybe but it might help you to understand that the sexual act means different things to different people."

Hearing this she gave a lop-sided grin. "Okay," she smiled like a schoolgirl. "But let me explain something first."

"Okay."

"I was twenty two, and in my final year at university, when I met Brian at a student party and after a rather long and drawn out engagement we finally married at the local register office."

"That was nice."

"No it wasn't," she countered. "Because I wanted the full trimmings."

"You mean the church. Pretty dress. Choir. Bells. The dreaded in-laws. And the honeymoon in a quiet backwater where your new husband could feel a twat and you could start getting to grips with something substantial."

"Put like that," she half laughed. "Then yes."

"I know this is going to be a bit personal," he leered. "But is your sex life good, bad or indifferent?"

There was a pause as she thought about it. "On a score of one to ten," she confessed. "Then I would put it's around the half mark."

"That good," he jeered. "So your sex life is more like a wham bam thank you Sam."

"Yes," she trembled. "I suppose it was!"

"What d'yer mean was?"

"Well to put it bluntly," she started. "I've not had sex with Brian for near on twelve years now."

"So," he started looking rather shocked. "Do you sleep in the same bed?"

"Of course not," she smiled. "We've actually got our own bedrooms."

His brow furrowed because he'd sometimes heard about this sort of marriage where the physical side goes on the back burner. "So you don't really understand what all the hype is when it comes to having sex?" He asked.

He could see what her answer was going to be by the lack of understanding chiselled across her face. "I'm not sure what you mean?" Erupted the frown.

"If you can remember the last time you and lover boy engaged in some good old fashioned rumpy pumpy," he suggested. "Did you manage to get the kind of feeling that made you realise that having sexual intercourse was, and still could be, a pleasurable act?"

"Not really," she answered. "Because if I remember rightly it was all over so very quickly."

"So you've never experienced an orgasm?"

Her expression of astonishment was priceless, as well as the necessary proof, and so when she said, "No," it was confirmed.

"So I take it that you've never played with yourself?"

"What?"

"You know," he suggested. "You put your hand between your legs and have a good old rummage with what's down there."

"That's a disgusting thought," she shivered. "And anyway why should I?"

"Because," he grinned. "You might find you like it."

"Where have you been?" Demanded Stuart when Alan finally appeared back in the pavilion.

Deciding not to tell of his shenanigans amongst the docks and nettles just smiled, "Walking." Having given his excuse he quickly noticed that the other players, of his team, were making their way onto the pitch hoping to prevent the opposition from reaching the gettable total they'd managed to score. They battled well in the hot sun. Catching some, but dropping most. Stopping boundaries, but the missed fielding cost them dearly because with the final ball the other team needed a six to win and as Brendan Case ambled up to bowl his usual donkey drops the spectators gasped their expectation as the ball rose high into the air with Alan watching. As it finally fell to earth he stepped back while making sure that he stayed within play and waited for the winning catch. Whether he was distracted, or not, made not the slightest bit of difference because the ball bounced from his waiting hands and dropped over the boundary rope. The applause was not from the home crowd but was very vocal from the away team.

It was late when both Alan and Brenda staggered home from the celebrations, or commiserations, depending on your viewpoint. The house was in darkness as they walked up the garden path, and after several miserable attempts eventually opened the front door and went their separate ways.

It was bright on the following Monday morning when he awoke and sat up. With the depressive feeling of irritation, especially in his bladder, he clambered out of bed and wandered across the landing towards the bathroom. Having finished his toilet crept back again, but was all the time wary that someone might be trying to catch a glimpse of him. He'd been in his room for a couple of minutes when a definite knock was heard on the door. So slipping into his rather battered looking psychedelic orange dressing gown moved towards the sound and quickly opened it. A broad grin spread around his mouth as his visitor slipped easily passed, and once inside went to stand beside the open window.

"I've been waiting for you to wake up so that I could say thanks!" Her sweet voice announced as she turned to give him a cuddle.

"That's alright," he smiled not having the slightest idea what she was on about but anyway he wasn't particularly bothered as she pulled him close. In doing this and with him feeling the softness of her bosom digging into his chest there was the usual consequences, well it was only the one really and that was starting to develop all by itself. Appreciating that it wasn't going to be long before his excitement would make an unannounced appearance, between the edges of his dressing gown, he was hoping that she'd hurry up and leave. Unfortunately, she only seemed to be making matters worse by instinctively thrusting her hips at him as well. Realising exactly what was about to happen he closed his eyes and smiled when recognising that his discourteous behaviour could be blamed on the fact that he was still in the world of alcohol poisoning.

"Now let me see," she suddenly asserted like the teacher having caught him behind the bike shed doing something naughty. "Exactly what are you trying to hide?" Understanding that it was no good denying anything stopped breathing when she opened his dressing gown and looked directly at his erection. "Oh! You naughty boy,"

"I'm sorry," he cringed while trying to close the dressing gown as if wanting to hide something.

She was having none of it. "Now let me see," she said. "What we're going to do with that?" Having spoken there was a pause and then quite unexpectedly she bent and kissed the very tip of the purple head. Alan was shocked. He was even more shocked when she slipped the whole head inside her mouth and looked like as if she was about to perform oral sex on him. It was exactly a millisecond before she stood up. "Right," she shrugged. "That's it!" And with that she left the room. Okay it didn't last very long but when push comes to shove she did actually suck his cock.

It was on the following Friday while he was laying on his bed at around three o'clock, listening to Test Match Special on radio 4, that a sudden knock was heard on his door. "Come in," he instructed.

The door opened and Brenda pushed her head inside. "Hello," she smiled. "I'm just going for a walk and would you like to join me!"

"Okay," he replied and got off the bed. They walked like they'd done the week before and when they'd reached the bridge it was Alan, again, who was the first to cross. Standing he watched as Brenda stepped onto the wooden plinth and started to walk. Also like the previous time she stopped about halfway but this time she peered over the rail and studied the calm water below. "Do you want to know something?" She said.

"What?"

"I'd love to do something really naughty!"

"Like what?"

"How about going skinny dipping?"

"But that would mean taking off all of your clothes."

"I didn't mean that naughty," she smiled.

"Then what kind did you mean?"

"I was only going to strip down to my underwear."

"Oh!" He huffed rather disappointedly. "I suppose that'll be alright."

She turned to look at him. "Is there anywhere that's a little bit more secluded," asked the question. "Because I don't want any Tom, Dick or Harry looking at me."

"Come on," he smiled as he led the way to an isolated bend in the river much used by people for the very same sort of thing. She returned the smile when climbing the last fence and saw the small white flowers of meadowsweet. Her smile was perfect when noticing a blue and orange kingfisher perched on the overhanging branch with its sharp bill ready for his next meal. "Here we are," he smiled with arms akimbo.

"Thank you," she returned, and then almost immediately started undoing the buttons of her pink blouse before taking it off. Alan just stood and stared. He licked his lips when seeing the flimsy material of her bra, and his grin got even greater when she removed her skirt to show off the fragile mystery of her custard yellow knickers. "Aren't you going to join me," asked the question as she slid down the bank and entered the water. He didn't need any encouragement as he stripped down to his underwear and stood, on the edge of the riverbank, looking down at her. Then like a graceful jellytot jumped into the water and surfaced beside her.

"Hello," he smiled as he instinctively looked at just how unmistakably erotic her tits were as they showed through the wet material. The two half crown sized aureoles looked perfect with each containing a rigid nipple that obviously didn't need any further sexual stimulation to make them any firmer.

As they played and swam about like two randy teenagers he was in paradise and it was at one point when lying side by side, on the grass, she calmly stated, "Do you remember telling me that I might like it if I put my hand down inside my knickers?"

For a moment he thought. "Oh! Yes," he smiled as an erotic picture developed inside his head. "Wasn't it when we were discussing what your mother had put in her diary?"

"That's right," she confirmed.

"So what did you do about it?"

"I went to the train station and brought a rather naughty book to read."

"What, the porno type," he wondered. "Where there are graphic descriptions about the sexual act in all its gory detail."

"No," she shivered. "It was better than that."

"How can it be better?"

"Maybe not for you," she ultimately stated. "But for me it was an eye opener."

"In what sense?"

"Because as I read the words I was taken on a sexual journey that allowed my fertile imagination to complete the story."

"Oh," he frowned. "So what's this got to do with putting your hand inside your knickers?"

"Well after reading the first four chapters," she smiled. "It got me thinking."

"About what?"

"Can you remember when I came into your room and I saw you in your dressing gown."

"Oh! Yes," he grinned as a corrupt, and immoral, picture developed.

"And if I remember rightly," she sighed. "You'd got an erection?"

"You know I had!"

"And can you remember what I did when I saw it?"

"How could I forget."

There was a moments pause as she got onto her elbows and looked him straight in the eyes. Well she wasn't actually looking into his eyes but was infact staring at the large bulge in his underpants. "What would you say if I wanted to see your little willy again," she grinned like a naughty schoolgirl.

"It's not that little anymore," he grinned like the schoolboy who was also behind that same bike shed. "And, only if I can see yours,"

Her response was immediate, "Okay!" And with that she rather awkwardly lifted her buttocks and removed her wet pants. "There!" He grinned with pure lust when seeing the rather hairy bush of her cunt and true to his word he removed his underpants. "Do you also remember the words that my mother wrote in her diary about the night you went into her bedroom by mistake?"

"How can I forget."

"And what happened after she'd put you to bed?"

"Remind me."

"She did something like this," she mumbled. Having spoken she clambered onto his chest and needing no instruction turned her back and got into the classic sixty nine position.

It was the next day and he was a little surprised when Brenda stepped into his room, with a parcel, and spoke to him. "I'm leaving in a couple of hours," she reluctantly said as they simply stood about a foot apart looking at each other.

"Are you," he smiled and then added. "So don't forget that naughty book you brought the other day when we were in town!"

"I shan't," she said while handing him the parcel. "And anyway I'd like you to have this."

"What is it?" He mused while undoing the paper and having finally unravelled its secret stared at the small model boat sitting on a wooden plinth.

"It was mother's favourite," she explained. "And I'm sure she'd like you to have it." Having given the present she simply watched him.

Alan gave a series of grunts as he scanned the small words etched on the metal band sitting below that infamous boat. "This is for all the help you've given me," read his stage whispered words and as this slowly sank in he awkwardly turned and stared at the woman gazing out of the window. With her back to him Alan could survey her with feminine appreciation. Her short, but well defined chubby legs disappeared beneath the floral hem of her skirt. Moving higher her large pear shaped buttocks drew his eyes if for no other reason than pledging their attraction. Her far from slender hips screamed in the quiet language of desire. Higher still, until spotting the white bra straps clearly visible through the transparent fibres of her blouse. Remembering the previous day he stepped forward and raced his arms around her rather bulky midriff. He closed his eyes as she fell back into his hungry arms, and all the while found the time to send his curious hands on a trip of erotic discovery. His heart pounded when feeling just how ripe her covered tits were. Beneath the hemline of her skirt he roamed before delving inside the silky threads of her pants. "Oh! Yes," she swooned as he started to work a single finger inside her cunt. "Please!" She begged as he immorally kissed the fine skin of her neck and then hearing this unmistakable command swung her around to directly look at her. He licked his dry lips, but drooled with uncontrollable desire when pushing her back onto the bed as he had her mother, and with that same carnal instinct ripped her blouse apart to send the seven buttons everywhere. But before those buttons had even landed he'd quite simply removed her lovely tits and eagerly began to play with them. It was some moments later that he stood before reaching and dragging her skirt away to reveal the pale pinks of her lingerie. He panted because there was nothing, absolutely nothing, going to stop him from ripping her knickers from her body. As they were tossed to the floor his heartbeat was explosive as he looked at the erotic way she opened her legs and showed off the vertical slit of her cunt. Seeing how lush it was his physical need was urgent as he tore at his clothes until posing as nature had intended. They performed like considerate lovers, but not a word was spoken only the occasional grunt of satisfaction as they wrestled together. He on top, then her, and then him behind.

Fully satisfied they must have drifted to sleep as they lay snuggled together, but he awoke to find himself alone. He searched the room, hoping to find a clue, but seeing no-one realised that she'd obviously gone to catch the train and return to the welcoming, but sexless, arms of her husband. Suddenly he spotted that gift she'd given him. He grinned like a Cheshire cat when also seeing the pair of knickers hanging so seductively from the yardarm because at that moment he understood. It wasn't the fact that Brenda might be sitting in a train carriage somewhere wearing no knickers because he was holding them. It wasn't even the fact that she might also be getting sexually aroused when reading from that dirty, and explicit, book she'd brought. It wasn't either of these because he knew what to do. He closed his eyes and began to laugh as he marched up to the gift and studied it. He had no conscious control when his fingers cleanly snapped the mainmast and held it like a jewel. He grinned as the edge of a piece of paper came perfectly into view. It read, "In the place where the girl will follow the Crusade you might find some borage."

It was late October when Alice finally decided to walk out on her philandering husband and move into Calder's with both of her children. It had happened quite unexpectedly and the first indication of her presence was when the front door burst open and in she strolled. "The bags are in the car," her methodical voice announced as she swept passed her open mouthed brother.

With him being delegated to bring in the cases Alan laboured, and complained, on that blustery afternoon so with each journey to and from the overloaded car he bided his time. But, patience had never been his greatest virtue and thinking that an hour was plenty long enough asked his rather insensitive, but logical question, "Why are you here?"

Alice took him to one side and masqueraded, like the dutiful but wronged wife, and placed both hands on her hips. She sighed at having to justify her presence and looked directly into his curious gaze. "It's far to complicated a reason to explain," was her only admittance and no matter how he tried to gather any further information he soon realised that what had happened was not open to discussion, or general debate.

It was a fortnight later when he lurched into the kitchen. "Morning," he snapped and as he blearily glanced around the room his heart sank with brotherly derision when seeing his mother grinning from ear to ear. She'd been in that state since her daughter's return and was probably due to the fact that Alice had told her a little, well it was gigantic really, white lie inasmuch as she'd come home to take care of her. As he shuddered with a guilty conscious he continued to look and smile because sat next to him was the amiable Clara, and on the other side was the precocious Wayne. Both youngsters had been, until two days ago, the apples of their grandmother's eye but what had happened Alan was never to know.

"You'll have to go to bed earlier," prompted his mother as she sipped from the cup of tea in her still shaky hand. Although she had made fantastic progress towards normality she still had difficulties in hiding the little quivers of cerebral injury. Her swaying movements, while walking, were hardly noticeable and only then because she had to make the point of informing the watcher. Everyone wrongly assumed that she'd reached the pinnacle of self reliance but never thought to give her any recognition for the constant battle to live in the real world. Whatever that is!

"I did," he scowled. "Infact it was half passed nine when I went." There was no more spoken until his finger pointed at his sister. "But, it's her."

"I don't know what you mean," returned the coy denial.

He knew he was onto a winner and so continued the attack. "I don't suppose it was you arriving back in the early hours of the morning," he barked. "And making plenty of farmyard noises outside."

"Alan," slapped the voice of his mother taking her daughter's side as she frequently did since the day of his birth. "Stop it!"

"But, it's true," he defended while buttering himself some toast.

"Well, that's as maybe," his mother insisted. "But, she's here to look after me and I don't begrudge her some time to herself." Hearing this Alan, who was about to speak, noticed his sister attentive scowl and realising the consequences decided that discretion would be the better part of valour and so bit his tongue.

The atmosphere now hung like a sleazy bordello until a voice of pure innocence, or was it mischief, piped up. "Why, what was mummy doing?" Hearing Clara's question Alan half choked on the piece of toast that had somehow become lodged in his throat. As he sputtered, for breath, his eyebrows rose in the mode of knowledge because how could he explain having seen the child's mother having a sexual wrestling match with Gary Chartenhouse, the village stud, on the bonnet of their car.

He spluttered as Alice, rather harshly, thumped his back. "Your uncle's being silly," she sniggered. Having finally regained his composure Alan smirked with delight when seeing that there was no colour difference between his sister's face and the beetroot red skirt she happened to be wearing. The playful banter continued as everyone sat around discussing various topics of interest and when the mention of the local fair cropped up it caused the congenial talk to become even more excited, especially from the two kids. I know the politically correct brigade will have a field day with that description but as it says in the front of the book; this is fiction.

"When are we going?" Erupted the combined question from both Wayne and Clara.

"Tonight," their mother offered. "If that's okay with Uncle Alan," her contriving voice explained. Hearing this he was dumbstruck, as again a lump of buttered toast seemed to become lodged in his windpipe, and for that he started choking again. "And that's of course he's decided not to pop his clogs." As he sat contemplating his existence he understood that his nightly jaunt to the pub had just been shelved, thanks to his sister, and with that though bouncing inside his head sighed.

After breakfast it was simply a race to see who had the courage to take over the bathroom and leave the other struggling with painful bladders and other functions. Eventually, having been given that final spot yet again Alan turned the hot tap and placed his flickering fingers in the stream of cold water hoping that enough had be left for him to enjoy the daily task of shaving. His heart sank, as it never even came close to being warm, and with a deep groan of annoyance splashed his face in preparation. Shaving soap does not froth very well when cold, and so with this handicap struggled to get barely enough to make the effort worthwhile and the five pink blotches of toilet paper highlighting the fact that he'd been unsuccessful. The cause was either a blunt razor, which seemed very unlikely since he'd put a new blade in yesterday, or more probably Alice who'd used it on her legs and other various locations about her body. Not wanting to be seen, and made to look the fool, crept into his bedroom and decided that today was the day that he'd start looking for work. What made the whole thing laughable was that he'd thought exactly the same thing yesterday, and the day before that.

"Post's here," shouted the familiar voice of his sister as he walked out of his room and stood at the top of the stairs looking down. There was a definite pause. "Alan, there's one for you," proclaimed her call while sniffing the envelope. "And it smells like you've got a female admirer." Down the stair he flew and literally snatched the offered communication being waved like a flag. With it in his grasp and without opening it scampered back to his room and hurriedly closed the door. Feeling excited; he fell onto the bed to lie prone gazing at the ceiling, and once there spotted another cobweb dangling from where two corners meet. His heart pounded tearing apart the seal, and with trembling fingers extracted the letter. He bit his tongue sharply as he read the first page. He grinned, from ear to ear, on reading the second. He threw out his arms in disbelief when seeing the signature beautifully inscribed at the bottom of the third.

The morning passed rather uneventfully as did the afternoon, but when half passed six arrived there came the call that brought both pleasure and excitement. "Are we going to fair yet?" Demanded two happy voices as Clara and Wayne ran into the sitting room. Glancing at his watch and having nothing better to do Alan jumped from the seat and hurried after them. According to his sister's travelling arrangements he was to take the children, because they'd been badgering her all day in wanting Uncle Alan to take them, and she was going to take their grandmother as well as picking up the Colonel. Realising that it was going to be pointless complaining agreed that on reaching town they were to meet in the car park. The evening had pulled in sufficiently for the black of night to be awash with the multicoloured glow from the stalls and rides. There were shouts of uncontrollable joy as punters kept exchanging money for the promised good times. "Who'll take me on the dodgems?" croaked the hoarse voice of Wayne as they gathered by the sparking brilliance.

"I will," cried the offer as the Colonel took the boy's hand and moved towards the kiosk. Once ready, the spectators witnessed the ruthless nature of the driver's skill. Everybody laughed as Wayne kept violently nudging other cars so that he was classically termed an annoyance, especially to other drivers, and as a consequence they were banished from that stall with a beady eye and hostile curse.

Moving around the crowded site, the smell of paraffin hung in the air, as did the aroma of sausages and overdone onions. As they passed the candyfloss stall a cry of want rose above the sound. "Can I have some," screamed the plea from both children as they pulled towards the swirls of reddish pink.

"No!" Their mother tried to enforce, and having said it everyone knew the consequence and true to form it was Wayne who threw the first paddy and refused to move. No matter what was said he turned down every offer of compromise until finally, to keep the peace, he got what he wanted. In time, and with the lack of muscular co-ordination, both children's faces were covered in the pink and white strands of spun sugar that just seemed to mass around their ever-eager mouths. It got everywhere. In their hair. On their clothes. In places that you would not think possible, but there it was.

It was after nine thirty when he thought he'd heard a female voice shouting his name. He turned and seeing no one carried on and having taken another two steps felt the tight grip of a hand resting on his shoulder. "Hello," the young girl smiled while naïvely thrusting her immature body at him.

"Oh! Hello," he sighed looking directly into the laughing smile of Tania Rutherford.

The Colonel had also spotted her, well he would wouldn't he, and had obviously noticed something immoral in the girl's conduct. "I think you might be on to a good thing," he insinuated looking directly at him.

"I don't think so," fired his defence as the young girl, who he'd often seen at cricket matches with her father, just stood with a very large and silly grin spreading across her face. She would be fourteen and five foot nothing tall. She had long mousey brown hair which was often pulled into a ponytail and tonight was one of those occasions. Even though she'd use plenty of make-up her face constantly resembled a Lunar Landscape, mainly due to the hormonal imbalance of puberty that caused the hills and hollows of the dreaded acne. She wore a brace across her tobacco stained teeth as well as wearing a pair of thick rimmed glasses, but apart from these little shortcomings she had all the hallmarks of a beautiful woman beginning to emerge.

The moment was shattered when Alice grabbed her brother's elbow and pulled him away with a quick question, "What's she want?"

"I don't know," he replied as Clara and Wayne returned with yet another stick of candyfloss. "Why don't you ask her?"

"I will," she grumbled while turning to their uninvited guest. Whether it was the atmosphere, the social occasion, or something entirely different but Alice looked directly at Tania before asking rather bluntly, "What d'yer want?"

Her answer was immediate. "Seeing that I've just split with my boyfriend I've got no-one who'll take me on some of the rides," she explained with a funny smile. "So when I saw Alan I was just wondering whether he'd like to take me on them." As they listened no-one could see her blushing, and if they had it wouldn't have made the slightest bit of difference. After a short discussion it was decided, by his sister, that her brother was to be the young girl's escort for the remaining time and at around eleven o'clock they would all meet up in the car park to arrange the journey home.

"Don't do anything that I wouldn't," teased the Colonel as he quaintly slipped his arm around his mother's waist. It was as the main party was disappearing, into the thick mass of revellers, that Alan quickly noticed exactly where the Colonel had now put his vibrant hand.

Now that he was alone with Tania he recalled hearing some rather juicy gossip, concerning this girl and her last boyfriend, from the infamous Betty Hasnik and so quickly demanded, "So why exactly did lover boy drop you?"

Almost immediately the answer came. "Because his wife found out about what was going on between us," Tania shrugged as if this kind of thing happened all the time. "And so he's gone back to Nottingham hoping to try and save his marriage!"

"Then good luck to him," he half smiled understanding the fickle complexities of an adult relationship.

"He'll need it."

"Why's that?"

"Because he told me that since the birth of their second child," she grinned. "His wife's put the kibosh on anything physical in the bedroom department."

"So he couldn't handle the fact that he wasn't getting his leg over at home."

"I suppose so!" She nonchalantly shrugged.

"And seeing as he's found someone," he continued. "Who's willing to drop their knickers, open their legs and allow nature to make a stand then he's fine about it?"

Hearing this rather nifty observation she frowned, "Oh! You mean that I would let him put his dangler in my wee hole."

"Of course that's what I meant."

"Well actually," she shuddered. "He never did put Percy to bed."

"Come again," returned his somewhat shocked response. "You're telling me that he never actually humped you!"

"Of course not," she shuddered. "What kind of girl d'yer think I am?"

Being tactful, if at all possible, he slightly moved his line of questioning just like any good lawyer and said, "So what are you saying?"

"Well," she giggled. "All he wanted to do was look and take pictures of my wee hole."

"Lucky blighter," he stage whispered while realising the condemnation he would get from various moralistic plebs even though they, themselves, would also be thinking along similar lines. "So when did he, as you so quaintly put it, have a look at your wee hole?"

Hearing the question she visibly became excited. "I once told him that I wanted to become an actress when I was older," she shuddered.

"That ole chestnut," he laughed. "And I suppose he told you that if he could take your photograph then he might be able to get you a starring role in the film he knew was being produced."

"How did you know?"

"Just an assumption," he grinned. "And were these photographs taken in a studio with a chaperone?"

"No," she smiled while thrusting her rather flattish chest at him. "Because he said it would be far better if they were taken outdoors as the natural light would bring out the beauty of my young and attractive body."

"Right," he goaded. "So where did he take you?"

"Down bull lane."

"Didn't you find it a bit funny that he wanted to take you there," he smiled because he knew that at the end of the lane was an old barn and he also remembered showing Erin just how isolated it was.

"He told me that it would make a lovely background to the photographs."

"I think he was going to be more interested in what was going to be in the foreground."

There was a pause. "Why?" She wondered.

"Think about it," he grinned. There was another pause before she abruptly grinned when understanding exactly what was meant. "Anyway, these photographs," he continued.

"Yes."

"What kind were they?" He speculated with a slight knowledge concerning their erotic content.

"Of me in my favourite dress."

"What, all of them?"

"Course not," she admitted. "Because he did ask me whether I'd be willing to pose without my clothes on."

"You declined."

"Definitely," she smirked. "That was until he suggested that a terrific shot would be of me lying facedown but naked on a bale of straw." He closed his eyes, in abject, horror when realising that here was another innocent schoolgirl caught in the sleazy world of the dirty Mac brigade. "But he did say that he'd make sure that there would be absolutely none of my naughty bits showing."

"And you believed him?"

"Of course," she smiled as she grabbed his hand and gave it a squeeze. "The man was most upstanding."

"I sure he would have been," he whispered. "So what happened?"

"After he'd taken maybe three, or four, he suddenly asked me to turn over and lay on my side."

"And did you?"

"Not to start with," she naïvely grinned. "But when he explained that producers wanted to see the real me then yes I did."

"Now that he could photograph you naked did he, at any time, try and grope you?"

"What d'yer mean?"

"Did he try and get you into a better position by using his hands to move you about?"

"What!" Slurred her first word while scanning his smirking face and realised exactly what he meant. "Oh! You mean did he touch my tits and fanny."

"Well, did he?"

"No," she owned up. "Though I've got to admit!"

"What?"

"That when he asked me to sit on a bale of straw with my legs open so that he could get a better picture," she admitted. "And I saw him staring I suddenly got a funny tingling sensation in my tummy."

"And would you like to try and describe this feeling?"

"I can't," she trembled. "But what I can say is that when I noticed the bulge in his trousers I so much wanted him to put his hands on me."

Realising what may have been happening to her grinned, "I presume the reason you felt that way was because your hormones were starting to kick in."

Whether she understood what he meant or not but suddenly she goaded in a voice that dripped a very young, but very sexy, teenage dare, "If you'd have been there would you have wanted to touch me?"

Hearing this rather double edged question he closed his eyes and instantaneously reopened them. He'd done that simply because in his mind's eye he was there taking those indecent photographs and realising that he'd just become another dirty ole man grinned. "Maybe not," he reluctantly offered as the word paedophile ricochet inside his head.

"Is it because I'm flat chested?"

"Not at all."

"Why then," asked her words. "Because my mum's told me that she had small breasts when she was my age but now look at the size of her tits."

"I hadn't really noticed," he lied. "And anyway not every man likes big knockers."

"Don't they?"

"No," he teased. "Some just like to get a nice handful."

"Which do you prefer?" She enquired while urgently taking his hand and placing it the outside of her pale cream anorak. "Mine or my mums."

"I'm not answering that."

"Why?"

"It might incriminate me," he ridiculed. "So let's get back to the Nottingham Lech."

There was a blank expression until the penny suddenly dropped, "Oh, you mean Tim."

"If that's his name," Alan indicated with a shrug of his shoulders. "Then yes!"

"Okay!"

"Is that all he did?"

"Pretty much."

His response was classic. "So all he was interested in was taking mucky pictures of an underage girl," he started. "With obviously no intentions of molesting her."

"Is that so wrong?"

"Only if the do-gooders, of this world, find out."

"Why, what's it got to do with them anyway?"

"Because in their eyes," he started to lecture. "They believe that every man who's ever had an erotic thought concerning a naked underage girl should be castrated and fed to the lions."

"But surely that's natures way," she answered. "The youngest. The prettiest. The sexiest will always attract a mate and help the genetic pool continue."

"So you did pay attention in the biology lessons?"

"Of course I did," she smirked. "But the sex lessons were a bit crap because we just concentrated on the reproductive cycle of an aphid."

"So things haven't changed?"

"Not really," she admitted. "Because I found out more about a boy behind the bike shed than I ever did from listening to Miss Guided."

"Is she still teaching?"

"You had her?"

"Unfortunately yes," he admitted. "And she was getting towards senility when I was at school."

"So how did you learn about girls?"

"Probably behind the same bike shed you'd used," he smiled as the memory of one Linda Caswell sprang to mind. "And we also had a varied selection of top shelf magazines to help."

"See," she frittered. "We girls don't have things like that to show us what a naked man looks like."

"Not a pretty sight," he laughed as he began feeling uncomfortable, especially in the groin region. Trying to change direction he asked, "So did you learn anything while you were with matey?"

"Only that his wife sounded nice when I rang her up."

"Why did you do that?"

She shrugged her shoulders. "Revenge," she admitted. Whether it was because someone bumped into them, or not, but they got extremely close and it was at one point that she pushed her small hand between their bodies and groped the bulge in his trousers. "That's nice," she cooed when he realised that here was a young girl trying to become a woman.

"Tania!" He scolded while hurriedly grabbing her wrist and pulling it into sight.

"Spoilsport!" She teased.

"That's not for little girls," he baited while adjusting himself. "And anyway it's illegal."

"Only if they find out," her truthful exposé proclaimed as she skipped towards one of the fair's notorious rides. Onto the boards of the swirling Waltzer they stepped, and into one of the buckets they dropped. It was slow to start with, but as the speed increased the centrifugal force seemed to take control. Whether it was the happy-go-lucky atmosphere of the occasion that compelled the girl to grab one of his hands and drag it towards her anorak covered body but he smirked lecherously, like any pervert, knowing full well that he could not prevent the Laws of Physics taking control as his hand ultimately settled on the smallish mound of an underdeveloped bosom. The thrill was magnified, some ten fold, when his heartbeat increased because he could actually feel just how soft it was as they spun wildly around inside that car. Eventually the ride slowed which allowed him to discretely remove his overheated hand and smile his thanks.

"Let's go in here!" She insisted while snatching his wrist and pulling him. Inside the Hall of Mirrors they roamed, as reflections varied with every gaze and it was about halfway through that she did the unthinkable. While posing in front of the mirror that makes the top half, of a body, look bigger she quickly undid her anorak and pulled up her pale blue T-shirt. Next she quickly lifted both cups of her training bra and thrust her chest forward. "Look at my tits now," she giggled as she continued to pose.

Hearing the instruction he stopped dead in his tracks and looked at the hypnotic illusion of her comely bosom. "Stop it," he insisted.

"But I thought you might like to see them," She smirked. "Because I know Tim did."

"He may have done," fired his concern. "But you're underage!" With that they left and continued around the fair and it was at one point they saw the Colonel with the others.

"How about going on there," she begged while moving towards the swinging carriage of the Big Wheel. They tried the coconut shy and failed. The Win a Goldfish stall proved profitable as they walked away with a cuddly bear and they ate their fill of hot dogs. "How about going to see the fortune teller!" She giggled as they strolled towards the white caravan displaying what might be inside. When seeing the photos, of various celebrities on the board outside, he was game for a laugh and so reached inside his pocket for the money. He paid for them both to enter and with surreal elegance stepped inside. Through the door they walked and moved through the thick curtain and into the splendour of that bordello styled interior. The place was empty and peering at everything immoral Tania would not let go of his hand, as they stood fractionally apart. The pure mystery was enhanced by the soft lighting that perfectly complimented the fine silk sheets that were everywhere, and the musty scent must have made the young girl's head swim with desire. "Hold me," she craved while shuddering with an uncontrollable appetite. "I feel faint." He thought for a second of any legal repercussions, but then did as was told. She fell into his arms as his hands struggled around her rather chubby waist. They remained like that for some moments until she grabbed his right hand. "Grope me," she implored while making him fondle the insignificance of her left breast.

"No!" He rightly insisted when realising the legal implications if he'd have been caught.

"But I want you to feel a bit of a tit!"

Suddenly there was a sharp cough which unfortunately announced that they were now not alone. "Who's first," the wizened looking crone smiled through broken and tobacco stained teeth.

"Me," Tania eagerly announced with a giggle. Understanding the privacy needed Alan turned and walked outside. He leaned against the caravan and sighed his thanks while watching various people walking by, and it was about two minutes later that the door suddenly burst open and Tania reappeared sobbing.

"What's wrong," asked his rather stupid question.

"It's what she's told me," she whined with real tears streaming down her face.

"And what was that," he endeavoured to discover as his arms went around her trembling shoulders as support.

"When she looked at my palms," her opening gambit started. "She saw that I was going to enter a monastic convent at eighteen both pure and chaste."

"But that implies you'll be a virgin?"

"I know," wept her words.

"But surely you've already sampled the earthy delights of having a quick hump with what's his name?"

"No," she remonstrated. "As I explained I never once let him have sex with me."

"That's probably why he finished because you wouldn't let him have is evil way," his rather simplistic view explained. "And anyway you have to appreciate that the gypsy's reading may well be completely wrong." She wasn't listening as she stormed away muttering rather crudely to herself. It took a bit of a struggle to catch her up, but eventually he did. They talked for some moments, hoping to clear the air, and having reached a compromise continued around the stalls. They stopped here and there to have goes on the one sided games that all fairs specialise in and in doing so soon discovered that he was being led towards the notorious Priesthood Alley and away from the fair. Slowly, as his eyes were becoming accustomed to the dark he started picking out couples exchanging very personal touches as the grunts and groans confirmed the obvious enjoyment that was being had. It was about two thirds along that he thought he recognised the woman, with her back to him, as a couple of male hands slipped down the back of the jeans and started to vigorously rub her sumptuous arse.

"That's what I want you to do to me," Tania explained as she deliberately stopped forcing him to reach out his hands in order to prevent any collision between them.

"I can't," he sighed as he accidentally, though it may have been on purpose, felt just how soft her arse actually was.

"Don't you want to touch me?"

"Maybe when you've grown up a bit!"

"But I'm ready now," she cooed as she walked away with the usual feminine strop. No more was spoken until Tania suddenly halted and it was here, where it was sufficiently dark, that she placed her arms around his neck. Now alone he reluctantly accepted her inexperienced attempt at a kiss and even allowed her to take his hands before carefully placing them on the taut material of her very short skirt which seemed totally inadequate to cover her bum, but when he refused to instigate what she thought sexually normal she scowled her disapproval. "Don't you think I'm sexy enough?" She questioned.

"It's not that!" He admitted as he valiantly fought the desire to get inside her knickers.

"What is it then?"

"For starters," he groaned. "According to the law of the land it's illegal for me to fumble with a minor."

"I know!"

"What d'yer mean you know," he grouched because he was staring at a fourteen year old girl desperately trying to become a woman and not quite knowing how to control the sexual chemistry that she'd been born with, and to make matters even worse never would. He sighed in frustration as he stepped towards the girl and with controlled anger snatched her wrist. His grip was tight as he pulled her to his side. Their bodies touched, but there was no physical attraction as they marched back to the gaiety of the fair.

"See that witch's prediction is coming true," she squealed in a high pitch that seemed to penetrate his mind. "And I'm going to die a virgin." Once back amongst the overflowing stalls she instantly spotted several of her friends who were just about to go on the ghost train, and with a callus wave left poor Alan grinning his salvation. He stood a moment and reflected on just how easily the young girl's disappointment changed into one of delight.

Wondering what the time was he glanced at his watch. It was a quarter to eleven, and deciding that it would make good sense he started to walk back to the parked car. He got there dead on time, but unfortunately his passengers came ominously into view about an hour later with no apology.

"Look Uncle Alan," proclaimed Clara as she held aloft the scrawny goldfish that she'd obviously won.

"Yes," he muttered while scowling at his laughing sister. "Very nice!"

Eventually they drove off, but not before the seating arrangements had been altered. "Can you take mum and the Colonel home?" Alice insisted as she got into her car with her kids.

Speculating what she might be up to he watched as she disappeared from view in completely the opposite direction. "I wonder who the unfortunate man's going to be," he softly stage whispered.

"What did you say?" questioned his mother from the back seat.

"Oh! It was nothing," he admitted, but very quietly added his envious footnote, "The one who's going to test the elasticity of my sister's underwear!" The drive back to the Colonel's house was fairly straightforward except for the fact that he kept imaging that a pair of headlights were constantly dazzling him. For the umpteenth time he gripped the wheel that bit tighter, but this time that apparent same car suddenly increased speed and started to overtake. When it came level he suddenly felt the steering becoming laborious, and as he tried to keep a straight line the other vehicle swerved violently towards the curb. The huge amount of adrenaline rushing through his body forced him to overcome the terror as the car slid from the road and started to skid. The moon shone its awesome glow as panic controlled his every muscle and his every thought. The clarity of his life flashed before his eyes as the darkened outline of a tree hurtled towards him. Instinct now controlled his action as his feet hit the brake and clutch pedals, in the standard emergency stop mode, but unlike the test situation his eyes slammed shut as well. Whether this was the right thing to do, or not, made very little difference because he'd done just enough to redirect the wooden bough from its intended path. Finally, having come to rest amongst the overgrown forest of cow parsley and briers of that country lane sweat pored from his skin and drenched his shirt, and as for his bowel movements his clean underwear had been stained with the stench of fear.

"Is everyone okay?" His squeaky voice asked as he twisted his head to look at his passengers, and as he stared his heart exploded. He'd been so busy concentrating on the his own route for survival that he was oblivious to the thick branch that had smashed through the windscreen and whipped over his left shoulder, but as he looked the shock was devastating when he saw just how easily it had been driven straight through the Colonel's chest. His mother's scream did little to relieve the horror as she stared at the lifeless features of the man at her side.

It was to be a long night for both Alan and his mother as they answered questions aimed with the subtlety of a loaded gun. It was nearing twilight when finally the detective inspector, and his overzealous colleagues, had gathered enough information to admit to it having probably been an accident but they would not go into details if they had their suspicions. Having given Alice a call to come and pick them up they waited and as time moved slowly by the feeling of being physically drained, probably due to lack of sleep, descended like the clouds around a mountain and once home they simply went straight to bed.

He awoke with a start when the bedroom door swung violently open and a head appeared. "Telephone," proclaimed the suspicious voice of his sister.

Still not in the land of the living he chugged down the stairs in just his pyjamas and spoke, "Hello!"

"Alan, is that you?" Asked a voice he thought he'd never hear again, and he suddenly smiled as the delicious image of her beauty converged inside his head.

"Erin!" His acknowledgement boomed. "Where are you?"

"Never mind that," she ordered. "Just listen because I haven't got long."

His heart was beating faster as he had to ask, "What is it?"

There was no delay with her words, "I'd come home un-expectantly yesterday afternoon when I overheard Patrick talking to." She never said anymore as the sound of an opening door was heard in the background. "I've got to go."

There was a moment's delay before the telephone went dead. "Erin!" He screamed into the mouthpiece when understanding that she didn't want to be discovered explaining something, or other, which may have been important and while listening to the dialling tone his active imagination played vivid pictures of a struggle flashing like stroboscopic lights.

Alan was just walking from the house, in the kind of weather that doesn't occur very regularly because it was really sunny, and as he thought about it the postman's van pulled up and Andrew Bird in his standard navy blue shorts sauntered lazily up the garden path. Having delved through his bag gave the five letters, doffed his fetlock and walked away. With the enthusiasm of an excited eunuch at a brothel Alan sorted them, and with nothing better to do returned inside and placed them on the hallway table. Whether it was coincidence, or not, but at that moment the telephone rang.

"Hello," he shrugged in the mode of nonchalance, and as he waited his nose scrunched up like an irritated child when no answer came. "Hello," he voiced rather forcibly as if trying to influence the caller. Still nothing was heard. Thinking that it might be another dodgy phone call, especially the type that his sister often got, he abrasively uttered his words. "If that's Noel Lake and you're after my sister," he started as an image of a scrawny looking excuse of a man came to mind. "Then from what she's told me you'll have to improve in the bedroom department and stop acting like a cunt!"

"Shut up and listen," demanded the trembling, but soft, voice. "Meet me beneath 103 at twelve thirty!" And with that the phone went dead.

The journey to his destination, which if driven at the legal speed limit would have taken just over an hour, but because of the weather conditions, took precisely twenty-eight minutes. He broke most, if not, all of the rule in the Highway Code but with his mind focused the bike twitched and behaved beautifully as he thundered across deserted roads and around blind bends. With the sweat pouring down his face he pulled up and parked. Reflecting on his good fortune left the overheated machine and clambered over the wooden gate before starting his trek across the very muddy fields. He knew exactly where he was heading because it was a glorious hot day in July that he and Erin had toured Rutland, and it was when going down the locally known Red Hill and baring right came across that most beautiful of manmade structure that had been built, with numbered arches, to span the Welland valley with rail track. Having left the bike and with an inquisitive desire they'd traipsed across a couple of fields before halting beneath a specific arch of brick and it was here they'd laughed as they fell to the bone dry earth. They'd giggled, like rutting rabbits, as they instinctively understood the other's smile. With eager fingers there was no reluctance when with deft appreciation Alan slowly removed Erin's biking leathers for her. She could have done it herself but where's the romance in that? They made love before watching the purest of sunsets lingering along the horizon to the west. With that intimate dream spurring him forward and it was as he neared that exact arch that his heartbeat increased exponentially. He trembled as he turned and walked beneath that canopy and felt weak when seeing Erin leaning against the brickwork. He froze in panic as she saw him because she never moved. Then it was as if a powerful spring had been released, because they literally flew at each other. Alan held her not wanting to let go. Erin wrapping her arm swiftly around his neck as the tears of joy soaked his flesh. As one they held each other as no words were spoken, although from time to time Alan kissed her head and ran his fingers through those auburn locks of hair. Time meant nothing when listening to the haunting wind rushing inside that cavern of brick. They stood together, but in different worlds of imagination. "Hold me tighter," she begged, and so he did.

    His arms were strong, and protective, and as he felt the softness of her body he whispered softly, "Let's go home."

    "No," she insisted while symbolically digging her heels in and refusing to move, and no matter how hard he tried there was no way that she would change her mind. Looking, with a little more intent, suddenly noticed the glow. He glanced down to detect that she'd put on a little weight since the last time they'd met and it didn't need a mastermind to fathom out the possible cause. "You're pregnant," he deduced.

"Yes!" She softly admitted with hardly any volume to her voice.

"So you finally got, what's his name, to participate in some up and down exercise."

She lifted her face, but a moment. "Oh! You mean Patrick?" And the tone of her voice sent the clearest of messages. "And you think he's the father?"

"Well isn't he?"

"I know you never passed your o-level Biology," she teased. "But surely even you can work out whose naughty tadpoles made me this way."

Whether he was deliberately trying to be thick but eventually even he knew the answer. "You mean mine," he acknowledged with an exaggerated stutter.

"Of course one of them was yours," she confirmed. "Because who else d'yer think I've been sleeping with?" This time she lifted her gaze and her eyes sparkled. She pouted and her luscious lips seemed to be glowing as she raced her tongue around them. She allowed her body to tremble; it wasn't a tremble of worry but was the tremble of expectant motherhood. The dimple, in the corner of her mouth, seemed to pulse as she grabbed his face and dragged it close. "Yes," she smiled. "It's yours!"

"Erin!" He craved while pulling her towards his excited frame and cuddled her like there was no tomorrow.

It was about half an hour later that they strolled into the pub where they'd stayed that July night. "Evening," welcomed the same red-faced landlord, of the aptly named Mucky Duck, as they walked to the bar.

"You probably don't remember us," Alan started. "But, we stayed here a couple of nights earlier in the year," he continued while taking out some money and paying for the drinks he'd just bought.

The landlord scrutinised both youngsters with his deep blue eyes, curled his lip and took the money. He turned his back towards the till and confidently answered, "If I remember rightly it was Mr and Mrs Smith." Why Mr and Mrs

Smith, well not being married they had to use some sort of alias and anyway they thought that because this particular set of names were seldom used in such an immoral context believed it to be quite appropriate.

Both smiled and partially coloured with embarrassment, and it was a second later that Alan came up with a suggestion, "Could we please impose on your generosity and stop again?"

The landlord thought while rubbing his chin. "Of course you can," confirmed the warm voice coming into view. It was after closing time that the portly looking lady cast her arms wide, and gestured for her guests to follow. They were led upstairs and shown into that same room, and once the door closed they were alone. With euphoric pleasure surging through his veins Alan helped as Erin slowly removed her clothes until finally standing in just her pants and bra. Like the story book hero he picked her up and carried her to the bed and once there she simply lay motionless looking up. As he gazed down he perceived the slight but definite bulge in her belly? He gave a smile a mile wide as he just stared at her.

"Come, lay with me," begged her voice, and like an adoring lover he removed his clothes and did as was instructed. "Hold me," she requested as he slipped an arm beneath her shoulders. They slept as one until the rising of the sun crashed through the curtains, and Alan stared because he could not remember closing them. He turned and saw that Erin was still asleep and for about a quarter of an hour grinned, like a doting husband, while watching how she twitched awkwardly before opening her eyes. Once awake, she returned his smile with one of her own that caused the hormonal attraction to force their mouths together. They sat up in bed, and then glancing around the room Alan felt Erin's grip suddenly get stronger when noticing that a change of clothes had somehow found their way onto a chair. Seeing what there was she deliberately threw off the bed covers and stood. Like any expectant mother she carefully examined each piece of clothing before smiling her obvious thanks. "I want to use the bathroom," she declared while turning towards Alan. Getting onto his elbows he watched her strip, and while watching was quick to notice that his clothes had also disappeared. Having stripped she turned and allowed Alan's gaze to absorb just how hypnotic her changing body had become. He smirked intensively at just how erotic the two discs of her aureoles were becoming and were also turning darker. He smiled to himself as she carelessly walked away and seeing this felt on top of the World watching the exaggerated sway of her arse as she disappeared from view.

"Alan," shouted a happy voice emanating from the bathroom. With concern he raced towards the door and stood watching the way she held her hands on her belly. She must have sensed his presence because she twisted her smiling face, and with no words being spoken grabbed his hand. "Can you feel it," she beamed as a kick was felt.

"Yes!" He grinned leaving his hand in place. "And another!" There was continued movement when suddenly the mood seemed to change.

"Alan!"

"Yes!"

"You can touch me!"

His pulse stopped, and he didn't know how to react when she rushed his frightened hand up against the astonishing firmness of her right breast. Having settled with his itching palms in place he could now savour just how rigid that nipple had become, for it felt just like a gigantic boulder. "I can't," his conscience pricked as he cowardly removed his shaking fingers.

"Why?"

He turned his head in embarrassment. He looked anywhere but at her worried frown. He knew he had to answer. "I don't want to hurt you," responded his natural concern as his gaze ranged over her motherly frame, and having delivered the statement returned to the bedroom. It was while dressing his mind fought the emotions that foraged out of control and it wasn't long before she returned to stand with impressive authority.

"Don't you find me attractive?" Her direct query posed as she stood her ground glaring like a volatile volcano about to erupt.

"Of, course I do," he admitted as he took her in his arms.

"No you don't," she squealed as her shoulders rocked with doubt. "How can you desire someone who's getting fatter by the day," she condemned as her hands lovingly moved over the gentle growth of that unborn child. He smarted when the next volley hit. "Look at my tits," she directed as she effortlessly cupped and offered them like two over-ripe grapefruits. Her words of self doubt shot across the divide, "They're ugly."

"No they're not," soothed his anxious words of comfort.

"Well, you don't want to play with them," she affirmed with a spiteful scowl. "You've made that perfectly plain."

"That's not true," he declared, and as if to justify the claim his not so eager hands reached and held the firm tissue.

Not waiting, and with an unknown strength she pushed him away. Was it anger in her actions when quite dramatically she twisted away? "Look at me!" She wailed and the tone of her voice trembled with uncertainty as the first signs of the dreaded stretch mark syndrome came plainly into view.

"To me you look beautiful," he smiled as his gaze travelled over every aspect of her body.

"Don't make me laugh," she started. "You men are all the same."

Alan shrugged his shoulders, "Why's that!"

Her next comment was below the belt, in more ways than one, "You were quite content to fondle and fuck me when I was slim and beautiful, but now I'm in this state you don't want to know!"

He felt hurt. He felt degraded and not quite knowing what to do just stared with eyes moving up and down, and it was when he'd reached her face that he saw the dimple beginning to twitch. He stepped forward and drew her close. She struggled gamely as he licked his lips and offered them as a sign of peace. They kissed, and as they were kissing he became aware of his hand being taken on a journey. "I want you," she softly whispered as her own steady hand delved inside his trousers. "I want you to fuck me," she begged.

He was now in a quandary inasmuch as he believed that if he did as requested he would breach, or tear, the delicate tissue that housed the unborn child. If he didn't then they'd both feel the frustration of denial? Finally, after a lengthy debate he trembled as he pushed her away, "I can't!"

"See, you're just full of hot air," clawed her sarcastic comment. Not wanting to be goaded he closed his eyes. "Please!" She begged as she fell onto the bed and posed like an expectant whore.

He strolled to the edge of the bed and gazed at just how alluring she'd become. He looked down and thought. He then realised that it might be the hormonal imbalance taking effect, and controlling her desires. He bit his lip and it was painful. He forced his eyebrows high as he glanced at the puffy entrance to her body. "But, won't it hurt?" Spluttered his concern.

"I'll tell you if it does."

"Then, say you're sorry," he teased and smiled.

"Shan't!"

"Why not?" He probed while starting to remove his shirt and trousers.

"Because!"

"I accept your apology," his lecherous voice usurped as he carefully lifted her buttocks.

They walked downstairs only to be greeted by the landlady standing by the telephone. "Did you sleep well?" She asked with a beaming grin a mile wide.

The youngsters returned the smile, "Like logs."

"It's the country air," their host continued with a giggle of knowledge. Then turning her head to look directly at Erin she continued, "I hope the dress fits."

Brushing down the pleats. "Like a glove," Erin thanked.

"It used to be my daughter's," smiled the reply as the woman carefully adjusted various pieces of the dress material. "That's better!"

Once everything was shipshape, and Bristol fashion, they followed the woman into the kitchen and were given breakfast. As they huddled around the table Jack Shears, because that was the landlord's name, started the conversation, "You must be wondering how I knew who you were?"

"I suppose you've got a fantastic memory," suggested Erin as she drank from the beaker of orange juice.

He glowed with pride. "Well, I think so," he admitted.

"And only then when it suits," sneaked his wife's retort.

As quick as a flash the man sniped, "I did remember your birthday."

"But, you tell our guests which year," continued the friendly onslaught.

"So, I forgot this one."

"And what about the others," came that cruellest of digs.

Sensing the man to be onto a loser Alan decided to get back to the original statement, "So, how did you remember?"

Whatever had happened, all those months ago, must have made a great impression. "Because it caused quite a stir the last time you were here," returned the answer.

Both Alan and Erin were curious as they turned their heads towards the man tucking into the large plate of bacon and eggs. "Why, what happened?" Asked the united question.

First he finished his mouthful, washed it down with a vast amount of strong tea and spoke. "After you'd gone," he started as another fork of breakfast disappeared. "A man and woman."

"Who we thought were your parents," instantly inserted Mrs Belinda Shears.

"Came knocking on our door asking questions," the man continued while finishing off the plateful of food.

There was a pause until Alan tried to influence, "What did they look like?"

The man simply shrugged his broad shoulders, turned to his wife and said, "I can't really remember." There was a moment's delay before asking his wife, "Can you?"

Mrs Shears turned her head away and thought. "Not really," came her reply. "But, I do remember the blue tattoos across the man's knuckles," she admitted with a smile.

Hearing this Erin froze. Her eyes were everywhere in panic. Her heart pounded against her chest as in her mind she saw her father's hand. Alan, on the other hand, saw the man in the paintings above the Colonel's bed showing tattooed fingers.

As one the two youngsters turned. The colour of their faces drained to resemble the lifeless skin of a corpse, and it was instinct that forced Alan to send his hand across and clutch Erin's. He could feel the tentative grip she gave as they tried to encourage the other. Finally, after the breakfast things had been cleared Erin turned and suggested, "Shall we go for a walk?"

It was about three o'clock, in the afternoon, when Alan and Erin returned only to watch Mrs Shears charging towards them. She looked concerned, she looked apprehensive and quickly explained that someone had called asking questions. "You didn't say anything," quizzed Alan looking somewhat alarmed.

"Only that you'd gone to London shopping and wouldn't be back until late tonight," returned the confirmation along with a sweet smile.

"Thanks!" The two youngsters sighed, and with that they raced up the stairs to disappear inside the bedroom.

They'd been in there for about twenty minutes when the door suddenly flew wide and in rushed Mrs Shears looking breathless again. "You'd better hurry!" Her strong statement declared.

"Why's that?"

"Because, as Jack was outside moving the crates of empty bottles a car pulled up and that same couple got out," she explained. "So I'm here to tell you that you'd better be going."

"Where are they now?"

"Downstairs in the bar."

Feeling brave, or was it stupid, Alan decided to see whether he could catch a glimpse of whoever they were. So along the landing he crept and silently down the stairs until looking through a sliver of light in the doorway. His heart pounded, with determination, as all he could see was the piano sitting in the corner. With aggravated survival surging through his sweating body he climbed the stairs yet again, and was about to step onto the landing when the shape of a man was seen emerging from one of the bedrooms which was about three doors before his. Alan pulled back a fraction, just in case he'd been seen, and stood panting for breath. Hearing another bedroom door open he quickly scanned ahead to see whether it was safe and seeing whoever it was disappearing into another room realised that he had but a fraction to respond. With his gut churning, as fear clawed its presence, he hurtled passed that open door before diving through his own.

"What's wrong," demanded the two women together.

"Someone's coming."

"I'll try and hold them as long as possible," Mrs Shears smiled moving towards the door and stepping onto the landing.

Panic now controlled their behaviour as they listened to voices discussing something or other. Feeling that they should make their escape quickly fled down the fire escape and towards the parked machine hidden beneath the over-hanging branches of a conker tree. His fingers trembled when he inserted the key, and as he turned it he prayed. The ignition fired first time, and now ready sped along the winding country lanes of Rutland. Travelling north through Oakham, and with daylight quickly dissolving into the pitch of night, they rode through nameless villages and it wasn't until they saw the name of a particular road did they realise that they'd actually reached Nottingham. Maid Marion's Way announced the metal plaque and as they cruised along the road Alan, suddenly felt a sudden thump against his back and for that pulled over and stopped.

"I need a wee," his passenger coolly proclaimed as she got off to stretch her legs.

"Well, there's Ye Olde Trip to Jerusalem," Alan indicated with finger pointing.

"But it'll be closed," the girl announced pointing at the blackened shell of the building.

"Well go down there," Alan suggested indicating a gloomy passageway near to where they were.

She looked at him. "I can't go there," she clearly stated. "It's not right."

"Okay, have it your own way," he grinned "But don't expect me to wipe up your mess when you can't hold it in any longer."

Appreciating the fact that nature was being unkind, and also becoming aware of the pressure in her bladder reluctantly made up her mind. "Shan't be long," she huffed slowly moving towards the dark. He sat astride that bike and waited, and as he waited became very watchful of the array of headlights rushing at him. He'd been sat about a minute when she reappeared. "Ah! That's better," she confessed while moving various pieces of clothing that had obviously got caught in something they shouldn't of. Having made herself ready clambered back onto the pillion and pressed her upper torso into Alan's back. "What shall we do now," asked the rather obvious question.

During the time she'd been away his mind had done metaphorical somersaults as he thought, and true to form an answer did eventually come. "I don't know," he shrugged as he switched the engine on. "But I'm getting sleepy!"

"Well!" She shouted against the throaty roar of the engine. "I do know there's a hotel, near the cricket ground, where father used to stay when he came up here on business." It took a further five minutes before they pulled up outside that very same building with the apt name of The Silly Point Hotel emblazoned across the front. Like proverbial lost sheep they sauntered inside and stood at the front desk, and with Alan feeling so full of confidence pressed the bell.

"Good evening," welcomed a voice. "How can I be of help?"

"We'd like to book a room," Erin announced as she took over the conversation.

"Certainly madam," came the reply and having spoken, the woman, paused for a moment to run her narrow eyes up and down the two intruders. "And how many nights would that be for?"

"Just the one."

There was no pause as she answered. "That'll be one hundred and twenty pounds," the slim woman declared turning towards the set of keys hanging on the board.

Realising that neither had, or came anywhere near to having, that kind of money Alan gentle pushed his fist into Erin's midriff as a kind of warning but wasn't prepared when she knocked his hand away. "Has Commander Forester still got an account here?" Erin calmly enquired.

Hearing that name must have sent warning bell chiming inside the woman's head. "Who would like to know," demanded the authoritative distrust.

"His daughter."

The woman furrowed her eyebrows. She pouted and stared. "Have you any proof of identity?" Asked the question and the tone resembled a headmistress's lecturing a group of teenage girls found trying to gate crash a party.

"Of course I have," Erin smirked as she went to look for it. Suddenly her smile changed when realising that she'd left everything at the Mucky Duck in the desperate attempt to quickly get away.

"Hurry up," encouraged Alan starting to whittle.

"I haven't got it!"

The receptionist was about to say something when a voice was heard, "It's alright Mary because I can vouch for their identity." Hearing this both youngsters stood totally amazed.

"If you're sure Miss Nuttell," the receptionist smiled.

"I'm sure!" Returned the authoritative confirmation of the woman, dressed quite elegantly in a long off white and ochre crinoline evening dress, who was now beginning to move towards the two stood open-mouthed. "Hello Erin," she smiled as she held out her hands in the gesture of goodwill. The two youngsters looked at each other and with a shrug of her shoulders Erin accepted the embrace. "Let me introduce myself."

"I think you'd better," Alan abrasively snapped.

"You're just like your father."

"How do you know?"

"All will be revealed," she smiled. "So if you'd like to follow me!" They were led towards the lift and got out on the third floor. Into room ninety seven they were shown and it was then the door closed. "First things first," came the introduction. "My name is Angela Nuttell,"

"Do we know you?"

"Probably not," flew the admittance. "But I know all about you two." Having spoken she sat looking directly at Erin. With an obvious sign of certain knowledge chiselled across her brow she spoke again, "Do you remember your wedding day?"

"How can I forget it," dribbled the response. "Why?"

"I was at the back during the service," she explained while going to the side board and finding a rather battered photograph. "And that's me with some of the others who were there," she indicated with a finger. Erin looked before passing it on.

"Do you know any of these other people?"

"No!" She admitted and then looking at Erin continued. "But when we were talking at the reception we all agreed that you'd obviously married in haste."

This was like a red rag to a bull. Erin's heckles rose as she shivered. Her anger forced her eyes to narrow. "But, I loved Patrick," Erin crossly exaggerated.

"No, you didn't," returned the simple words. "That was plainly obvious by your movements down the aisle." Erin was about to explode, but the woman never seemed to notice as she continued. "Then, how do you explain leaving the reception and meeting Alan."

"So we could say our final good-byes."

Alan's brow furrowed because had she married this other bloke to spite him? "And I presume that when your husband sent me the photograph of you with your daughter," he suggested. "Then I suppose that was to tell me that you'd moved on with your life."

"What fucking photograph?"

"This one," he admitted pulling it from his jacket pocket. His fingers trembled as she snatched it. The perspiration began to coat her brow as she scrutinised the three individuals as well as reading the accompanying letter.

"The bastard," spat the words as the whole of her body shook while trying to control the anger.

"Who's the girl?"

"That's Emily."

"Is she," his legal statement stared. "As Patrick's explained, in his letter, your daughter!"

"Of course she is," she declared as a tear of guilt welled and rolled down her cheek. "And she's also your daughter."

Alan's mouth hit the floor. His eyes swelled painfully. His lips formed words, but nothing was spoken. His drink crashed to the carpet sending it everywhere. Finally, after a moment's hesitation he mused, "My daughter."

"Yes!" Erin's fragile voice confessed.

It was now Alan's turn to feel anger, but it wasn't anger of the violent sort it was more like the frustration of discovering something he should have known. Eventually his head landed, and with it came the demand, "Why didn't you tell me?"

"I tried to," came back the quivering response.

"When?"

"With the letters I kept sending," she confirmed. "But, when you didn't reply I just presumed that you didn't want to know and like most blokes who'd been caught with their trousers down," her frail words continued. "Didn't really want anything to do with her!"

Erin was cowering, and so feeling sadistic the lad went for the metaphorical jugular. "But, you had the chance to tell me since we've been alone," he enquired.

"I know," sulked the admittance. "But, I was scared of what you'd do."

The confusion was infectious, "Why should you be frightened?"

Her eyes clouded as a tear continued to roll down her cheek. "I didn't want to lose you again," her soft words sparkled.

Realising exactly what had been said he stood and walked towards Erin. With the strength of an army he pulled her into his waiting embrace, and once there closed his eyes. They remained bound with not a word, but with his own feeling in a state of panic he shrugged and asked, "Where is she now?"

"With my parents," returned the answer. "In Gibraltar."

"So where's Patrick?" His direct question followed.

"I don't know, and don't care," her definite statement declared. "He's probably off on one of his security purges," she threw with contempt.

It was over the next couple of days that conversations were exchanged of little importance, and it was one afternoon when Alan took it that little bit to far. "How well did you know my father," was one such question.

"I'm not quite sure how to answer that," Angela admitted with noticeable guilt.

"Why?"

"Well," she mused. "Let me explain. After signing up I was sent, for my first tour of duty, to one of the naval bases in New Zealand where because of my outstanding language skills I was employed to translate the various messages that kept being received from around the world. It was on the Thursday of my eighth week, I think, that Admiral Low ordered me to appear before him to discuss some serious contradiction in something I'd been working on. Trembling with apprehension, as well as fear, I sat in his secretary's office to await the inevitable reprimand and punishment. I'd been sitting for what seemed an eternity when a junior petty officer, who I later discovered was to become your father, walked straight into the Admiral's office and closed the door. For two hours I sat and it was only when his secretary ordered me back to barracks that I finally went with absolutely no explanation as to why, or what had happened. It was a fortnight later when I'd gone down, with friends, to the Venus Arms for a drink that a certain Henry Young walked over and asked whether he could join us. It was from that meeting things started to happen, which in hindsight, should have started alarm bells ringing. One such incident that happened was when needing to raise some money for the local hospital it was decided, by the Admiral himself, that a good idea would be to organise a raffle with the prize being a tattoo. The entire workforce, which was well over a five hundred personnel, were ordered to contribute and to make it more interesting they were encouraged to send in suggestions as to the design and position of the tattoo. It was a week later when on the parade ground that the winner was announced and a huge cheer went up when my name was called out. If my face wasn't red before that then it must have been after I pulled out the ticket explaining exactly where the design was to be.

Hearing this something must have clicked inside he poor lad's memory. "Remember that photo you showed me the other day," Alan demanded with no please, or thank you. "Then can I see it again?"

"Which one?"

"The one of you in the wedding group," he insisted. She got up and rummaged around inside her drawers before he snatched it. As he looked he was totally unaware of the two women clucking like a couple of old broilers, about something or other, because he was smiling when maybe recognising a couple of the faces in that group. "You know the tattoo you said you'd won?" He nonchalantly insisted looking directly at the older woman.

"Yes!"

"Can I see it?"

"Certainly not."

"Why?" He ridiculed with some slight regret.

"Because it might have something to do with where it is!"

"Ah!" He mocked while getting up and walking to where both women were sitting. "If I'm right then it's in your knickers and just about there," he indicated with his forefinger pressing awkwardly into her dress and about six inches below her navel.

"It might be," she glared looking somewhat stunned. "And anyway what's it got to do with you?"

"Because I need to know," he pestered looking like the proverbial fink.

"It's alright," Erin grinned in that most condescending of manners that quite simply annoys the hell out of men. "He's got this fascination about middle aged women with a tattoo."

"He very well may well have," Angela sniggered. "But he's certainly not seeing mine."

"Okay," he cursed. "Because, now you don't leave me much choice." Having spoken; he quietly knelt infront of the woman's knees.

"What d'yer think you're doing," squealed her voice which was reminiscent of a suckling grunter being made ready for the bacon sarnie.

"This," he grinned while grabbing the hem of Angela's skirt and lifting it over her quaking thighs. His eyebrows rose as a sign of delight when he spoke again. "So you're," he smirked. "One of those women who don't like wearing any underwear."

"Maybe I like to feel the cool air around the ole honey pot," she erotically stated with a mischievous grin.

"And I also bet," he leered while staring at the faded image of the borage. "That you've had many a bee buzzing around that flower hoping to lick the nectar from it."

"Stop it," sneered Erin as she quickly grabbed his shoulder and pulled him away.

"Why?"

"Can't you see she's embarrassed."

"So?"

"What d'yer mean so?"

"I needed to see it."

"But the tattoo's there," she indicated with a pointing finger.

"I know," he smiled.

Hearing this Angela's voice became hysterical as she pushed him away, "Stop staring at me you pervert!"

"Sorry," he shamefully apologised. "But I had to know."

"What?" She screeched. "That I prefer to be clean and smooth down there."

"That's not what I really wanted to know," he smiled. "But it was nice."

"Right," she snorted. "You'd better have a good excuse for what you've just done!"

"How about," he mused. "That I needed to be certain as to whether you're the right person."

"Well," she whinged with a fair amount of hostility. "Am I?"

"Most definitely," he confirmed while still eyeballing her with erotic desire.

"Okay," she yelled as she quickly pushed down her skirt. "I think you've seen enough!" And as soon as she'd spoken the atmosphere became icy, well it did for Alan twitching rather uncomfortably as he went and sat down again with both women giving him the evil eye.

As he felt isolated Alan's patience got the better of him and so egotistically asked, "I don't suppose that you've got anything else that you find particularly odd." The blush was instant although she tried to cover it by picking up the silver cigarette case, from the table, and taking out a single smoke. Her hand was violently shaking, it was shaking so much that it was difficult to light the fag even if she'd have wanted to, and the look she gave hinted that she didn't really want to respond either. "Well!" He enforced staring directly into her rather jaundiced gaze.

After the continued brow beating she replied. "They're in the bedroom," her timid tone announced. Having been given the necessary information he stood and walked towards the door. It opened freely, and in he strolled to stare at the two pictures hanging on the wall and as he turned spotted a single photograph by her bed. The first of the paintings showed a group of Arab men smoking from a hookah as several pretty maidens dressed quite seductively in the colourful silks of a harem danced in the background. The second showed the naked Andromeda chained to a rock and waiting her rescue. The photograph, on the bedside table, showed a beautiful young wren on the bridge of a naval vessel somewhere.

Alan just stood and studied each picture in turn. "Who's the girl in the photo?" He asked.

"Oh! That's me." Angela answered.

"Nice," drooled his word while studying it with a greater interest. "And where was it taken?"

"On the bridge of the Tanmouth."

Hearing the name, and with some desperate hope began to remove the picture from the brass frame. "Who took it?" He asked and while waiting for the answer looked to see whether anything had been written on the back, or any other place that might hide a clue. Discovering there was absolutely nothing swiftly replaced it.

Her answer was a trifle apprehensive, if not slightly awkward. "It was taken by Erin's father and was going to be used as evidence against me at my disciplinary that never occurred."

According to the initiation folk law, of that particular base, all the new wrens had to be photographed aboard the latest arrival that was anchored in the harbour. Miss Angela Redman, because that was her proper name, was woken in the early hours of the Tuesday morning by a discreet knocking on the door and having been told the previous day, at her induction, of what was supposed to happen got dressed and followed her escort. They somehow managed to sneak aboard HMS Tanmouth and onto the Bridge. Leading Seaman Forrester had taken just the one picture, of her dressed in her uniform, when they were apprehended by the redcaps.

Hearing her father's name mentioned Erin crashed through the bedroom door and stood at Alan's side staring down at the image. "Did you just say that my dad took it," she asked pointing at the picture.

"That's right," the other woman smiled. "And it's not a bad effort if I say so myself."

"How come you've got it now," Alan asked looking rather confused. "Because wouldn't it have been kept it in your files."

"I suppose that it should have been," she shrugged. "But what I do know is that after about six weeks I was posted to the naval dockyards in the Caribbean and then a week later that photograph arrived."

"D'yer know who sent it?"

"No," she admitted. "Because there was no letter of explanation as to why I'd been given it."

"Is that all you got?"

"No," she said. "Because a week later the picture of Andromeda arrived and then a week before my wedding, to Sam Nuttell, the other one arrived!"

"Who's this Sam bloke?"

"It's short for Samantha," returned the whisper.

"So where is she?"

"She died," quietly grieved the voice. "But I'm using her surname as a mark of respect."

Whether she meant to or not but Erin destroyed the atmosphere when she rather sleepily asked, "Are we going to bed?"

"While we're in Nottingham," smiled the chirpy exuberance of Erin as she stood in her mothering bra and knickers, with her back to him, looking out of the window studying the world and his dog outside. She turned, smiled and instantly recognised what might be developing beneath the bedcovers. "Why don't we do some shopping," she asked.

"If we must," came back the rhetorical annoyance that mankind had endured since the dawn of time when realising that he'd been tricked, yet again, when staring at her.

"Well, that's okay," she grinned knowing full well that she'd won that rather one sided battle. At the breakfast table the two youngsters were greeted by the woman they'd previously met, and it was during this time that it was agreed that she could join them on the tour of the shops. Feeling like the proverbial carthorse Alan paraded in and out of the various establishments for what seemed like a pointless exercise dedicated to the maternity industry. It was exactly twelve o'clock when it was finally deemed necessary to locate a restaurant.

"What exactly have you brought?" The man questioned while trying to rummage through the over-full bags of shopping and then holding aloft a pair of rather innocuous looking navy blue knickers. "What do you need these for," he teased.

"Stop moaning!" Both women needled with large smiles racing around their mouths, and as Erin blushed she snatched the garment and stuffed it back inside one of the bags. "Anyone would think that you didn't like me shopping!"

Deciding not to be drawn into the one sided argument he inadequately smiled. He never said another word of complaint as they sat discussing various anomalies that would often crop up. One such instant was whether she should have brought the yellow skirt rather than the lime green one. Another was about whether a smaller bra size or larger would have made better sense. And yet another was what sort of shoes go with this, or that, particular outfit. Eventually, after every aspect had been thoroughly discussed they stood up and left.

"I'm just going in here," Angela announced as she walked inside yet another well known department store. Like the proverbial lost sheep he followed and stood beside the section of clothing items that varied from the relatively cheap Macintosh to the highly priced coronation gowns.

"What are you looking at?" Erin asked looking at him.

"Nothing," he lied as he'd been scrutinising the highly seductive range of lingerie that's constantly on display, in these places, and knowing that gave a wicked smile when realising that he was infact in pervert paradise. And to make the whole thing incredibly stupid both women knew it.

"Oh," she sighed as she turned and pushed her back into his chest. Then taking his hands she instinctively wrapped them around her waist before driving her large arse into his groin.

"Stop it," he smiled. "You know I like it."

"I can tell," she teased while give him an extra wiggle.

"Okay," he whispered into her ear. "You've asked for it." With the spontaneity of a lover he moved his right hand under her T-shirt and groped her covered tits hoping she'd take the hint and tell him to stop.

How wrong he was as she hurriedly unzipped his trousers and removed his stiffening cock. "Oh! Alan," she craved. "I need you to fuck me."

"What here?" He asked with a slight tinge of shock.

"Yes," she pleaded as she pushed his hand below her skirt and pressed it against the gusset of her knickers. "Because just feel how wet I am!"

"We might get caught," he explained looking about to see whether they could be spotted.

"So," she moaned as he made her spread her legs and in one quick movement pulled aside the sodden gusset and slipped inside her eager cunt. "Oh! Yes," she quietly moaned when he suddenly felt a hand tightly gripping his shoulder. With absolute horror he turned.

"Why have you stopped?" Erin demanded obviously not understanding what had happened to call a halt to the illicit proceedings. She instantly coloured, as did Alan, when seeing who was actually standing there.

"Couldn't you wait?"

"No," Erin replied. "Sorry!"

"You'll have to excuse her," he tried to explain.

"Why?"

"Because of the hormonal imbalance of her condition," he carried on. "She gets these occasional mood swings."

"Is she ill?"

"No I'm pregnant!"

"Oh," Angela smiled looking rather concerned at having destroyed the sensual moment they were enjoying and watched as Alan simply wiped his wet cock on the nearest piece of cloth. "Did you have to do that?" She asked with a modicum of disgust as he pushed it back inside his trousers.

"Blame it on her hormones," he shrugged as they all quickly left the store. They were walking down Clumber Street when he saw some paintings in the shop window opposite. "Let's have a look in here," he grinned hoping, like the majority of men, to see the odd female nude.

"Oh, I see he's found Joy Fisher's shop," smiled Angela grabbing Erin's arm and pulling her towards the window. Once there both women stood behind Alan, who was simply staring at the artwork, and it was at that point the owner emerged.

"Hello," spoke the word of friendship as the two older women hugged like long lost sisters.

"Joy," Angela returned. "How are you?"

"Fine," returned the other lady's answer. "Do you want to come inside and have a good look round?"

"Oh, I'm sorry," Angela warmly smiled. "Let me introduce my young friends. This is Erin Carlton, and Alan Young." The handshake and hugs completed the introduction. For the next hour, or so, everybody looked and studied the array of portraits that hung like drops of rain clinging to the walls of an Amsterdam Knocking shop. "Who painted these," complemented Alan's soft voice while staring at the vivid detail.

"I did some," Miss Fisher smiled with pride. "But the majority are examples of someone else's work."

"I wonder who that is," Erin chirped while scrutinizing one specific picture that had obviously caught her fancy.

"I see you've picked the best example," Joy smiled with pride. There seemed to be a pause until turning and quietly asked, "Are you here for the party?"

"Yes," Angela confirmed. "Because that's why we've been doing some shopping."

Hearing this Alan looked bemused. "I thought you were buying maternity things," he huffed. "Not getting party outfits."

"Oh! Didn't I tell you?"

"What?"

"That we've been invited to a party!"

"I do now," he laboured when realising he'd been left out of the loop. When at last they'd left the shop it took a moment, but eventually the question rose from his mouth like a match of curiosity, "Who was that?"

"Someone I knew in the Navy," Angela admitted with hardly any concern, and having given her reply started walking across the road. Alan dutifully followed as his two companions restarted their quest for that illusive bargain which always seemed to follow the same pattern. First into one shop, then to another, then onto the next until finally returning to the beginning and purchased the very first thing they'd seen. Boredom. Frustration. Annoyance were some of the terms that described the feeling dribbling through his body as he patiently waited. However, every so often he would focus his agile mind on the array of different women as they unwittingly posed for him. This was plainly evident especially when he was inside the rather personal domain of a lingerie boutique.

"I saw you looking," scoured Erin walking passed his innocent stance.

"I'm only human," he countered while looking at another woman parading around in just her underwear.

"It's more like being a dirty old man," she sniggered. He couldn't argue with that statement and so shrugged his acceptance. Feeling like a dejected lover he quietly followed as both Erin and Angela went to the counter in order to pay for the items of clothing they thought adequate. It was while waiting he was quick to notice that the woman from the picture shop had just walked in.

"Are you following us?" Alan, still feeling a tad pissed off, queried as she walked passed.

"Oh! Hello again," Joy smiled while picking out a rather formal dress and holding it against herself.

"No!" He mused. "That doesn't look right."

"What about this one?"

"No!"

"This," asked her soft voice holding a rather low slung dress.

"Well," his excited voice revealed.

"You'll have to excuse him," came the rather cross expression as Erin moved closer. "All he wants to do is have a good gander at your cleavage!"

"Erin," he stuttered going red.

"Well it's true," she continued with a stare that could have frozen hell. Having caustically spoken she grabbed his wrists and harshly pulled him away, and he was outside the store before he could utter any words.

"Shall we head home," asked Angela as they strolled down one of the narrow lanes?

"I'd think we'd better," Erin confirmed. "And anyway my back's killing me."

They finally arrived back at the hotel and decided to simply sit chatting, and drinking, the evening away. "I'm just going to the toilet," announced Erin as she abruptly stood and left.

With her gone Angela turned and looked directly at Alan sitting opposite. "Now we're alone," she started. "There's something I think you ought to know."

"I'm all ears!"

Her voice became very quiet. Her words seemed to be stage whispered, "You know Erin's father?"

A puzzled line of curiosity furrowed along his brow. "Yes!"

"He's not what he seems."

"Then what is he?" Alan demanded with interested. He waited with bated breath, but no answer was forthcoming because at that moment the toilet door opened and out walked Erin.

"What were you talking about," giggled her warm voice as she sat next to Alan before grabbing his hand.

"Nothing!"

"I don't believe you," she crudely emphasised. "And if I didn't know better then it was probably about that other woman we met."

"Which one?"

"The one who's all tit and teeth!"

"Oh! You mean Joy," Angela smiled as she interrupted.

"That's the one,"

"I was going to explain how we met in the Caribbean," Angela rather coyly continued. "And how we became good friends and what we used to do in the sweltering heat of the evenings."

"He would have liked that," Erin giggled.

"Would I?" He wondered aloud.

"Of course you would."

"Why?"

"Well," she smiled. "Don't men find lesbian relationships horny?"

"There's an exhibition," Alan indicated while pointing at the advert in the local paper. "Showing scenes from Greek Mythology and other erotic locations."

"Where's it at?"

"The Bacon Memorial Art Gallery."

"What times it start?" Erin enquired leaning over his shoulder.

"Ten o'clock."

"Are we going?"

"You try and stop me," he explained grabbing her wrist and pulling. "I bet some of the paintings are going to be a bit risqué."

"Then you'll feel at home," smiled the dig.

"To right," he grinned giving her belly a loving rub.

Climbing aboard a number twenty seven bus they kept looking out of the window at the world flashing by and it wasn't long before they reached their destination. Feeling a lot better, probably due to the fact that the journey was rather bumpy, walked the short distance before climbing the concrete steps and going inside the exhibition. "Just going to the toilet," Erin winced moving towards the correct door. "And I'll come and find you when I've finished."

"Okay," he answered moving towards the array of paintings that hung on the walls.

He was miles away. "Hey," beckoned Erin who'd just reappeared. "Come and take a look at the ones I've just found!"

"Be there in a minute," he offered as he started to move and having caught her up stepped inside another room a little further down the corridor. Once there literally just stopped dead in his tracks and stared open mouthed at the collection of pictures on view. His active eyes were everywhere. First he focused on Artemis, or more precisely Olivia Thomas, in the classic representation of footprints in the sand. Then, his gaze was drawn towards the goddess Hera skinny dipping in the flowing waters of the river Styx and remembering the photograph, her husband had shown him, realised that here was Irene Sutherland. Up and a bit further along was the majestic portrait of Persephone, or Catherine Hill, in her bedroom having just emerged from the cleansing water of her bath in preparation for the journey. His heart refused to beat as he scanned the fourth. His mouth went dry as he saw who it was. His breathing stopped because he was looking directly at Angela Nuttell posing as the beautiful Andromeda chained to rocks as Perseus knelt at her feet.

"That's beautiful," announced the admiring voice at his shoulder. Hearing the proclamation he swivelled and stared directly into the warm eyes of Joy Fisher the woman he'd met the day before.

"It sure is," he grinned, as he simply couldn't take his riveted eyes from the canvas. He couldn't wait for the next image and in two steps he'd reached the canvas because it showed a portrait of Aphrodite rising from that clam shell. He was staring, not at the model's face because that could have been anyone, but at a specific region below her belly button. It wasn't the fact that her feminine sexuality was clearly visible, although that did add the je ne sais quoi aspect to it, but was because like the previous four portraits there was absolutely no sprig of herb anywhere to be seen.

"Alan!" Shouted the rather hysterical toned voice of Erin as she raced, well waddled, into the room.

"What now?"

"Come and take a look at this!"

"Okay," he replied following her into another room.

"Look," she pointed while at the same time her face was getting redder and redder. "That's me!"

"So it is," he smirked looking at the illustration. It was breathtaking. It was beautiful. Well it would be wouldn't it because don't they say that beauty is in the eye of the beholder? It showed the image of a scantily clad Pandora, or Erin which ever way you want to look at it, sitting and opening a small silver casket of some sort. Still captivated he jumped, in alarm, when suddenly feeling two arms eagerly snuggling around his waist and it was probably the shock that forced him to twist and stare directly at the culprit.

"I see you've made it," Marsha Cooper whispered.

"I wouldn't have missed it," he smiled. "Especially as I've just seen this one." Having spoken Erin looked daggers at him, which was a bit unfortunate because several other people had put two and two together and realised that here was that Pandora in real life. Trying to be discreet, if at all possible, they all casually moved into another room where their identity hadn't yet been recognised.

As they walked Marsha suddenly pulled Alan back before whispering something. "Meet me, tonight, in the Trip at nine thirty," she smiled while turning towards some other people who'd recently gathered. "Because I've got something to tell you and be on your own."

Fortune favours the brave, so they say, which partly explained how Alan managed to slip away unnoticed. It also helped that Erin felt the need to go to bed early because of the physical aspect of her condition. Needing answers he walked the mile or so before slipping through the door of the drinking house and scanned to see whether Marsha had kept her promise. It took a moment before his eyes became accustomed to the cigarette smoke but eventually he saw her, in a corner, sitting quite alone at a table. "Can I join you?" He asked with drink in hand. She looked up and smiled. Her gracious gesture was all the indication he needed and so sat beside her. "Why exactly am I here," he asked. "And why did you want to see me alone?"

She gave half a smile. She allowed her left eyebrow to rise as a mark of respect. But, before answering her hand gripped his like there was no tomorrow. She then bowed her head, as if in shame, and quietly replied, "Please don't let what I'm about to tell you go any further." And as she waited for his reply her forehead glistened with a fine coating of perspiration.

It was over the next hour, between drinks and cigarettes, that she went on to describe how a young Marshall Forester had once brought an envelope with a sepia photograph of a young woman of no more than seventeen inside for her to paint.

The girl in question, because that's all she would have been, was at her parent's party that was being thrown to celebrate the couples' thirtieth wedding anniversary. The wine flowed as the festivities progressed and as the evening developed several of the gentlemen decided to escort the young ladies for illicit rendezvous in the Oriental gardens of that luxury house. The particular one of interest occurred around midnight when a dashing young officer, dressed in the colourful uniform of the household cavalry, walked up and began describing the daring missions he'd encountered in the battles for the Queen's empire. She was spellbound as they walked, arm in arm, on that balmy evening through the jasmine gardens and in return they laughed about the cloistered life she endured with the maiden aunts inside her house. They lost track of time, or where they were, when running for cover as the monsoon rain started to penetrate their clothes and they were thankful when spotting the sanctuary of the Summer House, which lay a short distance along the path. It was dark as they entered, and with the rain sounding like pebbles being thrown upon a tin, they ran inside. With a quick flick of a flint the lantern was lit and the fiery glow cast her sultry shroud about. Now standing fractionally apart the musky scent of their bodies hung in the air, and in that moment the cordial atmosphere changed to one of passion and desire. Her innocence was clearly evident for only being seventeen she trembled as the man ripped the bodice of her dress. Her body was hot as his strong hands dominantly removed the entirety of her wet costume and left her all but naked. She smiled with innocence as the man disrobed and when she saw his cock, standing to attention, an unfamiliar feeling raced around her young body. He was the perfect attendant to her needs and was gentle when stealing her virginity. They kept their affair secret as they frolicked and played beneath the tropical skies whenever the opportunity arose. He was nowhere to be seen when she screamed in abject pain giving birth to their illegitimate son, and neither was he there at the burial of the lifeless child. That was a private affair, and the unseen body was laid to rest beside the two other tiny graves at the bottom of the garden.

"Do you know who the girl was?" Alan asked as he looked at Marsha.

"No," she replied with a rather dubious shake of the head. "But after the painting had been completed Erin's father collected it and with it gone I never gave it a second thought."

"That's a shame."

"To right," she admitted. "Because I really would have liked to have shown it at this exhibition."

"What," he stuttered. "That was your exhibition?"

"Not quite," she answered.

"Then whose is it?"

"Mostly my grandmother's," she smiled. "With a few of mine and Joy's." Having finished she reached inside her handbag, took out a silver cigarette holder and then with deft expertise withdrew a single smoke to place it between her crimson decorated lips. Next, she rummaged and located her lighter. Whether she did it on purpose, or because her hand was trembling so much, but she let it slip and watched as it fell to the floor beneath the table.

"I'll get it," was Alan's immediate response as he collapsed to his knees and began to search. It took a moment until he saw the flicker of silver glistening behind her feet. As he reached and over-stretched his face unintentionally nestled in the crotch of Marsha's skirt.

"When you've finished manhandling me," her tease commenced. "Then, I'd like a smoke." Realising what he was doing quickly picked up the lighter and stood. Now, feeling rather guilty he instinctively looked at the silver case before handing it over. Sitting down again he watched as the cigarette spluttered to life and it was a moment later Marsha deliberately, well he thought so, dropped the lighter again and with calculated authority scanned him.

"I suppose you want me to see where it's gone," his disgruntled voice proclaimed and getting the welcoming eye dropped to his knees. Whether it was a reaction to something he'd done, like accidently touching her thigh, but she dramatically lifted her knees and caught him under the chin. That didn't really hurt but when he cracked his head against the table top he winced with aggravated pain.

"I'm sorry," laughed the apology as she grabbed his head and moved it into a more appropriate position further up her thighs. Which I suppose was her intension all along, and in doing so Alan sighed when he came face to face with that specific area of her skirt that would cause his hormones to run wild. Realising what would happen; he tried his damnedest not to get excited as the intoxicating smell of her pheromones started to invade his senses and as they did his eyes closed in pitiful anxiety when becoming conscious of his mouth getting dry. Slowly, and rather reluctantly, he pulled away but as he moved he was hopefully focusing on anything that did not require him to imagine what lay beneath her skirt? Suddenly, while twisting his face slightly to the left spotted an unknown couple sitting at the next table playing footsie with each other. He didn't want to do it but curiosity compelled him to look up the middle-aged woman's skirt and seeing what, if anything, was there smiled when realising that if the man played his cards right he may well be onto a promise. "Are you alright," quizzed Marsha's grinning face that suddenly appeared as if from nowhere.

"I don't know."

"Why's that?"

"D'yer remember where you put my face?"

"Yes," she giggled.

"Well," he teased. "It reminded me about whether I'd remembered to strap a plank across my arse."

"Why?"

"Well," he smirked. "I wouldn't have liked to have fallen in." As he waited for the usual female complaint he suddenly noticed, out the corner of his eye, a familiar looking hand reaching below a table close to the exit. In a flash Alan jumped to his feet. In that instant he'd swivelled around to stare at the back of the man, and woman, disappearing through the door. He raced across the room. He pushed aside other customers in an effort to get outside, and once there stood looking this way and that. He cursed with euphoric exuberance because they'd simply vanished.

"What's wrong?" Marsha asked when he finally returned.

"Didn't you see them," exploded his angry question as he grappled her shoulders and powerfully shook her.

"I wasn't looking," the excuse frowned. "And, anyway I had other thing on my mind."

"Oh! Yes," he fumed. "Whether you could use your thighs as ear warmers."

"Is that so wrong," came her defence. "Because I'm still a woman with a woman's needs."

"What about your husband?"

"He couldn't raise a smile."

The Saturday night finally arrived and through the doors, where the Masquerade Ball was being held, they all paraded dressed in accordance with the event. The music, from the beautifully arranged orchestra, was loud and claustrophobic. "Who wants a drink?" Alan offered as he watched the two women move towards a vacant table a little further down.

"Pernod and lemonade," half shouted Angela as she helped Erin weave in and out of the obstructions that lined their path.

"A bitter lemon," hollered Erin as she continued waddling until sitting down. Towards the long bar, which seemed to take up the whole length of the wall, he pushed and shoved. It took a long time before he was considered to be served and even then he had to wait. Eventually he carried the right drinks back to the women talking as if there was no tomorrow.

"Thanks," they shouted against the noise and although he never heard the appreciation smiled anyway. He quietly laughed to himself when realising that most of the female gender have the uncanny knack of being able to communicate through any level of noise, and with this idea slumped back into the chair. Now ready he scoured the room hoping to recognise any of the other guests and having no success puffed out his cheeks in frustration. Feeling the isolation he picked up his drink. With it near his mouth something must have caused him to look towards the entrance as a group of women entered the room. He smiled his appreciation as he stared at their costumes, and then he saw her. His eyebrows rose in disbelief because he wondered how he'd missed her the first time, and then it hit him. She would normally have her hair in a bun, but tonight she had as if blowing like the corn in a field. He was still staring when she looked across at him and gave a wave of welcome. She appeared to wait that fraction before walking to where he was sitting. Now there she grabbed his eager hands and pulled him into contact with her luscious body. She then tried to shout against the music and of course failed, but as her cherry coloured lips moved he read the words. His response was just as noiseless and with that they separated.

"Who was that," queried the hoarse question as Erin suddenly noticed his interest. His eyebrows rose as a mark of fun, and simply allowed his mouth to form the kind of smile that he knew would annoy. "Well!" She tried again. Realising the effect he was creating shrugged his shoulders as he wouldn't or couldn't answer. Sensing that the women were obviously becoming bored by his rather childish antics took a long swig of the drink which conveniently finished it off. With neither Erin nor Angela appearing to notice, or looking particularly bothered, he stood before going to the bar again. Just like the last time he had to wait but this time it was worth it because suddenly a warm hand touched his shoulders. Swinging his head he smiled as Margaret Bowler pushed through the mass before standing at his side. She spoke, but again he couldn't hear and hoping to rectify the matter twisted his head so that she could shout directly into his ear.

"It's nice to see you," screamed her words as he felt the warmth of her breath.

He smiled like a gentleman, but allowed his gaze to fall like that of a lecher. He licked his dry lips as he took her hands and pulled. "Where's Stuart?" He questioned as she fell against his strutting chest.

"He couldn't make it," she yelled as she innocently pulled away. "Something about improving his stroke play by not giving a quick tickle to the silly point," she grinned causing him to smirk when realising that she was talking about how her husband was trying to improve his batting average.

"But wouldn't it be far better for him to keep using his weapon, of a bat, and not caressing the odd ball towards the point area or force his on drive through the slips occasionally," he suggested. As he waited for her response he smiled when noticing how the fluorescent light perfectly showed off the fact that she was wearing an erotic set of black underwear that could be clearly seen through the white fibres of her dress. Whether she knew that people could see made very little difference because the delicious perfume she was wearing simply ignited the volatile pagan need to simply stare at her. So yes, she knew that her body was perfectly visible and in saying that a good allergy would be how the trap door spider lures the hapless victim into its web of fate. Suddenly a group of rather elderly men, who'd also been lured by what was on show, moved closer and started discussing something, or other. With them there Alan simply looked on and felt a little deprived, as well as left out, and so returned with his drink to sit watching both Erin and Angela still continuing their conversation whatever that was. It was about half an hour later that Margaret waltzed up with hand extended. "How about a dance," she smiled.

Feeling gallant, or was it the boredom, he accepted the offer and moved towards the dance floor. They found a space and made a grab for each other in that most innocent kind of manner, and since the pace of the music had slowed Alan felt perfectly entitled to wrap his strong arms around her waist. With curious anticipation he pulled her close, well as close as he dare which wasn't all that close if truth be known. She twisted her face as if to ask what exactly his intentions were and when his hands stayed exactly where they were probably understood. It was over the next couple of hours that more drink was consumed along with several further trips to the dance floor, and it was getting towards midnight when all three were dancing to slow melodies. Alan had somehow managed to entice Erin, onto the dance floor, and he'd even been allowed to caress and massage her mothering frame. Angela, on the other hand, was dancing with Miss Fisher who'd generally had her hands everywhere, if you understand what I'm trying to say. So when that particular piece of music finished both Alan and Erin wandered back to the table. Feeling thirsty Alan picked up his drink and was about to take a quenching gulp when he was accidentally pushed in the back. Staggering forward he collided with Erin forcing her drink, as well as his, everywhere. Fortunately, it didn't land on either of them, but absolutely soaked Angela who'd just happened to be passing. What happened next was like a bawdy seaside postcard as the liquid soaked the other woman's blouse to reveal the fact that she wasn't wearing a bra. Then like the teacher with a slimy slug on a plate of salad, very gingerly began moving the wet material clinging to her skin. Nothing happened for a moment but it was when two female hands, Alan recognised as being those of Joy's, wormed themselves around Angela's body that things started to get a little out of hand. If you know what I'm thinking? There was a flurry of laughter as those same two hands started groping the wet breasts, and a raucous cheer went up as Angela's nipples soon resembled a pair of nine carat gold nuggets.

"Come on show us your tattoo," yelled the delirious demand from the appreciative audience. The sounds, of both the men and women, clapping came as encouragement and a cheer went up as Angela climbed onto the table. When in position she seductively commenced to act the stripper and began to remove her blouse. In the smoky atmosphere, plus the party lights sending wispy shadows, the silky folds of material soon separated which allowed her heavy tits to swing perfectly free. Seeing the pure eroticism of her movements the audience applauded with gasps of appreciation. "Who'll pass my drink?" Her seductive words asked, no demanded, and almost instantly the glass was pushed forward. She took a mouthful and then dipping a single finger into the golden coloured wine skilfully massaged, and teased, both nipples. The passion it created was self evident as two, if not three pairs of hands, reached up and started pulling at the wet material clinging to her skin. Knowing exactly what she was doing sexily wiggled her hips as a raucous cheer erupted as she carefully, and erotically, started pushing down her wet skirt. A loud cheer went up as the blue, but damp, flower of that borage appeared and the applause was spontaneous when she ultimately stood naked with the pure magic of her sexual beauty clearly on display.

Whether it was Erin becoming self conscious of her condition, or for some other reason, but she grabbed Alan's arm and pulled. "Let's go back," groaned the plea, and it was while leaving the room that Alan turned to watch Angela pulling someone up to join her. Out into the pale glow of the city's lights they strolled hand in hand, passed the railway station and onwards to the hotel until finally settling for the night.

It was about a quarter to four in the morning when the bedroom light was suddenly switched on. "What's wrong?" Demanded Erin looking at Alan sitting bolt upright with the bedcovers hanging limply from his shaking frame. "If it's my body you want," sleepily wondered the tease. "Then think again." He said nothing while getting out of bed. So with curious eyes she followed his unrehearsed march as he silently opened the bedroom door and headed down the corridor. Because of her condition she struggled, but it was a moment later that she followed his progress, and was but a footstep away when he thumped hard against the closed door of number ninety-seven. Getting no answer he tried the door. It opened and so in he strode. He rolled his teeth over his bottom lip as they stared at the empty bed. As he looked he was quick to notice Erin's brow furrowed in confusion, but not taking the slightest bit of notice he paced towards one of the paintings and studied it in greater detail. Obviously still finding absolutely nothing of interest quickly moved to the other. Then like a table tennis match his gaze once again settled on that group of Arabs smoking from that hookah. He looked puzzled as he gazed once again at the stunning portrait of Andromeda. He trembled because he thought he saw something, but when looking again it was just a flicker of light dancing across the canvas. Standing with the wheels of confusion racing along his brow he started to laugh. "Look!" He demanded with finger pointing.

"What at?" Smiled Erin's confused declaration.

"That picture," he smirked.

She complied with the order, and then shrugged. "What am I supposed to be looking at?"

He sighed. He fidgeted, and then spoke, "What exactly can you see?"

"Lots of naked women," she mused. "Is that what you're wanting me to say?"

"No," his pitiful sigh grunted.

"So where am I suppose to be looking?"

He was cruel wrapping fingers around her chin. It was painful when he pulled her towards the specific canvas. "What exactly are the men doing?" Fired the question as if shot from a rifle.

"They're all smoking."

"And just look at the puffs of smoke," he insisted.

"They just look like puffs of smoke to me!"

"They may do," he returned. "But, can you remember what your Morse code looks like?"

"Yes!"

"Well," he smiled. "Imagine that the round puff is a dot and the elongated one is a dash."

"What's that got to do with anything," she interjected as if trying to help.

"The painting is trying to give us a clue."

"Okay clever clogs," she sniped. "So, what's it saying?"

Understanding what was needed he hurriedly found a piece of paper and quickly wrote the seven letters. "It reads CIGCASE," he shrugged with deeper confusion.

"Listen!" Directed Erin as she sat in bed and turned up the volume on the radio.

"With firemen still damping down the blaze at The Palace Hotel police will be investigating whether it was started deliberately."

"Wasn't that where we were last night?" He shrugged.

"Yes," she replied with a shiver.

Then trying to lighten the atmosphere he half-heartedly smirked, "Well, it must have got better after we'd gone."

The response was hostile to the point of being acidic. "Stop joking," she trembled as if the devil himself had just walked across her grave. "Because we could have been there."

"But, we weren't," he offered as well as a comforting arm.

"What about Angela?"

The sigh was deep, the look was painful but the offer genuine, "Okay, I'll just go and check her room again." He'd been gone about a five minutes before returning with a rather silly grin.

"Well!"

"She's fine," smiled the response. "And anyway she's asleep." What he forgot to mention was the fact that he didn't want to go into detail about taking a greater interest in the tattoo she'd had done. Nor to the fact that there was a very personal silver plaything, lying on the bedside table, that had obviously been used. He also forgot to mention that before leaving he'd picked it up a silver object and put it in his pocket. Not the toy you mucky minded people but something else and with it in his hand his eyes closed as a smile raced along his lips because he knew that what he had in his hand was what he wanted.

"That's alright," she sighed rather thankfully and then added. "I wonder what happened to cause the fire."

"Don't know," shrugged the retort. "And anyway I'm going to the little boy's room to contemplate my navel." While sat on the enamel throne he pulled the cigarette case into view and gave an ugly grin of satisfaction when throwing the four un-smoked tapers of addiction away. His determination was infectious while ripping the pristine blue velvet from inside the box. The smile rippled along his lips as he read the tiny words, "On the stepping stone this Titan used you'll find a French variety that tastes of lemon."

Everybody was talking about the fire at breakfast when they entered the dining room, but that all seemed to change as they moved. Not a word was spoken only the feel of curious eyes probing for hopeful clues. "Weren't you at the Palace last night," asked a rather stuffy looking gentleman perched by the window drinking tea from a china cup.

"Yes!" Alan returned while pulling the chair out for Erin to sit.

"Were you there when the fire started," cried a chorus of voices together that sounded like a bunch of cats squabbling.

"No!" He smiled. "As we'd come back before anything happened."

"What about Angela," queried that same man?

"She must have returned after us."

"I hope she's okay," asked another concerned question.

"She was asleep when I looked in on her," Alan replied and hearing this the man abruptly placed the cup on its saucer and hurried from the room.

With him gone several of the other guests turned to one another and formed faces that spoke in the silent world of a question. "I wonder who that was," asked a frumpy looking matron buttering a thick slice of toast. "Because I don't think he's a guest."

Alan was listening when suddenly alarm bells started to ring and as they chimed the image of the man's fingers, around the teacup, flashed inside his mind. He stared intently at Erin as she'd just started to eat her breakfast.

"We've got to go," he ordered snatching her hand and pulling. They left the dining room with an even bigger discussion than the one they'd interrupted with their arrival. Up the stairs they raced, well as fast as a slug on heat. Through the bedroom door they marched and picked up various items they thought valuable, and then back out onto the landing. "Wait here!" Alan ordered as they neared Angela's door. "I just want to check something." In an instant he was gone.

"Hurry," called the frightened voice. "Someone's coming." With this warning he reappeared looking a whiter shade of pale. There was no sound as they started to trundle away. They were two steps further along the landing when her curiosity got the better and so had to ask, "Is she alright?"

"She's still asleep," he lied knowing full well that she'd never wake up. Into the clear air of that late October morning they moved and never looked back as they motored away. Through the gears he crashed as the bike twitched along the road rushing onwards and upwards towards Chesterfield with its crocked spire. Then through Bakewell stopping for that famous tart. Next, was Buxton and the notoriety of the Roman Springs? Finally, travelling south the circuit was completed when returning to Calder's with the single headlight cutting a curious path.

"Where have you two been?" Offered the welcome as they walked into the kitchen where Alice was preparing three mugs of hot milk.

"About!" He replied. Suddenly, his mind must have worked overtime because with pointed finger he wondered, "And anyway who's here?"

She hesitated, but answered, "Erin's father."

To use the well-known proverb of being knocked down with a feather described was just how Alan looked and felt at that precise moment. He shuddered violently as if blowing the cobwebs from his brain and with hurried animation swivelled his blank face to study his passenger. Looking, he saw a flicker of paternal love rushing across her windswept face and realising he was fighting a losing battle demanded, "What's he doing here!" Waiting for the answer he smarted while watching the man's daughter skip towards the sitting room. He was about to follow when his sister snatched his arm and dominantly dragged him back.

"Leave them!"

"Why!" He demanded as he pulled against her strength.

"Because, he's got something to explain to her." Hearing the words Alan felt the anger build. He felt the claws of fury tearing inside his gut, and for that violently pushed his sister aside. With hostile intent he strode towards the room and crashed open the door, and once inside stared at Erin embracing the comforting frame of her father.

"I'm glad you're here," interrupted the voice of his mother beginning to stand.

"Why's that!" Spat the words. "So that he can keep us apart again." It took exactly two strides before the two men collided, and it was at that moment Erin was harshly pushed away. The sound of Alan's fist connecting with the bearded chin of her father sounded like two blocks of wood. There was no retaliation as the pent up brutality, of the younger man, was about to be delivered. The scream was pitiful as Erin pushed her way between the two of them.

"Stop it!" She hollered as hands flew towards her face as protection against the hostility.

"Why!" Alan screamed as he roughly started to push her away. He panted his authority as she stumbled, and as she struggled he tried to fight for his own freedom when other arms became wrapped around his body. Against just the one he could fight and win, but together the arms acted like a spider's web forcing him to pant his determination.

"When you've finally settled," uttered the authoritative tone of his mother as even she tried to restrain her son's anger.

It was Commander Forester who actually came to the young man's rescue by saying, "Let him go!" So with calm resolution he was released. The mood was on a knife edge as both men simply stared at each other. Alan trembled with hostility. The other calm. For exactly thirty seconds not a word was spoken as each tried to gain the dominance he felt he deserved.

Finally, with neither buckling with the strain it was Erin who tore down the curtains of stupidity, "How can I make a choice?" Hearing this, the two antagonists twitched and stared at the girl uncertain of her actions.

"Now see what you've done," Coarsely accused Alan's mother as she placed her arms around Erin and pulled her close.

"I didn't mean to," the younger of the two offered while strolling forward with arms akimbo. He was about to cuddle, and protect, his pregnant mistress when she took one step back. Looking bewildered his mind reflected upon how stupid he'd appeared, and while waiting understood her undoubted parental need. Her father paced forward with a smile of victory, but even he was shocked when she shrugged away his embrace.

"Sit down," trembled Erin's words looking at both men with harsh reality. "And talk!"

Over the next couple of hours, along with an adequate supply of drink, Alan sat listening to the various stories Commander Forester told and as is human nature he began getting bored when hearing the rather trivial episodes of someone else's life. "Are you paying attention," Erin suddenly asked having noticed what was happening.

"I'm all ears."

"That makes a change."

"Why?"

"Because," she smiled. "By this time you're usually throwing out the Zeds."

"Is it that boring," asked the Commander.

"Probably because there's no sex or violence in it," his daughter tittered.

"Okay," grinned her father and then turning towards Alan asked. "Do you remember that cold week in December when you were about sixteen?"

"How can I forget," he replied. "Being thrown out of the house and having to live in that godforsaken shed."

"Did you ever wonder why you had to do it?"

He thought for a moment and when nothing sprang to mind rather abrasively snapped, "Not really!"

"It was," the man started. "Because Henry, sorry your father, was conducting a military operation and seeing the need for secrecy it was decided that Calder's would be a more suitable place to use."

"What was it about?"

The look said it all as well as the next sentence, "Because it's still not officially been closed I'm not at liberty to reveal anything that might be of National Importance."

His mother suddenly joined in the conversation which happened sometimes, "Henry knew that Alice would be at work and that I could go and visit my friends."

"So that just left me!" He realised.

"That's right," she smiled. "So when I joked to your father one night about you going into the shed for a week he knew he was onto a winner."

"Thanks a lot," he begrudgingly smiled while remembering those exact days of his youth. It was a moment later that a curious doubt spun, as well as a real one, and metaphorically hit him. "If there was supposed to be people coming and going why didn't I ever notice anything," he pondered with eyebrows furrowed.

"I didn't expect you would," his mother postulated gazing directly at her son. "Because you obviously had other things on your mind!"

"That's right," confirmed the other man beginning to smile. "Could it possibly have something to do with my youngest daughter?" With hearing this definite, but true, account both Alan and Erin blushed. "And anyway Henry knew exactly where you were when he invited me on to go and visit him on the Thursday morning," he continued.

"So why were you called?" Alan asked looking slightly concerned at the fact that this man may have been involved in something dishonest.

Marshal Forester turned towards his mother and smiled, "Your father wasn't stupid and soon realised that maybe Erin was getting a schoolgirl crush on his son and not wanting to put at risk what he'd achieved called me over to discuss my possible posting."

"It wasn't," Erin culled. "Just another crush."

"I know that now!" Again there was a pause. "Has anyone got any questions so far?" The Commander offered taking a sip of Brandy.

Hearing this the younger man's mind twisted like a tornado, because after all this time he simply wanted to know the truth about a certain fact, and for that he stared directly at the man. "If there was to be no contact between our families then why, out of the blue, did I receive an invitation to Erin's wedding?" He speculated looking directly at him.

Commander Forester's shoulders drooped. "It was a paramount instruction from your father, my commanding officer, that there was to be no contact between us," started the reply. "But Erin, so much like her mother, simply could not accept that you were to be out of her life for ever. It broke my heart to watch her day after day yearning for any contact that might arrive, and I felt awful taking the letters you'd send. For two years we kept the constant vigilance and it came as quite a shock when discovering that she'd managed to book a flight to England hoping to see you. Fearing the worst it was a hurtful experience stopping her making that journey, and so deciding to break with protocol I contacted your father hoping for a solution. Having all the answers he arrived the following week, along with a set of photographs that proved that you had forgotten her to the point of getting married. It broke her heart and for several months there was nothing anyone could do to support the grieving girl, but time is a great healer and I think you know the rest." His voice now became very quiet, "I probably made a big mistake when I arranged with your mother, because I know Henry would never have agreed, that seeing my daughter getting married would close a door on the past," he openly admitted. "But, I never expected Kitty to do what she did at the reception."

"Father!" Erin's blunt expression naïvely scorched.

"Why, what did happen?"

He went on to explain how during the service his wife turned and saw Alan gazing down from the balcony. It appears that during the reception, and unbeknown to the Commander, Kitty had taken her daughter aside and explained about Alan's presence. The outcome was that Erin went AWOL, thanks to a little help from Carol, and it wasn't until six week later that he was told and if proof was needed then his granddaughter was born at the Naval Hospital some seven and a half months later with no complications.

"I'm sorry," Alan admitted. "But, I didn't know."

"How could you," the man began. "It's like I've already said we were under strict orders not to make contact under any circumstances."

It was Erin's turn to ask, "What about the letters I kept writing after I'd married Patrick?" Her curious tone demanded.

"I've only recently seen those," Alan admitted.

"So, why did you look so shocked when I told you about your daughter?" She wondered with lines of curiosity.

"They don't mention anything about her," announced his excuse.

"That's probably because I've still got those ones," his mother divulged as she stood and carefully walked towards the writing desk. Now there her son looked dumbfounded as she expertly prised apart a secret compartment and produced those opened letters. In frustration Alan's hand whipped around and snatched them. They were even quicker at reading the words, and as his eyes followed each sentence his jaw dropped.

"So you knew!" He shrieked at his mother.

"I couldn't tell you because I didn't want to jeopardise what your father had done for the other's safety."

Next Erin's father spoke while looking at his daughter. "And because I naturally thought Emily was Patrick's," he stated with confused words. "I just assumed you'd forgotten about Alan."

Erin's next comment was well below the belt. "Patrick's hasn't got a good fuck in him as he prefers batting for the other side," her vinegary tone stated. "So how the hell could he father a child?"

"So did he, actually, consummate the marriage?"

"If you call slipping it in, wiggling it about for a few seconds and grunting rather stupidly," she shuddered. "Then yes I suppose!"

As if in a lecture hall of a University Alan suddenly asked, "If my father wanted to keep everything he'd done secret then why on earth did he keep giving all those cryptic clues?"

After he'd asked the question his mother hands went up in the comical manner she'd always use while impatiently finding the right words for the conversation she was hoping to start. If you remember she'd had an accident which obviously led to the frustrating impression that she was stupid. "I presume," she stuttered as she got up again and returned with a single scrap of paper. "That after he'd received yet another warning letter he simply wanted to make sure that whoever was responsible was found and brought to justice."

Hearing this Alan's shoulders slouched. He looked stunned. He twitched with convulsions and stared open mouthed when realising exactly what he'd done. "After I'd found that first clue and worked out the others," his confession dribbled as if the weight of the sky was upon his shoulders because he now felt like Atlas must have done. "I've now realised that I've led the killer straight to his next victim."

"Why do you think that?"

"Because it was me who's worked out where these people were," returned the reply. "And I've simply put a sign on my forehead saying if you want to find the next one then just follow me!"

"Tell me if I'm being stupid," his mother started. "But how did you know whether you'd got the right person?"

"Easy!"

"Well!"

"As part of the clue," he smiled somewhat lecherously. "All the victims had the tattoo of a particular herb on their body."

"Where abouts?"

"About here," Erin indicated with her index finger pointing to the exact spot.

"Bet they were worth seeing," the Commander rather chauvinistically grinned and hearing this rather bawdy statement Erin gave her father a very dirty look. "Sorry," he slouched. "But it was you who said there wasn't enough sex in my stories."

"I meant for porno Pete here!"

Everyone laughed at Alan's embarrassment.

"So I could be part of the puzzle?" His mother suggested as the colour in her face immediately vanished.

"I'm not sure," her son confessed and then thinking about what had happened added. "You could be!"

Hoping to relieve a little of the tension Erin stated, "Angela's not dead."

"Oh! Yes she is!"

"What?"

"Remember when I went to see whether she was alright."

"Yes!"

"And can you recall seeing that man?"

"What man?"

"The one sitting alone when we went down for breakfast."

"Oh! Yes," she recalled. "The one who asked some questions before walking out."

"That's the one," he brazenly shrugged before adding. "He probably went upstairs and committed the crime."

"You think so?"

"Probably," he answered. "And anyway I did find another clue."

"Did you?"

"Yes."

"So where is it?"

"It's in my jacket pocket."

"Well, don't just stand there," Erin's brisk tone demanded. "Go and get it!" He was gone roughly twenty seconds, and with the cigarette case in his hand returned waving it like a beacon of death.

"Let's have a look," imposed the Commander holding out his hand in hopeful expectancy. Alan duly placed it within the man's grasp and waited. The wait was awesome. The silence even worse but eventually the man simply burst into fits of laughter. "It's Gibraltar," confirmed the declared destination.

Alan looked puzzled. "How did you get that?" He quizzed.

"Think about it!" Returned the only sliver of help he was going to get.

With agitated annoyance Alan snatched the trinket and quite literally focused his gaze over the words yet again.

"I am coming with you!" Erin declared as both she and Alan discussed what their plan of action was.

"How can you," he mused looking at her as she sat at the dressing table applying the finishing touches to her make-up.

Hearing this declaration she stood and twisted. Dressed only in her rather unflattering maternity underwear the delicate bulge was plainly visible. "I'm only six months," she confirmed as her hands roamed over the stretching flesh of her belly.

"You very well maybe but, I don't think they'll let you fly," he insisted as he homed in on her. They kissed.

"Well they're not going to know," she confessed moving his hands that were discovering just how hard her nipples had become. "Don't you think you've done enough damage," she teased while removing his curious fingers.

"I don't know what you mean," his innocent remark grinned as he pouted his frustration.

"Well, I didn't get this way by myself," she announced with knowing authority. "And if I remember rightly that's how it all started!"

He knew he'd lost. He grunted his smirk like a naughty child and walked to the window. He was still looking when two arms quickly wound themselves around his waist, and tightened. A warm breath was felt as Erin nuzzled his neck. A line of kisses caressed his skin. He fought the primeval urge for all of a second. As hormonal urgency ripped his control asunder he turned and grabbed her. They kissed, and as they kissed he fought the animal desire to tear her clothes away.

"Are you descent?" Came the curious question that came from outside the room, and it was a moment later Alice strolled in. "There's someone downstairs to see you."

Alan followed his sister and was quite surprised to see Marsha Cooper waiting in the hallway carrying what appeared to be a large picture. "Hello!" She declared with a wave of her hand. "I've got that painting you wanted."

He stopped dead in his tracks. He closed his eyes in pure panic when remembering the intimate design he'd commissioned. He slowly meandered towards the sparkling figure of the artist obviously waiting. "Do you want to have a look?" She smiled removing the brown paper.

"Go on," dribbled his apathy, and once it had been uncovered his attitude instantly changed.

"I've tried to do something different," Marsha explained as he stared at the pure majesty of the painting. Instead of the usual erotic portrait she was much renowned for there was a superb picture of Erin, wearing a deep blue ballroom gown, standing by an oak table similar to the one in the Colonel's dining room.

His heart pounded as he stared, and as he stared there was no doubt in his mind. "What do I owe?"

"Call it a belated thank you," she offered while giving a great big hug and a quick peck on the cheek.

"Please, fasten your seat belt," ordered the pilot's voice, over the intercom, as the plane circled the historic monolith of rock. Alan gently nudged his snoring companion and watched the way she twitched and grunted like an overweight buffalo. Eventually, she opened her eyes and carelessly rubbed the sleep away.

"Have we arrived," asked the sleepy question. Alan turning soon realised that someone, not to far away, had just done a silent but deadly discharge of the smelly variety. Trying not to become asphyxiated had noticed, over a short period of time that because of the physical condition, of her condition, had regrettably acquired that really couldn't give a damn attitude.

"Not quite" He explained while trying desperately to wrap the belt around her waist, and finally succeeding sat back breathless, in more ways than one. The plane landed smoothly, and taxied to the rather battered airport terminal. When ready they left the cramped interior and walked down the steps that had been placed by the open door of that old RAF Comet. Together they stood at the bottom gazing at the picturesque granite of Gibraltar where rumour has it that Atlas, a mythical Titan, had once used it as a stepping stone while supporting the sky across his back.

"Mummy," shouted a young girl's voice racing toward them holding her arms in welcome and when she'd reached them, Alan watched as Erin embraced her daughter. When, at last they'd separated they strolled towards another familiar figure waiting.

"Hello!" Kitty Forester greeted as she gave her daughter a loving hug and Alan a quick kiss of welcome. Having finished she looked over their shoulders and simply asked. "Where's your father?"

The man in question had just disembarked and was now pacing, with a couple of heavy looking suitcases probably bearing gifts, along the greyish black tarmac. Obviously seeing his wife, he dropped the luggage and simply waited for her to jump into his arms.

The journey to the Forester's home was suicidal in every respect, because it may have been the non stop aggression of the local drivers or it may have had something to do with every vehicle deciding that they had the right of way down the narrow side streets but after several close encounters they pulled up outside the plush exterior of number 47 Dockland View.

"This was my bedroom," Erin indicated as she fell onto the ready prepared double bed, and seeing the way she patted the space beside her Alan obeyed his natural instinct and went to be at her side. He'd been there but a moment when she rolled and started blowing lazily into his ear. It was so hypnotic and it was as if a mythological Siren had just called because he knew all about her needs and feeling every bit as randy allowed her to straddle his physique. Seeing the way she looked, he eagerly pulled her down and forced his urgent mouth onto hers. His hands instinctively roamed across the substantial bulk of her backside until slipping beneath the hemline of her light cotton skirt before feeling the silky threads of her underwear.

"Fuck me," she demanded as he masterfully pulled her knickers off and threw them to the floor. He'd learnt that the standard missionary position was probably not the best position to be using at that precise moment and so panted his need as she reached beneath her arse and held his cock ready. The tempo increased as he played with her motherly breasts.

They awoke to absolute quiet, and it was when he glanced at his watch that he was rather surprised when seeing the time. "It's midnight!" He said.

"So!" Was her first acknowledgement? "What do you want me to do about it?" Hearing this he didn't quite know how to respond, but eventually he stood and walked to the window. With him staring into the dull night Erin crept up and swung her arms around his waist. "Let's go for a walk," the offer sighed as she took his hand.

Along the sea front, arm in arm, they strolled as the aroma of freshly baked food hung deliciously in the air. Standing like a beacon against the darkened water the greasy looking man casually tossed pieces of freshly caught fish onto the charcoal embers of his brazier fire. Further along the front they walked until nearing a courting couple. "I'll be leaving tomorrow," bluntly grumbled the sailor as his arm indicated the Giant Battleship majestically anchored in the deep waters of the bay.

The young girl reached onto tiptoe and urgently placed a warm kiss upon the sailor's cheek, and when she'd finished her words were bold as they rose from the heart. "I will always wait for you," she promised as once again they kissed. Seeing this the two onlookers felt the love that had been promised, and for that clutched each other even tighter. How long they'd been walking they never knew but the sun was shining brightly when they awoke. Like two lame ducks they waddled downstairs and spotted a short note written on a card left upon the table.

"Taken Emily swimming," precisely stated the first sentence. "So when you're ready why don't you come and join us." Having read the words Alan shrugged his shoulders.

"They've obviously gone to Catalan Bay," confidently announced Erin making breakfast.

"Where's that," coaxed his uncertain question.

"The other side of the Rock."

Hearing this he panicked. "And how far's that?" He demanded tucking into the bowl of something edible. He'd taken a mouthful when he grimaced because the taste reminded him of milk that had been left on the doorstep on a warm afternoon in August.

"It's always like that," Erin teased when watching the facial expression. Bowing to her greater knowledge he continued eating until it had all been devoured.

It took less than a quarter of an hour before they walked down the slight slope that led directly onto the golden sand of that rather smallish beach. With his towel rolled under his arm he stepped onto the scorching sand and quietly cursed with pain from the heat. It didn't take long before they found Erin's mother laying face down on a rather large beige towel. With Alan towering above her, he looked down and noticed that she'd undone the guarding clasp of her mustard coloured bikini top to expose the dusty complexion of her skin. Whether it was his cumbersome shadow that forced the woman to beginning twitching but then with some agility she turned her face and glanced at him. She smiled when with expert dexterity she cupped her breasts, immediately sat up and looked directly at the man staring at her. Her smile was radiant as she pleasantly asked, "Who wants to rub some lotion on my shoulders!" And as if any motivation was needed indicated the bottle of coloured liquid sitting in a basket close by.

"Where's Emy?" Erin wondered while taking the bottle and casually starting to rub the pale pink liquid across her mother's shoulders.

"She's with your father," uttered the reply as Alan watched. He was hypnotised because although she was fast approaching middle age it could be seen that Mrs Forester had kept her youthful beauty and attractiveness. After some two minutes, or so, her mother softly whispered something into her daughter's ear that made them both howl with laughter.

"Why don't you go for a swim," smiled the instruction as Erin roughly pushed Alan away. Sensing that they might want to talk about certain topics, which women could never openly discuss in front of a man, stood and rushed towards the clarity of the Mediterranean Sea. He dived headlong into the water and started to swim towards the pontoon tethered but a short distance from shore. He climbed aboard, stood and dripped water everywhere while staring back at folk lazing on the beach. He smiled with a keen, and knowing, interest when he noticed that Mrs Forester had now removed her hands. His curse was stage whispered, because he was a little to far away to appreciate the stunning beauty of her uncovered bosom.

Trying not to focus he twisted his head. His eyes soon picked out other women seductively dressed in their beachwear. Concentrating, he never heard the teenage youth get out and stand beside him. They'd been standing for a couple of minutes when another pair of hands suddenly came into sight on the edge of the raft. Next a head appeared before a middle-aged woman started to pull herself out of the water. "You don't get many of those to the pound," whispered the younger of the two open mouthed men staring at the woman's bikini covered chest.

Trying to bring a little decorum to the situation, if at all possible because he was leering just as much, Alan offered his little snippet of advice, "Seen one pair; seen them all!"

"You may well have done," started the counter debate. "But, in saying that I'll bet you'd love to get to grips with them."

"And who do they belong to?"

"That's the infamous Eleanor Yardley," he lad grinned. "And if you ever get the chance then just have a good look at her when she's wearing her white bikini bottoms."

Erin was in a quandary because she didn't know what to do for the best. With the humid weather, thanks to the local climatic conditions, the wearing of mothering bras had become tortuous. If she didn't wear one her heavy breasts proved strenuous in the extreme, and if she did then the discomfort became unbearable. "I want to go shopping in La Linea," she explained while dragging Alan towards the solitary bus stop, and dead on time the old yellow rust bucket trundled its weary path. Along the dusty road it crept and with the midday sun beating remorselessly against the metal hull rivers of perspiration flowed down the faces of the passengers. Deciding to remain motionless Alan simply studied the scrubland, through the dirty window, and listened to the pounding throb of the engine struggling to keep the vehicle moving. For the umpteenth time the driver crashed the gears while trying to discover the correct one for that particular piece of uneven road. As the bus lunged momentarily forward it caused all the passengers to shift position and it was a second later that the Spanish insults flew, like swarming bees, as the inertia propelled everybody backwards. For the umpteenth time the large figure of a woman dressed in black collided with the seat directly in front and forced the whole of her twenty stone to land on top of the pathetic looking individual who just smiled as if nothing had happened. It was during one of these moments that several live chickens escaped their mobile coop, and became free to fly around. The bus finally pulled up outside the white washed terminal building and the door creaked open. If it had been hot inside the bus then as both Alan, and Erin, stepped off the stifling heat of the afternoon sun hit them. Tottering towards the obvious market, Alan spotted a stricken old woman struggling with several over-laden bags precariously hoisted around the frailty of her doubled body. Whether the weight was too much for her, but at one point a single bag fell to earth as she struggled onwards. As if undertaking one of the Labours of Heracles he raced and picked up the bag. If he thought the old woman was struggling with the weight his smile instantly turned to a grunt when trying to lift it? The short journey across the dusty square seemed a million miles, and having reached the path decided that enough was enough. His sigh was deep as the heavy bundle dropped to earth. His expression changed to one of awe as the old woman casually picked up that dead weight, as if she'd been doing it all her life, and smiled her smile of broken teeth. There was no word of thanks, as she scurried passed, but into his hand was pressed an over-ripe peach.

"That'll teach you," giggled the spontaneous smile as Erin flicked her bleached auburn locks.

Not daring to admit to anything Alan warmly barked his defence. "Got a free peach didn't I," he confessed throwing it high into the air.

"And you'll have to declare it through customs," her whimsical voice giggled as she caught the fruit rather easily. "So you'll have to catch me if you want it back," she giggled as she waddled hurriedly away. Alan chased her, and kept bumping into others as she craftily avoided his reach. Finally, down one of the side streets he made a grab and caught hold of her. As he pulled, the peach seemed to become squashed between their hot bodies and as the juice oozed the tingling sensation forced them apart. "Now, look what you've done," she explained pulling the sodden material away from her body.

As he looked he realised that today Erin had decided not to wear a certain piece of cumbersome lingerie. "It's a wet T-shirt contest," he teased while staring directly at the damp patches where, but a moment ago, her two heavy and mothering breasts were perfectly on display.

"Is that all you think about?" She abruptly demanded while trying to cover her large nipples. She failed of course, and now being self-conscious began to walk away. It didn't help when passing a group of elderly Spanish men who simply stared open-mouthed as if they'd never seen a woman's breasts before.

"It's the same the whole world over," he declared.

"What is?"

"How every man likes to see a nice pair of tits?"

It was nearly seven o'clock when they arrived back, and then onto the veranda, where Erin's mother and father were sat drinking some sort of alcohol.

"Did you get everything you wanted," asked Kitty as she stood and wandered towards her daughter. Once together, both women huddled as if in a scrum and talked. Every so often it was either Erin, or her mother, who twisted her head and looked directly at Alan before giving a grin of knowledge. This continued as the evening light began to disappear, and the view was breathtaking as they gazed across the bay towards Spain. "I've got just the thing," the words erupted as both women disappeared from view.

"Now, where are they going?" Wondered the Commander sipping from his glass and the shrug of Alan's shoulder confirmed that he didn't know either. It was about five minutes later that the two women reappeared. There was Kitty wearing a sunset gold evening gown that enhanced the gentle curves of her body to full effect. The silky chiffon material fell to earth, but as she pirouetted it showed the full length slit flawlessly exposing her bronzed legs.

"Do you like," asked the question.

Both Alan and the Commander sat studying the beauty. Suddenly, the older of the two stood and walked towards his wife before racing his hungry arms around her waist. "It would be better," he stated while a hand moved inside one of the slits. "If you didn't have to wear these." Having spoken his hand reappeared holding a pair of sunset yellow paper-thin knickers. "Because it just wouldn't look right having the ridges of your underwear so clearly visible!" As the man twirled the intricate fabric, in the air, there was a chorus of sniggers and innuendo that flew like chaff in the wind.

Whether she was embarrassed by her parent's antics, but Erin cordially announced, "I'm going to bed." But, before leaving the room turned towards Alan and suggested, "Coming?" Taking the hint he crisply walked after her.

They lay naked in bed, snuggled beneath the mosquito net when a mischievous looking intruder appeared. "I can't sleep," quietly mumbled the young voice of Emily as she stood in the bedroom doorway.

Her mother sat up and held out her arms in comfort.

The daughter moved gingerly forward and allowed herself to be caught and cuddled. It took a moment, but she cunningly sneaked between both her mother and her natural father and understanding the child's need Alan turned towards Erin. As he saw the intense love he smiled. "I'll go next door," he sacrificed while beginning to stand.

It wasn't Erin's hand that was offered, but was Emily's. The intensity of his paternal desire forced him to cuddle both mother and daughter, because he was there and could. He awoke, around six o'clock, to find Emily's arms locked tightly around her mother's frame. He smiled and twisted his face to look directly at Erin as she posed like a beached walrus. As they lay he could see the little ripples of life flowing over the naked bulge in her belly, and as he watched he smiled. Feeling so full of life, he sprang to his feet and crossed towards the shuttered window and opened it. He'd obviously forgotten that he was naked, but anyway felt the cool air refreshing his body while stretching his aching frame. It was after this moment of reflection that he peered into the enclosed courtyard below. Suddenly he felt embarrassed because there was Kitty putting washing on the clothesline. He simply didn't know what to do when she looked up, caught sight of him and gave him a courteous wave. Seeing this he panicked, but ultimately decided that in the best interests of politeness then a simple smile would suffice. Unfortunately his scheme was a little to casual inasmuch as she was also completely naked. His pulse raced when she smiled, and with that she disappeared inside the house once again.

"Breakfast's ready," announced the warmth of a voice that had just opened the bedroom door. Emily, who'd simply dressed according to the weather, ran passed her grandmother and hurtled down the stairs. "It'll be on the table in five minutes," finished the message. Whether it was the sea air but Alan felt as if he'd not eaten for a week, and so rocking Erin ventured towards the kitchen. He was about to descend when spotting Kitty stepping from her own bedroom, and as she came closer his imagination ran riot. "I see you're an early riser," she grinned knowing full well that he understood the double entendre.

"The early bird catches the worm," his immediate response grinned.

Her smile said it all, but no more was exchanged as they walked into the kitchen and sat at the table. Eventually everybody arrived, and it was over the next ten minutes that they discussed their plans for the day. "How about going Tangiers?" Erin wondered.

The sun was hot as they cast their eyes over the stern of the ferry as it ploughed its path towards the African Coast and the Atlas Mountains, and it was here Emily kept pointing to the numerous dolphins playfully chasing in the ferry's wake. It was about halfway across when a sudden gust of wind caught both women unprepared, and as they brushed down their billowing skirts they both smiled. Erin, because the whole thing seemed rather silly and inappropriate for someone in her condition. Her mother, on the other hand, because she'd obviously decided that the need for underwear was totally inappropriate. Alan looked, well he really couldn't do anything else, and remembering the incident that morning went deathly white.

"What's wrong?" Asked the Commander who'd just arrived back from where ever he'd gone. "Feeling a tad sea-sick."

"Maybe!"

Hearing this and showing their concern both women quaintly wrapped their arms around the ashen features of Alan, and decided that it would be better if he went below. "It used to work for me," declared Kitty starting to walk away. It was dark when the three of them stepped into the hot interior, and the smell of stale bodies lingered. After scrambling over the sleeping populous they eventually found a space and sat together. Suddenly, as if she'd done it a million times before Kitty took the lad's head and rested it across her lap so that with the heat and heady scent he must have dozed off. "We're here," the excited utterance erupted as well as a gentle rocking of his frame. His eyes slowly opened. His faculties took a moment, but ultimately they arrived and having woken noticed that everybody had, either disappeared, or were about to.

"Where's Erin?" He asked as a plan bubbled.

Kitty reached and took his hand. "She's gone to be with Emily," smiled the reply as she began to pull him up. He wasn't going to allow himself to be dragged into a standing position, and so pulled against her. His strength was just too great as she collapsed onto his body, and as she fell his arms quickly whipped around her waist. She lay, panting with the effort, and burst into laughter as they just stared at each other.

After a pause; his breath was hot as the question came, "Do you remember when the wind caused your skirt to billow up?"

"Yes!"

"Well," he began. "When I was inside Marsha Cooper's studio doing some investigating I remember seeing a portrait depicting that exact same scene."

"Oh! Really," she grinned.

"And there's always been a rumour about a painting that showed Carol, your daughter, sitting naked in a garden full of foxgloves," he challenged before asking. "Or was it of you?"

Hearing this; she gave a wicked smile that neither confirmed, nor denied, his thoughts and so with that they both walked on deck without a single word being exchanged. They joined the others as they walked the gangplank and stepped onto the dry earth of reality. Into the dusty streets they moved. It was here that old men, in dirty caftans, sat around in groups drinking and smoking long black cheroots. Camels constantly spitting their intolerance and contempt against the Bedouin who controlled their lives. Young urchins, dressed in rags, constantly badgering and bartering their way to happiness. The religious needs of the women that had them hidden from top to toe in the black of night, and upon their covered heads were caskets of water. Along side the barren roads sat snake charmers enticing their hooded friends to gyrate in tunes with no melody, or flow in time. There were lepers huddled in contorted corners away from the prying eyes of man.

The stillness of the evening air brought their excursion to a weary end as they trod, with heavy steps, towards that same vessel that had deposited them amongst that magical world. Eventually, the constant throbbing of the engine confirmed their journey home and it was under a lover's moon that Alan held Erin. The stars twinkled, as did his desires. The soft glow played a symphony across her body. He listened but a moment to the music of his heart. She was prepared when their mouths met in a frenzy of unadulterated passion.

Emily had gone to the local school and it was the middle of the afternoon when both Alan and Erin wandered along the beach at Catalan Bay. Although it was early November the sun still had the power to burn skin if not to careful. Because, of her condition Erin sat beneath the large parasol dressed in the frumpy outfit of a woman nearing her time. Alan, on the other hand, relaxed beneath the hot sun ever hopeful of improving his luke-warm tan. With his eyes closed, against the glare, he suddenly heard Erin's voice. "Wow, look at her," sniggered the slightly jealous tone of her voice. "She's colossal!"

He sat up. Gazed at the rather large contingent of bathers either still in the warm Mediterranean, or lazing on the beach. "Where, am I supposed to be looking?" He shrugged.

"There!"

He followed the pointed finger to observe a rather lanky, as well as skinny, woman moving behind a red and white-stripped windbreak. He was still looking when she reappeared, and as she ran passed and towards the water's edge his jaw simply crashed to the sand. He was speechless watching the ease in which she swam, not to the first raft, not even to the second, but all the way to the third a good hundred yards from shore.

"Where do you think you're going," demanded a stern voice. "As if I didn't know."

He was breathless when eventually he lumbered aboard that twelve foot square piece of floating wood and once out, of the water, turned to look directly at the woman lying on her belly. Creeping across the pontoon, like a thief, he allowed several drops of salt water to splash upon her back. "Hey," groaned the declaration as the woman twisted her head and stared at him.

"I'm sorry," he offered while stepping back. There was no response and so feeling like the proverbial lost sheep he was about to dive back into the water when he noticed another swimmer getting closer.

Not wanting to dive in and collide with whoever was approaching like the answer to the Mary Celeste he waited. "Hello," smiled the man as he got onto the raft. "I thought you'd be here." Alan looked stunned because he'd never seen this bloke before and was about to admit to the fact when the lady, still on her belly, looked up.

"I've been waiting for you," she smiled while standing up and quickly placing her arms around his shoulders. Alan smiled because the scene that was now being played appeared to have been taken from a low budget movie. As they kissed she ran her rather spindly fingers through the few wispy strands of hair that seemed to be sprouting from his bald head. The vivid green Bermuda shorts, which went all the way down to the bloke's knees, seemed quite incapable of supporting his well rounded middle-aged spread that was pressing against the woman's belly and acting as if a cushion. His eager hands were loving cupping the woman's arse and was carefully lifting the mature cellulite. Her tits appeared to be far to young for the age of her body because she'd obviously had a little nip and tuck to make them appear like every male teenager's fantasy. They were huge in every sense of the word; so big infact the white bikini top had trouble in keeping them from fall out. With him studying the gruesome twosome and realising that they probably wanted to be alone dived into the water and swam back to shore.

"Well!" Erin declared while packing away the various pieces of beachwear, which normally gets brought for any emergency, and never gets used.

"I just don't know," he puffed while looking out to sea. He scrunched up his nose as he thought that he saw the couple diving into the water. "Hold on, a minute!"

"Now what?"

"I think she's on they're way back," he hoped, and turning to Erin continued. "You go, and I'll catch you up when I've finished."

"Okay," she shrugged while carefully shuffling across the sand before climbing the rocky steps and disappearing. It took another couple of minutes before the other woman eventually arrived back and marched towards her forgotten garments. As she neared, Alan took the moment to stare directly at her. His eyes sprang wide when remembering the young lad's comment concerning what lay hidden beneath a particular person's white bikini pants and as he saw it he smiled. Not because of the image of her naked cunt, but because from her rather bushy pubic hair the delicate design of a white flowering plant was seen to be sprouting.

Realising that this woman could actually be the one he was after arrogantly walked to where she was drying herself and carefully asked, "Did you ever know a Captain Henry Young?"

She never flinched. She didn't even stop as her head became lost within a towel. He simply watched as she twisted her face, and the cold expression said her silent words. Obviously understanding that she didn't want an audience he felt frustrated and for that sighed. He began to walk away and was climbing the steps when suddenly a strong hand grabbed his ankle. He turned and looked down at the woman staring at him. "Who would like to know?" Her curious, but foreign sounding, words slipped as her gaze focused on him.

Having got her attention he smiled. "Let me introduce myself," he beamed extending a hand and announcing the name that came into his head. Pulling back his shoulders in confidence began, "The name's Otis Chaney and I'm conducting an investigation about the man!" The change was instantaneous. The colour drained from her body as if a magnet had been used. Her body trembled, and no words were uttered as she quickly vanished into the milling throng of holidaymakers. He felt confused standing watching her move. Needing some answers he jumped onto the hot beach and gave chase. He was breathless having caught her. He was rather rough snatching her elbow. He panted as he pulled her into the quiet of an alcove that seemed so natural. Now, ready he instantly threw a strong hand hard against her mouth so that she could not scream. Her gaze was scared as they stared into each other's eyes, and it was then that Alan noticed the tremble of fright rippling through her body. "Why, did you run?" He asked in a mode of authority. She tried to answer, but the French sounding expression was incomprehensible and the look of terror compelled him to loosen his grip. "I'm waiting."

Her knee was too quick for Alan's defence. The agonising pain soared around his body making him feel sick. He dropped to the sand clutching his groin, and watched her disappearing through tears of excruciating agony.

"That'll be my guests now," the Commander smiled putting his sherry glass down. He was gone for a couple of minutes before the door reopened. "This is Kevin Yardley and his wife Eleanor," he introduced.

Remembering being told that Eleanor was French Alan tried his somewhat limited use of the language. "Je voulais juste te dire un gros bonjour," he smiled while kissing Eleanor on both cheeks.

"Merci," she returned. "But please no more French."

"Why?"

"Because the British are pretty shit at it," Kevin responded. "Keep putting the wrong emphasis on the wrong words."

"Okay," he thankfully agreed.

"You know each other," asked the surprised looking Commander.

"I don't think we were formally introduced the first time."

The laugh said it all. "That's right," Kevin explained. "Because if I remember rightly it was when we were on the third raft at Catalan bay."

"That's right," Alan acknowledged. "And it was just a fleeting moment!"

"And weren't you the one dripping water all over my back," continued Eleanor and hearing this Alan grinned rather stupidly.

"Because I presume," her husband joked. "That he simply wanted you to turn over."

"Ah! You mean," she answered thrusting out her comely bosom. "He wanted to look at my nice new boobies."

"And, also, to see what else was on view," her husband romantically smiled.

"Pardon!"

"Don't you remember which of the costumes you were wearing?"

"Oui," she smiled. "The beautiful white bikini."

"That's the one," Alan confirmed.

Eleanor continued, "And doesn't it show off my figure quite stunningly."

Remembering what he'd been staring at when she walked towards him smiled, "It most certainly does."

"Why, thank you," the woman grinned. "And I must say that out of all the swimsuits, I've got, it's that particular one that always seems to attract the most stares."

"I wonder why," interrupted her husband's quiet words.

"I don't know," she shrugged. Whether it was the alcohol, the mood or something completely different but he leaned across, with a truly wicked smile, and whispered something into his wife's ear.

"Kevin," she remonstrated. "Does that mean to say that every time I've worn that particular bikini people have been; how you say; voilà ma vaginaux."

"And that's a very discreet way of putting it," he answered. "But the long and short of it is that everybody has been able to see it."

"Why didn't you tell me?"

"Because my sweetest," he defended in that most tactless of male tones. "I've learnt, over the many years of our marriage, never to pick fault with any of the things that you have chosen to wear."

"So you don't mind any Tom, Dick or Harry looking at my rude bits?"

"Is that why you kneed him in the nuts," Erin suddenly piped up with a classic laugh. "Because he was staring at, how did you put it, your naughty bits?" Hearing this Alan closed his eyes and smiled rather stupidly when remembering the fact that it bloody well hurt.

"No," she admitted. "But it's because of the name he used to introduce himself."

"And which name was that?"

"Otis Chaney," Alan answered as they all walked towards the veranda.

"Why him?"

"It was the first name that sprang into my head."

Over dinner, which was superb, Alan simply could not take his eyes of Eleanor's cleavage as she sat opposite. It was part way through dessert that she looked him straight in the eye before issuing those immortal words while indicating their exact position, "My eyes are up here."

"I know," he shrugged with some slight understanding.

"What's she saying," Erin asked.

"She would like it," Kevin remonstrated. "If he would stop looking at my wife's cleavage."

"He can't," smiled Kitty.

"Why's that?"

"Because," fired the standard feminine argument. "It's instinct that compels the male to ogle a woman's tits whenever they can!"

"At least she's got something worth looking at," Erin argued looking directly at their guest.

"Haven't you," smiled Eleanor thrusting out her chest with even more voluptuous emphasis. "Because being la jeune fille au l'école I can remember how all of the boys, as well as certain teachers, regarde moi."

"At least you've got something worth looking at," she huffed pushing out her belly. "I just look like a beached whale with a couple of volley balls stuffed up my jumper."

"No you don't," Kevin argued. "Because to me you look cuddly."

"Exactly my point," she insisted. "Cuddly I maybe." Here she paused while looking directly at him. "But sexy I'm most definitely not," she plunged like a dagger.

Then as if trying to make her feel slightly better Kevin rather amorously added, "If I was twenty years younger then I'd be more than willing to feel just how cuddly you are."

"It's not you I'm trying to make feel guilty," she scowled. "It's Captain Stud here." Alan instantly coloured because he knew it was aimed at him.

"I think what she's trying to say," interrupted Eleanor in her beautiful French accent. "Is that just because she's pregnant don't mean that all of the sexual urges she once had have gone into hibernation."

"See!"

"You can still play with her naughty bits," Eleanor added.

"Is that right?" Alan defended. "Because here's me thinking that now she's in the pudding club I really shouldn't be using my long handled spoon."

"Stop trying to be funny," Erin teased. "Because I wouldn't mind it if you tried dipping your finger and licking the bowl occasionally."

"Erin!" Her father's voice snapped.

"Sorry."

"I know how you must be feeling," her mother smiled. "Because when I was carrying you, and your sister, your father made it perfectly plain that he didn't want to feel a cunt either."

"Is that so wrong?" Her husband defended.

"It is when I was feeling horny," her words smiled before adding the kick in the teeth. "And you just turned over and went to sleep!"

"That's revenge for all he times you'd done it to me."

"Stop it you two," Eleanor interrupted as she stood. "Because it doesn't matter what moralist's say; sex still rules the world because Mother Nature has made that perfectly clear."

"I've got a nick-name," Eleanor interrupted during the conversations. "And does anyone want to hear how I got it?"

"And what name is that?"

"Sorrel," she grinned.

"Which one?"

"I presume it's the French variety."

"Why," asked Kevin. "Because you're rather lemony and a bit sour."

"Shut up," she groaned and then continued. "I'd been seconded from the Marine Nationale to help your father." Here she looked directly at Alan. "Concerning discrepancies about something, or other, that we were investigating when we heard a loud knock on his office door. When it opened a young nurse walked in carrying what I later discovered to be a test-tube full of red liquid and to cut a long story short I was ordered to go down to the hospital where they wanted to carry out further tests because it appeared that I've got a very rare blood group." Here she paused. "I think it was on the third day that while sitting on a bench, in the hospital garden, your father walked towards me and as he approached I immediately stood and saluted."

"Very formal," Alan agreed. "And very proper."

"But what I didn't expect," she added. "Was when a psychiatric patient ran passed closely followed by two, or three, burly porters trying to catch him."

"Bet that was fun."

"Not really," she started. "Because they knocked me into the flowers."

"Bet you came up smelling of roses."

"Actually no!"

"That was a joke."

"It might have been," she stated. "Had you mentioned the fact that I might have been able to get a prick from it?"

"Nice one," somebody laughed, and by the way she coloured it was probably Kitty who'd said it.

"You have to remember," Eleanor continued. "That because I was in hospital all I had on was my dressing gown and slippers."

"We're still waiting to discover exactly how you got your nickname."

"I'm coming to that," she shivered. "Anyway as I lay on the ground I realised that my dressing gown had fallen open and there was your father looking down at me."

"And could he see anything?"

"I don't think so."

"Why?"

"It seemed that I'd fallen amongst the French Sorrel that the cooks use in making a lovely tasting soup, and the broad leaves had slipped between my legs and covered my naughty bits."

"I bet father was a bit disappointed."

"If he was," she shrugged. "Then he didn't show it."

"But that's the British for you," introduced the Commander who was also leering at her. "Stiff upper lip and all that."

"But why couldn't he have tried the French way," she sighed as her eyes closed. "You know the kind of thing, a little soft here and a bit stiff there."

"I doubt whether he could get to grips with that kind of spontaneous idea," Kitty suggested. "As I suppose he was metaphorically hoping that you'd take him in hand and give him a good time."

"He may well have done," she pouted. "But he was just standing there."

"So nothing happened?"

"No," she sulked. "But after the arranged eight weeks your father did ask me whether he could give me something as a sort of memento of our time together."

"What kind of memento was it?"

"I don't want to sound unkind," she frowned. "But he must have forgotten."

"That's unlike father!"

"Sorry!"

"My father was much renowned for his attention to detail that I find it hard to believe that he didn't actually give you one."

"I don't know about that!"

"What d'yer mean; you don't know."

"After I'd returned to duty in Brest it was about four months later that I received a strange painting?"

"Let me guess," he asked. "It showed you completely naked with your tattoo in perfect focus."

She blushed. She refused to look at him. "Actually it didn't," she admitted. "Because all it showed was the back of me standing in front of a wardrobe mirror."

It was a couple of days later when Alan walked into Eleanor's bedroom, because that was where the painting was hanging, and just stared at how salacious the intimate decor was. "There you are," she indicated. The moment he saw it he just swooned. It was beautiful. It was highly erotic but above all else it was what he wanted to see.

"That's you," he responded while studying the canvas. "And can you recall what I asked you about the other night?"

"Whether you can see my tattoo?"

"That's right," he smiled while staring at just how sensual the profile of a woman's naked back could possibly be. "And from the angle used it's hard to tell at first glance."

"Quoi!"

"Whether my father did give you one," he grinned. "But, if you look at the reflection in the mirror."

"Oui."

"Then, he did give you one," he grinned while grabbing her shoulders and twisting her face so that she was looking at the impression of that herb just above her pubic hair line.

"And there's me thinking that the artist was being a bit generous with his brush strokes."

Not wanting to go down that route asked, "Did you receive anything else?"

"There was only the painting," she confirmed. He stepped forward and gently touched the canvas to begin gently stroking where the actual reflection was. He'd closed his eyes mainly because the image inside his mind suddenly became very real, and if you can picture what he was thinking then you're just as corrupt as he was. Finally, after a bit of fiddling about, he removed a small piece of paper and stage whispered the words, "You've found the clues now who's the foxglove?"

It had gone midnight, when both Alan and Erin, finally settled in the double bed they'd claimed as their own and drifted into the wonderful world of sleep. When waking and twisting he noticed the empty space and seeing the time ultimately decided that Erin had taken her daughter to school to discuss something with the teachers as to why Emily was being bullied. This may have had something to do with the fact of having to use a different surname to that of her mother. Anyway feeling rejuvenated and full of the joys of spring he got up and dressed in a pair of white tennis shorts, white socks and sandals which seemed to go with everything. Or more conventionally the British overseas uniform that can be spotted at a distance of about a hundred paces especially the socks. With nothing else better to do he wandered about until finding the empty kitchen, and it was in here that he managed to gather enough food to make breakfast, or lunch depending on your point of view. It was about halfway through the meal that the door suddenly burst open and Marshall Forester sauntered in carrying an assortment of maps and charts. "I'm glad you're up," whittled the welcome as the other man sat at the table spreading various paper coastlines. "Because I'd like a quiet word." Having spoken the man poured a tumbler of lukewarm milk and took a quick swig; now with it in his hand he took a deep breath. "How much do you know about what your father did in the Navy?" He asked while scrutinising the coastline of somewhere, or other.

Because of his military upbringing Alan was a trifle suspicious at hearing the question. But, seeing as the man was obviously an old friend still decided to give a shrug followed by his carefully chosen words, "Only from what I'd found, and read about, in his journals at home."

"So, you don't really know!" The man responded never lifting his gaze.

"Know what!"

"Exactly what he did do!"

"And I suppose you did!"

"Not precisely," returned the Commander's answer. Hearing this Alan's brow furrowed as uncertainties raced inside his mind; because in all the time he'd been reading those journals he'd never once seen any indication as to exactly what his father's job was. He knew for certain that he'd captained the Tanmouth on more than one occasion. He knew for definite each posting he'd received, but as for anything else he had about as much idea as trying to split the atom.

"So what do you know?"

The other man sighed with reluctant admiration. "Only that he was part of something very secret," he shrugged.

"Is that it," Alan doubted.

"Yes," he smiled. "But after his death your mother started digging around and asking questions."

"So why didn't I find anything?"

"Probably because I've got that information," he admitted while standing up and walking to the desk in the corner. Once there he opened it and pushed various papers aside until obviously finding what he'd been looking for. "Take a butchers' at these," he insisted pushing a couple of rather tatty looking sepia photographs forward.

"Who's that?"

"Your father."

"But he's got hair," Alan laughed. Taking the next he simply stared at a photograph showing a young couple, both in uniform, with their arms around the other as a mark of their love. As he looked Alan struggled to identify either of them. "Do you know who these two are?"

"No," the older man admitted with a shake of the head. "Not even with the clue that's been written on the back!"

Hearing this Alan turned the photo over and whispered the words, "Remember to add the polar bear!" He smiled. He tittered. He closed his eyes when remembering the painting in his mother's bedroom and the cryptic clue that went with it. He looked at the Commander and wondered, "Could it have something to do with the maps you're showing me?" He'd asked this simply because he remembered the interest Olivia Thomas had shown while he was up in Dundee.

The other man didn't answer the question directly, "You know when you were searching through your father's things?"

"Yes!"

"Did you happen to find anything that you felt might have been a bit out of character with your father?"

"In what respect?" Alan asked as his mind went back in time and cleverly focused on the make believe pages his imaginary fingers were quickly turning. "Because as I've tried to explain I'm not entirely sure what he did." Suddenly he smiled if for no other reason than seeing a crayoned drawing that his father had obviously doodled. The first time he'd set eyes on it he dismissed it as being totally pointless as it simply illustrated a single matchstick person with the words I know who you are written underneath.

He was still thinking when the Commander tried to jog his memory, "Well!"

"The only thing that might be of any use," he offered. "Is I kept seeing photographs of this one particular woman," he shrugged with wonder. "So d'yer think that she might have anything to do with it?"

"Is that her," asked the man pushing another photograph under his nose.

"Yes."

"Do you know who that is?"

"No!"

"Well let me tell you," the Commander rather officially announced. "Her name was Yvonne Parsons."

Thinking about the possibility of espionage, or something along those lines, he demanded, "What d'yer mean was," and as an afterthought added. "Did something happen to her?"

"Only inasmuch as that she's probably sitting infront of the television, at Calder's, with a nice cup of tea in her hand."

"I'm sorry!"

"That's your mother," he teased.

"Oh," he blushed with a comical snigger. And then wanting to change the direction of the conversation asked, "Why did father really want to see you when I was being made to camp in the shed all those years ago?"

He gave a creepy smirk like he did the last time before responding, "I remembering receiving a telephone call on the Wednesday evening to report to Calder's at 09.00 hours the following morning."

"Can you tell me what it was about?"

The man had that look of wanting to put him in the picture but officially not being able to. You know the kind of look. The one where it appears as if he'd just wet himself; and then trying his best not to divulge anything serious simply said, "When I arrived and met your father I was ordered to keep a watchful eye on Mademoiselle Eleanor Rochat in Gibraltar."

"Who?"

"You met her the other night," re-assured the Commander. "Because that was her maiden name before she married Kevin."

"Oh!" He smiled when realising who he was on about. "And do you why you had to keep an eye on her."

"Not really," he answered. "But what I do know is that there were four other people who were ordered to meet up with your father at Calder's."

"Could they," asked the question. "All have been ordered to safeguard various people?"

"Maybe," he shrugged. "But when a senior officer gives you an order you simply don't ask any questions."

Realising that he wasn't going to get any further help decided that another avenue might be better. "Are there any letters, notes, scraps of paper with information you've got that might be helpful?" He asked.

"About what?"

"The odd coup d'état abroad. Any political murders. Uprisings in the Far East. Any revolutions on the African continent. Any government scandal both here and abroad."

"Don't you think we've tried that?"

"And?"

"After years of deciphering various puzzles," he nonchalantly admitted. "We know about as much as you."

"You're a fat lot of good," Alan cursed as he began to brow beat the man. "Is there anyone you might think had a vendetta against my father, or something you felt odd at any time?"

The shrug said it all, but it was a moment later the other man asked as something must have clicked inside his head, "Can you remember the month you were sent to the shed?"

"December," Alan shivered. "And it was bloody cold."

"Right," the older man confirmed. "So why did Henry ask me to go into the garden and find him the purple digitalis?"

"I don't know," he shrugged. "Because surely that's a summer flower."

"Maybe it was code for something, or someone."

"Such as?"

There was a pause. A rather lengthy pause until Alan shrugged, "Can you get a pen and paper?"

"Okay," the Commander offered. "Now what?"

"Write these down," he grinned while repeating the ten letters flashing inside his head. "Now what have you got?"

It was like a bolt of lightning as they both mouthed a name, "Otis Chaney."

It was part way through February when Alan sat comfortably in the armchair beside the blazing fire at Calder's drinking from the half empty glass. With the fiery warmth of Brandy slipping down his throat he smiled at what had happened over the past months. With a feeling of utter contentment he summarised every facet of his life and smiled. His first was for Erin sitting opposite reading a storybook to Emily perched quite contentedly at her side. His next was for his mother who'd gone to stay, and live, with the Foresters' after celebrating the arrival of the New Year. Another was for Alice having returned to her husband with the understanding that their marriage needed a little more sparkle. His next was for the adventures of the past year, which still left a somewhat bittersweet taste in his mouth. And in the final chapter, which merged and melted like a good thriller, he'd managed to solve the perpetrator of his father's murder. Major General Otis Chaney had been brought to justice; and it was day after day that the idea of his innocence rippled through his mind, but come the dark of night the accused was still guilty.

The man, in question, had on every occasion been present at the death of each person that Alan had met. His undoubted mechanical expertise and driving skills pointed to the accidents that had occurred. On cross examination the man simply could not point to any facts that might clear his name, and the further the Court Marshall continued the deeper became the hole. The Isle of Man Boat Company kept detailed records showing that there were two people who'd hired a yacht during the week of Olivia Thomas's accident. There were witnesses who claimed to have seen him near the car that Alan's father, plus Irene Sutherland his passenger, had driven before that fatal crash. The stumbling block, for the prosecution, seemed to be the death of Catherine Hill. Was it the hand of God, as was claimed by the defence, or was the man actually there? It was day eight of the trial when a receipt was produced showing that a spare part had been purchased from Wright's Body Shop in Worcester which was later found by accident investigators to have been tampered with. This rather damning piece of evidence was found half burnt in a rubbish bin at the bottom of the garden, although the defence lawyer claimed that it had been planted, and it was this that clearly pushed the accused closer to the verdict. There was no emotion shown when questioned about his whereabouts in Nottingham as well as the death of Angela Nuttell. Alan smiled when realising that at least Eleanor Yardley was still alive and living quite safely in Gibraltar. Was the suspect at the inquest of Captain Young's death? Was he also present at Worcester and at the church talking to the Colonel? Like all nasty pieces of work he claimed, during heavy cross-examination, that these facts were merely circumstantial but in the reality of that courtroom the man simply had no alibi. As the trial proceeded, at the somewhat pedestrian pace of the military law machine, his guilt shone through the paper-thin defence of his barrister.

Guilty was the verdict, but the sentence was never carried out as the man was found shot in his cell with the smoking revolver dangling from his mouth and the back of his head sprayed against the wall. Suicide, returned the coroner and the case was closed.

"It's time for bed," Erin smiled giving her daughter a quick peck on the cheek.

The young girl returned the kiss before gamely skipping away. Having reached the door stopped and turned, just like her mother had once done, and asked her usual question, "Are you coming to tuck me in?"

Alan smiled, stood and playfully chased her. He normally caught her just outside his old bedroom, and tonight was no different. Taking her hand he led her inside and watched as she climbed into bed. She looked priceless as like any loving father he carefully tucked her in and bent to kiss her brow. He walked away, but not before looking at the painting above his old bed, that Marsha had reluctantly turned.

"Alan," screamed a voice. "The baby's coming!"

Racing down the stairs, two at a time, he hurtled inside the sitting room where Erin was clutching her belly. It was blind panic that forced him to appear in control. "Have your water's broken," came the standard question he'd read about in one of the many books dealing with that aspect of childbirth. He spotted the drops of fluid on the carpet, and as he stared her scream was deafening. "I suppose they must have done," he tried to tease as she fell like a bag of spuds.

Her arms were everywhere pulling at various pieces of clothing. "Take my knickers off," she wept as another contraction ripped through her body. With urgent necessity he pushed up the hemline of her maternity dress, and yanked down the sodden material. In an instant her knees went up to display the classic posture of a mother about to deliver her sprog and he was also quick to notice the intense contraction. "It's coming!" She panted in the textbook manner the midwife had obviously taught her but then she violently screamed, "Next time use a fucking condom!" He felt pathetic as he stood watching the bloodied head of his child slipping effortlessly into view. The transformation was truly magical as the screams of pain vanished only to be replaced with the love of a mother. He gazed down and stared at the child lying motionless in the elastic tissue of its afterbirth. Fear, now forced a cruel path through his uncertain body and for that he stopped breathing. He closed his eyes and simply prayed. His heart pounded and the pain made him pray all the more intensely. The first cry was from his throat. The second was Erin's, but the third was the child crying in desperation for its mother. He was frightened as the baby girl twitched. He fought the flood of relief when Erin's arms stretched in hope, and so with shaking fingers he bent to hold his newly born daughter in the single span of a hand. Having given the mother her child he stood back and watched. He felt so isolated. He felt so lonely that his mind went back to the man he'd seen on that painting in the Colonel's dining room.

"Fetch Dr. Cooper," rumbled the plea from Erin as she cradled her new-born. Hearing the instruction he raced from the house. He reached his destination and urgently slammed his hand against the door.

"Yes!"

"Erin's just given birth," Alan's excited voice shouted as the door opened and the Pointer's nose tried to push its way out.

For the next twenty minutes he was not welcome as the doctor, and his able wife, attended to the mother and child's needs. At last the bedroom door opened and Marsha eagerly welcomed him with an antiseptic smell. "She's beautiful," confirmed the doctor. "And Erin's doing fine."

With the noise that had been going on everybody had forgotten Emily, and it was only when she walked into the bedroom did anyone remember. "You've got a sister," smiled Marsha showing the young girl the baby asleep in the cot.

"What's her name?"

"How about Katie," Alan suggested.

"That's lovely," Erin smiled.

"I like that," was the confirmation from Emily, and with that comment turned and walked back to her room.

"What can you see?" Emily asked while holding up the scribbled drawing she'd done at school.

"Let me get in," smiled her father having just arrived from work and ever eager, to please, slipped off his coat. He studied and gazed intently at it. "I can see mummy!" He grinned being quite sure of himself.

The young girl scrunched up her nose, similar to how her mother would and turned the sheet of paper. "And now?"

"Me," he smiled, and it was an instant later she rushed to gamely swing her arms around his waist and gave a huge hug.

Erin must have heard the commotion, because she appeared and gave the kind of welcome typical of her love. When at last they separated she calmly announced, "Guess who's been round today?"

"Give up," came his standard response.

"Then let me tell you," she teased. "It was that Pond biddy."

"What did she want?"

"Something about wanting to talk to you," she suggested while returning to the kitchen and as she disappeared Alan smiled, because since the birth of Katie her figure had those seductive curves that all new mothers seem to possess.

"When does she want to see me?" He wondered rather aimlessly.

"I said you'd be round about seven o'clock," came her rather distant reply.

It was well after dinner, and rather dark, as he walked down the path that led to Miss Pond's front door. Knocking twice he waited. "Hello," the woman's rather soft veldt accent greeted after the door was opened. "Won't you come in?" He stepped inside, and it was as if he'd stepped back in time because everywhere there were pictures and paintings showing what life must have been like before, between and after the Two Great Wars. His gaze travelled over various portraits showing young women working as farm hands. Others were of nurses tending to the injuries of war. Some were even lines of factory workers chatting amongst themselves. There were mothers clutching their newborn hoping that the father would return. He was shown into the sitting room and having taken just the one step stopped dead in his tracks; because if the paintings in the hallway were breathtaking then no words could be found to describe what he was feeling when seeing what was hanging on the walls.

"Weren't these painted by Marsha," asked his confused question. "Because aren't they in her style?"

"Not really," smiled the answer. "She never did inherit my artistic talent."

"What!" He stuttered completely gobsmacked. "Marsha's your daughter."

"No!" She softly sighed. "She's my granddaughter." There was a moment's pause before she continued, "And I've allowed her to say that she'd painted them because I wanted her to have the chance I never had."

"But, I've seen the paintings in her studio," he alleged. "And you're telling me that she didn't paint any of them."

"That's right."

"But, what about the one I asked her to do of Erin!"

"Didn't you think it a bit strange that it wasn't what you expected?"

"I simply thought she'd changed her style."

The old woman grinned, in a flattering sort of way, and said, "That is her style!" Having had the wind metaphorically taken from his sails he just sat with his wide eyes everywhere. Her next question came straight out of the blue, "You know that portrait that was in the Colonel's?"

"Yes."

"That should have been mine."

If he was flummoxed before then there was no explanation as to how he felt at that precise moment in time. "Why, do you want it?" Was the only comment he could muster.

"Because when I'd gone round for tea, one afternoon, and saw it hanging on the wall," she blushed. "I asked the Colonel whether if anything happened to him then could I have it as a keepsake."

There was a slight delay as he stared at the woman's bloodshot eyes and wondered whether she'd been crying. "Well," he began. "The Colonel had obviously forgotten to put anything in his will and seeing as the executors couldn't settle on its final resting place decided that it would be better left with my mother until someone came forward to claim it."

"D'yer know why it was decided to leave it with your mother?"

"No."

"Because he was shagging her!"

Again he was dumbstruck by the sheer audacity of her statement and smiled when realising that maybe this woman was a tad jealous. "And anyway," dripped the sarcasm before adding his frustrating words "You have to remember that it takes two to tango."

"It wasn't just a quick paso doble," she condemned. "It was more like the slow waltz of unadulterated lust!"

"He probably just wanted to keep his hand in with all the new moves and techniques!"

"It was more like he'd become a bit stiff and needed someone to take him in hand," she giggled rather laboriously. "So unless you're desperately wanting to keep it," She asked. "Then can I have it?"

Alan scrunched up his nose, if for no other reason than realising that there was someone who might have wanted that portrait. "I can't see why not," he snorted, like a ruminating heifer, and made an offer, "I'll bring it round in the morning." And with that he left. Back at his home, he carefully picked up the portrait and held it at arms length. "I wonder who you are?" he queried staring at the Unknown Soldier.

He'd been studying it for a moment, looking this way and that, when an innocent voice asked, "Who you looking at?"

"I'm not quite sure."

"I'll go and take a look," she irresponsibly replied while walking behind the picture. "There's no-one here."

"Of course there's not," he smirked. "And anyway shouldn't you be in bed?" Having tucked in his daughter he stood looking at the picture, once again, when something clicked and using Emily's childish logic decided to carefully draw a line, with a carving knife, down the edge of the picture frame and gently remove the canvas. Then it was like turning the final page of a good novel as he smiled when seeing that on the reverse side was a young girl dressed quite beautifully in an evening gown and obviously wanting to be part of some celebration. He gave a lop-sided smirk when seeing that someone had scribbled Charity Power loves Michael Ledbetter along the bottom.

"Have you got it?" Smoothly enquired Miss Pond as Alan stood in the chilly weather of a winter's day.

He pulled his collar that bit tighter, rocked his shoulders obviously trying to keep out the cold and asked, "Can I come in first?"

"Please do," the frail old lady smiled and indicated the way forward. Because of her rheumatism she slowly shuffled, along the rather dusty hallway, until reaching the door of her sitting room. Feeling gallant, Alan opened it and allowed her to enter first. Once inside, he stood by the blazing fire and rather nonchalantly studied once again the numerous portraits that hung on every wall. With a modicum of enthusiasm he walked to the one that had most caught his attention, the night before, and again studied it. Like the awkward detective he quickly noticed that it showed a beautiful young girl sitting amongst the red roses and yellow foxgloves reading a book. With further investigation he also spotted that the artist had given the picture a title beautifully written in the bottom right hand corner. It simply read Charity. He thought for a long moment and then cast his curious eyes at the woman. "That's you?" He surmised as the pretty features of the young girl were perfectly captured in paint. The old woman, remained sitting, and smiled. They both looked at each other, and although the ravages of time had sculptured her face, the beauty was still there. He waited, with a dry mouth, and as her head never moved, or gave any indication, Alan's skin crept because at that moment a sudden question flashed through his mind. "If that is you," he wondered sitting down. "Then this is you as well." Having spoken he carefully removed the other portrait he'd found and showed it to her. His stomach tightened as he waited. Getting no response he turned the portrait over and simply asked, "Then who's the soldier on the other side?"

The old lady, sitting contentedly in the chair, would have been eight when her parents moved to South Africa to oversee the various claims prospectors would use when setting up Gold Mining communes. Now that she'd just celebrated her fifteenth birthday was to witness something that would change her life forever because having just climbed the stairs she heard the front door burst open and watched as five, or maybe six, outlaws rushed in brandishing an assortment of weapons. She stood trembling at the top, making sure that she was not seen, and watched as her father, the Right Honourable Reginald Power, ran out of the study with a silver revolver in his hand that he fired just the once. Having missed his target a salvo of rounds pumped into his dying body. Hearing the shots her mother raced from the room and seeing the lifeless figure of her husband falling to the floor screamed. The young girl on the other hand felt absolutely nothing.

Well that's not quite true because a smile raced to her mouth as she'd always wanted revenge for each night that her father would creep into her bed; and the grave of her stillborn child at the bottom of the garden was a constant reminder of his unwanted desires. Peering through the lattice railings she felt astonishment when one of the antagonists stepped up to her mother, ripped the honey yellow dress from her quaking body and tore away the lacy petticoats. Eventually naked her mother trembled as various hands began to grope, and fumble, with her nudity. The young girl felt pity as one after the other each of the men took turns to rape her. The man, or more precisely the boy, at the back stood waiting his turn and obviously feeling bored suddenly glanced up and noticed the young witness looking down. As their eyes clashed the frightened girl instantly realised what would happen if she'd been caught and so fearing for her life scurried into one of the bedrooms and hid. She was actually inside one of her mother's wardrobes when the door opened. She held her breath as hands kept moving the dresses when all of a sudden she came face to face with the young man who looked more frightened than she was. As their eyes clashed she stood trembling like a leaf because all he could do was to stare back at her. He was staring in a way that was totally different from the way her father would have done. Where his would have been a stare that held an unforgiving need; the boy's had softness to it. As she panted she'd become conscious of the fact that over the previous eighteen months her puberty had kicked in. She'd grown breasts. Although they were relatively tiny she had officially got a pair of tits. Her arse had developed the stunning curves mature women possess. Her face had a luscious sheen and her lips pouted with sensual desire. She smiled and he smiled in return when walking up and gently placing his rough hands against the bodice of her nightgown. As she looked at him the boy simply groped her tits for a second, or two, before stepping back and closing his eyes. Suddenly the bedroom door burst open and another of the gang stepped into the room. The girl stopped breathing, not because she thought she was going to be used as a surrogate fanny for these barbarians but because the door simply closed leaving her untouched. How long she waited was of little consequence because the next time it opened was when the police arrived and found her. After a painstaking and prolonged investigation it was finally decided that the identity of the perpetrators, of this heinous crime, belonged to a radical group of mercenaries locally known as the foxgloves. Having lost both parents and seeing as she was quite alone it was to be decided, by some bureaucrat somewhere, that the local convent take her as help in the hospital. It was about a year later when she was assisting with various patients that a couple of injured men were brought in to be treated. Actually they'd been shot in a frantic shoot out after the local constabulary had discovered the whereabouts of that infamous gang. It was too late for one of the men who died from the wounds he'd received but as for the other; he needed continual supervision if he wasn't to follow the same outcome. The statuary guard kept a constant vigil when one of the nuns quickly called the girl over to help change the bloodied bandages and as soon as she saw this man's face instantly recognised him. With trembling fingers she carefully lifted the bloodied shirt from the left side of his flank and stared at the appalling injury. Like any good nurse she tenderly bathed it with antiseptic and it was on the eighth day that he finally opened his eyes. Looking with a somewhat frosty, as well as incoherent, expression the lad didn't seem to recognise his attendant which was probably due to the fact that she'd developed in all the right places. It was part way through the third week that the girl went to the Mother Superior and after explaining the events of what had happened on the fateful night of her parents death it was decided that the two of them board a train, with new identities, and start their lives afresh.

"So what happened next?"

"We travelled from country to country," she smiled. "Earning our keep by doing various jobs."

"What kind of work?"

"This and that," she smiled. "Whatever was necessary?"

"So you were a kind of hired mercenary," he joked.

"I suppose you could call us that," she laughed. "And anyway we continued north until finally arriving in England."

"So how did you end up living here?"

"Because we'd done some work for the government it was decided that it would be in the best interests of national security if we became lost in an isolated community somewhere."

Hearing the description of the village he had to laugh. "What kind of work did you do?" He asked knowing full well that the prospects of getting an answer was close to being zero and seeing the expression she was using, as well as the half smile, said it all. "So what happened to your alleged partner," he wondered. "Because all I've ever known is that you've lived by yourself."

"Realising that people would start to get curious," she answered while giving a rather contrary smile. "It was decided that we lived separate lives because tongues have been known to wag especially when an unmarried couple unexpectedly arrive and set up home." He grinned when remembering that's exactly what had happened when an elderly gentleman and his niece, if you understand my meaning, moved into eleven Main Street. The clucking got even louder when ten months later an additional member of the parish was born.

"But didn't you tell me that Marsha's your grand-daughter?"

"That's right I did."

"So where's her mother?"

"She died in childbirth."

"I'm sorry to hear that," he sympathised. "So, have you got any other skeletons in the closet?"

"If you're talking about me having any other children?"

"What else could I be talking about," he stupidly sniggered. "That you're a hired assassin."

Taking not the slightest bit of notice replied. "Much as I'd have liked to have had a big family," she sighed. "I only ever had Shirley and after her birth she went to live with her father."

"So, d'yer want to tell who he is?"

"Think about it," she suggested while taking the painting from him.

"What's wrong?" Erin asked as Alan stood staring at the portrait above the sleeping figure of his eldest daughter.

"The answer to everything is staring me straight in the face," he confirmed. "But I just can't see it." The sigh was deep as he turned away. Then suddenly, something twigged that forced his gaze to concentrate on the slightly distorted face of each of the maidens in turn. His mind had the agility of thick treacle as he remembered each woman that he'd met and realising this looked again. He smiled, in a funny sort of way, when realising that this was not the actual picture that Erin had given him. Okay, it looked similar but why were the women holding a sprig of the distinctive herb instead of the single one he remembered. "Look," he instructed with a pointing finger.

"Where!"

"At what you've got in your hand."

"I know," she giggled. "That I've got this."

"That's not what I meant," he shivered when realising that she'd removed his stiffening cock.

"But, I'm feeling horny," she smiled as she reached and pulled him. "So let's go back to bed!"

"No! I need to find something first," he claimed racing down the stairs and moving inside his father's study. The house was silent as he searched various scrapbooks and files. He was getting more, and more, frustrated with each passing minute until a shout went up. "Found it!"

"Now, what have you found?" She asked while standing in the doorway completely naked.

"This," he smiled as he looked up and when he saw her instantly forgot about what he was holding. "Oh! Erin."

"I told you I was feeling horny," she moaned as they started intimate touches of the others body. He kissing her and started playing with her wet fanny. She, just letting him. They fucked like there was no tomorrow and it was only when Katie once again demanded sustenance that they called a halt to proceedings.

He stood looking at the trio of women who'd come into his life. First there was Erin, his mistress soon to be his wife if Patrick agreed. Next, was Emily his eldest daughter. And finally, Katy suckling on her mother's breast. He stared and thought. He thought and stared. Then, suddenly he knew the answer. Up the stairs he charged and stood directly in front of that portrait. He smiled when understanding his father's final request and quite dramatically tore it from the wall. Now like a sprinter he raced and never stopped for breath until reaching the house of Marsha. He knocked and waited. It finally opened only for him to charge passed and race up the stairs and towards her studio. Once inside fiercely opened the wardrobe door and picked up the original painting. Not a word was spoken as he raced towards the home of Miss Pond and burst through the door. Down the corridor he stormed and into the sitting room. Panting for breath he saw her crouched in a chair. With his right index finger pointing he instinctively announced, "I now know who that soldier is!"

"Do you?"

"Yes," he insisted. "Because don't you remember telling me about what happened in South Africa?"

"Yes."

"And how a fanatical group of anarchists murdered your father and raped your mother."

"I remember," she confirmed while closing her eyes.

"Well if that gang was so intent on murder and rape then why did the lad, who found you in the wardrobe, just have a quick grope before closing the door?"

"Maybe he felt uncomfortable about violating my body."

"Bullshit," he insisted. "Because if he'd have been sex starved, like the others, then he just wouldn't have been satisfied with a quick feel of your tits."

"Wouldn't he?"

"I doubt it," he provoked. "Because d'yer know what I think?"

"What."

"That you knew each other," he casually stated before successfully changing tact. "And with this in mind I went and looked through the scraps of newspaper, my father kept and realised that there was never any mention of a gang being known as the foxgloves."

"So!"

"But there was a tiny fragment of paper, attached to a specific picture in his book of herbs, on which was written the word; protect."

"Was there?"

"And thinking about it."

"Yes!"

"I'm almost certain it was my father's job to make sure that nothing happened to this foxglove fella," he hypothesised. "And do you want to know something else?"

"If it'll make you feel any better!"

"And I also think you know who it is," he sneered with about hundred percent certainty. "Because he's the one on the painting."

"Marsha's here," Erin shouted from the hallway after having opened the front door.

Hearing this Alan carefully folded the paper, put it on the arm of the chair and stood. "Hello," he smiled while walking through the door. "And what do we owe this pleasure to?"

"As you've probably read," she started. "My grandmother passed away last Thursday."

"I'm sorry to hear that."

"That's alright," she half smiled, if that's at all possible. "And seeing as we've just got back from the solicitors." There was a slight pause before she continued. "And according to her last will and testament I believe this to be yours." Having spoken she opened her handbag, pulled out a single letter and handed it over. Being somewhat bewildered he opened it and read the words.

Alan.

Now that I've gone to meet my maker and slipped off this mortal coil I believe you deserve an explanation, and the truth, concerning certain events. Hopefully you will recall the little talk we had and how I explained about what happened to me in South Africa? If so; then you'll remember me telling you about how my father was murdered by a notorious gang of cut-throats that went under the name of the foxgloves. Indeed he was killed; but as you worked out it wasn't by a gang. It all started one very hot summer's night when I was twelve. Feeling all grown up, and because it was so hot and sultry, I'd removed my clothes before lying on the bed hoping to keep cool. At some point I must have dozed off because I suddenly woke to discover a naked, and excited, man sitting on the edge of the bed with his hand nestling across my mouth. As I looked at my father the inborn panic I was feeling forced me to tremble as he just smiled while reaching and taking my right hand. It's what he did next that I cannot forgive or forget; as it still makes me shudder and cringe when remembering exactly what he made me do. It got worse because he made me pregnant and the baby boy was still born some eight and a half months later, or that's what my mother told me after he'd been taken away. For the next six months my father never came to visit me in the night, and it was only when I couldn't sleep that I discovered the reason. Hearing some unexpected groans, coming from down the passageway, I got up and wandered towards the source. When pushing the door ajar I saw exactly what was happening and you cannot image the disgust I felt when watching the way my father was sodomising one of the young maids like he'd done to me. Revenge is such an ugly word but, as they say, its best served cold. I'd just celebrated my fourteenth birthday when my father once again came to my bed and in the flickering glow from a candle I watched as he stripped. Now ready, in a sexual kind of way if you can imagine it, he quickly removed my bed covers and tore at my nightgown. As he knelt between my legs, which he'd violently forced apart, I reached beneath my pillow and grabbed what I'd hidden there. Now ready I drove the single knitting needle, which I think was a size two, straight into his chest and as it penetrated the look on his face miraculously changed from the undoubted smirks of pleasure to the colourless face of death. As I looked at the pathetic shape, of the man, I felt absolutely nothing as his eyes pleaded for forgiveness. To cut a long story short I was taken to the police station and placed in a filthy cell where there were only the four corners where I could squat for relief. I'd been there a week, or was it seven days, when again I felt a strong hand resting across my mouth and simply thought here we go again. Cowering with fear I looked up and saw one of the patients, who I'd treated in the local hospital, looking down at me. It appeared that he'd heard rumours about the crime I'd committed and because he'd been the victim of my father's sadistic anger he felt justified in saving me from a fate worse than death. So running through the back streets we eventually arrived at my house and opening one of the barn doors raced inside and decided to hide amongst the straw until morning when we would borrow, on a permanent basis, a couple of the horses. I'm not entirely sure when it was, but I remember being roughly shaken as it appeared that there was someone moving inside the barn. Peering over the edge of the bales my jaw dropped when in the flickering light I instantly recognised the woman laying down with her legs wide apart. Remembering the grunts and groans, my father would use when he was with me, I realised that the rather old and decrepit figure of someone I'd never seen before, was doing exactly the same to my mother. Wanting to save her from a fate worse than death I panicked and grabbed the pistol that Tommy, because that was my hero's Christian name, had by his side. My heart was pounding when in a flash three shots were fired, and it was then that I realised just how crap my aim was. It wasn't the fat looking bloke lying in a pool of blood, with his life having just been extinguished, but was my mother looking more shocked than me. Tommy came to the rescue as he snatched the pistol and pumped the remaining bullets into the oversized figure of the man. Realising the consequence, of our actions, like being hung, drawn and quartered we decided that the best thing to do was to run to the country. We travelled north through the Belgian Congo, Nigeria next before passing through French West Africa until reaching French Morocco. We boarded a pirate boat, in Rabat, before arriving in England at Weymouth and it was on our journey that our love blossomed. Having arrived in England the first thing we had to do was find some kind of work, and true to the idea of free enterprise Tommy enlisted in the sinister world of espionage. Due to his expertise in his particular field which I believe was the extermination of certain unwanted guests, a sort of latter day rat catcher, it was decided that it would make better sense to change our names so as we could blend in somewhere and not stick out like a pair of sore thumbs. Having said that; I became Isobel Constance Pond and Tommy David Humm, I know it's a bit of a silly name, became Michael Ledbetter. Also, another stupid idea put forward was that I was to become celibate. Can you imagine being a young woman, on her own, with a couple of tits and plenty of hormones agreeing to such a philosophy? I was so much in love with Michael that the idea of not satisfying my physical desires was just too much. With sex being such a powerful emotion we would take any opportunity to disappear for an afternoon and use that old country remedy for a bee sting. You know what I mean about getting a prick in your hand and putting it in cider. Sorry for that corny joke, so back to the explanation. I met Michael one afternoon for our usual apple bobbing games without the apples, and noticed the look of absolute horror chiselled across his face. When I eventually asked him what was wrong he told me that according to reliable information he'd picked up, you know the kind of thing that originates in the corridors of power, there was someone digging and delving into the assassination of Lord Douglas Bana-hepplewhite in Cape Town at the turn of the centaury. I'm sure the name doesn't ring a bell, as it didn't to me, but the location surely must as it's where I shot my mother some twenty odd years earlier. Why this suddenly interest to investigate what happened is anyone's guess but rumour had it that there was a pen pusher, sitting in an ivory tower somewhere, thinking what can I do in this spare half hour that'll either waste a lot of time and money or get up people's noses. After a little digging and talking to various colleagues at the home office, the most forthcoming being the toilet attendant in ten Downing Street, Michael discovered that there was an army officer by the name of Otis Chaney doing a lot of snooping. This may have something to do with the fact that the dead man was actually his late father.

Realising the consequence of him discovering certain facts like who actually did murder the man we broke with protocol and asked to meet up with someone from the Home Office. About three days later when answering the door Colonel Ledbetter, as he'd become, found your father waiting on the steps ready to talk with him. I can't go into much detail but the long and the short of it was that your father had been given the task of making sure that the identity of the foxglove never saw the light of day.

Because I had an artistic upbringing he asked me to do the painting that Erin gave you and it wasn't until I had a brainstorm of an idea that this could be used as identification that we decided to steal it and reproduce it with the ladies in a different sequence. Whether it was a pure fluke on Marsha's part, or sheer luck but when you'd solved the riddles of your father's making it spelt at the name of his murderer.

Having done my bit to bring to justice that godforsaken excuse of a man I could now paint the picture I'd always wanted. Knowing that I'd never be allowed to live with the man I loved the next best thing was to use the other side of a self portrait; I'd previously done, so that Michael and myself could always be together. Now can you understand why I so much wanted that portrait back? Here's a question. You found out who the purple foxglove was, but do you know who the yellow one is?

Charity Power.

www.ingramcontent.com/pod-product-compliance
Ingram Content Group UK Ltd.
Pitfield, Milton Keynes, MK11 3LW, UK
UKHW021317180426
11947UKWH00015B/1275